THE RESPONSE

We can travel with our imagination into the cosmos and enter its immensity.....Constellations with myriads of stars form Galaxies and Constellations of Galaxies integrate the Universe of Creation.

Here and there, we can visualize planets inhabited by plants and living beings similar to ones on Earth, our home.

We can also look into Time and Space to investigate our origin and our destiny through our imagination and thoughts.

We are beings who are born, live and die....Our life is just a wink in time as we try to understand the marvels of creation. But this lapse is so ephemeral that we are not able to understand the reason for our own existence.

A message has come to us as a special privilege through the generosity and love of superior beings. It is contained in **THE RESPONSE.** This book will give us a better glimpse of the Universe to understand the relationship between the physical body and the Spiritual Being and its divine origin. This explains the so-called mysteries. It is simply ignorance that has deformed man´s conscience.

This message tries to help us comprehend the "whys" of our own existence.

The message in **THE RESPONSE** can open your eyes to improve and ponder a new light....which will help you find true values and true love once again.

Pablo E. Hawnser

The response

*A testimonial regarding contacts with beings
from cosmic civilizations who visit us to help us
attain spiritual evolution*

Design and execution of cover
Tamara Meral Hanan

ORIGINAL TITLE
La Respuesta

Order this book online at www.trafford.com
or email orders@trafford.com

Most Trafford titles are also available at major online book retailers.

Sansores y Aljure Editores. S.A. de C.V.
Francisco Sosa 102
Col. Coyoacan
México, D.F., 04000

Note for Librarians: A cataloguing record for this book is available from Library and
Archives Canada at www.collectionscanada.ca/amicus/index-e.html

Printed in Victoria, BC, Canada.

ISBN: 978-1-4269-1447-8 (sc)

First Edition: August 1997
Second Edition: October 1998
Third Edition: August 2002

*Our mission is to efficiently provide the world's finest, most comprehensive book
publishing service, enabling every author to experience success. To find out how to
publish your book, your way, and have it available worldwide, visit us online at
www.trafford.com*

Trafford rev. 2/25/2010

North America & international
toll-free: 1 888 232 4444 (USA & Canada)
phone: 250 383 6864 ◆ fax: 812 355 4082

ACKNOWLEDGEMENTS

To my dearest and enthusiastic partners and friends who made possible the English version of this book.

DEDICATION

This book is dedicated to all who, regardless of age and sex, have an open mind and the desire to find their inner selves through an awareness of the TRUTH.

To all those who contributed directly or indirectly to the Message, this grain of sand on the shores of the Ocean of confussion in our present world.

To the real author, who sent us through Rahel and Mirza, the revelation contained in the "Eric Story"

CONTENTS

FEW WORDS BY THE AUTHOR 13
REFLEXION 15
PROLOGUE 17

CHAPTER I 21
VIRTUAL REALITY 21

CHAPTER II 29
WHERE ARE WE? 29

CHAPTER III 37
WHO AM I? 37

CHAPTER IV 43
WHERE DO I COME FROM? 43

CHAPTER V 47
ERIC´S STORY 47

CHAPTER VI 64
THE CONTACT 64

CHAPTER VII 69
THE FIRST APPOINTMENT 69
    THE CONSCIENCE 81

CHAPTER VIII 106
REMEMBERING 106

CHAPTER IX 122
APPOINTMENT IN CULIACAN 122

CHAPTER X 137
THE FIRST DREAM 137

CHAPTER XI 176
BIRKEN 176

CHAPTER XII 222
ENCOUNTER IN MERIDA 222

CHAPTER XIII 238
QUANTUM BIOGENETICS 238

CHAPTER XIV 248
ENCOUNTER IN LA MARQUESA 248
    THE CHAKRAS 251

CHAPTER XV 278
OUR SCIENCE 278

CHAPTER XVI 285
FROM HERMOSILLO TO GALIMOR 285

CHAPTER XVII 318
ENCOUNTER AT TANGAMANGA 318
    SPACE 330
    TIME 331
    ADDENDUM 349

CHAPTER XVIII 354
THE UNIVERSE 354
    DEVELOPMENT OF EVOLUTIONARY SPIRITS 364
    FIRST EVOLUTIONARY PLANE, ... 365
    THE HUMANOID 365
    SECOND EVOLUTIONARY PLANE, ... 366
    THE CAVEMAN 366

THIRD EVOLUTIONARY PLANE,.....................................367
FIRST LEVEL, THE MAN......................................367
THIRD EVOLUTIONARY PLANE,.....................................373
SECOND LEVEL, SUPER-MAN......................................373
FOURTH EVOLUTIONARY PLANE,.....................................375
FIRST LEVEL, SUPRA-MAN 375
FOURTH EVOLUTIONARY PLANE,.....................................375
SECOND LEVEL, DEMI-GOD 375
FOURTH EVOLUTIONARY PLANE,.....................................376
THIRD LEVEL, MAITREYA 376
FIFTH EVOLUTIONARY PLANE,.....................................377
COSMIC ENGINEERS......................................377
SIXTH EVOLUTIONARY PLANE, ...377
BIOLOGICAL ENGINEERS......................................377
SEVENTH EVOLUTIONARY PLANE,.....................................378
MONITORS 378

CHAPTER XIX 383
THE ISLAND IN SPACE 383
THE GENETIC PATTERN FOR REPRODUCTION..........393
THE METABOLIC PATTERN 401
PATTERN OF BEHAVIOR 401

CHAPTER XX.....................................424
OUR SMALL UNIVERSE 424

CHAPTER XXI 443
THE FINAL ENCOUNTER 443

A W A K E N......................................458

11

FEW WORDS BY THE AUTHOR

Dear reader:

Now that you are ready to get to know this work, I recommend calmly and patiently reading the Prologue and the first four chapters.

"Eric's Story" includes a lot of information passed on by our "Elder brothers", the self-named extra-terrestrials. Concepts of this origin are included in the chapters mentioned, which will prepare your mind. In the end you will be able to discover the real message contained in the teachings behind the story.

This story is not a science fiction novel, it is a true story. With the exception of error, omission or involuntary lack of understanding, all the concepts mentioned that are not already proven by science, will be one day when the required stage is attained. Remember that even if not scientifically proven, this does not mean something is false. And, it may serve, in the meantime, as a path to be followed.

Legend tells us that a few years before the discovery of the New World, at an extreme point on the Iberian Peninsula, the king ordered a sign that read NON PLUS ULTRA, which means "there is nothing more", because in those days it was believed that the Earth was flat and supported on the backs of two elephants who were standing on a turtle.

The wise elders, on the other hand, had informed the king it was necessary to deepen some concepts regarding literature and other branches of knowledge, but that the sciences such as mathematics, physics and chemistry had already been perfected.

Today, scientists are more humble in regard to the extent of their knowledge, because they understand science is a gift of creation to compensate man's efforts and uses his intelligence in an effort at comprehension.

Get ready, then, to learn something you have always wanted to know.....but didn't have the slightest idea where to look.

Thank you for taking this recommendation into consideration. I am sure the knowledge you will attain here will help you find within yourself that cosmo-spiritual being that is your true SELF in the universal dimension

.

Pablo E. Hawnser

REFLEXION

Religion and science had the same starting point; both seeking TRUTH have traveled great distances and have had to adjust their course continuously.

But now they stopped moving away from each other and have begun to converge. In a not too distant future they will converge, having covered two semicircles and, at the cusp when they come together, will understand both were seeking their beginnings and that this is one and the same, the beginning and the end of creation.

We must each draw our own circle with knowledge and faith until they coincide in TRUTH.

To have FAITH is to know how to perceive things with the spirit and spiritual perception is that which is able to contemplate the TRUTH.

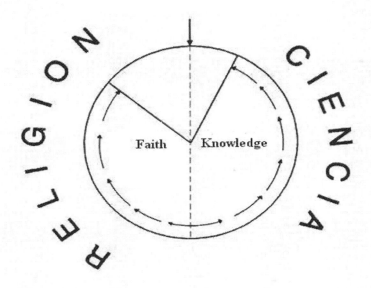

PROLOGUE

If I told your spirit (before sending it to the Earth)
would give it a WORLD of knowledge, today I offer:
A HEAVEN of wisdom.

Book of True Life (T.L.F.)

THE RESPONSE is the title of "Eric´s Story", as the actor guides us toward learning about personal experiences and situations that could be considered as paranormal or as science fiction.

As these situations and experiences unfold, many questions and doubts will arise in the reader´s mind; but they will also entice him to enter a world of knowledge that will allow him to experience a new dimension in life. Thereby finding his own RESPONSE to questions he may have trying to explain the reason for his own existence.

The supernatural is a topic that always awakens interest, however, even when the facts are real, it is natural, at first, to go through a process where initial disbelief will give way to reasonable doubt. Later, a conditioned possibility will be reached as the mind experiences natural confusion upon discovering it does not possess the necessary elements to accept or reject the assumptions put forward. The result will be astonishment, which is the reaction of our mind when we discover that we only needed to open our eyes to be able to see. But not our physical eyes which only pick up the reflexion of matter, but the eyes of our spiritual mind, of our faith and of our understanding.

Then, finally, a door is opened for an analysis leading us to understand and accept there is more of what we don´t know than what we think we know about the elements and the knowledge that will give us the capacity to form judgements with which we will

17

determine our own attitude toward what was put forth. A judgement to determine our acceptance or rejection of the story.

After the initial process, a kind of "awakening of the conscience" will begin, a light that seems to shine into each person´s sense of perspective, offering a new dimension of reality.

We are now living in an era of light, that will be of understanding for mankind as all mysteries will be explained. Faith is needed, because faith is the spiritual view that complements the understanding of human comprehension. Blessed are they that without seeing nor understanding, believe; because they feel with their spirit, and they rise above to be able to see with spiritual eyes and understand with an intelligence beyond human reason.

We are entering a NEW ERA, the planet Earth will continue rotating in space, it´s not close to being destroyed; but this world of mistakes, hate, ignorance and evil is about to end.

Our science, as it is now known, will not have the chance, at present, to draw back all the veils that prevent a wider understanding of the Universe. This comprehension will come when mankind reaches a spiritual evolution that will manifest itself in its behavior. It is necessary to attain a world of peace, harmony and respect where love rules, to show that mankind has been able to reach this goal in its evolution. It will depend on mankind if this will be achieved through love or if it needs the "Great Tribulations" announced by St. John in the Apocalypse.

However it is reached, it will not be until then that we will be able to receive the visits and open contact with our elder brothers, who will come to see us as naturally as we are now visited by our brothers of other continents of the Earth.

The extra-terrestrial visitors are really our older brothers (as they call themselves). Many people talk about them, but very few undertake this subject with due seriousness because their existence has not been "officially" recognized. From the scientific point of view, which is acknowledged "officially" by "serious" persons, the possibility of their existence is accepted, but their presence on our planet has not been admitted.

In 1967, conferences and debates were organized in Moscow, Prague, New York and Washington for the first time among the most distinguished scientists in the world. The project CETI

(Communications with Extra-Terrestrial Intelligence) was born to analyze the possibilities of getting in touch with any intelligent civilization in outer space. Talks began with representatives of scientific institutions from the ex-Soviet Union, United States of America and Czechoslovakia, who organized the study and at least 53 prominent men of science participated in the different areas.

Philip Handler, President of the Academy of Science in Washington, D.C. noted that the success of celebrating these conferences was an accomplishment to be registered in the history of mankind.

The final result was that the possible existence of intelligent beings on other planets of other solar systems in known galaxies was accepted; but, due to our impossibility to know where and how to look for them, it was decided that it was easier "to listen" to try and receive a communication rather than sending it ourselves.

At present, the Planetary Society is a scientific organization seriously engaged in the possibility of contact with human intelligence outside our planet. The prominent scientist, Carl Sagan, is the President and also the Director of the Laboratory of Planetary Studies at Cornell University. In addition to Mr. Sagan, Bruce Murray, Vice-President and professor at the Institute of Technology of California; Louis Friedman, Executive Director; Michael Collins, the Apollo XI astronaut; Thomas Payne, Administrator and also Chairman of the Space Commission of NASA; Steven Spielberg, renowned movie director and producer; Joseph Ryan, Henry J. Tanner and a pleiades of scientists and professors of universities in the U.S.A., Great Britain, Russia, Australia, France and other personalities, such as politicians, astronauts, writers and even an actor concerned with science: Paul Newman.

This society began the project SETI (Search for Extra-Terrestrial Intelligence), in addition to the BETA program of space study by radiotelescopes, and it is supporting the SERENDIP program of Berkeley University in California to monitor 4.2 million channels every 1.7 seconds through analyzers on the radiotelescopes. All these technological efforts are carried out to try to identify signs of intelligent life coming from outer space.

THE RESPONSE is a clarion call to awaken mankind. As the teachings and concepts received by our elder brothers range from

19

the known limits of science to universal   and knowledge were left as proof of their existence and their presence on our planet, even though they are not "officially" recognized.

TRUE LIFE is the life of the spirit because it overcomes the limits of what is perishable and is the life of our immortal soul.

CHAPTER I

The Supra-Conscience, the physical brain,
mental processes and imagination constitute
The MAGICAL POWER OF THE MIND.

Psychology, Parapsychology, Metaphysics,
Biochemistry, Quantic Mechanics, Astrophysics,
Cosmology, Hyperspace...are different areas,
but they all converge toward a knowledge of reality
that is our understanding of the UNIVERSE

and of OURSELVES.

Pablo E. Hawnser

VIRTUAL REALITY

We would all like, either consciously or unconsciously, with an occasional rare exception, to live a totally uncommon experience, to participate in an heroic deed and feel emotions we have only shared, for example, in an Olympic competition by putting ourselves in the place of a famous athlete.

When we involve ourselves more deeply in any given situation, mental vibrations can be so strong they could lead to tears, to make us feel how enthusiasm invades us physically and to share the event by identifying ourselves with the actor. It is as though we were there in person.

For example, let´s imagine this scene: a friend is competing in the finals for an Olympic gold medal in swimming. We see the presentation of the competitors on television and we recognize him taking his place. Sitting nervously on the edge of our seat, we are with him mentally. We keep silent during the seconds that precede the start of the competition.

Now, as the swimmers approach their starting positions and await the shot, we don't dare wink, we hold our breath...they're off! We try to appear cold and indifferent, but our palms are perspiring, we are transmitting our energy hoping he will win.

The names and nationalities of the competitors are announced, and suddenly we realize our friend is in second place. This is confirmed! Now, each second becomes torture, we push him on with our eyes, we follow each stroke with heightening emotion, we fervently hope he'll make it! After the first turn he's in first place! We can barely remain seated, we pray he'll hang on. He's still ahead! They are nearing the finish line, the swimmer in second place almost overtakes him; we sweat, we want to pull him. They get closer to the finish and our swimmer holds his own....and is in the first place again! He manages to gain a few inches. We can no longer take it! We jump and down cheering him on, he keeps on! More! HE WON!

Our eyes fill with tears, we jump, we hug each other, a flood of adrenaline invades our body, we are carried away with joy!

Now, the award ceremony begins: our friend gets on the podium; we can hardly see him as tears blind our eyes, with a knot in our throat. The notes of the national anthem and the flag rising while proudly waving...all this emotion is stronger than we are...we swallow saliva...laughing to avoid crying.

We were all able returned to normalcy; we keep on feeling as if we had been there. Moreover, mentally we had been! We participated, we urged him on and his triumph was also ours.

Our surrender and our acceptance of the experience are based on what we consider to have all the right elements of judgment to recognize that what had happened did really occur.

We can understand the physical and psychological state of a person who undergoes a supernatural experience. But...what does supernatural mean? As we mentioned before, it is not recognized simply as natural, normal or customary; it is different, it has unexpected turns and we identify ourselves with the actor as long as he reacts as we would. However, mentally we are drawing a parallel between the story and what we accept as true according to our knowledge, experience and reasoning.

When the lines separate, we stop believing the facts and automatically disqualify them, because we no longer agree! Now, why? Well, here´s the clue: we have judged. Our conclusion is based on A PRIORI common sense, but, could we be mistaken by sitting in judgment without all the necessary facts? Do we even know what they are?

The author asks us, then, to first meditate and analyze before accepting or rejecting these so-called paranormal phenomena (which are the result of our perception and in which there is an apparent contradiction in the fulfillment of natural laws) could be in reality THE PROPER COMPLIANCE of universal law which we sometimes don´t know and we are perceiving through our senses.

The apparent contradiction is based upon the fact that when something happens different to daily events, or what we know, or what is usually called normal, and that is why it baffles us. Here are two examples:

Example 1

We are having a cup of coffee at a restaurant while waiting for a friend. Locating him through a huge window facing the parking lot, we find that he is talking to an eskimo! Yes, there´s no doubt about it, his parka is covered with snow, as is his sled, his dogs, etc.

At this point it would surprise us a little; it would attract our attention as unusual or abnormal as there are no Eskimo in the parking lots in Mexico going about their business as if they were selling hamburgers from their carts. This does not seem supernatural unless...here´s the scene: At fifteen feet above the ground, the eskimo waves goodbye and takes off flying over the parked cars until out of sight! We turn around to see who else saw this. We need witnesses to prove we have not lost our senses! Is this a paranormal or parapsychological phenomena?

We go to meet our friend who seems to descend toward the entrance of the restaurant, then we discover a plexiglass ramp supported by columns of the same material, practically invisible at a distance. Also, there is a two-yard wide walkabout where the

Eskimo, with all his snowy apparel, is advertising a nearby supermarket.

The supernatural phenomenum has vanished, only the act itself remained, but now it is real and has a logical explanation. We only needed facts to understand, and these changed something unexplicable into what we could perfectly comprehend.

But what would a real eskimo have thought, supposing he was ignorant and newly arrived from the North Pole? Perhaps it would be more difficult to understand that the truth of what appeared to be supernatural was only a reality he could not understand.

Example 2

Let´s imagine it´s the year 1850 and a special part of machinery in the main sugar mill in Veracruz has broken.

January 10:	The Engineer reports the problem and immediately orders the spare part from England.
January 12:	A ship bound for England takes the order.
March 12:	The ship arrives in England.
March 15:	The supplier receives the order and immediately prepares the part for shipment.
March 20:	The spare part leaves England bound for Veracruz.
May 21:	The shipment arrives.
May 25:	The machine is repaired.

Hypothetically, if there are no delays or mistakes, it takes four and a half months (135 days).

The same problem in 1995.

January 10:	At 8:00 A.M., the problem is detected.
January 10:	At 9:00 A.M., an urgent order is faxed containing specifications and drawings for a replacement.

January 10:   At 9:01 A.M., Mexico time (4:01 P.M. London time) the supplier receives the fax.

January 10:   At 10:00 A.M., (5:00 P.M. London time), the spare part is sent to the airport by the supplier and at the same time the invoice and documents are faxed to Mexico.

January 10:   2:00 P.M. Mexico time, (9:00 P.M. London time), an airplane leaves London on route to Mexico with the order.

January 11:   2:00 P.M. Mexico time, Customs releases the spare part.

January 11:   3:00 P.M. Mexico time, the machine has been repaired.

Time taken: 32 hours (1.3 days). In 1995 then, it is physically possible to do this in one-hundredth part of the time it took in 1850, 145 years later.

Now, if we had been able to speak to the engineer in 1850 and told him that 145 years later, in our time, the problem would have been solved as shown, he would not have believed it, because it implies the perfection and use of technology he could not even begin to imagine, such as telecommunications with the speed of light, computer equipment, domination of space for transportation, jet propulsion engines, etc.

What do you think the engineer would say regarding this scene, if he could be transported in time to witness it? Extraordinary! Supernatural! Incredible! And yet, it is a daily affair for us, something that happens continuously.

These examples clearly show that if mankind had been told 200 or 300 years ago how we would live today, scientists themselves would have considered all this as something unconceivable or even supernatural. Yet science, step by step, has turned these marvels into happenings, so even children play with them. What was magical, incredible, marvelous, now is commonplace. In addition, all this and even more in substance and in spirit was prophesied for our time.

There are continuously natural phenomena still not within our full comprehension, because they are not within the scope of today´s science, yet continue to be total natural phenomena.

The understanding of parapsychological phenomena is not within reach of all human beings. Adequate criteria is needed, through study, having an open mind, with intelligence, bypassing prejudices that close the doors to understanding.

It is necessary to broaden our knowledge to allow our mind to perceive light that moves darkness into an explosion of color, and turns fictional dreams into reality.

Today´s truths are the lies of tomorrow. Scientific and technological progress have transformed all we live and enjoy, what were once dreams of inspired minds, into reality.

Let´s stop for a moment to ponder about IMAGINATION.

What does IMAGINATION mean? Is it a thought projected on a mental screen we can build on to our liking as we do on a computer? Well, it´s also that; but we can define it better as a way to develop a project. We cannot prepare ourselves for something and make it come true if we haven´t imagined it first. It is the result of a mental process. It begins within our physical brain, and we need "to be able to imagine" the necessary knowledge for the computer to take the data base to build on.

What happens when we imagine and then try to develop what we apparently know nothing about nor have the necessary facts? How have we generated this information?

Imagination is the result of an energetic process and the internal communication between several areas of our brain. It is the management of energy and the information in our mind that, as we shall see further on, not only can be attained by physical senses. Our brain also has other means to gather information and thus also generate mental processes. These are illusions that appear in such a way that for us they are dreamlike.

Dreams can be reprints of physical reality stored in our memory or editions of recently received impressions combined with data based information. They can also be the projection of information to our conscious sent by our subconscious, as well as information coming directly from another dimension through other types of energy.

This way, the solution of a problem that was in our subconscious can be revealed in a "dream". Imagining possible solutions, and using all the information we might have, the mind can reveal the solution it finds through a mental process in the subconscious and/or in our spiritual brain. Also, now marked by our conscious and acting according to our FREE WILL, we can obtain what we seeked. We can be sincere and honest or false and unjust; we may be able to fool everyone, but we can never fool ourselves. The mental print we file in our conscious will be indelibly etched, independently from what we make up through the action of our FREE WILL.

Concepts change fundamentally in the light of knowledge. When man believed the world was flat, he would never have understood how someone living on the other side of the Antipodes could point to the sky in the opposite direction and accept that both were right.

Just yesterday man believed to be the center of the Universe. Galileo risked his life for daring to put forth the Earth was only a celestial body rotating around the Sun and ended his days under house arrest . He saved his life only because he was able to recant in time.

The brilliant minds of Ptolomeus, Copernicus, Galileo, Arquimedes, Michaelangelo, Newton, Kant, Dirac, Rusell, Kepler, Maxwell, Eddington, Lemaitre, Planck, Pauli, Bohr, Weisenberg, Einstein, Hawking, etc. have converted their fiction into natural phenomena, and have changed the classification of paranormal and parapsychological phenomena into natural phenomena, for those they submitted a reasonable explanation.

We are wise to look back in history. We are proud of our culture and technology and we feel capable of making A PRIORI judgments on facts that require knowledge we do not possess nor do we understand enough to put forth our opinion. It is human nature. We usually accept what our limited senses and knowledge accept A PRIORI and thus become very vulnerable to mistakes, misunderstanding and intolerance. When parapsychology, religion or spirituality is linked to science, we have to be even more careful as we judge or express our opinions, as we must keep in mind that the surer we are, the more we can be mistaken.

To know the TRUTH, the first step must be taken with patience and humility, awaiting the fundamentals needed to permit our brain to pass judgment. This judgment should be flexible to modification, if it was a result of our ignorance in substance and our faith in spiritual matters.

It is necessary to be alert and prepared to comprehend that true reality can easily surpass the most daring and incredible fiction.

CHAPTER II

*I would like to know how God
created this UNIVERSE. But I'm not
interested in this or that phenomenon.
No, I want to know his thoughts;
The rest are just details.*

Albert Einstein

WHERE ARE WE?

It is a given fact that mankind exists in an almost permanent state of war in all corners of the planet. A true war of social, economic and religious ideas.

We live in a planet we call Earth, it is real. It is a place where substance has evolved as a result of the transformation of cosmic energy, that according to universal law is the presence of the Creator.

In philosophy, we can say we perceive the world of substance through our corporal senses, but feelings live in our soul.

But, what is matter if all is the manifestation of energy? We must understand that energy is vibration and vibration within the range of our perception excites our senses and is the only one we can perceive physically. Energy, whose vibration is not within this range, can only be conceived by the mind through its manifestations, or through our spiritual intuition.

Eventually, and under special circumstances, we can have extra-sensory perceptions to aid us in perceiving phenomena we classify as paranormal or parapsychological because there´s no explanation within our known physical laws. We can only interpret them using metaphysics, which is beyond what is considered natural.

However, everything that happens in nature and within our universe, is natural. We may classify it, momentarily, as supernatural, but only until we can understand it.

Man lives within his own universe, whose limits are set by his own physical perception, increasing these according to his comprehension. The size of the UNIVERSE as limited by senses becomes more real as seen by human eye. Let´s subdivide the universe into three parts, easily recognizable physically, to be able to understand each other better:

FIRST: The Microuniverse (in the field of quantum mechanics). Here we classify all that exists, but it is so small we cannot see it with a naked eye. To pry within this natural kingdom we need to start, a microscope, and from then on, we depend only on what our mind can grasp.
SECOND: The Universe (inhabited by human beings). This is contained within the smallest point we can see to the farthest star visible to the naked eye.
THIRD: The Macrouniverse (the field of cosmology). It is the Universe of all creation in which the human Universe is only a dot where our reality exists.

Therefore, we can conceive the Universe as space and our small planet is within, but parameters need to be established regarding the way our life elapses.

We consider our planet as our home, a quiet and stable place. But this is not so; as the Earth rotates in its orbit around the Sun, we are moving in space at the speed of 108,000 kms. per hour, and to this, we should add another 900,000 kms. per hour, that is the speed with which the entire solar system rotates around the center of the Galaxy. It is possible to establish coordinates through geography (latitude, longitude and altitude) to locate our positions on the surface of the Earth. Then we can do the same to define our surroundings in space and the positions of celestial bodies in our solar system. This field is known as Cosmology.

Geometry applied to Topography, on a planetary level, and Cosmology at a cosmic level, will place us geographically and/or cosmically without taking motion into consideration.

To consider the Earth´s rotation on its axis and its movement around the Sun, we need a new parameter for comparison, and this is what we call "time". The concept of "time", as normally measured, is what we call "before" and "after". We measure this lapse with conventional units of time to compare and to determine the transitory distance between two events.

We apply time in units such as a day (which equals a 360-degree rotation of the Earth on its own axis) made up of fractions of hours, minutes and seconds. Longer units are weeks, months and years. It takes a year to complete an orbit of our planet around the Sun, during which time it has rotated 365 times on its own axis.

Each unit of time corresponds to the distance traveled in space, and while we remain within our planet, the speeds of traslation we use internally are so small we consider it a dimension, and thus life in a dimension of space and time.

But, beware! This is only a conventional agreement, since in cosmic reality we live in a "space-time" dimension, in which time tends to revert to zero when its speed approaches that of light, and at the speed of light, time stops, has zero value, it does not exist.

If S = Speed of light
Then $T = 0$ (zero)

Are you aware how as we take a step back, our concepts depend on what we can understand? Our senses cannot see, hear or perceive time, it is our mind through reasoning, and using acquired knowledge that allows us to understand these concepts. Physical senses are the doors for knowledge to enter our mind. But beyond what we can see, hear, taste and touch is what we can comprehend.

We know that we cannot see nor touch a molecule, but we cannot deny it existence. Besides, we readily accept because we understand how and what it is.

In the same way we know that galaxies exist thousands or millions of light years away from us and even without having seen

31

them, they are within our understanding. These concepts correspond to the micro and macro universe, respectively, and we comprehend them with our mind.

Mankind is on Earth because it evolved here creating its own home. Man´s physical body requires certain conditions to live; such as an environment keeping within very narrow ranges of temperature, pressure, humidity and other conditions that exist on this planet, to be able to evolve physically, socially and spiritually.

The list of requirements that the planet must have is incredibly long and all are perfectly fulfilled. How lucky! Truly! How many planets exist that could have also been home for mankind?

Scientists tell us not many, since it is not easy to put together so many things so perfectly. How many planets are there in our galaxy?

The SETI program (Search for Extra-Terrestrial Intelligence) of the Planetary Society is a serious scientific program in the search of intelligent life on another planet. It was started by a group of scientists and is the result of much study and discussion by the most qualified men on the planet.

How should we do it? How and where should we direct our efforts? After great deliberations, it was concluded to be easier, cheaper and more viable to listen and wait to detect and receive intelligent signs coming from some other type of humanity in space than for us to try to contact them.

It was a smart decision and their equipment (radiotelescopes) are precisely placed to be as efficient as possible.

Meanwhile, Earth is REAL. Here we live, enjoying the transformation of energy in all surroundings, in a world that evolved under universal laws that are the presence of the Creator.

However, our mind goes out to space and men of science tell us that there are millions and millions of planets like ours. They expect to find intelligent life in beings like us in more advanced civilizations that might already be trying to find us.

If we consider our reality, we´ll conclude that today man has the moral obligation to take advantage of his knowledge and intelligence. To know how to listen to his own intuition, to accept facts within his reach, just by opening his eyes and trying to understand.

It could help to make a hypothetical comparison between two trips carried out under very different conditions and time spans.

The first one was in the year 30 B.C. when the Roman Empire lived years of glory, culturally and technologically. Alexander the Great had conquered Egypt and Adrian the Emperor thought it proper to visit the pyramids of Ghiza and the Sphinx. It was a feat then for a 90-foot barge to successfully make a trip from Aswan, in Upper Egypt, down through the Nile river passing Thebes, Memphis, Cairo, Heliopolis up to Alexandria in the Mediterranean Sea.

Let us imagine the possibility of continuing the voyage on that barge to where Sydney, Australia is found today. Taking into consideration the specifications of the barge and the nautical technology of those times, this trip would present insurmountable risks and difficulties. Nevertheless, the trip is physically feasible.

The second is the space trip by Apollo 11 taking the astronauts to the Moon. Considering the means and know-how of each in its time, which one, before starting out had a better chance of succeeding?

We agree that it would be the Apollo voyage, as they knew what they were doing, what they were facing, and although difficult, everything was under control. The other trip was riskier as to the possibilities of total success.

Now let us imagine another trip, interplanetary manned voyage to outer space with scientists to research biological life on Uranus, Neptune, Pluto or their satellites.

If there is one astronomical unit (AU) from Earth to the Sun equal to 150 million kilometers, planning a voyage to Pluto 39.4 AU away, (in a straight line), would mean a round trip some 100 AU including a little interplanetary touring, or 15,000 million kilometers, supposing they would be more or less in conjunction (aligned in the same direction).

We would visit three planets and their satellites. Uranus has 20, but only five are important, Neptune two

33

and Pluto one. The trip would take 30 days, making ten stops a day; that leaves 20 days traveling time. What would be the required speed? This is very simple:

> Total distance: 15,000 million kilometers
> Traveling time: 20 days
> Distance to cover per day: 750 million kms.

Five AU per day equal traveling approximately at a speed of 31.25 million kilometers per hour, which is 521 thousand kilometers per minute. At present we have space vehicles, astronauts, technology to carry out studies, but not the proper technology to obtain these speeds.

But, going back again in time, when our barge reached Alexandria, wouldn't it have been even more incredible in those days to think of the Apollo trip than it is today of travels in space? What would the ship's captain have thought? Wouldn't he have considered it even more incredible than what you can consider nowadays of the proposed trip to Uranus, Neptune and Pluto?

We are at the dawn of the NEW ERA of light and understanding for mankind; all mysteries will be revealed, but faith is needed as a bridge between comprehension and intellect.

The Bible notes, in other words, blessed are those who believe without seeing or understanding because they feel with the spirit. They acquire spiritual vision by rising above, to understand what is beyond human reason.

Our scientific knowledge will not be able to unveil all mystery. This will happen after a trial period when mankind faces the consequences of its irresponsible exploitation of the planet Earth. Physical suffering will come about for not respecting ecology, because of greed, in spite of having had the knowledge to foresee the results of its actions.

Man has upset the balance of nature for his own existence in the biosphere. Thereby provoking a reaction of the elements that are physical evidence of our planet as a living being to be able to recover the required equilibrium, that nature has to fulfill, in accordance to universal laws.

It is a given fact that mankind exists in an almost permanent state of war in all corners of the planet. A true war of social, economic and religious ideas.

Man is the predator of man; cruelty, intolerance and madness are set loose and destroy what civilization took generations to achieve. Apparently intelligent and enlightened men let themselves be swept away by fanatism. All go mad without even realizing the most savage of beasts would not behave in like manner.

Destroying their brothers by fire and blood, through technological, political and economic power, their own homes are flooded with blood, tears and despair. Can mankind such as this even be aware of the extent of this incongruence?

The nature of our planet is made up by the planet itself and the plant and animal kingdoms that thrive within. Man has invaded the whole planet and contaminates it without any respect. Plants and animals have become slaves and suffer the consequences of his clumsiness and stubbornness. Lack of intellectual evolution can clearly be seen in his behavior and thus turns himself into his own executioner.

Nature´s reaction has already begun to show its effects. Alterations provoked by mankind are already in a process of readjustment. All of us are aware of the climatic variations as shown by changes in temperature, humidity and the winds. By altering the metereological conditions rains, hurricanes and tornadoes act as though the planet wishes to cleanse itself of what irritates it (this is us). These elements could be scourges for mankind on the face of the Earth.

Besides, this imbalance could affect the delicate equilibrium of the lithosphere, and this will tend to find a new balance by adjusting the continental plaques. This readjustment will cause, of course, tectonic movements or earthquakes, shifting and sliding between plaques, fracture, etc., that will bring unpredictable consequences for mankind. If the tranquility and equilibrium of the oceans are altered, these in turn could even change the planet´s geography. In the new balance of the Earth´s surface, changes could occur up as some areas emerge and others disappear underwater. Frictions of adjusting plaques could cause faults over the existing ones, violent fractures or the fusion of rock plaques by reactivated fires within volcanoes.

All of the above would cause the Great Tribulation for mankind, and in turn, be the deciding factor for a change in man´s attitude. Realizing this impotence against the forces of nature, man in his despair, will listen to the voice of his conscience. Then all religious and economic wars will come to an end, when mankind will become, through fear and pain, in a new humanity where spiritual values and love for fellow man will be renewed.

Experience has already shown us that man, facing sorrows and tribulations, changes his attitude and becomes aware of his responsibility towards his brothers, and his behavior shows his highest moral and spiritual values.Would it be that this affliction is necessary as the only way to recuperate brotherly love and kindness?

If this is so, then it will only be after this trial, when a new world will begin with peace, love and progress (up to now we have only stood at the threshold of true knowledge) and scientific development could be renewed and advanced into the dawn of a NEW ERA.

CHAPTER III

In order to live, irrational creatures
are guided by instinct.
This is the light that paves their path.
Man is given that light,
directly by his spirit.
It is the voice of his conscience,
it is the voice of God.

Pablo E. Hawnser

WHO AM I?

As human beings are aware of our physical bodies and we are conscious of our material being, which has the capacity, through our senses, to store information as in a computer. This natural computer is our brain.

Throughout the course of our life, processed information becomes knowledge and is increased and illustrated by living our experiences. These are a graphic part of knowledge, as we remember them in third dimension and in full color, by the sounds, the aromas, the temperatures and any other environmental data registered by our senses at the time.

Also our brains work with energy, as computers do, work with energy. Without electricity, a computer would be no more than a useless complex gadget. Likewise, our mind could not function without the energy that animates our physical bodies, including the nervous system and the brain. Our life is the result of the interaction of physical energies within our bodies and their interactions with the spirit.

Now then, a plant manifests life transforming energy, fulfilling its predetermined functions and following the laws of nature. It begins with its birth, when the seed sprouts and continues with its growth, reproduction and finally, its death, as the transforming energies cease to give it life.

Life is also evident in an animal, fulfilling similar functions and besides presents other more complex, such as freedom of movement. Even so, it complies strictly with the laws of nature, as the plant obeys predetermined functions we call instinctive, regulating its behavior during life. Besides being able to move with freedom in his environment, the basic difference between an animal and a plant consists in the fact that the animal has a brain, from the smallest, simplest and least developed, to the larger and more physically evolved as in mammals.

A brain gives animals memory and other functions, hence their superiority over plants. This is the intelligence that requires a high degree of complexity in its neuronal interconnections. They can learn from experience, and it is evident they have freedom to make decisions. Although, this does not mean that they have free will, as true conscience and an evaluation of its behavior does not exist.

We accept plants and animals have life due to a creation animated by energies that fulfill universal laws of nature within a context oriented towards a predetermined end, within the evolution of the planet.

Where does a human being enter this natural symphony? He makes his appearance as an animal and later on, elevates his condition to become a HUMAN BEING, when he receives a SPIRIT from his Creator, in addition to a brain capable of greater development.

The spirit uses information received through his senses to generate mental processes and, through them, judgments and thoughts. Thereby taking advantage of experiences printed in his memory to make a mental decision. To be able to act he also receives spiritual gifts which are: a CONSCIENCE and FREE WILL.

38

A CONSCIENCE will be a guide to carry out actions a mental decision has determined as positive or negative.

FREE WILL is a SPIRITUAL GIFT whereby a human being is allowed to act in accordance to his will. This action will be taken after reaching a mental decision that is the result of a judgment where he considers all the facts within reach, he analyzes them and comes to a conclusion. Once he has reached this conclusion in his mind, his CONSCIENCE will evaluate it. Then, with full acceptance of this evaluation, he will be free to act according to his own will.

In other words, man has freedom of action and not only has to obey his intuition or a genetic prerecording, because he would not be responsible for his actions since these would be automatic reactions as the spasms of the heart pumping blood throughout the circulatory system or the spasms of the esophagus in swallowing and of the digestive system finishing the process. No, we refer to the actions carried out by a human being, with full consent, knowing the what, why, how and when to obtain a benefit or a loss for himself or for someone or something else by exercising his free will.

In addition to having his own physical energy to nourish his animal life, a human being uses another more subtle one, more complex, not physical, but equally real in his mind. He perceives sensations similar to those he receives from the senses and identifies them mentally the same way, through the transmission of another type of energy called feelings.

Through our sense of touch we can feel the pain caused by thorns or the delightful caresses of fresh water. But the sweetness of joy or the painful grief of disappointment are perceived through the spiritual senses.

In other words, emotional sensations reach the physical brain, but not through electrical impulses of the sensorial nerves. They are not images of electronic light nor vibrations of sound nor chemical reactions to taste or smell. They are vibrations that become electronic compilations that are identified by the mind and enter the brain to take part in mental processes.

We physically register happiness, sadness, hope, altruism, loyalty, generosity, selfishness, excessive pride or love in our mind in this way, while being sensations identified with the SOUL, participate in our material being as if we had received them through the sensorial organs of our physical body.

Therefore, man being a physical animal is classified as "superior" due to his rational capacity, mind and spirit that allow him to enjoy the guidance of his CONSCIENCE and of the freedom of action given by FREE WILL.

It is convenient to agree that:

--The physical body of man receives communications through the senses.

--The soul or spiritual body receives communications through the mind, where the CONSCIENCE influences mental processes in man´s decision making.

Let us remember two common sayings:

"He is a good soul!"
"He is mean spirited!"

These sayings demonstrate clearly how the spiritual feelings of a physical being can be identified by actions taken by FREE WILL. By this we are not talking about physical characteristics but spiritual ones.

Thus, let us accept then that a human being has two integrated elements: the material or the physical body, and subtle, which is the SOUL. This controls feelings and their sensations, which form part of man´s mind.

So, where do feelings like humbleness, patience, charity and love reside when not present and active in a mental process? As the physical body has a brain with its lobules of neurons to store information, and the organs of the senses (eyes, ears, etc.) that are there even when not in use; so the SOUL also has, within its spiritual brain, in a dimension of its own which are the CHAKRAS

The chakras are centers of energy through which vibrations of the third and fourth dimension are manifested internally in the PLEXUS. These physical areas receive influences of energy from each chakra.

Vibrations received by the material body of a human being are detected sensorially by physical organs under the influence of energy of the acting chakra and passed on to the physical brain by the spiritual brain at the same time.

Perfectly marked zones where pain or physical excitement correlates with feelings such as love and disappointment show up more intensely in the cardiac plexus or the heart; just as fear and insecurity are felt in the solar plexus and the stomach, even malaise or general euphoria are not related physically but spiritually.

Physical sensations are feelings transmitted by the nervous system. They are the perceptions of our senses and travel from the periphery to the central nervous system, through the cerebellum to the brain.

When sensations arise from the subconscious and /or from a spiritual origin, the path is inverted: from the center of our brain, where they are interpreted, they travel to the cerebral lobules and to the cerebral cortex. On their way, they cause biochemical reactions in the neurons that communicate and store information, to finally arrive at the plexus and the physical organs (heart, stomach and other areas of the body) where they manifest themselves to our physical being.

When the feeling is not generated by physical perceptions or by the senses, all body communications are activated. The nervous, lymphatic and circulatory systems operate as a whole and physical alterations as temperature, pressure and even of a glandular nature can occur.

The material intercommunication between the soul and the physical body, takes place totally through the plexus and is felt from the top of the head to the tip of the toes.

Let's establish the SOUL as our spirit, that element of our being of a more subtle nature within our physical body. Its matter belongs to another dimension as it is integrated by subatomic particles specifically of that dimension.

The SPIRITUAL GIFTS of divine origin are found precisely in this spiritual body identifying man as the preferred son of creation.

These gifts allow man to contact his spirit, also of divine origin, and thus be guided by his conscience.

A CONSCIENCE analyzes thoughts produced by a mental process, which no longer is an isolated idea nor extracted from memory. These are only the elements, and the final result is the complete thought where the brain proposes action. This complete thought is analyzed by the CONSCIENCE to determine its harmony with the universe and then passes judgment.

This "judgment" determines if the thought is good or bad, positive or negative, correct, just, truthful and in accordance with universal law. Thereby a human being knows, before taking action, if this is accordance with or against his own CONSCIENCE.

Thus, with full inner awareness, a human being decides to act according to his FREE WILL, whether he follows his conscience depending on his interests, his moral values, his physical well being or his spiritual inclination. He acts and by this selects the path to follow from options within his reach. As every action causes a corresponding reaction, so will his decision to act have consequences. Due to this marvelous symbiosis, the spirit will become the means for man's evolution.

When man becomes conscious of his physical body, his spiritual being and his mind, he surpasses the boundaries of limited understanding of his physical senses and is suddenly faced alone with big dilemmas. This is when his mind produces knowledge within his understanding and partially unveils the immensity and infinity of time; of the physical reality that limits him and the reality of his cosmic being that incites him to search for TRUTH. It is then, when he asks: Who am I? Where do I come from? Where am I going?

When a human being evolves enough to pose these questions, he is motivated and interested in this story and can live it with the author, feeling the excitement of someone about to embark on an adventure through the world of knowledge.

The reader will hunger to know more as, apart from his religious inclinations, he will also be aware that man's intelligence searches for an explanation, a justification giving meaning to his existence. Since he now has the capacity to understand so many marvels proving we are on the path to spiritual evolution.

The real message the reader will find in this story must reach his soul through his spirit. The metaphysical and extra-terrestrial information included will stimulate the awakening of his conscience, and dare him to accept the reality of the Universe with his mind.

CHAPTER IV

One can look...without seeing,
one can hear...without understanding,

but then one cannot comprehend.

Pablo Hawnser

Whoever has eyes to see, let him look,
whoever has ears to hear,
let him listen, whoever can comprehend,
let him also understand.

Quotation from the Bible

WHERE DO I COME FROM?

In "Eric´s Story", the reader will be able to share feelings and doubts with the actor, including the excitement of seeing fiction become reality, the encounter with a universe that had only been imagined but is real; discovering the horizon of nothingness from the origins of matter to the foreseeable fates regarding the spiritual immortality of after life, and his mission towards his Creator through the universe.

It is a human story, where the reader will be able to participate in unveiling the mystery of the universe where we live and our ability to easily understand the physical and spiritual marvels that surround us. To coexist physically and mentally with our elder brothers, who are as real as we are and with whom we have a common destiny, although they are a step ahead in evolution.

There are two areas of discussion and study to be addressed by mankind. This should be done now.

FIRST. It is necessary to find a way to make all human beings on the planet aware that the existence and life of other human beings outside the planet Earth is perfectly natural.

Any grade school child accepts this affirmation as naturally as he watches the Cosmos program of Carl Sagan on television. Why do adults see it only believable as a science fiction adventure?

Maybe because ignorance makes them fear whatever could happen. As man on Earth is so belligerent, he imagines the arrival of extra-terrestrial astronauts being the aggressive and mindless characters created in Star Wars or in cheap and irresponsible literary trash which fills children´s minds.

SECOND. It is necessary for authorities to promote open and scientific discussions regarding extra-terrestrial visits, instead of denying the facts, especially as they have been able to reach this planet and the atmospheric conditions are favorable. What is the reason we are not allowed to get in direct contact with them?

It is not hard to face the problem sensibly. The difficulty is, in that according to man's know-how a trip from another system is not possible because of the distance. Of course it is not! Not with the means, knowledge and technologies available to us today.

But, is it not too arrogant of man on this planet to think that if he cannot do it, no one else can?

It is time to be open-minded, meekly realistic, ban prejudices and have gentle ambitions. The NEW ERA will allow us to reach a level similar to that of our elder brothers.

When we refer to them as "elder brothers", we must understand we are alluding not only to their technological advancement. This, although important, is secondary, since it can be obtained by our own efforts or with assistance. No, in reality we are referring to the degree of their spiritual evolution, vastly superior to our own.

When we have attained a spiritual evolution through a change in attitude, we will reach a greater development and a new opening of our intellect. We will be able to comprehend the message of our Creator who is and always has been the same for mankind, ever since the beginning of his life on the planet: to love one another and to treat each other as brothers as all are his spiritual children.

When we have overcome evil, envy, deceit, greed, lies, false pride...and they will be overcome! Whether by good or bad, we will then deserve to be in open contact with them, who will visit us as naturally as we receive visits of our brothers from other continents of the Earth.

Let us agree on the following definitions as they are understood by mankind:

ENCOUNTERS OF THE FIRST KIND. They are distant sightings of UFOs that can or can not be extra-terrestrial vehicles, seen briefly. Whoever has had this experience enters the stage of UNCERTAINTY.

ENCOUNTERS OF THE SECOND KIND. These are sightings of extra-terrestrial vessels with or without crews, at a short distance, with clear images. Everyone is interested when these are reported, but nobody believes in them. The witness looses his credibility, distrust begins, his judgment is doubted and his state of mind is questioned. The authorities dispute them, and therefore are not officially accepted.

ENCOUNTERS OF THE THIRD KIND. These are direct contact with extra-terrestrial beings. Any reports place the speaker in a situation of little credibility. He needs to offer authentic proof, such as for example, a video where he would be seen with his contacts, entering and descending from the space ship, waving and maybe even making some announcement to create a more natural scene. If this is not possible, then he becomes a passive nutcase in the eyes of his listeners; as the authorities or any serious civilian will consider his reports as science fiction.

The majority of reports of encounters known at present, all refer to people who saw them at a distance repairing a vessel or carrying out some other activity and then going away. There are also reports of close encounters but the witnesses either lost consciousness and are not able to render more information, remain in shock by the experience. There is talk about research, surgical interventions, kidnappings, abductions attributed to extra-terrestrials that have caused grave traumas to the victims.

However, we now have this story; there is no video nor photographs as this was the expressed wish of the visitors, as is the managing of the information left to us that we present in "Eric´s Story".

Science is a means to turn fiction into reality, it becomes a peephole through which humanity can see the light to learn what Creation is, but we are still not able to comprehend the entire cosmic truth....

CHAPTER V

ERIC´S STORY

Eric was feeling a little tense while looking out the window as his taxicab sped through the city towards the airport. He thought he was on time, as at 5:30 A.M. the traffic was very light and in a few minutes he would get there, even a little early; so this was not the cause of his nervousness.

He was feeling happy, the fresh breeze of morning air was stimulating, but deep inside his mind a restlessness was beginning. He hoped his premonition was correct, but he decided not to think about his feelings to avoid disappointment.

The events that, all of a sudden, appeared in his life had turned it into a whirlpool of emotions. There was even a moment when he felt loosing control, but an inner force of strength provided a peace of mind that, little by little, was permitting him to get over his confusion and accept the experiences naturally, with serene patience and a capacity of comprehension he never thought he had.

A clarity of mind with which he could understand and accept many of the concepts that previously had caused him confusion was evident! His mind allowed him to understand problems without any major effort, that previously would have caused him to dismay before solving.

The taxicab driver glanced at him a couple of times through the rear view mirror and when their eyes met, he asked, "At what time does your plane leave?"

"Don´t worry," Eric answered, "I have to be there by 6:00 A.M., but we´ll arrive at the airport much earlier, thank you."

"Really, I could go faster if you want me to," said the driver.

"No, it is not necessary, really. Please continue at the same pace. I do not want the risk of a traffic officer stopping us. I don´t want complications, not today anyway. But, thank you all the same."

The driver looked at him and didn´t say anymore, but Eric glanced back at him through the rear view mirror and smiled realizing he had tried to be helpful, sensing his passenger´s stress.

Well, he really shouldn´t press himself, as everything was in order. This would be just one more trip, much like the ones he usually took for his job, up to three times a month. He couldn´t avoid thinking about his experiences, but this time had a feeling of expectancy that something different was about to happen.

This time, like many others, he would combine air and car travel. He liked to drive and preferred to leave earlier, but the flight to Monterrey would take an hour and fifteen minutes and catching an earlier flight was unnecessary.

The taxicab entered the unloading zone amidst the congestion formed by rental cars and baggage boys with their carts hurriedly receiving passengers. Eric paid his fare and after thanking his driver, turned and entered the terminal.

The cold on his cheeks brought memories that were related in a way with the experiences and events of the last months, but that in reality, came from many years before; in fact, almost all his life.

The usual comings and goings of an airport and the local broadcasts of flight departures calmed him, while he went to the counter to pick up his boarding pass. The clerk was helpful and pleasant as he courteously assigned the requested seat and wished

48

him a good trip. He also was starting his work day and was a little prophetic when he wished him an "extraordinary" day. Eric nodded with a smile and said, "I hope it is, thank you!"

Now, more at ease, he slowly made his way to the airline waiting room. As he concentrated on his thoughts, it seemed to him all external noises and voices became muted. He needed a mental rerun of everything and be calm. He had to do this with serenity and self-possession, so his head would not start boiling over with ideas, doubts, repressed emotional impressions and tensions so as not loose control. It was clear that his brain was in such a fragile state that control could disappear suddenly and he wasn´t sure he could be able to recover easily.

He felt the danger of lingering in anguish or was it fear? But fear of what? Maybe of not knowing what to do with the responsibility he had been given. It was the fear of being surrounded by people and the obligation of telling them something urgent; but nobody could see him, he was invisible. How should he address them?

His flight number had not appeared on the screen assigning the boarding gate yet. He breathed deeply and sat down trying to relax; he did not want to think, but couldn´t avoid it.

How did everything begin?..............

Eric was ten years old when he became aware of an uncanny experience. One day he saw himself in a strange place; he was beside a window watching the snow fall. Instinctively he stretched out his hand to touch the window pane and he felt how cold it was even with gloves on. Standing on his bed, leaning on the wide wooden window sill, he looked around and everything was familiar, yet he know this was the first time he had seen it.

After getting up, he felt like someone waking up for the first time in a strange place where he had arrived the night before. Everything seemed different to him. He knew the people, the things and the places, but notwithstanding, he felt he was seeing them for the first time. The dream of the window, the snow, the coldness of the glass, everything fitted within the novelty of daily life. Yet, watching the people he knew who they were, but had the feeling of seeing them for the first time. It was like being on a visit and having the sensation of knowing a place, a life, a surrounding he only had in his memory.

That was the first experience, little by little he got used his life and to identify his surroundings from within, he experienced the discrepancy between what he had to express and what he really felt inside. For example, a classmate looked him up repeatedly, this did not displease him too much, but it did not correspond to what he felt. Even though he remembered in a dreamlike way that they had been inseparable and used to walk together as great friends.

The same thing happened to him in many ways: his clothes, his family, his food, his friends and his surroundings didn´t totally satisfy him. Without understanding why, he had felt as an outsider to his own life, until in time, he had gotten used to it.

The loudspeaker announcing the flight departure brought him back from his reflections. On his way to the gate he kept on remembering that feeling of change.

It happened several times, some within the space of months, others after years had passed. He always had the impression of remembering things about his life, but without consciously having really lived them. Also, the dreams from another place that repeated themselves, the remembrance of knowing another life, another place, another family, other customs, everything was different, except a small ceramic figurine that showed up alternately in two places; on his night table or on the window sill.

He boarded the plane and made himself comfortable. As he looked out the window, he remembered the long hours of watching out the window where he could see snow, rain or a brilliant sky highlighting the colors of the forest. Yes, he clearly remembered what he could see from the window and of having walked through each one of those places, in such a way that they were familiar even to the most insignificant of details, like the fence that separated the backyard from the field, the details of the part where he used to jump out to run through the trail up to the forest. And the sight of the house from there! Feeling the cold air on his nose and eyes while playing with the snow. He could remember the feeling of happiness when playing with snowballs and the cold wind that seemed to freeze the uncovered parts of his face. The memory of walks to town with the family to go shopping and the long tiring trip back on foot or on a cart pulled by a white horse he used to feed. Dreams, repeated dreams, leaving a sense of sadness or nostalgia.

The voice of the flight attendant on the plane´s loudspeaker brought him back from his reverie. The routine announcements for the flight were always a little nuisance, but he overcame this by ignoring it and thought of Rahel.

In his mind, he had gotten used to accept the reality of his presence, his friendship and all it meant to him, and also the responsibility of the knowledge entrusted to him and of his great effort to absorb the reality alone with his spirit. At the beginning it was difficult, but the fear of being disbelieved or ridiculed was a help. Afterwards, he learned to keep it stored away in a special locked corner in his mind, to avoid the temptation of allowing the contents to escape. Although he felt calm, he was restless as well.

Every time he spoke to Rahel, ever since the beginning when Mirza introduced him, he received the necessary tools to get used to and to learn how to carry the inner burden of that reality with the same ease as the memories of daily life.

He began to daydream and remembered something he had analyzed several times. He imagined an ant was traveling on a small branch floating down stream, looking desperately for a way out. Then just before falling into whirling waters, the branch got stuck on the bank, and the ant feels it is his chance and quickly goes from one twig to another, just in time before the current sweeps the first away. What a fantastic coincidence! Mathematically exact for the little ant to be saved; but if ten meters upstream we would have wanted to calculate the probabilities that this would happen, maybe it would be one in a million. Was it saved by a miracle? Of course not! The elements involved were: the current, the turns of the branch on its route downstream and its position to be able to stop with mathematical precision in the only possible place. All this was going to happen, and it did. And, if we had filmed it and reran it, we could study everything that was necessary for it to happen. When it did, the ant took advantage of the only opportunity it had. Was it smart or intelligent? Was it conscious its life was in danger? Or was it coincidence? The fact is that it did the right thing at the right time.

In much the same way in our life, the participating elements are there already and are going to take part exactly when their time comes and we will reach the necessary place at the right moment. Only then, at that moment, will it depend on us, the only beings of creation with free will, to act this way or another and therefore modify our journey through life. This happens every time we make a decision with our free will and we go on modifying or building our own destiny.

Yes, it is us and us alone who can decide our path in life, and we modify our destiny by our own voluntary decisions. We lose the divine opportunity to participate in our choices when we remain passive.

Now it was the stewardess who brought him out of his reflection, with a gentle voice said, "Would you care for breakfast?"

Eric nodded with a smile and hurriedly ate to continue with his thoughts, trying to make sense of all the ideas that occasionally engulfed his mind

That Thursday of October 1989 was, without a doubt, when the swirling began. He could clearly remember the emotional impact on his stomach when, surprised and elated, he saw Rahel´s space ship for the first time. It appeared gliding across the road about 50 meters off the ground and then sliding silently behind some trees on a small ravine to his right.

He saw the chance of getting off the highway onto a little dirt road that led toward the area where the vessel had gone. Without a second thought, he took it to find and see that "thing". (Figure 1)

As he left the road he didn´t see any ongoing or oncoming traffic and the need to have someone with him crossed his mind. If he had seen another vehicle, maybe he would wait to have someone accompany him to investigate, but since he did not see anyone, he decided to go by himself to see the apparent UFO or space ship or whatever it was, as its whereabouts were very close by.

He advanced softly some 150 meters off the road to the point he had seen it descend, and according to its angle of descent, it must be down to the left. He stopped silently, he did not feel nervous nor frightened. Upon analysis, he realized he was puzzled. He got off the car, but thinking it over, he changed his mind and turned the car around pointing to the way back, as a precaution in case he had to run away.

He then got out, quietly closing the car door to avoid making much noise so his presence would not be detected. He went to the ravine and after a few steps....There was the apparatus, vessel or whatever it was!

FIGURE 1

When the space ship had crossed the road, a searchlight of approximately two meters in diameter pointing downwards was lit, giving off a conical halo similar to the rays of the sun, lighting up the surface below. Now the light was off, the vessel was silent, posed on a tripod about a meter and a half above the ground. It appeared to be made of a very smooth dark lusterless gray plastic.

He calculated the total diameter to be 14 or 15 meters and its height at the center, some seven meters approximately. It was similar to placing a soup plate upside down on a flat plate, but lacking flat surfaces. All the perimeter followed a soft aerodynamic curve from top to bottom. The area of greater diameter was one third from the bottom to the top. The supports were wide at the bottom like concave skates at the end of a tripod at a 30 degree angle.

There it was, silently standing out clearly under the last lights of the afternoon. It was approximately 6:30 P.M., only about half an hour was left until darkness fell.

Without thinking, Eric slowly made his way towards it like a robot, concentrating his five senses only what was ahead. He tried to discover some sign of life inside some window or traces of a door, but there was nothing visible from that distance. It was about 100 or 120 meters away, and from there, it seemed to be made of one solid piece.

He stopped enraptured in contemplation. He couldn´t believe what he was seeing, but there it was, it was real, right before his eyes. Then he heard (or was it his imagination?) a voice telling him, "Be careful, do not get too close."

However, he still kept on until he was about 40 meters away. He then felt a very soft humming sound, much like high tension wires; at the same time, he sensed the proximity of a magnetic field. Cautiously he backed up a little, and to prove he was right, he took a stone the size of a baseball and threw it towards the apparatus, not to hit it, but simply having it cross the area where he had felt the sensation of a magnetic field. The stone was in the air, when all of a sudden, it seemed to hit an invisible wall and was repelled violently by a greater energy. After seeing this, he preferred to slowly back until he reached a safer distance from the magnetic field. He believed they were definitely watching him, they knew he was there. Why then, didn´t they show themselves?

He was sure he was standing before a vessel foreign to Earth. There wasn´t the slightest doubt. He was not ready for more surprises, he was only trying to live this experience to the limit.

Nothing happened for some time, he then tried to communicate with its occupants by telepathy. He made an effort to remember what he knew and concentrated as best he could to send a mental greeting, some words of friendship and of peace....but to no avail.

Darkness was falling, so he decided to go back to the car. As he got closer, he got a great surprise: a black pickup truck was parked only a few meters from the car. This made him react, and immediately started looking for the driver. Would he be the owner of the place? Or was it someone who had also seen the vessel and had come to investigate? He returned to the vessel and was astonished to see a person was approaching it; it was a woman in trousers! Clearly it was a woman, walking slowly, elegantly and sprightly in spite of the uneven terrain. She looked young, with beautiful blond hair, slightly combed back. (Figure 2)

Eric, in his confusion, ran forward and shouted "Hi!". He stopped short of the magnetic field and saw how a hatch, resembling the boarding ramp on a plane, slowly open.

The inside was softly lit and in the doorframe of the hatch a tall man appeared dressed in a one-piece uniform. The woman seemed to be wearing something similar, it appeared to be a one piece suit, including the footwear, although the boots seemed to be of a darker color. She reached the entrance and turned back to see Eric, who was paralyzed observing all this. He then impulsively raised his hand in greeting. They returned the greeting and entered the vessel, closing the hatch behind them.

After a few seconds, as if a band slid horizontally, some small windows surrounding the upper part, lit up. They were rectangular, approximately 40 x 60 centimeters in size, and were placed in vertical positions at regular intervals and showed a soft interior light of a slightly greenish tone.

The two characters appeared again, one in each window, after watching Eric for a few seconds, they raised their hands again signaling a greeting or a farewell. He again felt or heard something within him saying: "Until next time, we'll see each other later; do not tell anyone what you have seen, make believe it did not happen. Until next time. We'll see each other again….." (Figure 3)

The band turned again, the windows disappeared and the vessel remained motionless as a dark shadow. In a few seconds a light on the bottom went on, the supports had been drawn back, the vessel was motionless, suspended in the air!

Only a very light humming sound was heard and the vessel started to float vertically, slowly rising and gradually increasing its speed. A halo of light lit up the area where the vessel had been so clearly it looked like sunlight. It even lighted all the surrounding area. The circle of light widened rapidly and when it reached Eric's observation post, the vessel must have risen 100 meters. The cone was about 60 degrees and its intensity seemed to be an afternoon sunlight filtering through the clouds. However, it rapidly paled and in seconds became only a star in the sky. It drew a semicircle and became ever smaller and then disappeared.

FIGURE 2

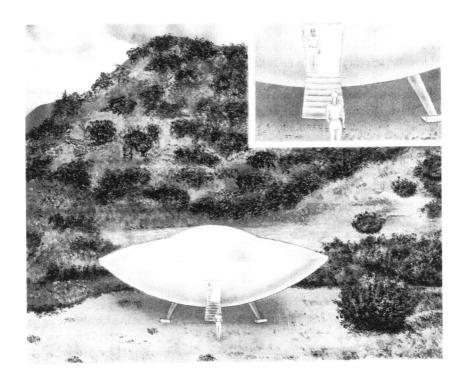

Eric was petrified in place. After a few moments, he began to feel chilly in the cold wind and walked slowly back to his car. The pickup truck was still there, he recognized it as the same one. Two searchlights mounted a frame behind the cabin and two other red ones were on the ends, facing the back as if they were stoplights.

He got closer and touched the hood of the pickup truck, it was hot. He looked inside, there was nothing special about it. The back part was covered by a material resembling a waterproof quilt and was perfectly fastened with hooks. Underneath there was a load of one-gallon plastic jars lined up in perfect order.

FIGURE 3

He got in his car, started it and then stopped on the road without knowing what to think or what to do concerning the encounter and all that had happened. He turned and saw the pickup truck again, its image came to mind as seeing it through his rear view mirror. It had been while he was in the city of Queretaro when, on his way back, before taking the exit to the highway, he had almost taken a detour to visit a friend. He remembered that when he slowed down, an inner voice said, "Come on, don't stop or you will be late for the appointment."

He didn't have any appointment he could remember nor did he have to be back in Mexico City at a certain time. He only wanted to do most the driving in daylight, although night would fall before the two hour trip ended. As he started up after that small pause, the pickup truck overtook him rapidly. After driving a while he reached the Sauz gas station. The pickup was parked there, without a driver; it was unmistakable due to the search lights. However, it was all insignificant and not giving it a second thought, he filled up and went on his way.

It was then when he clearly understood it was the women guarding him. He was sure it was her voice saying: *"Don't stop or you will be late for your appointment, " "be careful, don't get too close," "until next time, we'll see each other later" and "don't tell anything to anyone."* All those sensations were exactly the same, as if coming from the same source just as he had felt when he remembered having heard those words. Maybe that is the way to listen through telepathy? If so, why didn't they say more? Besides, that meant that they had understood his efforts to communicate with them.

What he was trying to tell them became more important, because of this. "I don't know if you can receive my transmissions, but I am trying to contact you, I have no doubt you are extra-terrestrials, your space ship confirms this. I have already had other experiences, and am convinced that you visit us, but I don't understand whey you do it secretly; why don't you come out in the open? We are friends, we accept your reality, little by little everyone will get used to you and it will be like when the Spaniards came to America, I only hope you will not treat us as badly....".

He smiled remembering his phrase, surely he didn't have the mental strength, the technique or whatever was necessary to transmit his thoughts. And, besides, they wouldn't know what he was talking about when he mentioned the Spaniards. Or would they?

"More coffee?" asked the friendly flight attendant, making Eric return to reality.

"Yes, thank you," he answered and prepared another cup.

Now he began to remember his inner struggle since he had left the sighting area and the pickup truck. On the highway, he felt a knot in his throat, wanting to scream, stop all the cars and tell them what he had just seen, to take them to see the pickup truck to look for its owner, to analyze the area, to search for clues. The excitement of arriving home and telling all the family

59

everything…but almost audibly this time, "Until next time, we´ll see each other later. DO NOT SAY ANYTHING."

Was that a reality? "Do not say anything" would return again and again in his memory. But he thought that these ideas or phrases could not originate in his mind. He obviously must have "received" them. He couldn´t have produced them since his natural impulses and wishes were all to the contrary.

He kept on driving automatically, slowly calming down. He remembered every detail, absorbing and digesting the experience. With growing excitement he realized he was going to make contact again, and understood it was not by chance, but something perfectly predetermined.

The place had been chosen, the pickup truck could have blocked other cars, to leave him alone at the moment of the encounter; the space vessel crossed the place at the precise moment. Everything had been thought out. Another question arose: Why me? What could be the reason to precisely choose me?

He tried to think of the characteristics needed for a person to be eligible for a contact such as this: previous knowledge, academic schooling? No, he didn´t believe so. There are many known cases of encounters of the third kind with very simple people, sometimes even ignorant. It could even be said they looked for them like this purposely.

But…were those contacts casual, accidental or planned? Were they locating a certain person with special characteristics? And if this were so, what were they? What characteristics did he possess that could be useful for this? He certainly had a willing disposition, he wanted it. If there had been a contest, he would have done everything within his reach to win the designation.

The preparation? Well, he had always wanted to learn more. He liked cosmography and was very interested in esoteric teachings, as also the functioning of the mind. Could it have been his wish to communicate by telepathy? But, how would they have known that? He didn`t believe he had exceptional skills to make a difference.

Could it have been his search for metaphysical knowledge and of paranormal phenomena? These were subject of great interest to many people, but he was neither the exception nor did he stand out. Was it his research and studies on quantum mechanics and physics, trying to understand the theory of relativity and its effects on human beings? Well, maybe, if someone knew him well enough and was aware he had had previous experiences, and of his complete belief of extra-terrestrial presence in the past and in the present on our planet.

But there must be something more to do with this. He remembered the practices in telepathy and studies of mind control with his late friend, Christopher D., whom he thought he had contacted after death. Would that have something to do with it or his bizarre experiences of "interchanges between persons". A shill went through him when he felt he had definitely been chosen.

If these people really considered his personal characteristics, this meant the extra-terrestrials had an information service regarding the intelligence and knowledge about each one of us as if they lived here. Besides, they must live among us. How could the arrival of the woman in the pickup truck be explained? And who was to retrieve the vehicle? Or is it that, by now, they had returned her and she was on her way home with the pickup? Anyway, they would have needed only a few seconds to bring her back immediately after he left.

As he thought about this, a mental image of the pickup truck came forth. What did the jars contain? Could it be some chemicals required for their vessels or at their base, wherever it was? Suddenly, it occurred to him that she could be in the vehicle and was behind him. He had been driving slowly, in no hurry, and in one hour anyone who had left a few minutes later could have caught up with him.

Before arriving at the toll booth in Mexico City, Eric had already realized that he couldn´t tell anyone about his experience if he wanted to deserve the opportunity of being contacted again. "We have perfectly identified and found the persons who are to be our contacts. Besides, they are classified to know what kind of contact can be had with them", Rahel would confirm later.

Another thought came to Eric, either by association of ideas or some mental mechanism, as the mind is like a computer and tries to find similar links. He remembered Rahel later made the following comment: "Some people have the opportunity of sighting space ships out exploring, but we have no control over these, as we don´t even know who they are. We pass a predetermined route to allow the sighting. We include people with some kind of schooling and evolution in this type of sightings, so they can see us from the surface of the plant, as can also aircraft crews, military plane pilots, ship crews and all those who, by chance, see us."

"These are awareness shows, something like making people believe they can see us, without our knowledge, but it is not like that."

"You can well understand we have the means to go anywhere and not be seen nor detected, not even by your tracking devices, whether by sonar in the water or radar on the surface or in space. We can come and go and carry out all sorts of missions and work in uninhabited areas, or in populated ones, without your ever being aware of it."

"The contacts, on the other hand, are very specific, in a certain place and with the persons we have selected. Contacts like the one we have with you are decided upon previously. Those selected, due to a large number of personal characteristics, physical and spiritual, intellectual and emotional, must also possess the social human conditions to allow them to fulfill the mission we wish to assign to them."

The plane shook a little as it started to overfly the mountains. Eric observed with great interest, as always, imagining what faults had caused the formation of those solid rock mountains. It impressed him to think that, at that altitude, it could have been possible to watch safely, the formidable earthquake or cataclysm that must have taken place when the layers of rock broke up and became those capricious shapes.

He amused himself for a moment watching a road from high above resembling a small ribbon winding through the mountains.

The entrance to Mexico City through the tedious Tepotzotlan road was always a nuisance. Excessive traffic, bad road signs and the continual dangerous repairs, made this stretch very tiring. Every time he passed through there he thought the same thing: "I hope whoever is responsible and has the proper authority passes through here, and fixes this. At least putting up proper signs, this stretch is a disaster."

However, that night he drove on , he didn't even remember having passed through there. He was so immersed pondering the encounter with the space ship. He felt a little nervous, but it was more stress, not so much thinking about the extra-terrestrial vessel, but wanting to talk about it.

The subject itself is interesting for many people, but only as a topic of conversation or a subject to be discussed, in that it is possible, but there is no real proof. However, those who rely on a strict scientific approach believe interspace travel is impossible because of the distances involved. But when someone dares to claim: "I saw it," suddenly we pay close attention.

"Come on, tell us! What did you see, how, when....?" Showing great interest. The sighting can be simple, fast and in the distance, and possibly all a mistake. Even so, people listening to the narrative wish they had been the spectators. Although, deep inside they are more inclined to believe it was something else and not the real presence of a space ship driven by extra-terrestrial beings.

It becomes an exciting experience to consider the story is probably true, but with an enormous possibility that the teller, even in good faith, is mistaken. A well-thought out analysis indicates, as far as we know, there are no planets inhabited by intelligent beings in our solar system, and the trip from a more distant place is apparently impossible.

With this in mind, Eric realized that to talk about what he saw, without any proof, was simply an invitation to doubt, not only whether the story is true but his sanity as well. He then decided to keep silent and felt greatly relieved

The initial excitement and euphoria had faded now, leaving a hollow feeling in his stomach, but he had hope, that if he had had a real telepathic communication, then, the promise made to him was still pending.

He lived several emotionally packed days. Then, little by little, he recovered his peace of mind and after reliving each and every moment and had filed them away in his memory.

CHAPTER VI

When humans receive the rays of spiritual reflections
they will not even have to make an effort to look for life outside
their world, as they will be seeked, at the same time, by those who
inhabit higher dwellings.

B.T.L.

THE CONTACT

Eric was on the phone with a customer, looking towards the mountains above the skyline of the city. Deep in conversation, he noticed his secretary had entered and was waiting to speak to him. He turned to her and she signaled he had a call on another line. He nodded, but did not interrupt his phone call.

As it ended, he automatically reached out to take the other call. He turned towards her and raising his eyebrows asked who it was. The secretary raised her shoulders and, at the same time, winked in complicity, saying: "I don´t know, but she has a very nice voice."

Eric smiled in amusement.

-"Good morning, may I help you?"

-"Good morning, sir, my name is Mirza. Do you remember me? We saw each other last week on the road to Queretaro, when I left on a voyage. We agreed to see each other again. Did you receive our message?"

Eric felt numb, he know perfectly well who she was, but the surprise call paralyzed him. He breathed deeply to recover and shyly answered, "Well, yes, if it´s what I am remembering....but..."

"Yes, I had to leave the pickup truck next to your car, then I left. You saw me, remember? All right, the person that left with me, or to be more accurate, came to pick me up, is what you call a captain or commander. He is a commanding officer, a person of higher rank, older and more knowledgeable that the rest, but he is a brother, a friend and our guide. Do you understand me?"

Eric got over the initial surprise while she had been speaking. He answered with the greatest courtesy and aplomb he could muster. "I understand you perfectly. What is the name of your companion and boss whom I suppose arrived on board the space ship?"

"His name is Rahel,"- slowly and clearly she spelled- R- A – H- E- L-, pronouncing the intermediate "H" like a soft throaty "J". Eric again had the feeling of remembering as he listened to the name articulated with soft clarity.

Noticing it, he immediately thought: "Is this telepathy?"

"That's right," answered Mirza. "We are having vocal and mental communication at the same time. Does it surprise you? Unconsciously and as beginners, you already do this and you practice in telephone conversations as this one very often, without realizing."

"I imagined that, but couldn't believe it," answered Eric, totally fascinated.

"I am making an appointment for us to meet with him. Is next Saturday at eight o'clock in the morning all right with you?"

"Of course, yes, it seems all right. But couldn't it be sooner?"

"No, you must keep on with your life as usual. This conversation will be repeated, but only in such a way as you can handle it naturally as meeting another friend. Do you understand me? To help you, I can tell you that you will not find any difference between speaking to us or talking to a companion…except for the subject matter and that we will communicate also through mental telepathy. It is very important for you to keep an emotional balance in order to trust your discretion. It is clear that, if it is not possible for you to fulfill these requirements to keep our relationship at that level, we will simply suspend it for your own good and the well being of the mission we are trying to carry out. Do I make myself thoroughly understood?"

"I understand perfectly, I agree and we´ll do it as you have indicated."

Mirza´s tone had been very clear, showing authority, but now became gentle and human. "It will be next Saturday at 8:00 in the morning at Wing´s restaurant on the corner of Mariano Escobedo and Copernico street. Do you agree?"

"Yes, I agree."

"Well, please be on time. Until then…", and she hung up.

When Eric put the phone down, he felt weightless, empty, that only his skin was left. A revolution of ideas, thoughts and memories began. For a moment, he felt extremely nervous, almost out of control. But at that instant he remembered Mirza´s words: "If you can´t control your emotions…..we´ll suspend the relationship…."

He got up and left the office. He went down the street, walking briskly with clenched fists and tightened expression. He headed for a nearby park and, little by little calmed down, breathing deeply slowed to a walk. He ended up sitting on a hard and uncomfortable concrete bench where he totally relaxed regaining control of his mind and his nerves. After that small explosion, he went back to work, calmly and with his emotions and feelings completely under control.

He decided he would have the necessary self-possession, serenity and control over his reactions, his mind and his nerves. Really it shouldn´t be difficult. How many times had he spoken with foreigners? Many times. And what was the difference? Except for the place they came from, none. This was the way to look at it in order to control his attitude. He had to show them he could do it and this way have the chance to ask all the questions he could….He wondered how much time would be spent on him and besides: What was the mission mentioned by Mirza?

The days dragged on slowly, but normally. In his free time, he began a list of questions. But as he did this, he remembered his dreams of experiences in unknown places. He preferred to mentally classify his doubts:

a) First of all, Who are they? Where do they come from? What are they here for? How long have they been here? How many are they? Where do they live? And what do they expect to get from us? How many more contacts are there and where? Why don´t they do it openly? How many space ships are there? Where are they? How do they fly? What energy is used, and at what speed can they travel?

b) About their "walk-ins"? Could they give him an explanation? Why was this method selected by them?

c) Regarding his past experiences with UFOs, had they been spontaneous or were they programmed? Was there any reality concerning his dreams or attempts for astral travels? And what about the knowledge of quantum mechanics on Earth being of extra-terrestrial origin?

He had to talk to them about all this, and more to take advantage of this unparalleled opportunity, although it was also undoubtedly necessary to prove they were really extra-terrestrials. He still doubted himself and whatever he would have to face.

He slowly got used to the idea that his encounter should be as natural as if he were meeting a friend, returning from Europe, China or any other place. After all, they seemed to be human beings like us. If they really were extra-terrestrials, the similarity was so great they could be taken for human beings from Earth. Maybe it could mean this physical form in reality is the common denominator of intelligent beings belonging to humanities having technological evolution on different planets.

If they really came from another planet, would it be one from our solar system? But, which one? Venus and Mars were eliminated based on what has been discovered to date. The possibilities were even less concerning more distant planets. But it seemed more logical for them to come from a closer planet, another star, from another solar system. The closest one is so far way that it would take years of interplanetary travel and that was even more difficult.

If Rahel and Mirza were really interplanetary travelers and came from some place in our system, their presence definitely destroyed the myth of the martians as being little green men or other such fantasies. If they came from another system belonging to a star in our galaxy, then our physical form is definitely a common denominator for mankind or human beings wherever they exist.

The resemblance was not only in appearance, if they didn´t need a space suit, it would mean their environmental conditions and our atmosphere were the same regarding the air, humidity, temperature and pressure, or very similar to those of their place of origin.

Besides, there was nothing to fear, I wouldn´t even be alone with them. It would have been more stunning if they had allowed him to get closer and to talk to them on the space ship. Also, reports and news of extra-terrestrial abductions of human beings and animals and other weird events came to mind, but as far as he could visualize he would not have to face either.

CHAPTER VII

Our universe is enormous, but finite.
What we do not know is infinite.
Intellectually we are on an island in the middle
of an ocean of mysteries which we will be
able to comprehend only through
the efforts of our mind.

Thomas H. Huxley

THE FIRST APPOINTMENT

Eric woke up very early that Saturday, he got ready and minutes after 7:30 A.M. he was arriving at the designated site. He parked on a side street, and as he got out and locked the car, he felt a slight chill. The weightless feeling returned, and although he felt nervous, it was not something he couldn´t control or even feign. He imagined the sensation would be similar to a blind date; exciting yet uneasy. He went to the entrance wondering if it was appropriate to go inside at once or wait for a while at the door. Maybe it would be better to do a bit of reconnoitering, although he didn´t expect them to have arrived.

As he went up the ramp, an attractive women, looking like a tourist, walked out and smiling addressed him by his name. "Good morning, Eric, I am Mirza. I saw you arrive and came out to greet you. We were already expecting you."

"Good morning," he said at the same time as he looked at his watch. "It´s early, isn´t it?"

"Yes, I´m glad you came early. Come with me." She had a slight foreign accent, it wasn´t British nor French, maybe German or Belgian, but very pleasant nonetheless.

Mirza seemed to be around 25 years old; she was tall, approximately 1.75 mts., wearing elegant and not too high heels, a pink and yellow suit and a white blouse. The image of a pretty blond with her hair pulled back. When meeting Eric she put out her hand and when he was about to take hers, she grabbed him by the wrist, as in the style of Roman centurions, but Eric managed to touch her hand, it was soft and warm. Mirza turned and guided him inside, gently and calmly, as if they were old friends or relatives. Her movements were distinguished and very feminine.

Rahel was sitting at the first table, by the windows. He stood up and went forward to greet Eric. He also was tall, approximately 6 ft., slim, blond, blue-eyed, wearing a suit and tie and a white shirt. He looked like an international executive.

Eric shook his hand, and was no longer surprised by their wrist holding as a greeting. Rahel slightly squeezed his shoulder and said, "This is our way of embracing friends. We have been waiting for you, we are glad that you are here with us."

Mirza smiled at him and Eric admired the beauty of her deep blue eyes and perfect teeth. He thought she could even be a model.

"You are very kind, Eric." Mirza said with a smile, letting him know she had "read" his thoughts. Eric sat next to Rahel and Mirza took her place, facing them.

"Eric, don´t be afraid," said Rahel. "We can only perceive what you want us to know, we can´t enter your mind nor listen to your thoughts. Do you understand?"

Eric hadn´t had time for anything, not even to be surprised. Everything seemed so natural....so nice and simple. His nervous tension had disappeared and he suddenly felt very happy, as if he were with two old friends.

Rahel continued, "Thank you very much for your greeting and welcome when we saw each other, by the space ship, and yes, we do want to take advantage of your offer and friendship."

Eric was surprised to note that the words of the last phrase had not been uttered by Rahel. He confirmed this while watching Rahel say "at the space ship'" without moving his lips. Also, the phrase, "Yes, we want to take advantage of your offer and friendship," was transmitted by telepathy.

Eric took a few moments to reflect on this and then Rahel repeated, "You have to get used to it. It will be very helpful to us if you learn to receive and transmit by mental telepathy. Now pay attention and try to tell me what I am thinking."

Eric tried to listen, to penetrate his mind. It was as if he were remembering Rahel´s voice repeating: *"We were expecting you, we are happy to be together"*....but he didn´t really hear anything.

"You see? You repeated my greeting and you got it clearly. Isn´t this so? Telepathic transmission is simple, you will soon be using it too. Longer distances require more effort. You have to transmit with greater energy, but it can be done, although it needs the help of your contact. You did it very well the first time, and surely you have done this before. You only need to practice...and a contact, not all your brothers can accomplish this."

A waitress approached their table, and Eric noticed that each of them only had a glass of water. Mirza smiled at the waitress, "Thank you very much, but I am leaving."

Rahel ordered, "Lemon juice in pure water and honey, for me, please." Then addressing Eric, he added: "You have whatever you are used to for breakfast, we already had ours."

"Do you want anything else? Not even a glass of cold milk and a piece of cake?" insisted Eric to Mirza.

"No, Eric, thank you very much. Besides, I have to go. I only wanted to thank you and introduce you to Rahel. We´ll be seeing each other again, I promise." Saying this, she stood up. She took Eric´s hand in hers with a gentle farewell squeeze. She looked at him intently and Eric received: "You must not worry, everything will be all right. Rahel will help you. Until next time."

Then she looked at Rahel, Eric watched them for a few moments. They looked at each other, then she smiled at both of them and was gone.

The waitress came again and Eric ordered a plate of fruit, and followed by toast and marmalade, coffee with cream. She took the order and left.

Eric, without hesitation, tried: "Rahel, did you and Mirza connect through telepathy?" Rahel looked at him and answered: "Yes, but we use our own language, and that´s why your mind can´t perceive comprehensible ideas nor identify words and therefore rejects the vibrations. It´s as if you hadn´t "heard" anything.

He continued: "Like you, we have phrases for short ideas, greetings, farewells, confirmation of previous engagements....it is a language similar to yours. Some day you will do the same. Our language is based on ancient tongues and has now been perfected in accordance to our needs and usage."

Eric nodded and suddenly he felt eager to start his interrogation, but before he could begin, Rahel said, "I believe it is the moment to set several rules we must follow in our conversations. You must understand I will not be able to satisfy your curiosity and answer all your questions. There are many things I must not tell and many things you wouldn´t understand. It´s not a matter of being mysterious or of trying to confuse you."

"I have to obey and follow rules that have to be respected and protected. In addition, keep in mind that since our contact is not direct, or as you would call it, it is not ´official´. Our contacts are not with religious or political authorities who handle your affairs."

"My mission is to give you the knowledge we want you to understand in order to reach the immediate goals set for mankind living in your planet. At the same time, I will entrust you with a mission, but not for your personal benefit. You will be a spokesman so many will understand our message. We will give advice and help, but we cannot actively nor physically interfere."

"Through your own efforts, it is your responsibility to obtain a physical, social, political, technological and spiritual evolution suitable to your mental development and the understanding of your spiritual development."

"We are physical beings similar to you. We have had to overcome in the past the same development problems you have, in addition to having the same intellectual and religious faults."

"Like you, in the past we had economical, political and religious wars. But we managed to overcome them when we recognized the reason for our existence. When we understood our evolution, our origin and our spiritual destiny; only then, were we able to acquire true knowledge and enter an age of peace and harmony that has also given us technological development and spiritual superiority."

72

"The main problem here is that you have converted your planet into an enormous battlefield. On one side is the law of force supporting selfish fallacies and egotism, thus becoming slaves to materialism. On the other side, your religious war with a fanatism based on ignorance, hypocrisy, arrogance and lies that also keep you enslaved."

"It is really sad to see you destroying each other by hate, freeing your baser instincts, where dignity, honor nor understanding exist. Furthermore, this is carried out in the name of a God who is love and truth. Isn´t it ridiculous?"

The waitress brought their order. In the meantime, Eric began having his fruit and thoughtfully watched Rahel. He took a sip from his glass and continued:

"The majority of you do not know who they are and what they are here for. Your main interest is material well being, it doesn´t matter how you obtain it. You don´t understand nor are you interested in knowing that often whatever you obtain as a benefit is the result of sacrifices made by your weaker brothers."

"Human behavior must be ruled by spirituality or be totally destroyed, and we won´t be able to avoid it, if you don´t change."

We wish to help you, we grieve and suffer watching how you kill each other, destroy Nature that gives you life and you degrade yourselves not understanding your origin nor your destiny. You behave like primitive beings and do not make an effort to become better humans. You have developed intelligence, but your mental evolution has been very slow, because you are behind in spiritual evolution.

Suddenly Eric again noticed that Rahel wasn´t speaking physically, his lips were not moving nor making any sound, but he was listening clearly as if he were talking out loud.

Rahel looked at him with a slight smile softening his expression and said, " I know you want to take notes because there are many concepts and you believe that you won´t remember them easily. You can do so, if you wish, even if it slows us down a little today, try it."

Eric started taking notes, and on several occasions, while doing so, he received a confirmation or correction of the idea presented. He easily learned how to transmit, it was like reading aloud what is being written. But after a while Rahel told him, "As you may have noticed, your mind gets distracted while taking notes, and more physical and mental effort is required in order to understand and express this in your language. Besides being tiresome, takes too much time. You'll get a headache and I will have to talk to you as you can't receive my telepathy and take notes at the same time. It doesn't work."

"Also, you must have realized it isn't possible to cover all the subjects we will be dealing with, in a single conversation. We'll have to have several meetings, and you won't have to bring your notebook, I assure you."

He looked at Rahel and asked with disbelief, "How do you expect me to remember everything you are saying?"

"I don't expect you to learn it by heart. I expect you to understand and to comprehend the concepts well and therefore remember the idea clearly. Just as you remember everything you learnt at school, and what you have learnt and understood later, like memories of your trips...and your dreams. Besides, I'll help you. The mind can be stimulated to remember what we have talked about if it was well understood. Do you want to ask me any questions regarding the ideas I have put before you?"

"Yes," said Eric, who had brought the long list of questions he had prepared during the week and more that had just come to mind. "Why do you say that we don't know who we are nor what we are here for? What must I understand by evolution? Who set the rules for our friendship and what will you tell me? Why isn't there any official contact? What do we have to overcome to evolve? What spiritual development are you referring to? Do you have any religion? What is the spirit? Where do you come from? How many are you? Where does Mirza live? Does the pickup truck belong to you?"…..

Rahel stopped him, extending his hand gestured him to calm down, and nodded, "Be calm, I'll answer little by little as I told you at the beginning, not everything, but enough."

Rahel took an apparatus from his waist band that looked like a cellular phone or a walkie-talkie. However, when it was open, it looked more like a complicated remote TV control. It had a recorder, and seemed to carry out other functions: in addition to a small screen monitor and a graph-lined one. He used it for a few seconds and evidently received an answer, as there were light signals on the monitor and graph screens. He closed his telecommunication apparatus, placed it on the table and turned back to Eric saying, "I am trying to follow a logical sequence, but I have to use words whose meaning I must explain. They are not only words but complete ideas."

Eric couldn´t resist the temptation and looking at Rahel said, "May I see it?"

Rahel agreed with a smile and slowly pushed the apparatus towards him. It was a computerized high frequency transmitter-receiver. Clearly it included several other different functions. It seemed to have audio, video and other incomprehensible purposes. After examining it, he automatically asked, "Will you explain it some day?"

"Some day you will have one and will use it," Rahel returned to their interrupted conversation. "Look, I am what is called an astronaut. I had to acquire many special skills and knowledge to be here. I am also a professor with specialized studies in what you would call biochemistry and many other specialties in physics."

"There exists an intergalactic organization controlled by our superior brothers. The norms are dictated by them and obeyed by us. We come into physical contact with the inhabitants of the planet getting help for their evolution. They are our superior brothers and teachers. They guide us, as maybe soon we´ll be able to do with you. But not before you deserve it. That means, you have to fulfill a preset goal for evolutionary development."

"In order for you to accomplish this, a special authorization was discussed to permit this type of contacts and was approved. You are not the only one. We have had others in a distant past, through time and now at present. We have contacted many persons, all over the planet, having different characteristics, but the same goal. The result we look for is that of making you aware of the reality you are living and to provoke the manisfestation of your spirit through the mind."

"Excuse me, Rahel," Eric interrupted signaling him to stop for a moment. "You say that they discussed and approved an authorization. Who discussed what and where?"

"There is an intergalactic organization that embodies all the evolutionary worlds there are in each galaxy. The only planets that participate are those with technological humanities at the level of "super-man" and that are organized and transported like us, by our superior brothers, who exist on the next evolutionary plane."

Rahel intentionally paused so Eric could "digest" this information and then continued, "For now, only take notes of the answer to your question. We´ll see this in detail later. O.K.? The most outstanding scientists of your planet observe the local universe through the equipment available and make a mental effort to understand the why, when and how of the behavioral pattern of the celestial bodies in space. Their efforts are admirable. But they still are limited by their research equipment and by their own mind."

"Evolution is change. A positive transformation attained by mental and physical effort. Physical evolution is the result of changes and mutations of transformations through acting energies that modify forms and spaces following always the Universal Laws that rule the galaxies and the atoms, with equal precision."

"Step by step, you have been following an ascending path. But you cannot skip stages. For example, you are in grade school, first you have to learn arithmetic, then algebra and afterwards, calculus. You cannot skip from arithmetic to calculus. It´s not possible. When a bird is born, it doesn´t have feathers, therefore it cannot fly and it won´t be able to until it has feathers. Do you agree?"

"Spiritual evolution occurs much the same way. It is a transformation toward perfection. There was a physical evolution on this planet as the elements were transformed by complex combinations, generating the formation of vegetable life and then animal life, aided by the action of diverse manifestations of energy, such as electricity, magnetism, heat, etc. Evolution is similar to a metamorphosis, it is the perfecting of plants and animals to attain the level that they have now."

"The evolution of the primate consisted of the development of the nervous system and his brain to reach the point when it was

76

ready to be used by the primitive man. That first man evolved with the proper energies to become the man of today---intelligent beings capable of formulating two extreme theories regarding the interpretation of the known Universe. You can understand this. Mankind has a theory they call "relativity". It is the most progressive one attempting to understand the macrocosmos. They have another theory for the opposite extreme. That is the "quantum" theory, with which they try to understand the microcosm of the same Universe."

"Those theories don't work as two parts of a continuous whole. They have to find the common denominator that joins and explains them. That common denominator is millions of light years away from their calculations and within themselves. Today the solution escapes their physical, not their spiritual capacity."

"That common denominator is God, Allah, Yavhe or whatever they wish to call Him. In other words, superior knowledge is needed that goes further than what can be seen by instruments that help your physical eyes and your material brain."

"To understand, first you need to become more spiritual and thereby enter a dimension where natural phenomena can be explained. This cannot be grasped, as yet by your actual perspectives."

"This implies talking about the spirit, and you already have an idea of what this is. Don't you? The spirit is the true Self of each being, the subtle part of a physical body.
Part of the spirit giving life to the material body is what you call soul. This is real. It is the energy condensed by the Father of Creation. Our Father who is also the origin of matter that makes up the physical and mortal body of the human being."

"A soul that animates a physical body is evolving with it. It takes part directly in the sensations the body received through the physical senses and in all the knowledge being acquired and stored away in the brain. It participates through emotions and feelings or spiritual gifts, and it experiences them while the being is alive. The spirit acquires knowledge and experiences directly through the soul in that body, and when there are positive, then it evolves."

"The soul does not die with the body it inhabits, when the latter dies. It simply separates and integrates with his spirit at another dimensional level. You shouldn´t be surprised at this, in fact, the soul does this many times while the body is still alive. You call it "out of body" and it truly is something like that. Many times it travels to other places outside of this planet, in the Universe. It can even visit other planets and acquire knowledge and experiences that at times can filter to the physical brain and there are registered as "dreams" or "intuitions".

"The soul does not need to sleep as the physical body needs to rest to recover its functions. This time of rest for the physical body, is used by the spirit, for its own evolution."

"It is necessary that you understand that when we speak of the spirit we are talking about something real, even more real that the physical matter you perceive through your senses, since it´s more enduring and has superior characteristics."

"You should not talk about subjective or complex or elevated things to a child. It is beyond his capacity of understanding. His reaction will simply be to turn his attention to something he is capable of comprehending. At present man, your brothers, will behave more or less this way when spiritual topics are touched upon."

"However, man already has the maturity and knowledge to understand, and using his intelligence, can comprehend metaphysical and spiritual matters."

"Man must understand he needs to listen to the voice of his conscience, and comprehend that this comes from his spiritual brain containing knowledge far beyond his material cognizance."

"This should be identified as the origin of intuition, the human mind in contact with the spiritual world. Conscience is the voice you have listened to since you were a child, and this is the voice of the spirit. I know this is hard to understand, but it is the basis of everything I must teach you."

"A little animal, soon after it is born, and as it reaches the necessary physical development, can do simple and complex things without being taught. Walking, feeding, swimming, flying, moving from one place to another and returning without getting lost, as pigeons and migratory birds do, or weaving a spider´s web would imply very complex knowledge. All this happens by what you call instinct, but in reality is a physical genetic, purely biochemically engineered recording."

"Tell me. Does man know, through science, when or how it was recorded? Who recorded it? Of course, it will be difficult to accept at first that "someone" had to do it. Why, if it is the simplest solution to the enigma? Don't you think so?"

"This is only in the case of animals. A prerecording of knowledge, a genetic inheritance received by their ancestors has been transmitted through generations from the true origin of how and who set the orders to be followed, according to the superior knowledge and techniques, to those of your brothers."

"Genetic recordings are conduct implants, something like a software disk for a computer, different from the recordings obtained by physical evolution. These are physical and behavioral modifications in animals and plants."

"It is a very complex process, resembling a metamorphosis, adapting to the environment and individual needs. These changes are gradual and take generations to occur."

"Your science is relatively young, but you have already been able to determine that the pattern of behavior for living beings has been predetermined and not learnt. You ask and investigate how, when and who did it. Isn't this true?"

"The necessary knowledge and the recording techniques that indicate what to do and provide the means by which to do so, goes further than what you can control."

"Just as I tell you about animals, I could say marvelous things concerning plants, whose reactions and functions your science is just starting to detect. But they are there, acting since their perfection to put them to use."

"Also, nothing happens just by chance in this planet's atmosphere; it is not accidental coincidence. Has it ever occurred to you, any time, to think about flowers? The colors, their shapes, their aromas. Can you imagine the requirements in manpower and equipment needed to manufacture an orchid? You don't have the means nor the knowledge needed to attain it, even if you tried. And, of course, by this I am not referring to modifying what is already done. But to create it!"

"What do you think of water? You only use it, or better said, misuse it, since you waste and contaminate it. You cannot generate the volumes that are needed, nor take care of what there is; even though it´s a vital element. What effort and at what high cost is it transported to where it is needed? But how does the planet move it? By evaporation from the oceans through solar energy, clouds, winds and rain. Then rivers, lakes and back to the seas. During this process, together with other factors and energies, it nourishes human life and even then, you don´t respect it."

"Do you think all this happens by coincidence? Of course, you have the answer in every religion, when science isn´t enough, their opinion is, "It is the work of God." But, how did your God do it? Since each one has his own. The consideration is "This is easy for Him, because He is Almighty." And in this manner, the matter is settled."

"Upon analysis, the simple answer is that somebody "real" planned, designed and accomplished it. Of course, our Universal Father, the Creator, is the originator. But, how did He do it? An "almighty" king wants to build a palace and orders the work to be carried out. Thousands of workers could be needed, from engineers to laborers; this doesn´t matter, they come and build the palace. The same happens in the Universe, only the existence of the engineers and the laborers of God has to be accepted."

"Now look up to the sky, watch the stars, and if you have understood me, you cannot but think, someone really is specifically taking care to create all that exists; that nature was not created by accident or by chance."

"No, Eric, it wasn´t a "a lot of luck" for the conditions of the Universe and its contents are as you know them today. Absolutely everything has been carefully predetermined, calculated and prepared, without omitting a single detail, since very long ago. And it is continued to be watched and led by very evolved beings, who with a lot of effort, superior knowledge and great love take advantage of the Universal Laws by means that even I am not aware of, to keep the house of our Father , that is the whole of Creation, going; where we are only beginning to take our first steps. Remember this, they and us, each at its own level, all of us are "God´s laborers".

"In this planet, which is your home, is precisely where you are showing the greatest disrespect and lack of responsibility. You mistreat and misuse the elements that provide the means to live. You don´t know how to regenerate them, but allow their destruction as if it didn´t matter, and you don´t use your technological development to improve, but to destroy yourselves."

Rahel leaned back, taking a sip of water, giving Eric time to take a breath to analyze and absorb all the ideas and concepts. Eric also ate a little while his mind filed all these away in the data base of his brain.

THE CONSCIENCE

After a brief pause, Rahel again began his monologue, speaking slowly and softly, trying to made his words easy to understand.

"You see, Eric, it must be clear to you. There are two very important words, which are very much alike, but have different meanings. It is necessary to understand them well. The first is CONSCIENCE, you are or can be CONSCIOUS of something. For example, you know who you are, where you are, why, with whom, etc. You have no doubt. It is clear in your mind where, why or what we are here for. To be CONSCIOUS is TO BE AWARE of all that happens around you."

"On the other hand, your CONSCIENCE tells you if what you are doing is right or wrong. An INNER VOICE answers an unasked question. It is as if, prior to acting, you ask yourself: "Is what I am about to do right? And someone who "is not you" answers only with a "yes" or "no". This answer is judging your action being committed by your own "free will"."

"In other words, before you act, someone tells you: "That´s not right, it´s unfair". This is independent of what you intend to do. Be it fast, slow, easy or difficult, sooner or later. The judgment refers to the act itself from your inner point of view. It lets you know if it is right or wrong. You´ll briefly listen to the voice, but its echo will remain in your mind much like the vibrations of a bell."

"Before your mind orders an action to the physical body, it studies the requirements to carry it out, as knowledge, physical force, dexterity, etc. It considers the risks, consequences and the material benefits we´ll obtain by acting one way or the other. Also the losses, damage, and/or sufferings the act could cause us or to others, and what we will get as a result of the harm or benefit."

"The implications of our actions are scrutinized by the mind by referring to the cerebral files of memories and experiences before giving the physical body an answer. The decision that is made, supported by our "free will", and the course of action, are our full responsibility. The physical brain only has to figure out the details of how, when and in what way to act."

"Once the mental process is over, it´s as if a messenger showed up at the window and told us something. That is the CONSCIENCE working and forming its judgment. The messenger doesn´t expect an answer. He doesn´t threaten, nor give reasons for or against a certain decision. His role is only to inform."

"The spirit of each human being gets in touch with the physical being through the mind, whereupon the CONSCIENCE acts."

"The physical brain is a computer with a data base. The mind is the result of the acting energy that synchronizes the functions of the mental spheres; the zones of energetic influence at different levels of CONSCIENCE."

Eric was positively hypnotized, concentrating one hundred percent, trying to follow and understand the explanation. No mental effort was needed to do this, on the contrary, it was like being thirsty and drinking fresh water. This is how he perceived it when being given the information.

"Allow me, Rahel, let me see if I am understanding the process. The conscience communicates with the brain, I understand that. But, how? When and physically how does the conscience send her voice to the brain? It isn´t through sound waves that the brain can hear, is it?"

Rahel looked at him, calmly taking another sip. Then he began to explain, "Energy reveals itself in different ways. Energy changes its vibrations as it is transformed and is present depending on the characteristics of the vibration. The awareness that the human being has of energy depends upon the sense through which he captures the vibration at that moment."

"It can be sensed in the form of matter. For example, if you see a wooden log burning, you perceive the solid matter through your sight; the thermic energy that it radiates with your touch; you detect the combustion, through your sense of smell. That also is a product of the same energy that was wood and is being transformed. The flames produce light, and the transformation continues until the original matter as such, disappears. All the range of vibrations within, which energy transforms, from solid, liquid, gas, sound, radio waves and even light, have a level of variation within the same dimension."

"There are also other dimensions: these can coexist in space and time. Imagine the projection of a movie on a screen. The rays of light from the projector open up in a conical way until they reach the screen and produce an image. If you place another screen 90 degrees from the first, then you do the same thing with another movie, you'll see what you are projecting in each one. Right? Well, now imagine the beams of light crossing in space. Each one has a number of rays of light for any given area you may consider, and all cross each other without apparently being affected, as the image they produce is not distorted. Several beams, with their projection light can cross all colors and intensities. The physical phenomena is different, but you can get an idea of what I'm saying. Two or more different vibrations can exist simultaneously in time and space without affecting each other. (Figure 4)

FIGURE 4

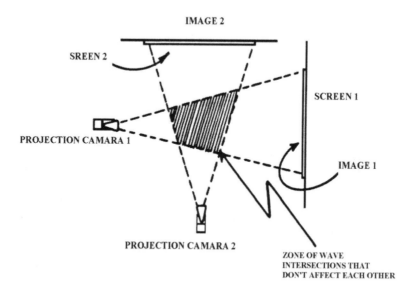

IMAGE 2

SREEN 2

SCREEN 1

PROJECTION CAMARA 1

IMAGE 1

PROJECTION CAMARA 2

ZONE OF WAVE
INTERSECTIONS THAT
DON'T AFFECT EACH OTHER

"You can see another example when two or more vibrations cross each other without affecting each other, as several stones simultaneously are thrown on the surface of calm water. Each stone will generate a circular wave that will enlarge until the energy has been scattered, and you will notice all the circles cross each other without being destroyed or deformed."

"Using another of your senses, you can be aware that the same will happen with sound waves. You can listen to sounds coming from different places. For example, if you stand in the center of a circle formed by musicians in an orchestra, you could listen to the sounds of each one of the instruments, exactly as they come out, without being affected by the intercrossing waves."

"This physical phenomenum is the result of energy behavior obeying the natural or Universal Laws, and it happens to corresponding vibrations on an equal plane or dimensional range."

"If the previous phenomenum can exist with vibrations in the same dimension, surely now it is easier for you to imagine that there is also no interference with corresponding vibrations of different dimensions."

"But now, let´s go to the spirit and how it reaches the mind. Allow me to use an imaginary situation to exemplify what I want to explain:

Imagine that you have made friends with a very small animal; let´s say an insect, that lives on the smallest leaves of a plant. He is so small that the little fuzz on the leaves seems like a forest to him. We´ll call our little friend, Eli. He, although small, is intelligent and very willing to learn and understand the world he inhabits.

After you have talked a while, Eli asks you if truly you can lighten up his small world at will, and you know that it will only take a battery light or to turn on a nearby light bulb. When he realizes of how big the world is, and that he lives on a little plant of millions, and that, besides, where you live there are cities full of so many things that he can only imagine. He asks if you can communicate with your kin far away without having to be there. You let him know that not only that, but you can see them and they can see you. When you show him a telephone and tell him that you can send and receive a voice through it, it is going to be difficult for him to understand and more so, if he doesn´t have ears, but he is communicating with you through a vibration system similar to radar."

"In spite of this, he has the will and the intelligence to understand, and you are going to make an effort to help him. But, you will tell him that is necessary for him to learn many things first, so he can understand how everything works in his environment. He accepts and believes you. In the same way, you will have to accept many things that I will tell you, as true for now, even without understanding. I need to mention them to explain some phenomena you don´t understand, but in the end, things that at the beginning you took for granted, were based on faith. That is, believing, trusting, looking above the obstacles you still can´t overcome, and which will have their explanation, then you will understand. I hope, Eric, that just like your little friend, Eli, you, too, could have faith."

"Almost magical concepts are expressed within those words that are energy and its manifestations, such as: electricity, gravitational force, electromagnetics, light, etc. and its applications, in addition to appliances, machines and instruments that can generate and transform it for its own use."

"The Spirit that animates you as mine does, were created by our Universal Father in an area of the universe where the necessary conditions and elements exist."

"Our spirit was created, formed, nourished and transformed with the approval of our Universal Father, from his residence in a very high place. It was formed by a special substance or matter, that is a condensation of his divine energy and is manifested in the seventh dimension. (Figure 5)

FIGURE 5

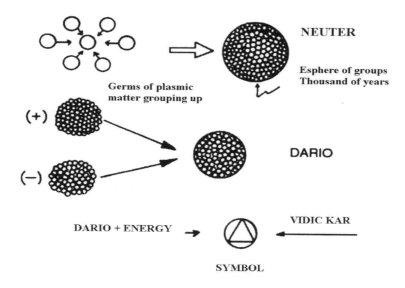

NEUTER

Esphere of groups
Thousand of years

Germs of plasmic
matter grouping up

(+)

(−)

DARIO

DARIO + ENERGY

VIDIC KAR

SYMBOL

THE VIDIC KAR

Formed by germs of plasmatic matter grow until forming an inharmonic PULSATING charge (inharmonic −9+6).

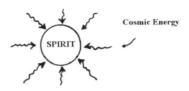

This seventh dimension is very elevated and is beyond your human comprehension. This energy has been concentrating and evolving for a long time and when it was ready, it received even more energy that it used to form two more denser bodies with a different polarity. These bodies detached themselves physically from that dimension, although remaining linked to the original spirit that stayed in the seventh dimension. These bodies descended to integrate themselves fully at the level of the fifth dimension."

FIGURE 6

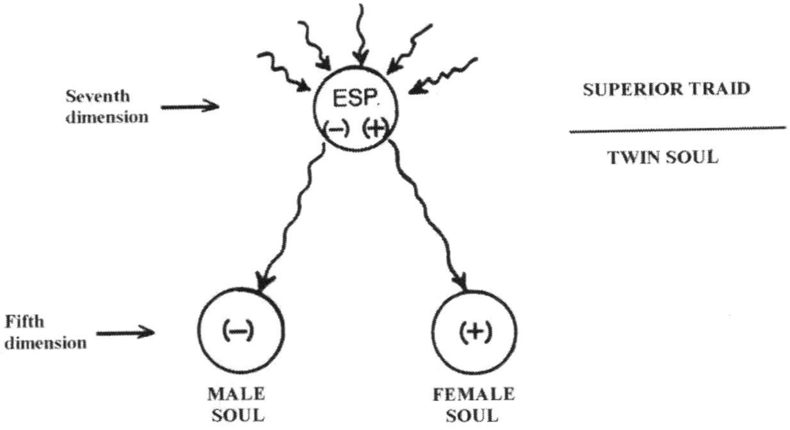

87

"These perfected bodies coming from the same spirit, in the fifth dimension, make up the twin souls of that spirit and will be their means of contact with lower dimensions, where they will animate matter that will be their teaching tools and material experiences to evolve. Each of these twin souls has an energetic polarity; the soul of the negative polarity will animate and evolve with the male beings and the positive polarity will do the same with the female beings."

"The complete diagram of the superior triad with its two inferior triads is what is called SEPTUM." (Figure 7)

FIGURE 7

SEPTUM

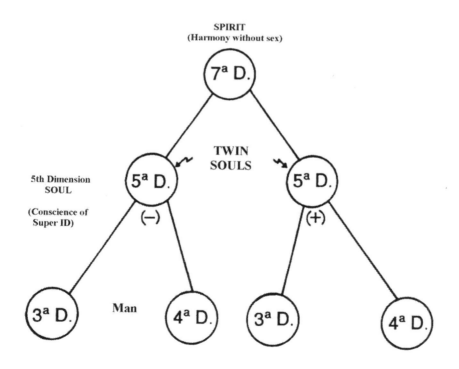

"In the diagram we can observe as the spirit already formed in the seventh dimension received more energy, it polarizes and creates two entities in the fifth dimension. One has positive polarity and the other, negative polarity; they will be the SOULS of two human beings, belonging to the same spirit."

"The soul of negative polarity (-) will belong to a male being."

"The soul of positive polarity (+) will belong to a female being."

"Souls in the fifth dimension go through a period of evolution once again. They are nourished by energy coming from the Island of Light, where universal energy and planets in evolution originate."

"When souls have attained the necessary development, each will create two bodies that have to fulfill their role in the evolutionary mission and must accumulate experiences. One of these bodies will be placed in the fourth dimension and the other in the third dimension, installed in a human being. Both together with the soul that created them will integrate a whole called inferior triad." (Figure 8).

FIGURE 8

NFERIOR TRIAD

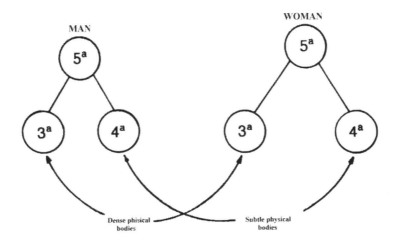

"The energetic-genetic conformation of the manifestation of the soul in the third and fourth dimension, is also the result (everything functions by cause and effect) of the condensation of energy and of subatomic particles from both dimensions. In this way, the soul will integrate in a material body of the third dimension in a human being´s body, which while being formed, also has his duplicate in the fourth dimension. A man will receive a soul of negative polarity and a woman, one of positive polarity."

"A human being in the process of being formed, even within the womb, is only a new live being in gestation. This physical body is the means of evolution for a soul and it will remain there while it is alive. During this time, the soul, which is the true BEING, having the personality and characteristics of its spirit, will be the vehicle of communication between its own spirit and the human being it inhabits."

"All this information has been given to you several times in different ways, but it seems as if we have made bubbles with it and tossed it into the sea."

"During the time it took to perfect the animal to be converted into man, the superior spirits identified as Biological Engineers, some of God´s Laborers, carried out tests and experiments with different anthropoids before the ape, already a perfect animal, was ready to become man through his evolutionary development. When this happened, the biologists had the MENTAL SPHERES ready."

"At the beginning, these spheres were the equivalent of the pre-recordings of the animals we mentioned before. They were programmed to energize and control certain areas of the brain you call cerebral lobules. They wield different energies for different levels of conscience and coordinate the workings of the mind in the third and fourth dimensions. They coordinate, through different vibration frequencies the level of conscience in the brain. They are part of the spiritual brain."

There are six levels of conscience. We´ll make a little sketch where you´ll be able to see them more clearly. They begin with the pre-consciousness, the continuous consciousness, the supra-consciousness and the subliminal; and each of them works at different levels as you can see in Chart No. 1.

CHART NO. 1

Function	Located in	Sphere No.
Pre-Consciousness	Encloses the brain and the occipital lobule	1
Sub-Consciousness	Encloses the pineal gland, hypophisis, hypothalamus thalamus, callous body	2
Consciousness	Encloses the right frontal lobule, the motrix and sensorial cortex	3
Continuous Consciousness	Encloses the left frontal lobule, the motrix and sensorial cortex	4
Supra-Consciousness	Encloses the left parietal and temporal lobules	5
Subliminal	Encloses the right parietal and temporal lobules	6

"The mental spheres are located inside the head of the human being according to the next diagram. Two of the six spheres work at only one level, one works in three levels and four work in four levels." (Figure 9)

91

FIGURE 9

ILLUSTRATIVE DIAGRAMS OF POSITIONS

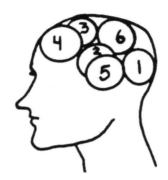

"There are four levels of consciousness and they depend on the mental
vibrations you have named alpha, beta, eta and delta."

"When a living being is assigned a spirit, he will receive, as I told you before, according to gender, a corresponding soul of the third dimension. Besides, the mental spheres will be installed and he will begin the mental recordings of his patterns of behavior."

"A pattern of behavior is a physical recording of the individual on a small sheet of seroglobulin found in the hypothalamic region in the center of the human brain."

"The soul also relies on seven generators we could equate with the physical senses of the body, except those of the "spiritual body" who are generators of GIFTS AND POWERS, that are characteristics belonging to the spirit. You have already received, since long ago, a lot of information concerning this matter from the East where it was passed on to help you. The result was contrary to the West´s reaction. They involved themselves too much in trying to learn and practice spiritual matters, and neglected the knowledge leading to the development of technology. In the West, they have done precisely the opposite."

"In both cases, they didn´t know how to keep the necessary links and balance. That´s why the development and knowledge of spiritual matters practiced originally by the Easterners, was transformed into rites, mystic traditions and fanatism. While the Westerners turned to pragmatic and selfish materialism. Fanatism blinds understanding, doubts reason and leads to intolerance."

"Just notice how much time has passed since the beginning of the evolution of this humanity having material living beings or the third dimension on this planet since mental spheres were planted for the first time in apes so they could begin to function as human beings in an evolutionary world."

"This perfected breed of apes produced the first human beings that were the Humanoids; who already had mental spheres, although small ones, still without knowledge, but starting learning experiences, functioning like this in an almost automatic way through electric reactions caused by the impulses received from the outside, of their environment of a perfect world at their disposal."

"The electric generators of the soul, already known by you as CHAKRAS, surround the body with a magnetic field called AURA, which was the first method to receive and identify electric impulses from other fields. These were classified as good if they triggered attraction or bad if they provoked rejection."

"Not having the help of a language, nor the capacity even to reason, and only rudimentary recordings in the patterns of behavior, twin souls were attracted to each other activating the sexual chakra to instinctively provoke reproduction."

"An harmonic energy, in this way, is generated and directed to the fifth dimension and there by beginning evolution."

PROCESS OF EVOLUTION

1.	Material support in the animal:	Ape
2.	First plane of human beings:	Humanoid
3.	Second plane of human beings:	Caveman
4.	Third plane. First level:	Man
5.	Second level:	Super-man
6.	Fourth plane. First level:	Supra-man
7.	Second level:	Demi-God
8.	Third level:	Maitreya
9.	Fifth plane.	Cosmic Engineers
10.	Sixth plane.	Biological Engineers
11.	Seventh plane. First level:	Planetary monitor
12.	Second level:	Solar monitor
13.	Third level:	Galactic monitor

"We´ll see in detail on some other occasion each one of these planes and levels. For the time being, just take notes of the classification so you have an idea of what is ahead in the evolution of your spirit."

Rahel paused while Eric wrote down the levels and their names. Afterwards, he continued:

"The first two planes are conditioning and development so the physical body can adapt to operate with the participating spirit through mental spheres and charkas. The Humanoid is the first plane and it receives spiritual support through the twin souls. At this stage, these incarnate simultaneously to be together in the material life of the bodies given to them. This only happens in the first plane and at the end of the third plane." (Figure 10)

FIGURE 10

DIAGRAM OF A HUMANOID

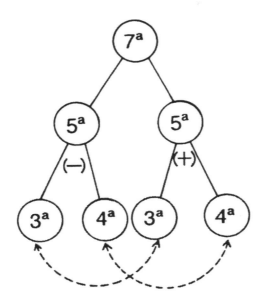

THERE IS A UNION OF TWIN SOULS

"Jumping ahead a little, I can tell you that this beginning is difficult, since the human being found himself in an apparently hostile world. He was weaker than the wild beasts, and his main strength depended on his intelligence, which he would be forced to develop precisely because of his need to survive."

"His soul passes to the fourth dimension upon death. Where it will stay for a short period until the accumulated energy has been used up. Then it´ll go to the fifth dimension. Here it´ll receive help to return to the material life and thereby continue evolving. The spiritual brain retains all the experiences and knowledge acquired in the physical life of the third dimension. But, these memories are blocked when the spirit is incarnated into a material body. However, filtrations to help the physical brain are allowed."

"Preference is given, in these stages, to psychic perfection and to the nervous system in general, obtaining genetic recordings and mutations that will keep on perfecting the human being as a whole. Although it is the beginning of non-evolved human beings, their physical bodies are already perfectly integrated with their spiritual being."

"The human being is similar to a marvelous antenna receiving external influences through particles and energies obtained from creation, such as electrons, photons, radiations and quanta. Besides, cosmic web rays covering the range of solar radiations and electromagnetic fields that made up the planet´s magnetic field, will influence the human being in his development and in his biological and psychic behavior."

"The internal protoplasmatic and intermolecular circuits are sensible to such influences and reflect the third dimensional body as biological reactions of chemical and of a physics-chemical origin."

"The mind and the spirit also receive external influences and, at the same time, will be sent out with renewed physical energy through electrons, photons and electronic quanta."

"Remember that all are vibrations, and as such, being received from different origins, be they cosmic, solar or from the planet itself, under certain conditions, the phenomenum of resonance or harmonic synchronization can be present."

"Photothermic vibrations are received from solar energy, ocean kinetic from the planet, and electromagnetic from the atmosphere which, combined with cosmic ones affect the metabolism of the physical beings."

"Biorythms are nothing more than pulsations with cyclical variations of vital energies in an organic being. They are the changes that the physical, spiritual and psychic energy experiments with and that influence the behavior of the individual during all his material life. The serpentine and solar energy of the planet affect the biorythms of the physical body, and cosmic energy that of the psychic energy of the mind. All this is as real as the direct influence of the climate on a living being."

"Astral influence is the sum of the electromagnetic and gravitational influences of the celestial bodies of the system, also combined with cosmic energy. These affect the delicate equilibrium of the living beings and influence them subconsciously, predisposing their psychic behavior."

"It is possible to detect changes in the propagation of vital liquids in the capillary tubes of plants caused by this effect. This shouldn´t surprise you, as it is precisely the means for life to regulate itself. Although this is being discovered by you, little by little, it has operated precisely this way from the beginning."

"The physiological balance of energy shows us marvelous reactions of the organism. All the influences of energy are, subjectively, God´s messengers. Our Father Creator, with His intelligence and foresight, has surrounded Himself with all the necessary means (part of these are you, me and our superior brothers). He uses the elements I have mentioned and many more, that you, at this moment, cannot comprehend, in order for everything to work in accordance with His wishes." (Figure 11)

"You may ask yourself, why twin souls? Evolution, which is the education of the spirit, needs all the enriching experiences to give it wisdom."

"The Soul in a male being will experience and feel through that gender, characteristically active, physically strong, aggressive, conquering, materialistic and with an analytical mind."

"These feelings will be different in a female being due to their life styles, responsibilities and experiences, especially everything related to motherhood, such as physical resistance, passivity, moral strength, tenderness, intuition, and in general, a greater understanding of love."

"The spirit thereby has the opportunity to receive both experiences. All thought and action is registered simultaneously on the physical and spiritual brain. They will come together in the fifth dimension and the spirit will then possess, for its evolution, a fuller knowledge gathered by both souls."

"The CAVEMAN is on the next level of evolution. It is the same being, but now the fifth dimension decides there will be no synchronization for the twin souls to unite in the third dimension. This stimulates the development of mental spheres to aid the function of the mind."

"When empathy with twin souls is nonexistent, developed intuition and the need for sexual energy release motivate the individual to look for a mate, defend her and care for their offspring. Thus violence and the need to protect all this develops the survival instinct in his mind, thereby provoking mental growth. The energetic activity of the other CHAKRAS nourish the mental spheres with adequate atomic particles for the development of an analytical mind."

"This being develops basic instincts: family, home, community, food, etc."

FIGURE 11

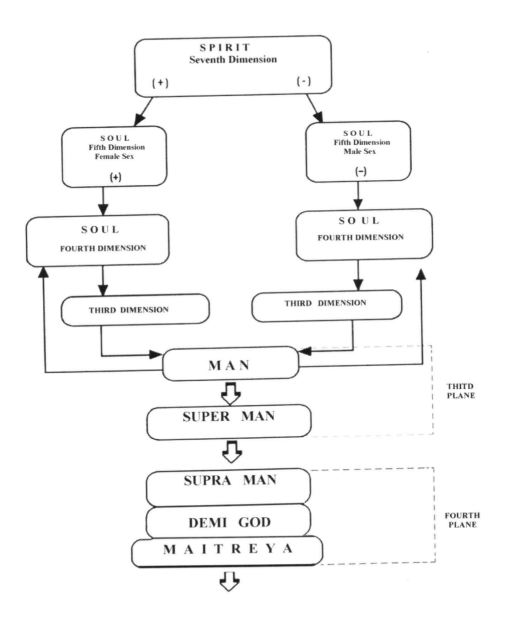

"MAN is the next plane of evolution. It corresponds precisely to the era about to end on your planet. Man has evolved in this era ever since the first Egyptian dynasty 25,000 years ago. One would suppose man should be ready for the next step, and is, but with difficulty. Mankind on this planet has been especially rebellious and has not acquired adequate harmony between spiritual and technological development."

"Man has achieved civilizations and scientific and technological development, but has not completed a material and spiritual balance, and therefore has not be able to move on to the next level."

"The SUPER MAN is on the second level of the third plane. It is the same man, but now has the sufficient spiritual evolution to be aware of the duality of his being and his physical and spiritual bodies. He must be conscious of his reality and will understand his triad. There will be, at some point, a joining of twin souls, so together the twin triads will integrate to form the superior triad and thereby continue evolving."

"This is precisely the moment and the reason for our encounter. All this explanation was necessary to continue to answer your questions. Where were we? Your question was: How does the spirit communicate with the brain? Well, I had to establish their relationship first."

"Today's mankind, your brothers, have lived on lower planes, developed their mind and acquired knowledge in their spiritual brain, which is the same as their soul. Also, they can obtain the knowledge and experiences of their twin soul by intuition enabling them quite a complete view of their reality."

"Knowledge of life at present, together with evolution, gives them an idea of their own history. However, physical knowledge has been divorced from the spiritual, thereby neglecting their own development and have left the spiritual responsibility in the hands of their religious leaders. These, be they pastors, priests or any other name given by their religion cannot obtain for each human being what each must achieve by themselves; and that is, to relate to their own spiritual being."

"Religious leaders must tend to the union of both lives that divide man's existence: the human on Earth and the spiritual in the

Universe, to guide through love. Those who remain in power, supported by twisted interpretations or deformed doctrines of revealed truths, will have to answer to their spiritual responsibility."

"Much interpretation of spiritual life is far from the truth and the first step to correct this is to eliminate their blinding fanatism. The day will come when man will discover that theories and dogmas given as truths, were false. Then he will understand, through his intelligence, the content and essence of truth. Analyzing with honesty, justice, charity and love, man will find spiritual light and men of science will, with this light, find the unimaginable through science."

"The spirit that is in a dimension of light and universal harmony should have obtained this through his own effort, as well as his wisdom and experience."

"Yes, Eric, you are thinking correctly. We are precisely at this level, and our superior brothers, who we will be addressing later, will participate with you and us in this adventure."

"But, let's talk further about your brothers. A human being animated by his soul, receives the judgment of his mental processes by his brain, the spirit is informed by the soul, as the latter communicates with the brain through the conscience."

"Materialism not self-controlled by spirituality, tends to direct man physically and mentally to satisfy his material desires. Arrogance, pride and vanity nourish evil, without the control of the conscience; mistaken decisions made by free will, will distance the truth."

"Man believes to be powerful due to his wonderful inventions and his scientific achievements. He closes his eyes, through arrogance, to the proof that someone before him created that which he is merely trying to understand."

"Scientists, through their knowledge, better understand their insignificance. But men in power do not, they have used that power and scientific progress to impose their will provoking evil, flooding the world with injustice and pain. The more material power man has, the less attention is given to his own spirituality, which is the truth and the means for evolution."

101

"Spiritual gifts are beginning their manifestations more and more each day. They are a message for humanity; to sensitize man to a spiritual presence."

"Real values only exist in the spirit. Analyze your feelings, and you'll see LOVE, in all its expressions, is the most beautiful and sublime, and this does not come from your physical sensations. Happiness, hope, nobleness and loyalty are feelings, as you say from the heart, but in reality come from your soul, from your spirit."

"I am talking to you about this because it is necessary for your brothers, who are so far from peace and harmony, understand the concept of GOD, who exists and is all around us. The essence of His word is not material, but the light which can only be understood by the spirit. When I mention the concept of GOD, you immediately turn to the Universe and wonder how many thousands or millions of light years away His divine presence is. Don't you? You ponder in a materialistic way, because in reality all you have to do, with a little effort, is communicate with your inner spirit, with your soul who gives you life, and you will be with Him, because your soul is you yourself and part of your spirit and this is part of GOD. Do you understand, Eric, why I asked you to have faith?"

"Conscience is the information, the guide the soul transmits to man's physical brain. Here's an example: John is on a road in his car, and suddenly sees another man called Peter, who has caused him grief in the past. The following physical and spiritual phenomena occur:

1. Physical: John's eyes look at Peter.
2. Physical: The image leaves the eye and through the nervous system arrives at John's brain, the cerebral cortex and the grey matter for intelligent analysis.
3. Spiritual: Simultaneously, the image is sent to the spiritual brain, transforming the vibration to a change in dimension for the emission antenna in the center of the brain. This is mental sphere number two, which surrounds the hypophysis and the pineal gland above the hypothalamus.

102

4. Physical: The image is registered in the cerebral cortex and is sent to the lobule where the memory files are kept to be identified.

5. Physical: Peter has been identified now, together with his life story and the events affecting John.

6. Physical: A mental process begins, which includes on one side, all the experience , knowledge and memories John has of Peter, and on the other, all the information in the brain plus the actions John might want to take concerning this.

7. Physical: Vengeful thoughts could be so strong John plans how to take advantage of the opportunity.

8. Physical: The mental process indicates the need to revindicate the harm done, and since this is so great, Peter has to be killed.

9. Spiritual: At this moment, the spiritual brain consulted its own spirit. The decision is: Forgive him, forget whatever he did to you, and continue on your way.

10. Physical: Peter continues walking on the side of the road, there are no witnesses, the opportunity is still there.

John is facing his destiny, he has two options, and each ends differently. Good or bad, doubtful, satisfactory, frustrating, etc., his destiny is in his hands:

a) Take his revenge, he could run over him and escape; nobody will see him (apparently). He could possibly destroy him without any physical nor legal consequences. He knows that his conscience said "no", but he has free will to act.

b) He could turn away without harming Peter.

c) He could rely on human justice, look for a policeman, etc.

"If John chooses alternative "a", even when nobody sees or accuses him, he knows he has done wrong. His conscience told him so, and he heard it in time, so he can't take justice into his own hands. He may not have all the basics to judge and, in any case, there is a judge, the Father Creator. The message of spiritual order was "No!" If he decides to carry it out and does, he will have to face the consequences of his action."

"If John chooses alternative "b", he is leaving justice in God's hands. That man, just like him, one day must face his actions and their consequences and will have to live up to his responsibility."

"If John chooses "c", both he and his aggressor will face the fallible human justice and, later in any case, some day both will have to face the consequences of their actions."

"Both Peter and John have listened to their conscience, they acted with free will influenced by material convenience supported by self justification according to their culture and evolution."

"Do you now clearly understand how the brain obtains spiritual information?"

"Always, invariably and without being requested, spiritual advice is present in all decisions requiring a mental process."

"As man becomes more spiritual and is aware of his physical-spiritual duality, inner contact with his soul and his spirit will become easier, and through them, to his Creator, the Universal Father."

"Eric, I think this is enough for today. You must digest our conversation, reason and analyze these concepts in the light of your intelligence. You must understand, not memorize."

"Do you see how some of your questions were less important? The space ship? The extra-terrestrials! What would you call them now? Your friends? Your brothers? We'll start with the "what" in our next talk. Is this all right?"

"Agreed," replied Eric, who was really tired of listening. "Shall we set a date?"

"Don't worry, Mirza will do so in about a week."

Rahel stood up, and gave Eric money to pay the bill brought by the waitress, and said, "Allow me, please you are my guest, this is the custom here. Please pay the bill and give the change to the waitress."

Eric nodded automatically and went to the cashier. Rahel smiled and mentally addressed him: *"Take it easy and be discreet as you are now.* We'll see you soon. Until then" And raising his hand to say goodbye, went out the exit.

Eric watched him leave, as if he were just another customer. He looked around and saw several totally indifferent people immersed in their own affairs.

Two young women with children were arriving. Eric smiled and asked himself what would they have thought if they knew who was just leaving.....

CHAPTER VIII

If the essence of things
were as obvious as they appear,
science would not be needed
to understand them.

Man is not powerful,
big nor wise through the flesh,
but through the spirit.
Only love can lead him
through the path of light, peace and truth.

B.T.L.

REMEMBERING

The flight attendant´s voice broke into his reverie, with routine landing announcements, their arrival in Monterrey. The weather forecast was clear and warm.

Eric mentally reviewed his working agenda, forgetting his thoughts. He imagined the beginning of the work day. He was a long time client at the car rental agency and the girls at the counter knew him well. It was always to pleasant to deal with people who made him feel good, especially being away from home.

He was able to meet a lot of people through his work. He liked to make friends and guess what they were really like. It gave him great personal satisfaction to earn their esteem. It was rare to have traveled alone, he usually made friends with his seating companion; one met so many different persons in this way.

However, it had been better to be alone on this flight as he had wanted to think.

He loved to fly, had it not been for his nearsightedness, he would have been a pilot. He had learned to fly during his youth, and had taken a course to be a flight engineer. This was when commercial airlines used propeller airplanes, like DC-7´s or Superconstellation, the most modern carriers owned by Mexicana Airlines. He thought of Captain Torruco, who had helped him in the company, Guest Airways de Mexico and, of course, memories of that time in his life crossed his mind. He had already finished his engineering career and this had opened many doors, but fate had something else in store for him.

He always imagined to be in control of the landings and take-offs, while flying, and felt very happy when under "his" guidance, the wheels touched the ground.

The plane rolled softly on the runway and, at last, stopped in front of the telescopic hallway.

It was hard to get up early, but it was so pleasant to enjoy the sunrise and morning dew; it was all so energizing. It was just 8:30 A.M. and he had a feeling it would be an exceptional day.

He rented a car, checked the air conditioning and then suddenly changed his plans. He had business to attend to in Monterrey and had planned to stay there all day and spend the night, to leave early the next morning towards Monclova and Nueva Rosita. But this could be the other way around. He could start by going to the more distant place first to take advantage of the good weather and preferred not to face the storms of the past few days on the highway. If the weather changed, then he could sleep in Monclova and later return to Monterrey. The change would not affect his work, as the people he planned to see would still be there upon his return.

He loaded the car and departed towards Monclova. He reviewed his plan, driving conservatively and in Apodaca, bypassing Monterrey, took the road to Escobedo, and then the highway to Monclova.

He turned on the radio for the news. Floodings were reported in the northern part of the state due to overflowing rivers, but the day was glorious. A musical program, featuring the famous northern "redoba" he liked began, but he decided to turn it off and return to his thoughts.

Three days had gone by since his first encounter with Mirza and Rahel. It was remarkable how he could remember with such clarity of mind all their reasonings and explanations.

It was like having many restless spheres in different colors and sizes, yet they all clearly looked the same. However, when moved they came apart orderly by colors. Thus, the concepts regarding different topics seemed to group and each were enriched upon receipt of the corresponding concepts.

Eric liked to arrive early to the office, giving himself time to tend to his business calmly before the hubbub of the office hours began. Mirza´s call came through as had been agreed and as he picked up the phone, he "knew" it was her. He wasn´t wrong.

"Good morning, Eric!"
"Hello, Mirza, I was waiting for your call. How are you?"

"Well, thank you," she sounded joyful and gave forth a feeling of friendly familiarity. "I hope you have been able to relate more to the concepts of your talk with Rahel during these last few days. Is this so? Are you ready to continue?"

Eric felt sure of himself and tried to project that image. "Yes, Mirza, I think I am understanding everything we talked about, although to be perfectly honest, Rahel did not give me much chance to speak." Mirza laughed, Eric could see her clearly, her lovely face, perfect teeth, well-lined lips, all in perfect proportion. She had, in his opinion, great beauty, but...there was something special, a characteristic stamp similar to that of Rahel. Their head and face gave the impression of being shaped like a rounded off rectangle.

"Yes, Eric, that´s his way, he always tries to make each topic perfectly understood. He´ll explain it in several ways; using examples whenever he can. Much like the parables in the Bible, "Would you agree?"

"Yes, Mirza, I am grateful because I need all the help I can get."

"Good, would you like to continue next Saturday?"

"Great, that's just great. Same time and place?"

"No, Rahel would like more privacy so you can concentrate more. You will be coming through Mariano Escobedo Avenue, when you get to Reforma Avenue, take a right and come up the street that goes around the park toward the museum. You will see my pickup truck parked and we'll be there. Any questions?"

"No, I think I know how to get there."

"Is 7:30 A.M. all right?"

"Yes, that's fine."

"Very well, we'll see you there then. Remember to be calm and don't worry about a thing. I'll take you something for breakfast I know you'll like. See you then."

When Mirza hung up, Eric had the feeling of hearing something more: "You don't have to bring anything, just your good will." Well, that was similar to what Rahel had said, and it would not be strange for her to confirm this by telepathy. Or, was it his imagination?

It was exactly 7:30 A.M. when Eric parked his car behind Mirza's unmistakeable pickup truck. She and Rahel were strolling along the sidewalk by the woods.

Eric joined them and they greeted him as they had the first time. He couldn't avoid recognizing a feeling of friendship and peace when he had expected the opposite. Since the night before he had felt tense, under pressure, as if he were to present an exam or have a stressful meeting.

He looked at Mirza. She had on black trousers of a soft cotton-like material, a long blue blouse, elegant and very feminine necklaces and golden sandals matching the necklaces. She really looked quite beautiful, like a tourist or a college student going to a meeting.

"Thank you, Eric," said Mirza. "You flatter me, I am a woman and my feelings are quite similar to the women's here."

Eric blushed and was upset he had not controlled his thoughts. Rahel smiled and added, "Don't be ashamed, its natural. It's like returning a greeting. Your mind permits thoughts to leave, if there is no tension. When there is something on your mind needing the advice of your conscience or your reasoning to address a mental process, your mind blocks spontaneous projection. Mirza, exactly what did you receive? Explain it to Eric."

"You were saying you received something pleasant and calm when you noticed my clothes and expressed: "You look very elegant and beautiful, a girl dressed as you are, at a party, would look great."

Eric smiled quietly and promised himself to be more careful, so he wouldn't betray himself.

"The feeling you got was our greeting," smiled Rahel. "We felt you were tense and we sent you our love and friendship. Today, among other topics, we will be dealing with AURA, that electromagnetic bubble that surrounds your body and is produced by generating energies of your soul. Your size, shape, color and vibrations depend on your emotional and physical state. Anything wrong in your organic body will be reflected there."

"When you send good wishes and love to a human being, you are generating and sending high frequency vibrations in the third and fourth dimensions. These vibrations are received by the aura, that is also an antenna, and are transmitted to the charkas who create, form, produce and harmonize the AURA. These vibrations are detected at the physical level as you did, and provoke a feeling of well being, of relaxation, of rest, of good disposition…and many pleasant sensations, as they come from a harmonious vibration in your physical and spiritual senses."

They crossed over to the inner garden that was fresh and pleasant, while they spoke. It seemed a peaceful oasis surrounded by avenues and buildings, but the trills of the little birds in song erased the hum of faraway traffic. "I offered to tell you about the "why of our visit" today," Rahel continued.

Mirza interrupted them a moment, and without speaking, said: "I'll catch up with you in a while, do keep on talking," and she returned to the cars. They nodded and slowly went on.

"Eric, you are going through a period of transition with your brothers. It is time to end an era of evolution of this humanity and join the New Era that´s beginning. A change of era does not happen from one day to another, remarkable modifications come about affecting everybody´s lives."

"As I have explained to you, there are many stages of evolution. There are beings in each, living their process of evolution in the most different ways, planets and dimensions."

"I spoke to you about MEN like you, of SUPER MEN, like us and afterwards many other levels of evolution await us where we will no longer have bodies of flesh and blood. These are made up of a material adequate for a rapid disintegration upon death, that is when the fountain of vital and harmonious energy generated by the body of the third dimension is lost."

"The physical body we use is sufficient for these levels. Later there will be substantial changes to allow beings at that level to take better advantage of the energies to fulfill more difficult missions of evolution. Further on, in superior dimensions, we will carry out missions we can´t even imagine now, yet we can perceive the results." He said this as he extended his arm encompassing all of nature´s gifts where they were: the garden was just a small sample. "Bodies in third dimension," he continued, "living beings, plants, animals and humans do not last long. The length of this life depends on many environmental factors, external influences and genetic causes."

"The bodies that have life possess a reproductive genetic pattern, their genes have specific recordings. The step from the electronic level to the physical one is a consubstantiation by the action of glutamic acid, using the notes of your scientists, the CAN (oxyniacidic acid) changes to DNA (desoxyrribonucleic acid), basis of the life of beings on this planet. In the development of a new life, the fetus develops in parallel dimensions of simultaneous coexistence in the third and fourth dimensions."

"During the first stage in the development of a human being, the material body is prepared adequately for the implant of mental spheres."

111

"Independently from the behavioral and acting patterns of genetic origin, the spheres are installed in the encephalus of the babies and are ready to function a few hours after their physical birth in the third dimension."

"The creation of the mental formation in the new being, is formed by vidic electronic charges. These come from his spiritual origin, from his "karma" energy, which is the origin of his soul and of his genetic-electronic-reproductive pattern."

"As I told you last time, we have already transmitted, through other brothers of yours, knowledge of quantum mechanics and, in greater detail some of the physical phenomena you already know."

"That's true," Eric dared to interrupt. "I took a course about that type of information, which at the time I didn't call it knowledge, since I couldn't even understand it. Tell me, Rahel, if all this is really scientific, why didn't you pass it on to our scientists? There are several centers in the world, mainly in universities, where very well prepared men are carrying out physical research related to quantum physics."

"Remember, Eric, what I warned you about. Ours is not an "official" visit, we are not here openly to contact you. Of course, we could contact scientists and scientific organizations and correct their mistakes and teach them what they don't know. But that is not the goal of the contact; they must continue working and getting ahead in all the different areas of scientific disciplines. They, politicians and religious leaders are those who guide the steps of mankind."

"To talk to them would provoke a complete frontal collision and, besides they would have to obey us. In the case of scientists, it would be easier. Once they recognize our superiority, they could automatically accept the changes of direction in their research and be students eager to learn. But merit cannot be gained without effort, and it is necessary they attain their goals by themselves before receiving our help. If they weren't so proud and a little more humble, they would already be seeking the information we have passed on indirectly as a guide, to supplement their theories and to make their research more productive."

"Any contact by us with politicians would cause confrontation because of their interests and materialism. Who should we help or overthrow to end violent wars, that are nothing more than mass murders? Who, of all of them, has the moral authority to be considered our ally? Just for us to show ourselves openly would be enough to provoke negative reactions in others."

"Ignorance and self serving interests would cause disorders and uprisings needing our intervention, our control by force. If we would want to help some, others would consider us their enemies and declare war on us. Would it be fair to have to destroy you, to protect our lives?"

"Although physically, we are similar beings to you, our spiritual evolution is superior; but our bodies, which are the means to evolve in the plane are as sensitive and fragile as yours. The physical difference is attributed only to our way of life, the way we eat and our customs."

"We live on our planet in a similar way to yours. We have proper organizations and institutions for government, education and production so it is easy to imagine our needs, according to our civilization, technology and evolution."

"We live in harmony with our brothers and our mission here is not one of conquest nor of submission; if it were, we would have already done so as we have the means to achieve it easily, but that is not the reason of our presence here in your planet."

"I am making an effort to make you understand the means and goals of our mission. Do you believe it is fair for us to risk our lives, letting one of your brothers, in his ignorance, underdevelopment and fanatism, hurt us physically or even cause our premature death, all for not understanding we are trying to help you? Or do you believe we should take you by force, savagely, causing panic and destruction to be able to help you? No, that is precisely what you would do, not us."

"What we try to avoid is mass destruction, pain and despair that you are about to cause to yourselves, in a general way."

"In the religious aspect, this humanity easily tends to irrational fanatism. Who should we call upon? Which of the religions you profess should we support? They all have a spiritual background of truth, but in a retrograde organization, humanly materialistic and with a tendency to fanatism. They are supported by self serving interests, traditions and rites, and their leaders do not show their followers to use their intelligence to understand the voice of their spiritual conscience."

"Suppose that, as you suggest, we present ourselves. Ignoring the problems that would arise, let´s say we are already having a dialogue in plain sight of all mankind."

"At the beginning, we would be heard because of the impact of surprise and novelty, but soon fanatism, intellectual blindness and material interests would dominate, and chaos would result. Everybody would have reasons, first to ask, and later demand, our support and direct intervention."

"The powers that be, politically and economically, would try to impose, by every available means when their interests are in danger. They feel left out whenever they hear talk of equality and love as they consider themselves superior. Love, they only know the word by name. Charity, humility or generosity are accepted as concepts they could apply to their servants. They grant, give and authorize, but share? To give without expecting anything in return is beyond their comprehension."

"No, Eric, that is not the correct way, because they are not ready for it."

"Do you understand now why we need to do it through one of your own? It is necessary to carry out a campaign of progressive awareness, so each of you can be informed and,
little by little, understand it."

Mirza returned carrying a box. Rahel allowed Eric a few moments to absorb and digest his last concepts. They sat in silence while she opened the box; it contained three little glass containers with a lid, some five centimeters deep, like dessert plates. Each took one and she opened a steel-chromed bowl, some 30 centimeters in diameter by 20 centimeters high, that also had a glass lid and three inner compartments. In each one there was some kind of different colored ice cream: light yellow, pink and pistacho green. The bowl had a small serving device in the center that pumped the paste straight to the plate through a special adaptor. Then, as there wasn´t any dust in the air, they took off the lids and ate with a very small flat eight-sided teaspoon with a long handle."

Is it ice cream?" asked Eric, knowing that they were inviting him to taste their kind of food.

"It is not ice cream, it´s not cold, it´s food," answered Mirza. "The colors differentiate flavor and content, sometimes it is necessary to receive proper energy for cold, heat or special risk conditions through contaminated air."

"Taste it, you will understand why it doesn´t bother us too much not being able to eat your food, that must be very savory, but is very harmful. We have tasted it, taking precautions, as our digestive chemistry is different. It would severely upset our health. On the contrary, you can try these without being in danger of having the slightest discomfort, and will increase your intestinal flora."

Eric tried the cream colored one....."It´s delicious!" And it really was. Soft, creamy, tasting between pathe and pork...scrumptious! A small amount was enough and easily swallowed.

He sampled the pink one...it had a fruity flavor with a flowery aroma, also delicious. It was smooth and not overwhelming. The green one was sweet, not too rich, with a fresh scent of aromatic plants. These were also easy to swallow and very filling.

Each ration was the equivalent of a medium ball of ice cream.

Rahel laughed watching Eric´s expressions, and said, "You have eaten enough for three days! The energy of a single serving is enough for 24 hours or more. Of course, it´s easy to digest and, what you don´t absorb, is eliminated without harmful residue. There are no undesirable side effects. This will also be your food in a not too distant future."

It was true, even though Eric hadn´t had breakfast, he felt satisfied. The effect of the meal was long lasting, he didn´t feel hunger, even at the end of the day.

Mirza, returning to their conversation, told him, "The predetermined time to end the level of "man" is practically over. There will be physical changes caused by the planet itself and by the effects of the cosmic zone it must cross."

"All this was prepared and calculated by Cosmic Engineers, who are your elder brothers in a higher dimension."

"This destiny will bring about grave sufferings for your humanity. Sufferings that cause great physical pain, will make your spiritual senses to react forcing you to listen to your own conscience. Because of your rebelliousness and indifference in following the call of your spiritual conscience and having used up the time to act with your own free will toward a positive evolution, you are forcing pain to be the element that will make you react and correct your physical behavior."

"Panic, despair and impotence before natural forces, will make you conscious of your weakness, of the superficiality of human evil. Courage and spiritual gifts will spring from your spiritual being to oblige you to overcome your present attitude of self-sufficiency and return to the path of spiritual evolution. This will be necessarily manifested physically through the gifts of kindness, sacrifice, nobleness and other demonstrations of love."

"When this happens, you will stop thinking and acting selfishly. You will forget the evil that incites attachment to all material things. Arrogance and ambition will disappear when your weakness and materialism has been identified. Then, spontaneously, you will realize that unconditional love is uniquely inexhaustible. Loving others will be an imperious necessity to calm your own grief and will become a balm of happiness and peace for all."

"Your life has been instinctively materialistic and ignorance of your spiritual evolution has not allowed your free will to be guided by your conscience."

"It is necessary for you to become aware of this. This is the only way you can ask for the intervention of higher planes to modify the colliding path that will make you evolve through pain. We can only intervene after to help you recover what has been lost, but only at the level of SUPER MEN."

"The level our Maitreya (who incarnated his spirit to help you) hopes you can achieve by yourselves will, by evolution guide you to spiritualism, through the divine energy that is love. Only then will you understand his message in its totality. That inheritance of truth you still can't use to elevate your spirit and obtain your evolution."

116

"The spirit that left you the guidelines is now at a very high level in creation, we know him by the name of MICAEL. He is the head of our local universe called Nevadon, and you know him as Jesus of Nazareth, as he was called during his incarnation on this planet."

Mirza carefully watched Eric, trying to help him absorb her message.

"The master universe is very large," continued Rahel. "Just think that a very, very small part is our local universe, yet that part is infinite, for us. If it would suddenly disappear with its galaxies, composed of 25 billion stars, it wouldn´t be noticed. Faced with a concept such as this of the Universe, we have to accept that our Universal Father is inconceivable to our small mind, and his representatives, all of them, are his children in different degrees of evolution. At the same time, they are part of creation. Even we were deified by you several thousand years ago, since we have already contacted you on two different levels of your evolutionary process. One previously and now, because we are physically and spiritually closest to you."

"But, of course, you had no way of understanding who we were, how and why we had come, in your previous level. Now, you are only lacking the will to."

"Science is only the mental process to understand matter; religion is the need to seek your origin and your identification with the creator. Spirituality is the understanding of your origin and the knowledge of reality. Do you understand now, the why of the need for you to accept the integration of the spiritual body in the physical one? Together they form the evolving unit, but as they belong to different dimensions, there had to be a link for contact and dimensional interaction."

"Many men with some degree of scientific knowledge believe that only what they can conceive, exists. They try to establish the impossibility of our presence, which is already a proven reality, instead of reasoning and coming to the conclusion of "why" they don´t allow open contact with you. They don´t want to see, listen nor understand."

"Humility and good will are needed to understand. Whoever is blocked by vanity and pride believing that he knows enough to

117

deny us, will also not be able to accept nor explain his own spiritual and physical being in harmonious dimensional coexistence to himself. He will only accept religious dogma for his spirit, and in his fanatism due to lack of evolution, will despise the use of his intelligence and capacity to reason."

"Men in high political positions, even those who, by referral or by own experience are convinced of our presence, do not dare express themselves "as officially in favor". They prefer to align themselves with scientists who, through their primitive instruments and knowledge confirm the impossibility of our presence on this planet."

"Religious leaders, who are also sometimes politicians too, as each has his own god and his own truth, are emerged in the traditions and rites that keep them in power, interpret and deliver their ideas to their followers as a dogma of faith."

"Hardheadedness, stubbornness, arrogance and meanness of spirit in some, and ignorance in the vast majority. Do you believe we could openly reason with mankind?"

"It was prophesied that the war of ideas and beliefs would be more ferocious and bloody than the one defending material interests. It is a war without warriors, in their place, fanatics kill and destroy maddened by pain and fury for revenge. Cowards murder without risks, as traitors kill defenseless beings. Mankind, in general, is the victim whichever is their creed, culture or race."

The Son of Man said, "Love one another", "Do not unto others what you don't want for yourself". All religions say the same, translated into your languages and adapted to your "gods". Why then fight, offend and even kill each other? Instead of trying to understand, forgive and evolve?"

"Besides, your country, Mexico, has a special destiny. It was marked since the beginning of "time". Since the evolving process began for mankind, and to be able to continue to the 3rd Era, which was the work that Jesus of Nazareth started in Israel, in his time, must be concluded here. Christ himself in the New Testament says what will happen at the end of time. This is now, today, and here."

"Eric, your mission is to get your brothers to wake up, to try to explain the existence of their spirit to them, and to teach them to communicate with it. This is the only way to pray and ask for a transformation with LOVE."

"There is a main motive why we are here talking to you. For unknown reasons and purposes but pointed out to us by our superior brothers, upon reaching this step, this era is the transition of man to super man. Your country is marked as the place where spiritual knowledge must be spread. This doctrine of UNIVERSAL LOVE must reach all the corners of the Earth to surround it as if it were its own atmosphere."

"A religion, whichever its name, is the union of precepts aimed for man to find God. All religions try to teach the same and have the same origin, which comes from the lessons given by evolved spirits, incarnated into human beings. They are known as prophets."

Rahel stopped and looked deeply into Eric´s eyes, saying, "All of you will soon be able to interpret better the teachings left behind by our MICAEL".

"The FIRST TIME spiritually for this humanity corresponds to the first occasion a teaching, other than material, was given to you. This happened when the Ten Commandments were delivered through Moses. This was the introduction of a moral code to follow. Of course, it was delivered in a way, adequate to the intellectual and social development of the time."

"The SECOND TIME spiritually for mankind began with the human life of Christ, Jesus of Nazareth, our MICAEL. His teachings began having mistaken interpretations because of human participation, even from the gospels themselves. Imagine, if his own disciples with their love and good faith made mistakes, time and humans made deformities easy, and these have not been corrected."

"To end the differences, and sometimes erroneous interpretations of the teachings left behind by Jesus himself to his disciples, who substituted the old prophets, Our Universal Father has had a special deference for the Mexican people, permitting His word, by direct teachings, reach you spiritually, fulfilling the promise he made to the people of Israel, of the Second Coming."

"The essence of his word today to men of your time, of cultural and scientific development and considering you are ready to understand the spiritual gifts, is the same as was transmitted before. Only that now, you are capable of understanding and ought to, not only in your mind but with total spiritual consciousness."

"Our mission, through you, is of awareness. The science of your brothers is worthy of great merit, their efforts to understand the origin of the Universe has led them to be more knowledgeable of their environment. They have comprehended that time and space belong to the same dimension. They seek and understand cosmic energy, which is the origin of matter, and anxiously look to space to find the reason for the balance of gravity. Cosmic energy is the origin of matter that constitutes the volume of the third dimension. But soon you will also learn that energies making up other coexisting dimensions are generated by the same cosmic energy."

"They are struggling to uncover the mystery of subatomic particles to learn the quantum mechanics of the atom and will close the circle again with cosmic energy. But all this is material, it doesn´t elevate your thoughts to higher dimensions where, you are an integral part through your spirit."

"Do you see how religion and science are two sides of the same coin?"

"Without becoming spiritual, you cannot advance in your evolution and the imperfections of matter are degenerating you. You have to use your intelligence and your mind to understand that, it is in your perfection and elevation in spirit, where you will be able to carry out the transition."

"There are two elements that act from the world of matter to that of the spirit in order to attain elevation and eliminate the negative quantum charges that are their KARMA or degeneration. These negative charges accumulate in the spirit every time an act has been carried out by FREE WILL against the recommendation of the CONSCIENCE. Physical and emotional pain and LOVE generated by the spirit and sent to our fellow men are the elements that supply the positive charges called DARMA to counterbalance KARMA."

"Now we must go, and while we meet again, think and analyze all the concepts we have transmitted to you on this occasion."

It took Eric a few seconds to understand. He reacted to find Mirza´s warm smile and her deep blue eyes shining brightly and an equally nice "invisible" voice saying: "See you next time, Eric, don't worry, I'll be in contact with you for our next talk."

They started talking toward the cars, Eric had been looking for a chance to question Rahel about the doubts that arose when he was alone. Rahel noticed his intention and, placing a friendly arm around his shoulders, told him through telepathy: *"I am receiving your unrest, be calm, don't overdo it. When the time is right, I will clear up whatever you want. We are helping you and you will easily remember everything."*

"Rahel, but you have not given me a chance to ask," answered Eric. "I have many things to ask you, you offered me…….."

"And I will," interrupted Rahel, "but if you notice, the answers will come even before the questions."

They stopped beside the vehicles. Eric still wanted to say something, and when he was about to speak, Rahel answered: "No, do not change your work plans for us. If you go on a trip, and we don't interfere with your activities, we'll see you there to talk for a while. For us, it is the same to come down here or in any other place. Mirza will be in touch with you."

Eric accepted and went to his car, waving a last farewell to his friends.

CHAPTER IX

Absolute truth is not possessed by any man,
nor is it contained in any book.
That divine clarity, that omnipotent force,
that infinite love, that absolute wisdom,
that perfect justice, is within God.
He is the only truth.

B.T.L.

APPOINTMENT IN CULIACAN

The car ran smoothly, arriving at Apodaca, Eric took the toll free road towards Monterrey and soon he would be on the highway to Monclova. His thoughts slid away as the car....suddenly an incident of that second interview came to mind. While they had been eating, Rahel pulled out something similar to a multiple stethoscope from a case, and showed it to Eric, saying, "Would you like to see a graph of your cerebral impulses? This is something like an electroencephalogram, but not exactly."

Eric happily accepted and adjusted the apparatus on his head. Rahel place the electrodes on several points. Then, using some kind of translucid disc, he placed it in several positions in front of his head without touching and asked him to try to relax, concentrating on a conscious level known as "alpha".

He asked him to make an effort to transmit a message by telepathy to a person far away. He made some measurements with his minicomputer connected to the support and some colored graphics appeared on the monitor. After, through telepathy, he asked him to try to remember if he had had a dream the night before.

Eric closed his eyes and tried to remember…..images of aerial views came to his mind, and were beginning to make sense when Rahel made him come back as he was falling asleep.

Rahel, pleased showed him the recorded graph of the emissions of energy and said, "Great, your pulses and emissions are clear and strong. We'll help you have some very enlightening and pleasant dreams."

Eric realized he may have been naïve, and now….could they control his mind? Suddenly, he felt uneasy. He feared they would read his distrusting thoughts! Although, apparently, it wasn't like that and he tried to think of something else. Rahel put the equipment away and the incident was forgotten.

The third interview was in Culiacan on a business trip. Eric had wanted to be able to communicate with Rahel or Mirza to set it up. He tried to made contact by telepathy during the night, apparently without result.

Very early the next morning, he personally received Mirza's call. She reminded him they had a monitoring system to detect the efforts of telepathic contact of certain persons whose capacity of transmission was known. That's all they could do. Detect someone's intention, but only if that someone had been identified previously. Eric told Mirza about the trip and she offered to inform Rahel.

"Continue your normal plans, as we agreed. If it possible for Rahel, he will find you there. All right? Thanks and congratulations for the success of your communication. Have a nice trip, Eric. See you later."

Eric kept on remembering that third visit. He saw Rahel waiting for him at the entrance upon his arrival at the airport for his return trip. He smiled to himself, his urgency to get to there as soon as possible was precisely because he expected to see Rahel there. As he finished his lunch, it seemed as if he heard Rahel's voice, saying: *"When you are free, I'll be at the airport,"* but he had thought it was just his imagination.

"Hello, Eric. I see you received me," Rahel said with a smile, at the same time he took him by the shoulder.

"Hello, Rahel, thanks for coming. You know, I sincerely thought it was only my imagination."

They went in, and since the place was practically deserted, they easily found a seat in the waiting room to be able to talk without being disturbed.

"Tell me, how can you monitor my intentions to communicate by telepathy?" Eric decided to ask before Rahel went into the subject he had selected.

"Well, it's a matter of having the right equipment; for example, you have an automatic answering machine in your house. The principle is similar. If somebody calls, the apparatus receives the call and the answering part is activated. In our case, when you want to communicate, the energy emitted by your brain with spiritual force is captured by a special receptor. There are very high frequency waves that exceed the capacity of the equipment you manufacture.

"Your projection can be noted, at those levels of width and frequency, if there is specifically calibrated equipment for the range. It registers the signal's reception and we do the rest."

"I will take advantage of your question and extend myself on this issue. You wanted to know something about your dreams and, there was more. What is it?"

"Well, I mentioned something happened to me on several occasions and I cannot decipher it. The first time was when I was about ten years old. It was like waking up in a place, without knowing where I was nor with whom. But curiously, the place and people seemed very familiar."

Eric explained those "moves" in detail, of his other life in another person, of another gender and in a different place. It was as if he remembered bits and pieces of another life, not only physically but emotionally as well.

Rahel listened carefully and when a pause in the story gave a chance to intervene, he began to explain, "Well, Eric, we have talked about the soul, that is as real as your body, but in another dimension. Dimensions are, physically, the coordinates that determine the position of something."

"We have to examine the coordinates in greater detail, since they are also the guides in space to go from one place to another."

124

"If you have a blueprint, you can locate anything on it through measurements and the use of coordinates. If you use two perpendicular axis and place them in the right position, you can by referral, determine points you need. You could even baptize them by their position according to the axis. This you learn in high school. You need three axis for three dimensional bodies. Then you can study their position and many things more about the bodies in space. This is learned in trigonometry and space geometry. It is studied in mathematics, which helps us calculate and exactly measure the physical phenomena in that field."

"That's your field, three-dimensional physics. Bodies that have length, width and volume and cannot be penetrated as each body occupies a place in space. But only one body in the same space at a time. Then comes another factor: time. It is said that a body occupies a place in space at a certain time. But afterwards, when it moves, another body could occupy that same place."

"Now, you have one more coordinate, which is time. It works like this for the tranquil life on Earth. Speeds where things can move on the planet or beside it like airplanes in the air; for objects as small as grains of sand, one hundredth of a millimeter, and as large as the distance between the Earth and the Sun, in three dimensions and time, as the fourth dimension, for comparison, is enough."

"But, if you may want to reduce the size and measure molecules, atoms and subatomic particles, or augment it to measure distances between galaxies. If you´re interested in knowing how long it will take you to reach a star, you would need to use the speed of light as reference for those distances. Then you would require knowledge that, at present, is beyond the science known here on Earth."

"The science of the minute is called quantum physics by your brothers, and the opposite is astrophysics or cosmology. We have already passed information on to you regarding quantum physics or "quantum mechanics" as we call it. In it we explain the origin of matter, and how energy overlaps to create mass particles and its different manifestations. Plus the use of basic forces of energy that rule in quantum mechanics with the nuclear forces of fusion and fission."

"On the other side, the basic forces in the field of cosmology are gravitational and electromagnetic. This is where the science your brothers call "Theory of Relativity" is found. Pondering it made you understand that time is the fourth factor or coordinate to place bodies in third dimension. As this is part of the total system, there is only one dimension called space-time."This knowledge can be applied to the real universe where your planet belongs as part of the solar planetary system in the galaxy known as the Milky Way. At the same time, this forms part of the local universe that is an integral part of a super-universe, many of which integrate the master universe of creation."

"The Theory of Relativity explains how "time itself" of any object can be altered. The alteration of time is in accordance to its speed, if this reaches the speed of light (300 thousand kilometers per second approximately). At that moment, the coordinate time would have a value of "zero"; that is time would stop."

"It is not easy to imagine "time" stopping because it is not something you can see. It must be understood in an abstract way only, since to imagine a world where time stopped would be like a picture or a fixed stage. It is easier in any case, to change the context and to think of it as another dimension."

"Imagine you are wearing crystal green-colored eyeglasses. You are in a green room and you see everything clearly in tones of green. Now, you go on to another room and you can't see anything with those eyeglasses, only emptiness. So you put on some pink-colored eyeglasses and you see everything clearly in tones of pink. But if you have the pink eyeglasses on and go to the green room, again you won't be able to see anything. But, you already know what is in there, and even though you cannot see it, it continues to exist. Something similar happens with the changes of dimension, each one exists even when you, in another cannot see it. However, you understand its existence and the phenomena with which it could be manifested."

"If you force your imagination to understand what I have just described, you will be capable to think and accept that other

126

dimensions could exist further away. In this way we can proclaim as the FOURTH DIMENSION, that region in space where matter is integrated in such a way, that time no longer exists as a separate dimension, but is integrated in to itself."

"I´ll try to explain this to you in other words. When a body is able to move with the speed of light, time as you conceive it, ceases to exist—it has no value."

"Coming back to the subject of the soul, you must understand your soul is incarnated in your material being which is its means for evolution. It lives in the physical body when it is awake, but when it rests to recover energy, the soul (not needing this type of rest) carries out other activities."

"It could take advantage to think, using the knowledge and elements it has received from the spiritual brain. With this knowledge and through mental processes, it can reason, deduct, establish premises and reach conclusions that permit a suggestion to filter to the physical brain, to solve a pending problem."

"Thanks to this process, often upon awakening, the physical body finds the solution to some problem in his subconscious. It is then, when brought to his conscious, he can act with his FREE WILL. The concepts and judgment of his CONSCIENCE are clear in his mind."

"The soul can "detach itself" and travel to different places in space on certain occasions. Ubiquity is no problem, as the soul is not matter of the third dimension, and can travel at the speed of light and even faster. Remember it is in another dimension."

"There is a link between the traveling soul and its physical body. The latter cannot awaken being alone, and if something forces to return to the awake state, the soul will be there instantaneously to fulfill its duty to accompany that body. The Easterners call that spiritual bond, the Silver Cord."

"On its trip, the soul can consult with its spirit, found in the FIFTH DIMENSION. This is only allowed under special circumstances. And, if its twin soul should also arrive, it could be that, while the latter receives instructions from superior spirits or teachers, who advise and help in that world of light, it will be allowed to return, not to its body, but to that of its twin soul for a brief stay."

"This phenomenum will last as long as they have the opportunity to coincide and then, each will return to its own incarnated body. It is not a frequent occurrence, but isn´t rare or exceptional either. It could last only a very short time and then would remain only in the subconscious of the visited body, like "in a dream". When one person dreams and sees himself as the opposite sex, it is possible that there had been an "interchange" of this type."

"A soul that temporarily occupies the physical body of its twin soul, does not have the same knowledge that is found in the physical brain of that person. Therefore it doesn´t have the recordings in the spiritual brain to act through the plexus in synchronization with the physical brain."

"The spiritual brain takes part giving the person, through the plexus influence of each chakra, the vibrations corresponding to the feelings and emotions in synchronization with the memories that the physical brain projects on the mental screen of that individual."

"The soul has in its spiritual brain all the emotional information that is linked to each image, sound and aroma. The vibrations are emitted by the chakras and the physical body perceives them in the organs under their influence. For example: imagine somebody committed a crime using a gun. When that person sees the weapon, his physical brain will show the memory on the mental screen, including all the scene´s details, such as smells (maybe of gunpowder) and sounds."

"His spiritual brain transmits, through one or several charkas, the vibrations that correspond to love, hate or fear he felt at that moment and could well have been the main cause for his action, which sometimes can be stronger than reason or material motives. The vibrations felt by his heart, stomach and other organs will make him feel depression, pain and even nausea. Grief, similar to physical pain, could activate his tears."

"Another example: when someone sees a loved one in a picture, he remembers the voice, or the person itself, and the physical brain presents an image of everything related to that person in movement, as it's liked best or the way he or she is seen."

"The spiritual brain transmits the vibrations of the emotions linked to that person and his surroundings, which will also be felt in

128

his physical body, interpreting happiness or sadness, as the case may be. In this way, enthusiasm, happiness, love or grief will show up in the person's physical body influencing even his facial expressions and movements."

"Now, coming back to the subject of twin souls. It is clear that during the visit of the soul to the physical body of its twin, it doesn't have the prerecorded emotional elements to identify persons and objects synchronized with the memories existing in the physical brain. The spiritual brain immediately, as images and perceptions are received through the senses, looks into the physical brain and makes his own recording but, as it doesn't have "history", it cannot transmit the emotional vibrations through his charkas to the physical body."

"As you can see, Eric, many apparently complicated and difficult to understand things that happen in your world, are simple and natural when you have an explanation. Of course, it is necessary to include new elements, such as spiritual vibrations that are as real as the vibrations in the world of the third dimension."

Rahel took a break to allow Eric to absorb the concepts and express his doubts. Since Eric didn't make any comments, as he was digesting the mechanics of interactive functions between the spiritual brain of the soul in fourth dimension and the brain and body of a person in third dimension, he continued, " As you recall, twin souls have polarity; one is negative and the other is positive, determined by their gender at the level of the third dimension. The visiting soul will leave a slight influence characteristic of its personality during his stay. For example: of tenderness if it´s female, or if it is male, a tendency towards physical effort. How can I explain this to you? They are temporary and superficial."

"In cases such as yours, where they can alternate, another phenomenum can show up in both beings. Let's suppose that a soul returns from the fifth dimension when her twin soul is in her physical body. When it is awake, they cannot interchange, so they have to wait for the right moment for the visiting soul to leave the body. Meanwhile, the proprietor soul can take energy "prana" from its own body. "Prana" is the name the Easterners call the energy composed of easily condensed subatomic particles in matter of the third dimension, being able to reflect light as if applying a light coat of paint to a cloud, but still revealing the shape and form of the physical body of that soul."

"By this same quantum-physic phenomenum, human beings can sometimes "see" spirits, hear their manifestations or simply "feel" their presence as a magnetic field, being detected by the aura. I am referring to all the spiritual bodies of the fourth dimension (the souls) whose physical bodies have died and can no longer provide them with energy of the third dimension."

"When the soul take only a little "prana", only a faint sillouette would appear to be moving and can pass through solid bodies of the third dimension. It could, also, give the impression of "floating", as they do not need to walk to move their matter in a world of gravity being themselves weightless. If they have enough "prana", they could even be seen as a physical body of the third dimension, even in daylight."

"With small quantities of energy, spirits can make themselves be seen, carrying out small physical and material tasks. A soul can be seen if it has enough energy, in the world of the third dimension, by making noises, moving material objects and even communicating directly with people. The soul will establish a direct communication, through telepathy, which to the receiver, it would seem as if he physically heard a voice."

"They won't do much more, as the stronger and clearer the manifestation is in the third dimension, the larger amounts of "prana" would be consumed, and therefore, would last only a few seconds. Besides, to get close to the people, they have to overcome the force of electromagnetic field of the aura. If the person reacts in anger, there is a notable increase in the emission of energy by his charkas and the aura enlarges with that forcefully repelling and breaking up the scarce material energy of the spirit. Then this soul remains isolated, being able to see from his dimension, but being unable to manifest itself."

"When a person in the third dimension perceives the presence of a soul and gets scared, an energy that carries "prana" is emitted and the soul will use it up. Sometimes, that´s what it wants, so it tries to "scare" someone."

"A soul, when it's separated from its body by death, will use the available "prana" of its physical body plus that of his loved ones present at that moment, to manifest itself if it wants, for a few seconds and under favorable conditions, in some place of the planet it is about to leave."

"The soul of a person who died, even months or years ago, if dense, can't rise to spiritual levels, as it is under the gravitational action of the planet. This is caused by negative charges or karmas not in harmony with the Universe. This soul no longer has a physical body to provide it with energy. It is a soul whose spiritual brain is confused, in darkness; it is undergoing great grief, unable to determine its state and looks desperately for a way to acquire "prana" and "materialize itself" to contact physical beings."

"Not being conscious of its spiritual state, outside the material world of the third dimension, it tries to ask for help to learn its situation. This state of confusion will be endured until, through natural action, it will be free enough of negative charges (karma) to detach itself from the gravitational force of the planet. It needs to do this to be able to rise and get away from the surface of the physical planet of the third dimension and reach the region in universal space where it can complete the return to its own dimension, where it will clearly know what must be done."

"The apparently inexplicable phenomenum of "clinically dead" persons who return to life, is like this: When the body is in deep rest the soul, probably due to weakness caused by physical sickness or by being in a state of shock through some trauma can be freed, but is aware of the danger its physical body is in. Although the physical brain doesn´t know what happened or what the situation is due to unconsciousness, the soul knows and its spiritual brain is recording what happens."

"The soul can consult its spirit in the fifth dimension, but if the final hour of its life in the third dimension has not ended yet, as this depends exclusively on the Father, it has to return to its physical body. By doing so, on its way, it can see, hear, understand and remember the surrounding world."

"Normally during these separations, the return of the soul is sudden because the body awakens, but in this special case, it can calmly return to the body. After, it passes on the information of this detachment and what happened, to the physical brain. The person then thinks of it as a vague forgotten dream, or remember clearly whatever his soul saw and heard.

"When a soul returns to its body, which is temporarily animated by its twin soul, it can take advantage and go to other places and visit persons it wants to see. It can even also have enough energy (from its own body) and prana to become visible. When this happens it is not a matter of ubiquity, it is a fleeting phenomenum of the dissipation of energy that is not volitional and happens without the will of the soul itself. However, physically the image of that person could be seen away from its own physical body at the third dimension."

"Now we are on this subject, there are other phenomena that can be explained and are caused by spiritual manifestations in the third dimension. Telepathy, which is the transmission of thought, is carried out by passing the ideas to be transmitted from the physical brain to the spiritual one, which then sends them through high frequency waves to the spiritual brain of the receiver and, from there straight to the physical brain. In both cases, there is the phenomenum of internal communication from the third to the fourth dimension and vice versa."

"Telekinesis, levitation and teletransportation are physical phenomena caused by the use of high frequency energy through the mind in the third dimension. Look, Eric, the human brain is a true marvel of the creator and when working together with the spiritual brain, which is very superior, they sometimes produce, unconsciously, high frequency emissions at the level of the third dimension which result in the phenomena I have mentioned."

"The wish to do something is, in itself, a mental order that puts the spiritual brain to work, and it uses the charkas, as means of communication through frequencies in their dimension and can, as in the case of telepathy, take images and sounds that will be received by other spiritual brains to whom the transmission is directed. These phenomena are known as clairvoyance and clairaudience. Also, at the same time, the emissions in the antenna of the fourth dimension, which is our own aura, go to the body itself through the plexus, and even more so to the intellect. These vibrations can be synchronized with those of the mind in the third dimension forming an HARMONICA."

"The harmonica are nothing more than strengthened waves that would cause, unconsciously, a person with a subconscious wish to unleash very powerful energy, physically capable of manifesting itself with the phenomena of telekinesis (moving physical objects from a distance) or causing physical alterations in a certain place where energy is concentrated in an unpredictable way."

"When energy is used on a purely spiritual wish, it can flood the auric cocoon with such intensity that an ant gravitational effect is produced causing the levitation of its own body."

"Another effect of harmonic vibrations is the teletransportation of physical bodies. I will leave this phenomenum for later because it can be used in high technology, although it is not easy to understand."

"A positive result of the harmonica force coming from spiritual energy acting in the physical body, could be a feeling of enthusiasm, a self-confidence, a kind of self-hypnosis that helps the physical being attain what it wants, thereby increasing the probabilities."

"Now that we are on this subject," inquired Eric. "Is what we are seeing related to the unexplained phenomena of mediums, witchcraft and fortune telling?"

"Yes, definitely. The strange phenomena you mention are precisely the reckless and dangerous use of energies beyond your understanding and control."

"We are on a subject that easily could surpass the limits of our information. I can tell you that there are spirits in the process of shedding those karmic charges, who have for a long time, have been in that state of confusion and find a source to obtain prana in those human beings blindly looking for contact with the spiritual world. They establish then a contact of intercommunication that distracts them from their confusion and sometimes obtain DARMA from the human beings grateful for the intervention. However, as they don´t have a conscience, in that state, they could do harm and receive karma, since as many of those who contact them are acting blindly. The danger is unpredictable and incalculable, since both are acting outside of their dimension. A human being has natural and adequate transdimensional contact through his spirit, which must always be under the control of the conscience."

"As you see, Eric, the soul has its own life in its dimension, but it is so united to the physical being that it is natural to perceive different manifestations. These are part of life in common with the body of the third dimension that is, as I have told you, its own vehicle for evolution---the other self that lives in the dimension of mass and matter, where it receives experiences and knowledge in gravitational worlds that are centers of learning and evolution. Sometimes that ephemeral and weak physical being, is the one we choose as our real self and it worries us more that the true one, which is the soul."

"Now you can understand that when you hear a noise, it could be a sign without apparent origin, a "here I am" of a soul that, making an extraordinary effort, has managed to gather enough energy to manifest itself. That "here I am" could be a desperate call for help. Perturbed spirits do not try to harm anyone, but to ask for help in their loneliness and confusion."

"Being used to matter not having a spiritual conscience, they feel lost in the darkness of reason and become desperate when nobody can see them as they have moved into another dimension."

"A prayer is a gift of love from the cosmic energy to help them shed the karmas that don´t allow them to see the light and rise to spiritual life in other regions of the universe, where they could find their identity and be conscious of their own spiritual brain to learn who they are, where they are and which is the next step in their evolution."

"It is the right moment to mention that your brothers try to visualize "life" after physical death as it happens with matter on Earth. They even imagine that the way human organizations are managed in this planet is the same as in the spiritual world. They expect to go directly to the Father to render accounts, and who will reward or punish them according to their material concept of justice."

"It is natural, with this kind of logic, for heavens or hells to exist only for material beings of the third dimension. Spiritually we are our own strictest judge. We will know the result of our spiritual evaluation of our actions during life. We will accept the need to mend our faults, spiritually or physically, in a new life, to get rid of karmas representing our spiritual debt, to be in harmony again with our spirit and therefore continue evolution."

"There are no severely imposed punishments, only love and just restitution so the spirit can continue being perfected to rise to higher levels."

People had begun to arrive little by little; suddenly Eric noticed they were surrounded by passengers waiting for their flight to Mexico City. Rahel hadn't said a word for a long time, but his expression of satisfaction, smilingly conveyed he was sure the complete message had been received.

A voice announced on the loud speaker, "*Passengers bound for Mexico City,* we will shortly be boarding through gate number two.
Eric and Rahel stood up and made their way over there.

"Are they coming for you or are you staying here?" asked Eric.

"Well, to be honest, they are waiting for me."

"Is it possible for you to give me a ride?" joked Eric, with a smile.

"It isn't so easy," answered Rahel. "Everything is planned, we are a team. Look, when Mirza travels there is always another vehicle with two companions, Misha and Elim, who have lived here and know your customs well. They have money and all that's needed to solve any problem, even in case of an accident, to pick her up and call base to take her there to be attended to as soon as possible. We cannot be cared for by your medical procedures, as we could die. Our blood chemistry is different and we don't have any defenses against your bacterias and viruses. There are many precautions to be taken, and have to act as an interconnected team. Do you understand? But yes, I promise that some day you will have the opportunity to come with us on a real trip, as you have surely done so in your dreams. It will be a great experience for you."

Rahel turned and looked towards the people by the entrance. Eric clearly distinguished Elim by the peculiar lines of his face. When they caught each other´s eye, he smiled and transmitted clearly: *"Hello, Eric, I am Elim. Have a good trip!"*

"Hello, Elim, nice meeting you. I hope we'll see each other again," Eric transmitted back. He picked up his boarding pass and with a wave, said goodbye to both.

"Mirza will be in contact with you," added Rahel.

"Thanks, Rahel, until next time."

Rahel said goodbye with a smile and transmitted: *"We'll talk about your DREAM TRIPS next time."*

"My dream trips?" answered Eric, with a doubtful look.

When Rahel referred to the spirit he had the habit of touching the top of his head with the middle finger of his right hand, signaling the position of the cosmic chakra called Shahasrara. When he was referring to the mind, he pointed to his forehead between the eyebrows, and signaled upwards with two fingers making a motion of departure when he referred to trips to outer space. So Eric understood when he answered with a signal from his hand that pointed to mind, spirit trip.

Eric was already about ten meters away, entering the waiting room when he realized practically all the conversation had been done by mental telepathy. He was happy and excited, satisfied he gave a last sign of goodbye to his friends, on his way to the airplane waiting to take him speedily and comfortably back home.

When the plane took off with great power, the strength of the turbines could be felt lifting it with ease. He looked out the window hoping Rahel´s vessel would show up somewhere and he daydreamed……..imagining it to appear. He would go the pilot´s cabin to let them know and would tell them: "Now it will move to the other side." And the vessel would move according to his prediction, as he would be in telepathic contact with them. Then he would tell the pilots: "Now it will go once around the plane and then leave straight ahead of us, on its way up until out of sight."…….and it would! Then he would have witnesses on his side!!!!

He smiled at his childish wish, but kept on staring out the window, until all visibility was lost in the clouds. He felt calm, his imagination was at rest, he fell fast asleep.

CHAPTER X

Whoever dwells deeply on the mysteries of
nature through science,
has a glimpse of great divine marvels,
but will only find the truth when
the investigation is inspired by love.

B.T.L.

THE FIRST DREAM

The highway from Apodaca joins the road from Monterrey and Nuevo Laredo through the northern exit of the city, not far from the Holiday Inn Hotel. Eric had thought of having lunch around there before leaving for Monclova, but was not hungry, so he started his trip. In a few moments he took the road and returned to his memories.

He began to summarize his first visit to Milburek, his stay in Milgar and the clear images of Parthelia, Galimor and Birken.......

The crowd was impressive. Eric was a little upset as he walked with several persons coming out of a very large station resembling a magnificently lit subway. The comfortable and elegant aerodynamic train stopped silently. The passengers were very well mannered persons. They all talked and walked in a hurry, but did not push and shove. They were very courteous, as if leaving an opera house.

The explanade was gigantic. There were circles, about thirty meters in diameter marked where very silent circular vessels descended, opened their hatchway, about 150 to 200 enthusiastic passengers came out of each. Complete families could be seen with

137

several children of different ages. The night was cool, but pleasant, and everyone was dressed in good quality casual clothes of different styles and colors. Shorts and mini skirts worn with colored tights and low, soft cushioned shoes seemed the fashion.

In spite of the crowd and normal murmur of voices, there weren't any jarring noises of motors. The floor was made of ceramic-like material decorated with figures in different shades and colors, and no footsteps could be heard. Not a single vendor could be seen.

They arrived at the entrance of an enormous hall with colored glass windows (maybe they were plastic, but looked like glass). There were many other entrances, marked with signs, where people passed rapidly and easily. There were no shops, vendors, attendants, police men nor uniformed guards.

As he entered, he could see that it was like a gigantic oval bull ring, something like the Plaza Mexico, but ten times larger. The passage ways were all carpeted, the seats were comfortable armchairs, ten to each section easily accessed on both sides, plus a wide passageway between each row.

It gave the impression of being a sports arena where the playing field below, at the center, was covered with a kind of enormous glass bubble. In reality, it was the immense lens of a magnifying glass. The public then had the impression of being only ten meters away from the players and the action.

Eric didn't understand the game very well, it resembled basketball. The players were all athletes, but the game wasn't rough and depended more on skill and speed. In any given play, although it was fast and sometimes violent, the players got hurt or hurt another player. When that happened, they treated each other as if they all belonged to the same team.

The people cheered their team competing against another from Galimor, but nobody was fighting. All the good plays were applauded and everyone celebrated. Nobody ate or drank anything, everyone talked and laughed....nothing more.

As the game ended, the local team of Parthelia won; everyone celebrated, even the opposing team. The prizes were framed diplomas. Joyful music could be heard in the background played by an orchestra, was at times full of rhythm and others, a march.

As they went out and the crowd started to disperse as easily as it had arrived. Eric's group back tracked to the station, but didn't board the train. They walked through wide, well lit, carpeted passageways with a soft musical background until arriving at a kind of platform where a two-meter wide transportation belt passed. The wide accesses
were marked with acrylic tubes of different colors. It was as easy to get on the belt as taking an electric staircase. Then, running parallel another belt passed at a faster speed. Going from one to another was as easy as taking the first one, and then on to a third, which tripled the speed.

The opposite side of the platform could be reached as these interconnecting belts of varying speeds passed under each other, as needed.

The support hand railings were placed about 50 centimeters inside the belts. That way it was very easy to hold on to them when changing belts. These were in 3 meter long sections, with a one meter space in between each. Therefore, one could pass safely and comfortably from one belt to another. The fastest belt was wider and also had some long, comfortable and cushioned benches in sections for four persons. All this became an underground subway of conveyor belts! The lighting in the tunnel resembled a living room, the different colored carpets made identification easy and there was no risk of danger. The walls also were painted in different colors to inform the passengers of their arrival at each access.

The fastest belt traveled at some 15 kilometers per hour; comfortable walking could add another 5 kilometers to the speed. This way, walking a few minutes would get the passenger to the train station faster. Although the train went underground in certain places, it was elevated most of the way, so beautiful views could be enjoyed. In places where there weren´t any belts, small electric cars could be used and, when no longer needed, were left where someone else could use them. They were kept perfectly clean and in good working order.

Leaving the station at Milgar, the intercommunication through passageways consisted of wide belts and electric stairs, at least 1.25 meters wide with comfortable handrails. The floor appeared to be wooden. Indirect upward lighting gave a sense of spaciousness.

Then they walked through a very wide hallway with large windows and well lit indoor gardens with grass, trees and flowers. This building looked like a huge hotel. On the fifth floor, another wide hallway led them to a door, where Eric was told:

"Here is your apartment, welcome to Parthelia, you are on the planet, Milburbek. Just rest for now, and tomorrow we'll come to take to see interesting places as instructed by Rahel. You won't have any problems. May you sleep well and we'll see you tomorrow."

Eric entered the apartment; it was not locked, and had an interphone. When he was alone, he started to become aware of his surroundings. He had practically remained silent from the beginning and had felt he was with "friends", but he didn't even know who they were....nor where he was or what he was doing there. But he didn't worry, his mind was only interested in what was happening, as if in a dream. Nevertheless, he noticed his reflexes were slow, and a kind of mental numbness didn't allow him to think clearly. He felt as if he were seeing himself as a spectator.

The apartment was ample, beautifully furnished and with large windows, or better said, glass walls! Everything lit up upon entering and he could observe the furniture. There was a spacious sitting room with a sofa, two arm chairs and a cute looking concave glass table supported by wide highly polished legs. As he touched it, it seem to glide over the rug.

The sliding door gave way to an adequately furnished bedroom: bed, night table, dressing table and chair. Another door led to a private bathroom. The furnishings could be identified, but there was no shower nor bath tub, only a vertical cylinder about 1.80 meters high, full of holes in what appeared to be a thick blue acrylic plaque. On one side, it had small handles and a button. The water in the wash bowl was activated automatically, by placing your hands underneath the faucet. To a side, a hand shower (similar to a telephone) resembled an electric toothbrush, made up of many small

140

tubes in an area of two square centimeters. The pressure, triggered like a gun, released thin threads of warm pulverized water. It really was a water brush!

The toilet had a cover, but no water tank, and was also activated automatically. When the water brush was unhooked, the toilet would flush, and it took the place of toilet paper. When it was put back, a current of air came out of the bowl to dry the wet part of the body in seconds. The wash bowl also had an outlet to dry with a twisting movement towards the face activated by a button on the floor. A liquid soap dispenses supplied a small dab by pushing a hand lever.

After investigation, Eric got to thinking how the bath would work. He would soon find out. He continued looking over the rest of the apartment carefully. There was another door, near the entrance, that gave way to a half bathroom for visitors, similar to the other, but also had a soft tissue dispenser.

There was also a kind of kitchenette supplied with cups, glasses, spoons and an apparatus which served food in three different colors. There was also a tea and pure water dispenser, and a box with straw like delicious cookies, one centimeter thick. These had to be chewed to powder as they didn't dissolve in the stomach. Later he found out that they were designed to keep teeth in use and healthy.

Plaques with a control button were imbedded in the wall. Upon entering a room an indirect light was turned on. If one wanted more light, just turning a knob would provide the desired intensity. Concave ceilings had a smooth dull finish to reflect the indirect lighting projected from lamps sets into the walls two meters high.

The windows of the sitting room that looked out onto a spacious garden had a control button. Pressing it once, the glass turned smoke color; twice, became darker; three times, it cleared again. It seemed to have two internal screens that changed colors and were transformed by some special mechanism.

The very comfortable soft armchairs were upholstered in velour. Soft background music filled the room and a large 40-inch television screen was set into the wall.

The next building was about one hundred meters away and no windows faced that side, ensuring total privacy. A small wood, flowering plants, grass and water ponds made up the garden.

The interphone rang, Eric hesitated before answering, "Hello..."

The voice of his guide could be heard clearly. "Eric, I hope you have toured your apartment. Do you have any doubts?"

"Well, yes. I have seen it but, how do I take a bath?" he asked.

He heard a laugh on the other side of the telephone. "Very easy, just to into the "shower", the water comes out when the sensor on the floor is activated by your weight. Adjust the temperature with the control and use the soap from the dispenser. When you are through, pull the lever next to the temperature control, up to substitute the water for air to dry yourself; the one on the right is the water pressure control."

"If there's anything you need, just call me. Pick up the phone and press the button with the crossed out circles, I will answer. Ah! Do eat! But only one serving of the green food. In the morning, have one of the pink after your bath, it will make you feel good. If you plan to have a shower now, afterwards, put on a pijama, they are in the lower drawer. Tomorrow wear the clothes from the upper drawer. You will be awakened on time, just set the sound control by putting it upwards at the intensity you want. Do you have any questions?"

"I don't think so," answered Eric. "Thank you very much. We'll see each other tomorrow."

"Until tomorrow, then. Have a good rest!"

Eric followed his instructions to wake up the next morning, and thought to himself, "What a nice man Elim is."

Then he went to look for his clothes. There was a closet set in the wall; by pressing a button, a door opened and out came a drawer. A carrousel of rotating drawers would appear, always at the same height—some 1.20 centimeters from the floor—when certain buttons were touched.

The pajamas were made of soft silk like material. A pearl gray bathrobe, his size, was also provided.

The clothes consisted of comfortable underwear, light trousers, long and short sleeved sports shirts, fitted socks and soft, moccasin type cushioned shoes.

He undressed and went into the vertical compartment. His weight on the sensor caused a spray of water like fine rain to come out. The sensation was really pleasant. He adjusted the temperature and noticed the change from hot to cold was practically instantaneous. It was truly a body massage, if the pressure was raised or, a soft humidifying cloud if lowered. The liquid soap had a delicate fragrance and made lots of bubbles. Eric felt clean and fresh!

Two bars, one fixed to the ceiling about two and a half meters high and another, about 20 centimeters from the wall, provided massages. He got on a 50 square centimeter cushioned bench, about 20 centimeters high, to reach the higher bar and it started to vibrate, giving a simply delightful massage to the soles of his feet. He did a couple of push ups and laid on the bench to massage his back. Fantastic! He could have even fallen asleep there.

His bed had two eiderdowns, one covering the mattress and the other to cover himself. The silk like texture was light and soft. The temperature was automatically controlled, only enough to keep the body heat.

He got into bed and, with a very satisfying sense of well being, soon fell into deep sleep. The following morning he awoke feeling rested and fresh. He took a shower, ate the recommended breakfast and was ready when his guide arrived.

Eric and Shem walked down the hallway of the building, people alone or in groups joined them on the way out. Shem explained that all the buildings in that area were alike.

"The majority of the residents are young couples, either still studying or already working," Shem said. "Transportation to their centers of activity can be reached within minutes on the belts and train. The belts go almost from their doorsteps to the stations, and the train is very fast and comfortable. After, there are more belts or surface vehicles. Today, I will take you to a food factory and later we'll go to a school."

143

They walked meeting more people each time, until they arrived at the belts. It was all very cordial, everybody smiled easily. Everyone dressed well in different colors and styles in varied fabrics. Nobody carried anything—no bags, no packages, no books. It was a rare exception if someone had a book or notebook.

Eric asked if it was possible to go out to the gardens.

"Of course, the entrances are on the lower levels. Although there are certain rules to be followed as a courtesy to other residents, but anyone can see them from their   homes." Milgar was truly a very beautiful residential area.

"If someone wants privacy," continued Shem, just by darkening the windows that look like mirrors on the outside, ensures total privacy."

"What happens is, as you will see, everyone has access to other parks and gardens, where there are recreational and sporting activities and they prefer to go there with their friends. There are young people who belong to the same sports team and spend a lot of time together, even though their homes are far away. Sometimes the equivalent to a thousand kilometers in your planet. Nevertheless, they can arrive within a few minutes, and sometimes reach their homes even before others, who live closer. They only take the belt and an air vessel carrying 500 passengers on a ten minute flight at an approximate speed of 10,000 kilometers an hour."

"Our distribution of time is slightly different than yours. We have a decimal system, our day is 20 hours long—an hour equals 18 degrees in the 360 degree rotation of the planet. People try to travel large distances within the same "time zone" so as not be affected by time changes for the different activities in their lives. Distances are really not a problem."

"What is the cost of transportation?" Eric dared ask.

Shem smiled and said, "Absolutely the same as their housing, food and education: nothing. We don´t pay for anything in money as you do. Here everyone works enough to have everything. There are some differences to acknowledge special merits for quality on the job, more than for quantity. We all have time to rest, work, study, and to get together, practice sports, read and other artistic activities like painting and sculpture, when this is not their work."

"How?" Eric asked. "You don't charge to work?"

"Well, yes, we do charge; but not money. Its equivalent in services and basic products. To charge, for us, means receiving all that's needed in food, clothes, education, housing, transportation, medical services, medicines, hospitalization, memberships to our recreation centers where sports, games, etc. are practiced."

"We all work in what we know best, and we all have to cooperate to have the food, clothes, transportation and everything else according to what is needed. Depending on what your work is, you participate in its organization and know how many three-hour a day shifts are needed and at what time. In a twenty-hour day, three hours are the equivalent to three hours and thirty six minutes of a twenty-four-hour day."

"You mean to tell me that you only work three hours a day?" asked Eric, thinking of the long work shifts on Earth.

"Yes, there can be three, or a little less or much more. Everything depends on the amount of work required to fulfill the production quotas or to meet the goals required in the factory."

"Then, if everyone works without getting remuneration for what they do. How can they be honest? How do you find out if some work more than others, and know when they have fulfilled their obligations?"

"According to the quality and the degree of difficulty of the work, acknowledgements are attained. There are jobs that produce many acknowledgements for a three hour shift, but to do them requires a lot of study and practice. If you have them, you can earn three or four times the acknowledgements of what you can get in manual or technical work that is easier."

"Well, that is the same as earning more. But if you eat and dress the same and travel without paying, how do you take advantage of your acknowledgements?"

"There are several ways. You can select a change of housing, if you live in one for two people, but if you want to be in a different sort of place, or want to live near your children, you need more acknowledgements. Also you may want more free time to travel and see other places, or want to study to learn more about what you are interested in, practice sports or spend time with your

145

friends in recreational centers. Or if you have another partner, you can go with her to other places."

"I believe I have understood. But, what is this of "another partner"?

"Well, when you have a partner and you get along well, you can live apart from each other and have a family. The number of children you want to have depends on the merits you have, since when they are born they will need all the help until they are older and independent. What they will receive has to be compensated by the parents, and they do it working more or less according to the number of merits they have and depending on their work."

"When a baby is born, as you would say, the country provides all it requires; in this case it is the whole planet. Everything has to be planned from conception."

"Is it necessary to have an authorization from the State, Government or whatever you call it?"

"Definitely, yes."

"And if the authorization is not requested?"

"Why shouldn't it be? There is no reason for not doing so if everything is going to be needed, from prenatal care and medical check-ups until birth, and then its care as a baby and later, the education."

"Is it necessary to be married to get the authorization?"

"Yes, of course. Couples ask for it together and accept the cost it will have for each one."

"And, do they remain married all their life?"

"No, not married as you understand it. Our society is very different from the one on your planet. There it is necessary because as parents, you are irresponsible and do not take care of the children and nobody else does. The child is left without parents, without a home, without education—like a little abandoned animal that becomes a social problem and a burden. Here, it is a contract between both to cover the cost of the newborn until he or she can support itself."

"How long does it last or what is the contract or agreement known as?"

"The couple is joined by an agreement of LOVE. They make the necessary arrangements to have their own home furnished with all that is needed. There are no complications until they want to have a baby. The contract is filed before the authorities and both agree to work until they cover the social cost. Nobody would even think of entering a new agreement with another partner, until the contract to cover the expenses and education of the offspring is complied with and a fund for these expenses has been set up for children under the custody of Society. When this has been done, then they can separate and be free to have a new agreement with another partner, if they so wish."

"The children, as I was telling you, usually remain with their parents until they are ten years old. Only under extraordinary circumstances would they go to a foster home for minors. After they go to school, they can continue living with their parents until they leave to make their own home. While in college or university, they can live in student dorms at their centers of learning. But they do so by choice, not obligation. If their parents are alone in the family home, they will keep on living with them and go every day to continue their education."

"By that time, if their parents have separated, they visit them, but will no longer be dependent on them for support or education. However, it isn´t generally this way. The more they know and live with each other, the more they want to continue together forming a true family and ask for more permission to have children."

"But if they want to have more children, is the previous contract cancelled?"

"Yes, that's no problem, because there's a guarantee that child can continue with his life without problems."

"Has it ever happened that the authorities have to intervene if one of the two does not fulfill their part of the contract?"

"It doesn't happen, because everyone fulfills their duties, and punishments are not necessary." The way of thinking is very different to yours, and the basis is RESPONSIBILITY through CONVICTION, not by obligation."

"When something extraordinary is required, such as an unexpected medical treatment due to an accident or illness, it is perfectly defined to be within everyone's right to have it."

"Could they separate before everything regarding the child has been paid for?"

"Yes, they could, but it will be a very special case. What usually happens is that they don't want to separate, since they had decided to get together because they understand each other, they get along well and their decision was made through LOVE. If you analyze it, you will see that the problems your brothers have in your planet do not exist here, so they don't easily change their minds. You, due to your organization, do have many problems. The main one is money, since you need it for everything; and if you don't have it, you do have a big problem. 80% of the disagreements are caused by money, the other 20% is due to education, because of moral principles and lack of spirituality or evolution."

"You are right, everything is moved by money on my planet."

"Money, in a commercial society such as yours, practically cannot be substituted; it offers many advantages, but carries implicit risks. Money gives power to its owner, even though he doesn't deserve it. When it's acquired cleanly, it is the fruit of honest work and becomes a loyal servant; but when it is ill gotten, it is a terrible weapon against society itself, and one of its victims is the one who uses it."

"What impressed me the most when I was with you, was precisely that. Everyone struggles desperately to have money and thereby have power. This power makes you materialistic, polarizing your spiritual gifts and decreasing your good will. It deafens you to the voice of your conscience and, by abusing your free will, you destroy each other and delay your evolution."

"Do you have any churches? Religions?"

"We all have our own temple within our body. Our religion is the knowledge we have of creation. Our behavior corresponds to the respect and gratitude we have for our Heavenly Father, Creator of the Universe, and we show it to Him by our love for Him, and all our brothers in creation."

"Our organization is easy and efficient because we are not under any obligation nor threats of any kind. We act voluntarily, each person is responsible for himself and his spiritual evolution. We are aware of what everyone expects of us and it is an honor and priviledge to fulfill these expectations, be efficient and respectful of the rights of all our brothers as they are of ours."

"If you love someone, you do not wait to be asked, you offer what that person needs, if you have it. And if not, you help them obtain it without expecting anything in return. Isn't it true? That is all, it's that simple, there is no mystery. Love everyone and treat them accordingly."

"If you give love, you receive love, respect and consideration from others. This is our concept of religion, as in this way we are also showing our gratitude to our Father."

While they talked they continued on the short route Shem had planned, they passed the recreational center of Milgar, that would be the envy of the most luxurious and exclusive country club on Earth. The accumulated natural beauty was exciting, the beautiful buildings with glass walls to enjoy the outdoors. All the comforts were displayed as usual, game rooms for couples or groups, billiard tables...well, very similar, but in the form of a U with right angles. A kids room resembling a bowling alley, to be used from both sides for games of soldiers and marbles, swimming pools, track fields, and courts for games like our football or baseball, but different in shape and size.

They arrived to the dining room, similar to those on Earth; ample, with tables and a large self service bar. There were fruit platters, similar to ours, only different in color and size. Besides there were the known food dispensers of colored paste, plates and teaspoons. Water dispensers, containing ades of several fruit flavors resembling ours, only with different names were on hand.

People didn't stay long in the dining hall, not more than ten minutes. They chose what they wanted, served themselves, went to the table, ate and left to continue their business.

"Normally, one eats in ten minutes," Shem explained. "People can have several meals, depending mainly on their activities. The rush hours of the dining halls, in the equivalent of Earth's schedule, are: from 6 to 7, from 10 to 11, from 14 to 15 and from 18 to 19 hours. Even when the dining halls remain open for self service, after that, there are few customers. Normally, if someone wants to have something after that hour, it´s done at home."

"In the morning, we usually have juice and fruit before going to work and we also drink tea at any time."

149

The food dispensers had about eight or ten different colors and flavors. Some were special for sportsmen who consumed large amounts of energy. Their presentation was practically the same and had the consistency of ice cream, totally healthy and nutritious. Their delicate and delicious flavors also smelled like the exquisite aromas of fine herbs. In addition to these foods, many fruits were eaten to improve digestion.

There were serving employees, but only to pick up used plates and teaspoons. They only served spheres with fruit to the customers. It was the only place in the club where one could eat; only tea was everywhere since there were dispensers all over to have it any place, and anytime. It could be said that it was the substitute of coffee, cigarettes, candy and "junk" food.

At some point of the completely automatic and telecontrolled train trip, they passed through a practically endless area of the city of Parthelia. In it there were huge buildings, always surrounded by large green spaces and lakes, where exotic birds lived. Bright colored swans, red, blue, yellow and combinations of black and white, obtained genetically for beauty could be seen. Also, there was a huge variety of birds of gorgeous colors and birds of song living in total freedom.

After leaving the residential zone, the train passed through small orchards of fruit trees and fields of different colored flowers, grown to supply the ornate decorations found everywhere.

The train entered a tunnel and continued underground. Shortly, it stopped in Golemisbek station, the city's airport. Goleman meant a vessel for passenger transportation and Golemi was the plural.

They traveled on a train made up of five very large 40-meter wagons, and very comfortably furnished. Even during rush hours they were never crowded; the passengers always traveled sitting down. In spite of the large population, when "crowded" there was space between people, no pushing or shoving, always with calm elegance and comfort.

The underground station was ample; on the platform there was a belt that brought people closer to other LUBA belts to exit. There were four LUBI on the ramp, three meters, and a 20 degree slope. Halfway up, there was a landing where the ascending belt for the second section of the ramp could be taken, to arrive at a distribution center.

The distribution center at Golemisbek was a round gigantic lobby, about 1000 meters in diameter. The beauty of the hall was impressive because of the peace and calm that could be felt.

A 50-meter dome at the center had other smaller domes around it. They were all painted or had stained glass panes. The drawings on each dome resembled a daisy whose petals had different shades of color that combined with the dull white in the background.

The main one had tones of blue and red, the rest yellow and orange. The combination produced a strange feeling of joy and peace. The floor was covered by a carpet in different tones of gray and apricot, very restful to the eyes. The lighting was splendid. The structure supporting the domes rested on arches above eight svelte columns at the center of the hall, that also served as supports for the "sariyas", or information screens regarding each boarding gate.

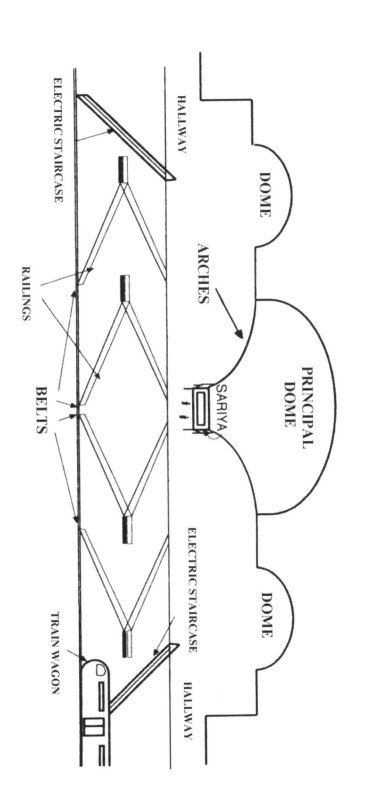

ELECTRIC STAIRCASE

HALLWAY

DOME

RAILINGS

ARCHES

BELTS

SARIYA

PRINCIPAL
DOME

ELECTRIC STAIRCASE

DOME

TRAIN WAGON

HALLWAY

(Golemisbek de Parthelia)

Eight passage ways, symmetrically spaced, opened out from the center of distribution. The main one was about 20 meters wide and had two sets of belts (one set of two parallel belts went in one direction and the other set in the opposite direction). Three mechanized walking bands, two between the belts and the walls, and a central one between the sets of belts.

FIGURE 13

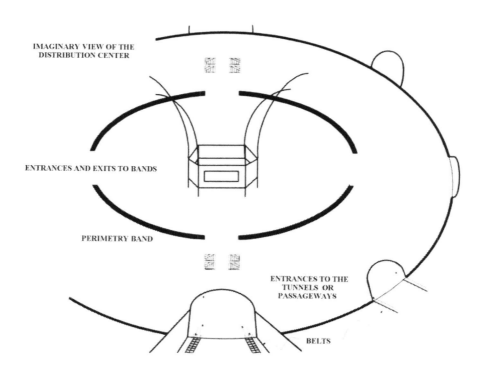

This mechanized walking band led to another lobby where the passengers arriving in surface vehicles could get off. Then it continued to another distribution hall similar to the first.

Some young people and groups of children went by on the walker bands at the ends; the center one was used by electric cars carrying cargo or airport employees and crews.

All the radial passageways were about eight meters wide and accessed the departure and arrival waiting rooms, via entering and exiting belts. The boarding halls on each passageway were always on the left, so the belt on the left went to the waiting rooms. When getting to the access of each one it was cut off and continued after passing the entrance, so that the passengers going to a waiting room farther away walked across this space and took the next belt. The band next to the opposite wall that went in direction of the lobby was continuous, but with accesses in front of each passageway of the boarding waiting rooms.

The "sariyas" (screens) that were in front of each hallway from the center, supplied flight information of departures of each waiting room and its colors of identification. Each passageway had a different color and the waiting room to which they led had a combination of the color of the passageway and the color of the waiting room. For example, the blue passageway had exits to waiting rooms color green, yellow, red, violet and blue. The walls of each passageway had painted stripes combining the colors of the passageway and the waiting room. This way, the first waiting room in the blue passageway had a blue stripe and a green one, meaning that all the first waiting rooms were green with the color of its passage way; the second ones were yellow, etc., so it was difficult to go to the wrong waiting room. These colors appeared on the "sariyas" indicating the destinations and information about each place. The first waiting rooms were used for smaller vessels that were able to land closer, and the parlors farther away were used by the larger vessels.

FIGURE 14

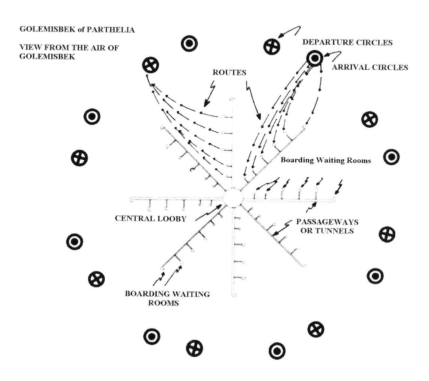

GOLEMISBEK of PARTHELIA

VIEW FROM THE AIR OF
GOLEMISBEK

DEPARTURE CIRCLES

ARRIVAL CIRCLES

ROUTES

Boarding Waiting Rooms

CENTRAL LOOBY

PASSAGEWAYS
OR TUNNELS

BOARDING WAITING
ROOMS

To land, the vessels had to follow a pattern similar to that of our airports, but simpler due to the easier handling equipment. At an altitude of about 500 meters, they placed themselves over a large colored circle that signaled the vertical landing point. In each radial section of the departure and arrival passenger waiting rooms, there were two circles,
one with concentric circles with the color of the waiting room for arrival and another a little smaller with a cross to signal the place of departure of the vessels. (Figure 15)

FIGURE 15

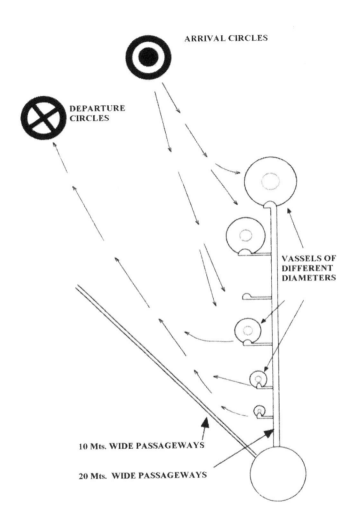

ARRIVAL CIRCLES

DEPARTURE
CIRCLES

VASSELS OF
DIFFERENT
DIAMETERS

10 Mts. WIDE PASSAGEWAYS

20 Mts. WIDE PASSAGEWAYS

    The vessels made their last vertical descent and remained
floating at about five meters above ground. Then they got into
position directly above their exit waiting room. They looked like
giant spangles floating softly and silently. Upon arrival, the exterior
roof of this room would open vertically, in such a way that the vessel

157

landed delicately on a supporting ring, which when lowered to the right level, the roof turned downward and covered the vessel.

The larger vessels had two types of gates, one was vertical that turned upwards, it opened like a roof and uncovered the other gates that slid horizontally embedding themselves in the fuselage. Thus, the access could be from about eight to fifteen meters wide, according to the size of the vessel. The "golema" connected to the waiting room and opened its access gates; at the same time, the door of the waiting room would connect to the vessel adjusting it to the floor and the protection of the roof. This could not be seen from the waiting room as the sliding door of the wall was closed. When everything was ready, the door to the waiting room would slide open and the access to the vessel would be similar to going from one room to the next.

Departures were the same, but the process was reversed: the vessel closed its gates, the exterior roof of the waiting room opened up completely uncovering the vessel which softly rose from the ring and floated upwards to the departure circle.

The departure circle was about 200 meters further away from the arrival one. When the vessel was in place above it, the first stage of vertical ascent would begin. From the time it closed its gates, the roof opened and it got to the vertical take-off circle, it would take one minute.

Each boarding room had an ample area facing the large access gates to the vessel. Also, there were huge windows on both sides, enabling a view of the airport's movement outside and the gardens; the feeling of spaciousness always prevailed. The sliding doors opened to the sides, so there was a wide passageway to enter or exit the connected vessel. (Figure 16 and 17)

FIGURE 16

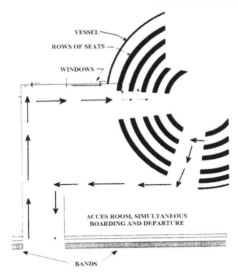

VESSEL
ROWS OF SEATS
WINDOWS

ACCES ROOM, SIMULTANEOUS
BOARDING AND DEPARTURE

BANDS

FIGURE 17

IMAGINARY VIEW OF PASSAGEWAY OF ARRIVAL AND DEPARTURE TO BOARDING WAITING ROOM

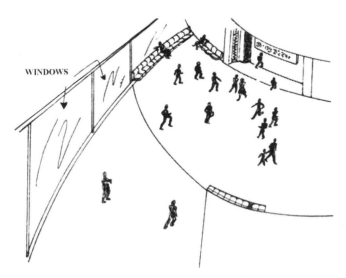

WINDOWS

IMAGINARY VIEW OF PASSAGEWAY OF ARRIVAL
AND DEPARTURE TO BOARDING WAITING ROOM

In the main lobby of Golemisbek there were, in addition to the "sariyas" pertaining to each passageway to the waiting room for boarding, a central panel and a set of monitors where special personal information could be obtained.

The same language was used on all the planet. To the ear, it resembled a mixture of a Germanic tongue with inflections and soft combinations of Italian or French; but Eric, in any case, didn´t understand a thing. To him, it was like hearing Japanese, Chinese or Arabic, that don´t resemble Spanish at all.

However, although he couldn´t understand the language, when they transmitted through telepathy he could perceive by intuition what it was about. If they were simple, general or preconceived subjects, such as comments on something everybody was looking at, then it was easy to understand what was said.

When a word of international use is pronounced on Earth, such as "restaurant", or the expression "O.K.", it is sometimes not understood because each language has its own accent and is not easily recognizable, but in telepathy, it is always possible to understand their greetings and many other expressions that were received only as ideas.

The Golemisbek in Parthelia, from where they departed, had two distribution interconnected by belts. In each, there were three main corridors and four secondary ones. The main ones were very wide and had two belts going to waiting rooms further away and were used for very large vessels.

The passengers´ cabin on the vessels was round and ample, four meters high in the center and approximately 2.5 meters at the sides. The center contained the heart of the vessel, where the motors of the rotors and all the electromagnetic system were found. It occupied one third of the total diameter. (Figure 18)

All the passengers entered calmly, comfortably chatting with each other. Some served themselves a cup of tea. Afterwards, the sliding door closed and the vessel began the flight. This type of vessel could make a 1,000 kilometer trip in approximately 15 minutes, counting from the time the access gates were closed, until they opened at its destination; where the passengers simply got off. Even when the vessel began its flight at an ascending speed of one millimeter per second as soon as it was disconnected from the support ring, one minute later it was already about 50 meters above the departure circle. The next minute it went up vertically and then changed to a helicoidal elevation, moderately accelerating until reaching a height of 50 kilometers before the fourth minute. Then it accelerated with force and by minute ten, it was already descending at its destination. In three or four more minutes, the passengers were already leaving the vessel. Usually there were direct flights, although very large vessels did make intermediate stops during their route.

FIGURE 18

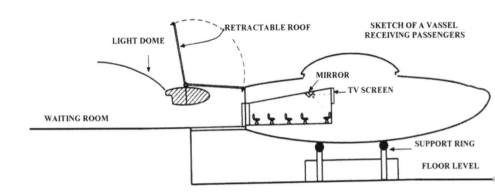

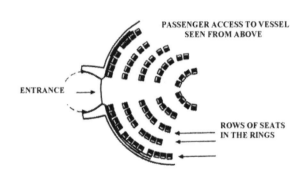

There were no document processing, no reservations, no ticket buying, no waiting in line, no waiting for luggage, no nothing. It was as simple as going on a trip in a comfortable and luxurious subway.

Also, there was no need for flight attendants nor seat belts. The passengers realized they had started their flight through the inside screens, and could see their arrival. If a passenger sat down, closed his eyes and only waited for the door to open again, he wouldn't feel a thing and would arrive rested to his destination.

The passengers would usually have tea, continue their reading or talk with friends. When only two carried on a conversation, they did it through telepathy; and only when they were in a group did they speak vocally. People used both communication methods with equal frequency and combined them easily and naturally.

The floor plans in the passenger cabin in the vessels were very similar in all models. As the area was round, the seats were distributed in concentric circles. The separation in between the circles was wide and besides there were radial aisles. The main aisle to enter was the wider one, a space the whole width in front of the first row was left free, the next row had less space and so on. Normally passengers, upon entering filled the vessel clockwise, walking towards their left through the circular passages.

The seats in the concentric rings were distributed in groups of four with a 30-centimeter space for magazines and periodicals in between each one. (Figure 19)

FIGURE 19

HORIZONTAL VIEW OF VESSEL
IN PASSENGER CABIN

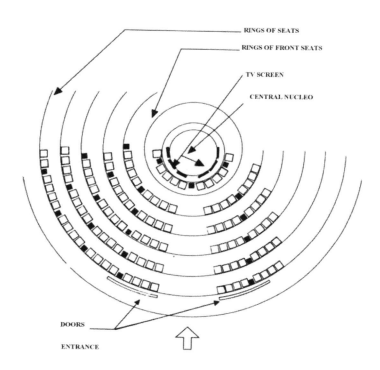

HORIZONTAL VIEW OF VESSEL IN PASSENGER CABIN

RINGS OF SEATS

RINGS OF FRONT SEATS

TV SCREEN

CENTRAL NUCLEO

DOORS

ENTRANCE

At the entrance, the access corridor to the rings of seats was as wide as the door. This way one could enter and take the circular passages in front of each ring of seats over to the opposite side. Therefore, passengers didn´t stop until they got to the seat they wanted, and sat down without interfering with the free circulation of

164

those who chose seats further down on the same row. The aisles were so wide passengers could get by without any trouble, even if some were already seated. Also, the seated passengers could be comfortable, and not have to draw up their legs to let others pass, as the space between was almost 1.20 meters wide.

On a medium size passenger vessel, say having a 35- meter diameter, it had five tiers of seats and a capacity of about 500 passengers. A 60-meter in diameter vessel had a capacity for more than 1,000 passengers, but were so ample, that if needed, any vessel could transport up to three times as many passengers without problems of weight load.

The seats of the center tier faced the outside and had a very wide circular aisle in front. There were about two meters between these seats and the ones of the first row in front of them that faced the center of the vessel, so they were also facing each other.

The television screens were placed above the passengers in the seats next to the central part of the vessel. The monitors, on a small vessel, were the size of a 40-inch television and almost twice the size on the larger vessels. (Figure 20)

The smaller vessels, measuring about 30 meters in diameter, had four radial aisles and five concentric tiers of seats. Those which had 60 meters in diameter had nine rows, of which the first four, from the center towards the outside, had seats facing the sides of the vessel and the other five tiers from the one next to the side fuselage, had seats facing the center of the vessel. The television monitors were placed between them, facing both sides so everyone could comfortably and clearly see the outside views.

In groups of three screens, the middle one showed the front view (as the vessel traveled), and the other two had the left and right views. The three moved vertically and were synchronized, in such a way that the passengers could enjoy a practically continuous 220-degree angle view. This was much better than the outside view our airplane pilots have. Their pilots also had another monitor with a large angular camera lens facing backwards which allowed a peripherical 360-degree vision.

FIGURE 20

VERTIVAL VIEW

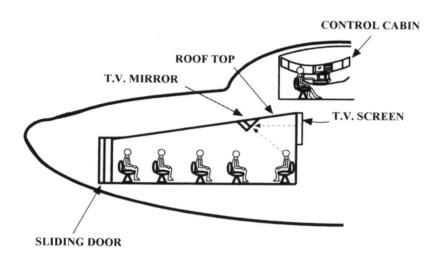

The front camera also had a telescopic zoom lens to observe details and these could be shown in the passenger cabin. The monitors had a sign indicating the vertical angle of the take. (figure 21)

FIGURE 21

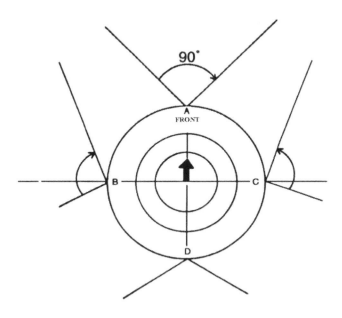

A. Front camera with telescope
B. Left side camera
C. Right side camera
D. Back camera

A 1,000 passenger vessel could carry out maneuvers to unload its cargo completely and be ready for departure in only three minutes. Boarding of departure passengers could be simultaneous to the exist of arrivals. The passengers, by the way, practically didn't carry any luggage at all; at the most, a portfolio, a small box or bag, nothing else.

The vessel in which Eric and Shem left carried about 250 passengers and boarding took three minutes, more or less, for everybody to be seated comfortably guided by only two attendants who remained on the ground after the door was closed.

A soft zooming sound inside the vessel could be perceived, but soon after stopped, indicating departure. Seconds after lift-off, a panoramic view appeared on the three sets of television screens. During the flight, the central T.V. showed close-ups of some mountain, valley, forest, lake or aspects of the city, which could be of interest to the passengers. What generally could be seen were planted fields or seacoasts and cities.

The vessel made the 1,000 kilometer trip at an altitude of approximately 100 kilometers (ten times higher than commercial planes on Earth).

"For the distance on this flight, one can distinguish three stages of the trip," explained Shem.

FIRST. The ascent begins very softly; the first ten seconds it goes from zero to ten centimeters per second. In the next five seconds, it goes up to one meter per second, and continues to increase its speed. After one minute, it is traveling at approximately 100 kilometers an hour at an altitude of 1,000 meters.

SECOND. Now it starts to move horizontally, but since it´s within an atmosphere of certain density, it inclines slightly to start a helicoidal ascent that will give it a faster rising speed, taking advantage of its aerodynamic line. This speed is held at about 1,100 kilometers per hour (300 meters per second), taking care to not go over the speed of sound to avoid causing problems to the neighbors on the surface of the planet and not provoking stampedes generated by the shock waves occurring when this happens.

THIRD. Five minutes after take-off, the height is almost 50 kilometers and the vessel accelerates to its cruising speed. In this case, it is 10,000 kilometers an hour (2.8 kilometers per second). It will continue rising helicoidally until it reaches the air route it will follow to its destination. At cruising height, it continues a geodesic route, parallel to the planet, and in five minutes will be arriving at its destination. The next three minutes will be used for the descent and a decrease in speed, similar to those of take-off.

The passengers do not notice the angles of ascent or descent, nor the increases of speed. The screens show the destination, instructions that may be pertinent and some additional information, then they are turned off. A few seconds later, the access door opens to the waiting room and the passengers have taken about 15 minutes to arrive to their destination.

Eric was fascinated, watching the views on the screens. When they were nearing their destination, the cameras showed close-ups of the area. It was huge; many large and beautiful buildings, surrounded by gardens, woods and small lakes. The typical airport dome could be seen, it was not too big, it had only one central bubble and 20 waiting rooms around it.

The screens were turned off and a few seconds later they were exiting the vessel in Galimor. This was a phonetic translation of the characters displaying the name of the city, according to Shem.

They went down the passageway to the central lobby, when Shem asked Eric to give him a few minutes to make some arrangements and went to an office at the far end.

Although he was not surprised by the belt transport system, it was astonishing to see them working for kilometers at a time, at varying speeds, as if it were the most natural thing in the world. Also, the magnificent, ample, comfortable, automatic train that had taken them from Milgar to the airport at Parthelia.

He entertained himself watching all those people, trying to imagine where they came from, what were their hopes and worries.

Reviewing his trip, so many new things made him a bit uneasy, as it usually does on the first day in a new country where everything is slightly different. Another language, other customs, another environment, other people....Nevertheless, he did not feel he was another planet, God only knew how far from his home on Earth. It simply seemed like a trip to Disneyland 25 years before. And maybe, he had probably been even more impressed then.

However, he did feel a knot in his stomach...the subway, the belts, electric staircases were not out of the ordinary...it was just knowing he was not physically in his world what was caused his emotional upheaval.

He remembered boarding the vessel together with all the other passengers, who calmly and courteously took their seats. Although it was in a different place, it really seemed to be as though entering a DC-10. But there the similarity ended, after a few seconds, a very smooth take-off appeared on the screens set at about

10 meters high. It was like a movie, absolutely no vibration had been felt.

He remembered he could see how it went up and, accelerating little by little, reached a high speed and even when it tilted, nothing could be felt inside the cabin. It was a 90-degree inclination, but the passengers would only know it by seeing the images on the screens. Nothing was felt because the vessel had its own gravity. Even if the vessel made a complete turn, the passengers wouldn't be aware of it.

The vessel provided the passengers an artificial gravity similar to that of the planet it had left. It was totally independent of the forces of gravity. As to the passengers comfort, they could stand up and walk over to the tea dispensers, serve themselves and return to their seats as if they were in a waiting room. If a person got up for tea when the ship started upward at a vertical speed of some 20 kilometers an hour; a few seconds later, when the tea was being served, it would already have a 45-degree inclination and would be traveling at 500 kilometers an hour. By the time the passenger returned to his seat to enjoy his tea, after about five minutes, the vessel would have reached a cruising speed of close to 10,000 kilometers an hour.

When Shem returned, they went to a ramp and walked down about 5 meters to a level that led them to an ample covered parking lot. There were some 30 vehicles, all resembling electric golf carts, but larger and more comfortable, for four passengers. All the vehicles had a device that fitted a retractable tube, which served as an electric switch to recharge the energy of the batteries. Shem disconnected one and they got in.

The car responded smoothly, and when traveling over a paved road, it seemed to glide. What a delight! They cruised a stretch of about 15 kilometers on an avenue surrounding a lagoon to the right. It had a small island in the middle, about 300 meters in diameter. It was practically covered by some buildings with what seemed to be, glass roofs. Shem explained it was a factory run by solar energy. The aquatic plants were produced underwater and the island itself was the processing plant.

"It seems a little strange to me; this road is almost empty, and besides I don't see any transport vehicles picking up the production," commented Eric.

"Yes, there are. You don't see them because they are under the surface; they are special ships that work all the time, as the harvest of plants and fruits is continuous."

"Fruits?" asked Eric.

"Yes, they have the consistency of your pumpkins and are very big. They are collected by robots, and placed in special containers. Then a ship comes, goes underwater, and connects the loaded container to deliver the cargo faraway, about 1,500 kilometers of your planet. There it leaves part of the load and....look!"

Eric turned around and saw a ship, about 80 meters in diameter, coming out of the water silently. The vessel had the usual shape, but clearly, a lower section measuring some 50 meters in diameter and 7 meters wide, was attached. It rose to the surface and remained afloat a few seconds. After, it started a slow vertical ascent, increasing its speed. Little by little, it started to tilt and began the helicoidal final take-off at high speed. In a few seconds it seemed to be a metallic button in a blue sky and then disappeared on its way to its destination at an impressive speed. (Figure 22)

FIGURE 22

CARGO VESSEL

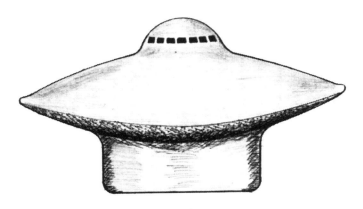

"The leaves and stems are processed on the island," continued Shem, "and then are sent to the food processing plant."

"How many inhabitants are there on this planet?" asked Eric, unable to contain his curiosity.

Shem looked at him for a few seconds, surely wondering if he should answer the question, and said, "This planet is three times the size of yours. Our sun is five times bigger and we are in fifth place from the center of our system. We have a population of about 15 thousand millions."

"The distribution of land and water is geographically different to yours, but of similar proportions. The inhabitants of this world have worked for many years to keep the surface of the planet as natural as possible, in order to maintain the meteorological conditions regulated and the rain fall, temperatures and winds to good use."

"All the residential and productive areas are balanced so as not to affect our ideal environment. The natural green areas, as forests, are completely protected; the irrigation areas have ponds of water and, arid areas are used to store solar energy and construction sites. The "albedo", which is the quantity of heat that the surface of the planet reflects to space, and its effects on nature is not altered."

They arrived at an area where no building could be seen. Some domes, approximately 40 meters in diameter, stood out in a small valley, five kilometers long and three kilometers wide. All the area in between the domes was covered by very green plants, like alfalfa, and groups of small very bushy trees.

The parking area had about 150 identical vehicles and ten 30-passenger vans that opened to the sides; all properly parked and connected to recharge their batteries. All the area was clean and fresh, a soft scent from the plants permeated the air.

As they got out, Eric saw a strange vehicle arriving with large wheels, wide low pressure tires and well equipped to get near to the trees and harvest fruits, like mangoes the color of apricots— between yellow and pink. The truck passed by silently, full of fruit and entered a tunnel to its unloading site.

Shem guided him to a belt that took them inside the vessel, Eric felt like a midget when he saw its enormity. It was like a bee hive of activity. The fruit was transported by conveyor belts, from the unloading zone.   On its way, the fruit was automatically classified according to size. Workers eliminated what was defective; certain sizes and characteristics would be later packed. The rest continued to another process.

There was a large variety of fruits and vegetables; each processing line had different products.

After going through a very large nave, they arrived at the center of the factory, where different types of fruits were packed in crates to be transported. The process of grinding and crushing took place in another nave. The juice was transported automatically where laboratory personnel took samples to be analyzed.

On an upper level, an enormous laboratory was as long as the production line. Large, transparent containers were placed, from section to section, where the juice was collected and another product was added; then it continued to other steps of the process with different machines. A light and homogenous paste was obtained which was pushed along to continue its processing.

Ground or crushed products, from other naves, were mixed with the paste. All of them were vegetables, except a product from the sea, very similar to a giant starfish, which had also been bred and grown to ensure quality.

These fishes, which ten minutes ago had been in the sea, were unloaded and classified by size. The bigger ones measured about three meters in diameter and 60 centimeters wide at the center. On top, they were red to yellow in color, and underneath, a whitish gray. After being processed, their paste was similar to that of fruit and vegetables.

"The end product is treated to have a delicate and appetizing aroma," Shem explained. "The texture and the colors that identify the flavor must be enticing. These are the characteristics of our food."

"Ingredients may vary according to regions, but as the food is not regional, but global, everybody can obtain all the flavors. The food is pleasing to the taste and smell; the texture also is very attractive. We eat very balanced meals; healthy, nutritious and easily digested thanks to great biochemical technology. Fruits in their natural state are eaten as a satisfying supplement. Agricultural technology and graft techniques, combined with fertilizers, produce truly delicious products."

"Health is most important, and nutrition is the basis of longevity. Today we live an average of 150 years with complete mental and physical fitness."

"Product packaging, distribution and transportation are as efficient as their production."

After a general tour of the plant, they went to a dining hall where Eric could taste a little of each of the different food he had seen prepared. A taste was more like it, as they were so many, and eating all of them would have been heavy on his stomach, although the excess would be easily eliminated.

"Some foods have special additives, such as revitalizing juices to prevent dehydration after a sporting event. There are very complex medical laboratories where close attention is given to health."

"Although it isn't apparently necessary, all of us periodically undergo very complete medical check-ups for timely detection of problems, which are immediately attended to."

"Nevertheless, mistakes can cause premature deaths. People know it, yet as humans, at times abuse, and do not follow the doctors´ orders. As a result, they die before the 150-year average. Under normal conditions, it is from this age on that situations could appear and cause death by natural causes. Death, under 150 years, only occurs due to accidents or human error."

Later, they visited some warehouses and the shipping department, where special large vessels, posed on a kind of lower half of a vessel, were adjusted to receive them, to be loaded. 500-ton cargoes seemed weightless. They were, so to speak, space "super-trailers".

"Do all the workers live at the units ahead of us?" asked Eric.

"No," answered Shem. "They come from varying distances, sometimes places up to 1,000 kilometers away. It´s not the usual thing; sometimes they are temporary workers. Full time employees live anywhere from 50 to 500 kilometers away and it takes them the same time to arrive. While some come in a vehicle, driving calmly and enjoying the outdoors, others come by train 100 kilometers away, and still others by air and belts. Transportation schedules are very flexible and synchronized to their working hours."

"And, what about the cost? Do they pay? I didn't see any ticket office nor controls."

"Everybody pays all the time to have all they need and more," said Shem, with a smile. "But remember, it has nothing to do with money."

"It seems nice to be organized like this, but isn't this a way to be owned by your government?"

"Owned by, why? We are not obliged to work at something we don't like. On the contrary, each of us is in the area we prefer. We are not limited by zones, we can work in whatever we like, what we know more about, even though it is thousands of kilometers from our home, or we can move to be closer. Remember, the better quality of work, the better homes and family and personal opportunities one has. Although there can be differences in material goods, more importance is given to the additional benefits, be they artistic, scientific or spiritual satisfactions, to be enjoyed personally."

"If you have easy access to food and board, don't you have problems with the idle who want to enjoy life without work?"

"No, there's nothing that gives you greater satisfaction than doing your duty. If someone doesn't see it this way, he probably needs help. He gets it until he finds the road to happiness, which is one of self-respect, and to learn to love oneself by earning the love and respect of others. When this satisfaction is attained, you don't fool yourself nor others. You do your part happily and look at things from a more spiritual point of view, that in the end, will help your evolution."

"How nice it is to be where everybody thinks this way," Eric said. "Where are we going now?"

"We'll fly to an education center nearby that you must see, called BIRKEN. It is like a University City."

175

CHAPTER XI

Life appears with a boom.
Cells multiply instantaneously as crystals
propagate in a saturated solution.
The smallest beings appear in microns,
in measurable multitudes, and the cells in myriads.
It is the beginning of matter,
it is the model and evolutionary structure
of native multiplicity.

Teithard de Chardin

BIRKEN

Eric thought they would return for the vehicle, but Shem went to another section on the opposite side. The belt took them to another exit station on the surface where there were about ten different sized vessels, parked under an oblong vault whose roof was slid back halfway.

The largest vessel, 25 meters in diameter, had a capacity for about 350 passengers. There were others 10 meters in diameter; three of them were under the uncovered section. Shem had made the necessary arrangements, on his intercommunicator, when coming on the belt. So, when they arrived, the stairway was down on one of the vessels, and a pilot was waiting. Shem introduced them; the pilot's name was Kunn. He was a young man, on Earth he would look about 25 years of age. He was blond, with grayish-blue eyes, and was keenly interested in the visitor.

Eric clearly received a friendly greeting, through telepathy. Kunn also sent his regards to his brothers on Earth. Eric noticed he was not the first man from another planet that Kunn had met. He decided to ask Shem, "Is it true he has met other persons from other planets?"

Shem nodded with his usual smile.

Kunn transmitted again: *"You are the third person to come with the same purpose and I have attended to all of them. The other two didn't come from your solar system."*

"How's that?" asked Eric. "Then they do come here from other places, from where?"

"Excuse me, Eric," Shem answered. "Although I would like to answer I must not, you must ask Rahel; he controls the information given to you. I can only answer questions regarding what we see. I hope you understand."

Eric had to resign himself to this. At the same time, he did his best to answer Kunn's welcome. He seemed to understand, Shem confirmed it. "Congratulations, Eric, that's it, ideas not words!"

Eric recognized Kunn's suit was similar to the one worn by Rahel and Mirza when he first saw them.

"Look, Shem, that suit looks like the one Rahel and Mirza had on when I saw them the first time. Is it a space or special suit?" asked Eric.

"That's not a space suit, it's a uniform," said Shem. "It's required at base to wear the uniform that identifies your origin, work area, and rank in the organization. It has special functional and informative characteristics. Space suits are only used on missions where your physical body could be in danger of decompression, of not being able to breathe, or the risk of gases, temperatures and some other external cause."

"It's exactly the same as what you do. Your astronauts don't wear the same clothes to repair a satellite in space as they do flying a plane or driving their car."

"When you have seen strange extra-terrestrials, it's because the conditions where they come from are different and that forces them to take precautions to protect their health. These could be special clothes with head gear attached, which they have to use every so often to regulate their body functions. Besides, there are those who can't stand the conditions of your planet and they need proper attire on their visits, that obviously seems odd to you."

"So there are visitors from planets having different atmospheric conditions?" Eric noted.

"Yes, that's right, so much so as to require special equipment."

The three boarded the vessel through a three-meter corridor around the center. After passing a closed door to the center, they entered an elevator for two persons about one meter in diameter, made of a dull gray thick acrylic. After the semitransparent sliding door closed, a light went on and the elevator could go up or down one level automatically. The door wouldn't open again until it was level with the floor. (Figure 23)

FIGURE 23

INTERIOR VIEW
SMALL VESSEL WITH ELEVATOR

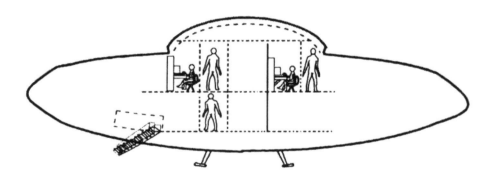

The control cabin, two meters wide, had a round table in the center and four arm chairs facing the instrument panel. 20 small rectangular windows, about 40 by 60 centimeters, faced the outside and slid open by pressing 2 buttons located on the sides, leaving a polarized pane uncovered.

When the vessel was in motion, the windows locked and couldn´t be opened without the approval of the central command.

In any case, the windows were unnecessary, as the monitor screens showed the 360-degree views captured by the T.V. cameras. These were placed in such a way for each to get 90-degree vistas and could also tilt vertically.

Eric concentrated and tried to transmit to Kunn another telepathic message: *"I see the vessel is turned off, so the lights, elevator and everything runs on batteries, don´t they?"*

Kunn tried to understand, but couldn´t. He turned to Shem with a questioning look.

"He can´t understand, Eric," Shem intervened. "You used concepts that, as he doesn´t speak your language, are difficult for him to get the idea. He is receiving your question as if you are asking something about the elevator. He didn´t understand the rest because you expressed unknown words, not concepts."

"A problem in your technology, at present, is precisely the storage and transmission of electric energy, because of loses. I can´t give you more details now as to how these vessels work because it implies something you are already perfecting and could apply anon. Do you understand me? It would be better for you to ask Rahel later."

"I will do so, thanks," answered Eric.

Kunn and Shem sat down, Eric took the arm chair in between. He was amazed watching the monitors and trying to decipher them, when he felt Kunn saying: "Come on, let´s get started." He smiled as he watched Eric absorbed by his computers.

"Do I have a duplicate of your controls?" Eric asked him.

Kunn nodded and proceeded to switch on the systems of the vessel. The monitors lit up. He quickly verified what showed up on the computer screen with color graphics. Then a vessel appeared and one could see as the hatch closed after the steel step ladder had been drawn in and the supports retracted.

The characteristic zooming could be heard. Eric again asked telepathically: *"Is that the motor?"*

"It´s the isolation system, now we are independent, we have our own gravity," Kunn answered making a sign with his hands as if he were holding a volley ball.

179

Eric was very interested in learning more about the vessel's operation, so this time, he asked Shem, "How does the propulsion of the vessel work? I know the engines that NASA uses in the rockets and the space shuttle, and the latest jet engines on our military or civilian airplanes. Obviously, these are very different here."

"Yes, that's right, Eric. Your have propulsion engines, and the objective is to propel the vessel against the existing forces of its surroundings. Our Golemi move under gravitational influences we control with magnetic fields."

"Our system is not propulsion by reaction, but rather something like, "allowing oneself to be pushed". It's as if a drop of water could chose the crease on the surface it wanted to trickle down on. It is complicated because of the technology it entails, but you will easily understand we only take advantage of the existing gravitational forces of equilibrium where we are to move. This is one of the many technologies that are more advanced than yours. But we are going to give you a guide to show you how to improve your performance in many areas."

The take-off began. The screens showed a view of a moving elevator; ten seconds later, the view was a ten story building; then the view seemed to be taken from the back of a soaring rocket, and extended to be seen on all four screens.

Shem asked Eric to turn a knob and see the monitor. He did so immediately, as he was eager to put his hands on an operating control. On the monitor, he could see downwards according the selected angle. To the left and the camera turned until it was almost vertical. Then he turned the knobs of the other monitors and he could simultaneously see ahead, behind, to the right and to the left. He could also see up and down, easily with any one knob. When the controls were released, the cameras returned automatically to the horizontal position, unless otherwise set.

While Kunn controlled the speed and direction, he also set the horizontal route to be followed, Eric eagerly continued turning the cameras 45-degree downwards and enjoyed the flight as if he were a flying dove. A couple of minutes later, they flew over the sea. What a breath taking beauty it was! Kunn lowered the vessel to an altitude of 300 meters (about 1,000 feet) and reduced the speed so they could all enjoy the trip, which was already an unforgettable experience for Eric.

Soon they saw some constructions on land. The vessel flew over the area so Eric could see the gardens, sport arenas and buildings. They descended to about 100 meters, and glided softly over that extraordinary center of learning and research called BIRKEN.

Groups of people were everywhere. It was about three o´clock of Earth´s time, and all the activities took place outdoors. All the people seemed concentrated in a given place playing or in groups, nobody seemed to be just roaming around.

"Mobile belts are used to come and go on campus," Shem explained while pointing out the pathways seen everywhere. They stood out about a meter and a half high and were covered by an opaque translucid roof, the side walls were also transparent.

"It´s the same in the rainy season. They leave the paths and get wet while playing or chatting without caring. Then they go to their baths and come out as if they had been playing in the sun."

They flew over the children´s facilities, where hundreds were everywhere, wearing different colored uniforms with designs to distinguish the grades they were in.

Then they saw classrooms with large windows overlooking forests and lakes. Further ahead, there were buildings where older students attended schools of higher education with laboratories and work shops.

"Small children live with their parents until they begin their studies at ten years of age. Before then, time is taken advantage of to develop healthy minds and bodies, learn moral principles and good living habits."

"From age ten on, they can continue living with their parents, or go to boarding schools. However, even though they are in boarding schools, they are not prisoners; they can go every day to visit their parents. Little by little they get used to boarding, and then it´s the other way around, the parents come to visit them during their leisure time. But if they want, they can continue living with their relatives, if there is enough space. You may recall, one family homes are earned by merits by the parents in their jobs and professions."

181

"When they don't live in this type of home, rather in multifamily ones, the children prefer to board at school to avoid so much traveling."

They descended on a parking lot where they were two similar vessels. Next to this, there was another parking lot for land vehicles connected to the electric recharging posts. These vehicles were designed differently than the ones that took them to the factory, but in any case, all of them could fit only four passengers.

They crossed the yard and entered the chemistry laboratories, where students here and there worked alone or in groups, showing interest, enthusiasm and concentration. There were five floors of similar laboratories in all, divided into sections, 15 by 12 meters and had windows on both sides. It resembled one of the best universities on Earth. The big difference was, in our planet, access is limited to a priviledged few, and there everyone had an equal chance to go.

Eric felt he would like to be one of those students, radiantly happy and healthy. Shem perceived his thoughts and transmitted: "It's a good wish and I assure you that soon you will also be like this."

Then he continued orally, "That's why you are here, to talk to your brothers about what they can attain when they decide to join forces for progress in peace and harmony, instead of using their intelligence to wield power over others, with no love for their fellow men, being carried away by negative passions and only obtaining hate and destruction."

"For love and good will to be felt by all, it's necessary for you yourselves to step up your evolution. This first step, taken by many, is the material and spiritual awareness of your own existence."

"The next step for your planet is what you have learned. I whole heartedly wish you can help your brothers to want it and obtain it. But let me introduce you to someone who is waiting for you. Let's go over."

Eric was surprised and curious to learn that "someone awaited him". When they got to the top of the section of building, they walked up a ramp to the fifth level. A central corridor was lined by ample private offices divided by plexiglass divisions, polarized to control the intensity of light coming in.

182

There were two large elevators, at the opposite end, about 5 square meters in size, whose front and outside walls were also made of plexiglass. The lower part of the walls, about 1.20 meters high, seemed to be wooden panels, but were also plastic.

A very pretty opaque plastic ceiling would provide a white light, at night, easy on the eyes. There was almost no lighting by spots, lamps or light bulbs, except where unavoidable, as the headlights on the vehicles. All the buildings had indirect lighting aimed towards the ceiling, thus preventing the reflection of shadows.

They entered the first private office on the eastern side, according to their sun. Elegant and practical, furnished with a table for six, movable arm chairs on a beautiful light brown tiled floor, decorated with geometric figures to break the monotony.

The computer equipment was mounted on a special panel and had a 1.5 square meter monitor, similar to a movie screen in the center of the dividing wall to the next office. On the left, between the dividing wall and the windows, there was a sort of book shelf with a framed empty space, and above it a television camera.

The professor saw them arrive and came out to greet them. Shem did the introductions speaking out loud. "Professor Krinnell, this is our guest, Eric."

The professor was a man about 55 years of age, about 1.85 meters tall, agile and strong, looking like a sports coach. He had a penetrating look in his eyes, and an air of contentment. He wore an elegant, comfortable white robe with light blue lapels, gray trousers and darker gray suede shoes. The robe was the uniform for teachers and professors.

"Messers" was the term used for teachers who worked directly with their students, and "Yunners" were the research professors who also doubled as advisors and counselors for their pupils. The colors on the uniforms identified the different areas of research.

Yunner Krinnell extended his hand in greeting, but when Eric took it, he only closed his fingers without moving his forearm and transmitted to Eric: *"Your greeting is like this, isn't it?"*

Eric laughed out loud and explained what a handshake on Earth was; they shook hands again to practice. Then Krinnell, as

Rahel had done, laid his left hand over Eric´s shoulder and transmitted: *"Welcome, what do you want to know?"*

The question took Eric by surprise, he didn´t know what to answer, and only managed one word: "Everything!"

Krinnell smiled and invited them to take a seat; he went to his place and operated a control, similar to the one Rahel had in the first encounter. Eric watched him with great interest. All of a sudden, he heard Rahel´s musical voice behind him, "Hello, Eric!"

Surprised he turned, and saw Rahel smiling at him from the stage of a holographic projection, in living color. It seemed as if he was watching him through a window. He was leaning on his desk, and could probably see them the same way as the transmission light of the camera was on. When the audio was on, the sound seemed to be coming over a telephone, or images could be transmitted by audio and video.

"Are you coming with us?" asked Eric, delightedly.

"No, I am very far away, but I do want you to take full advantage of your visit. Yunner Krinnell will show you some things to help you strengthen and understand your knowledge of quantum mechanics, and will be happy to answer your questions. This is important because it is the basis of what I want to teach you later on. We´ll see each other again soon on Earth. Until then". He waved farewell, which they answered and the image faded.

Yunner Krinnell spoke to Shem, who translated to Eric. "The transmission of images in third dimension is already known by your brothers. It only needs to be perfected to be used everywhere. Yunner Krinnell, or Yunner Krinn as he is known here, is a specialist in physics. Do you have a question for him on this subject?"

"Yunner Krinn, our science on Earth is starting to explore quantum physics. The course of quantum mechanics Rahel referred to was given on the planet by some superior brothers of unknown origin, but I have heard about it directly from a brother on Earth. I didn´t give it much importance, at the time, because of ignorance, so now I ask you."

Professor Krinnell received Shem´s translation by telepathy, almost simultaneously answered, "I took part in preparing it, so I know what you are talking about. If you allow me, I will explain. We´ll use a holographic illustration."

He stood up and went to a bookcase where he chose a cassette he placed in the hologram receptor. Before turning it on, Yunnder Krinnell said, "You will see a live animation of the origin of matter. This is what your scientists are trying to discover, but still do not possess the necessary elements."

After sitting down, he continued, "The origin of matter is closely linked to the knowledge of astrophysics and the divine origin of cosmic energy. If you don´t know this, it´s more difficult to interpret the behavior of energy and matter in an expanding universe. But it is necessary to understand and accept that the origin is not in the matter itself, whose physical characteristics are sensitive and measurable in the worlds in the third dimension."

"Our planet worlds are designed ex profeso to develop humanities having evolutionary spirits like ours. We find in them all the necessary elements to be transformed and develop an entire civilization; which together with science and technology will lead us to a mental development able to conceive a spiritual existence."

"Comprehension and acceptance of other dimensions is therefore, implicit; as the origin of the transformation of energy and our spiritual one is found there. Only then will we understand the love of God, of our Creator Father, that is manifested as the infinite source of energy where its transformed and is the origin of all creation."

"You will see a descriptive allegory to help you understand. Try to imagine the home of our Universal Father as if it were an immense planet, whose size is unconceivable—as large as a universe—but completely full of light. We´ll call it ISLAND OF LIGHT and it will be represented as a golden sphere."

"Imagine you could see divine energy coming out to flood the cosmos as if it were the magnetic force of your own planet. That energy, the manifestation of his love, will travel through the universe and return through the opposite pole. It will be transformed, on the way, and become the origin of all creation. In this way, as if coming out of nowhere, all will be created. This "all" will evolve and become divine energy upon its return to its Creator. Watch."

The professor activated the hologram projector. Lovely music played by a distant symphony could be heard; then the holographic stage lit up with a soft orange coloring like the dawn.

Yunner Krinn sat down as Shem and Kunn did as well on the armchairs for visitors. Eric moved to be by the professor´s desk.

A bright dot in the center, like a brilliant spark became a golden sphere the size of a melon. It glowed, floating in the center of the stage, slowly rotating.

A vent of blue steam puffed out of the golden sphere from the south or negative pole. It formed a ball at the end, which separated and turned into a ring that followed the same path as the magnetic lines of a planet like Earth. Later, the ring broke up and became a group of floating cotton-like puffs. Soon, another vent went through the same transformation until seven groups were floating in different positions in space.

The musical background was perfect. The listeners were fascinated and drawn into contemplation. Later, steam again shot out of the same pole of the sphere, faster this time. Silver threads could be seen as they spread out following the same path as the previous emission.

Gradually the sphere got smaller and smaller, until becoming a dot, as if they were leaving on a ship.

The light blue steam represented the release of energy from the Island of Light. It was projected in a straight line to measure about 100 diameters larger than the sphere; then it opened up conically like flower petals to form the ellipsoid to return. (Ellipsoid is a geometric figure, whose perimeter is the longitudinal cut of an ellipse and the path follows the forces of the planet Earth´s magnetic fields to go from the south to the north pole) (Figure 24)

FIGURE 24

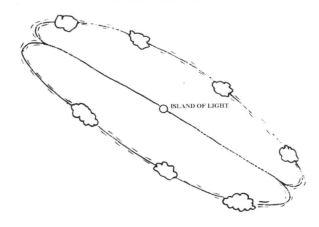

ISLAND OF LIGHT

The silver lines marked the path and the steam that had filled all the space in between the lines and the sphere, spread out. Soon the ovoid was formed and the lines curved to return to the north pole of the Island of Light.

The animation was perfect; a little blue steam vent was emitted at the south pole and followed the ovoidal path returning at the opposite side; all the space inside was immersed in a flood of energy.

The music in the background changed when the blue steam vent caught up with the one before; thousands of bright lights appeared as they crossed and mixed. Now the imaginary observation ship rapidly got closer, and submerged in the zone where two emissions collided. While the first steam vent advanced slowly, the second continuous emission was much faster.

The cosmic energy was represented by colored clouds. Getting closer look, they noticed that the bright dots appeared out of nowhere and lit up to be seen. (Figure 25)

187

FIGURE 25

FORMATION OF A CESNA DOT

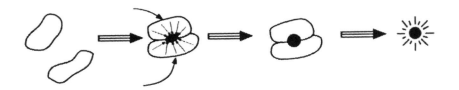

Yunner Krinn explained, through Shem, "The bright dots are concentrations of energy, and we'll call them as they do in the quantum mechanics course you took, CESNA DOTS. Soon you'll see how they group together."

The dots lit up everywhere being generated when crossing the currents of energy. They multiplied in amazing numbers, and then started to cling together as they passed near to each other. They were trapped forming groups of ten dots that melted into a red luminous sphere; if the group had twelve cesna dots, they melted forming a bright violet cube. (Figure 26)

FIGURE 26

GROUPS OF CESNA DOTS

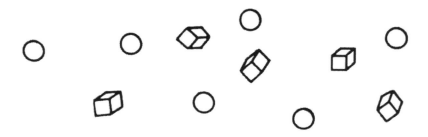

Soon there was an abundance of spheres and cubes in that iridescent sea of cesna dots. Then when getting close to one another, pairs of cubes and spheres, trapped each other as if attracted by an electric charge caused by the difference of potency due to the different number of cesna dots they contained.

Shem, with Yunner Krinn's permission, broke in, "We'll continue using the same course you took. Those groups of spheres and cubes are called CARPINS. (Figure 27)

FIGURE 27

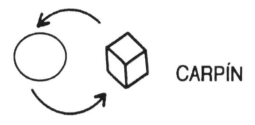

CARPÍN

Late, pairs of carpin systems flooded the stage They attracted each other forming groups and took their place in order in the elliptical orbits until creating groups of one million carpins, which was a MEGACARPIN. (Figure 28)

189

FIGURE 28

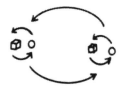

PRESSURE

*M*AGNETISM

"As you can see," Shem added, "there is a kind of halo that surrounds that system called megacarpin. The cloud that seems to rotate around the ring drawn on the system, is a primary magnetic field and is composed by the difference in accumulated potency in all the carpin systems. That way a current of energy is established forming the field it encloses.

What later will be an electromagnetic field that will generate the terms of some natural universal laws, with its behavior and characteristics, is born here. These laws, that are acting and manifesting themselves, will be the ones to keep forcing the process being illustrated in this animation. The cesna dots and the carpins are so small you cannot even imagine them. But let us continue watching the transformation from the imaginary vessel. Watch how small rings of megacarpins are formed—they are seen in a sea of carpins, cubes and spheres joined together to form systems, rings of megacarpin systems, and then these, having multiplied, start to also unite forming triangles of megacarpins. (Figure 29)

FIGURE 29

NEUTRAL MYRIAD

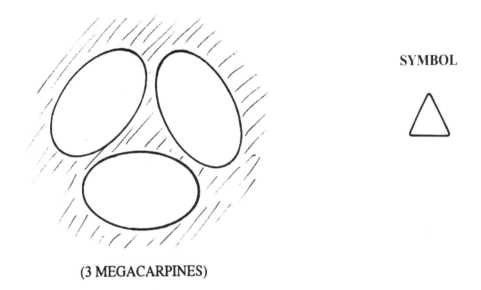

SYMBOL

(3 MEGACARPINES)

Three megacarpins have already defined their orbit of the pole zones. They define a positive side (entrance of energy of the magnetic field) and a negative side (exit of energy of the field) are attracted to each other and form a NEUTRAL MYRIAD.

The neutral myriad is integrated by three systems of megacarpins, and are oriented according to their poles attraction. This system, which already has characteristics of electromagnetic pressure and affinity, is in balance and does not rotate. It has a neutralizing effect on any element passing through its structure.

The animation then focused on the three megacarpins that had already constituted the myriad, when another myriad formation was seen getting closer. When it was near enough, it joined the first one and both started to rotate counterclockwise. (Figure 30)

FIGURE 30

POSITIVE MYRIAD

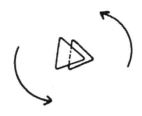

Shem′s voice was heard again, "This pair of myriads is called POSITIVE MYRIAD and the sum of the charges of its six megacarpins produce a reacting and rotating effect due to the charge in the center of their triangles. Its rotating speed varies between 1,000 and 625,000 turns per spin."

The positive myriad, in the animation, floated away while rotating counterclockwise increasing its speed. Meanwhile, three other myriads got close enough to each other to unite and form a NEGATIVE MYRIAD that also started to rotate; but this time, clockwise. (Figure 31)

FIGURE 31

NEGATIVE MYRIAD

This negative myriad is formed by nine megacarpins and has a rotating speed of 626,000 to 1,210,000 cycles per spin.

The professor stopped the holographic projector for a moment and showed them a table that appeared on the computer´s screen, and was as follows:

1 Hour	= 60 Minutes
1 Minute	= 60 Seconds
1 Second	= 12 Instants
1 Instant	= 60 Quarz
1 Quarz	= 60 Spins
1 Spin	= 12 Quantas

"These time values are all relative and correspond to your planet. Our numbers are different, but the rotating speeds in the Universe are the same."

In one POSITIVE myriad: Mc = 1 million cycles (1 megacycle) Sec. = 43,200 spins
Therefore, we have:
From 0.001 to 0.625 Mc. X spin (megacycles per spin)

Which equal:
From 43.2 to 27,000 Mc. per second
That is: from 43 200 000 to 27 000 000 000 cycles per second.

In the NEGATIVE myriad, the rotating speed is:
0.626 to 1,210 Mc. per spin

That equal:
626 000 to 1 210 000 cycles x spin

That also equal:
$270\,432 \times 10^5$ up to $322\,704 \times 10^6$ cycles x second

These numbers will seem inconceivable to you and in fact, they almost are, but you must consider that we are talking about the micro-Universe and it is, precisely that, a Universe.

Yunner Krinn returned to his seat and turned the hologram´s projector on again.

Hundreds of small reddish brown and green whirlpools floated in space. There were also some triangles with vibrating sides that represented the three types of myriads. Suddenly they started to join together, uniting two neutrals with one positive and one negative, forming a tetrahedron. This geometric figure was also balanced. Soon there were thousands of luminous tetrahedrons. (Figure 32)

FIGURE 32

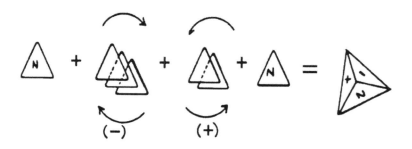

TETRAHEDRON

4 myriads one (+)
one (-)
two (N)

The tetrahedrons started uniting in groups of two to twelve units. These formations are called RAMAS. (Figure 33)

FIGURE 33

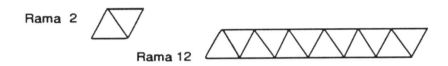

Rama 2

Rama 12

At the same time, the ramas began floating and joining the same number of bodies, alternately.

"…..and we´ll call these organizations, CHAINS," concluded Shem. (Figures 34 and 34-A)

FIGURE 34

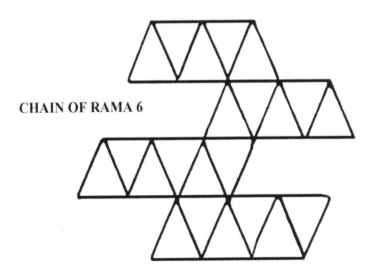

CHAIN OF RAMA 6

The chains of combined ramas with equal number of tetrahedrons seemed to attract each other and soon began to unite. The ramas interlocked and curved to become the surface of a sphere; that is, real bubbles or spheres were formed by the same type of ramas and developed into brilliant blue spheres.

FIGURE 34

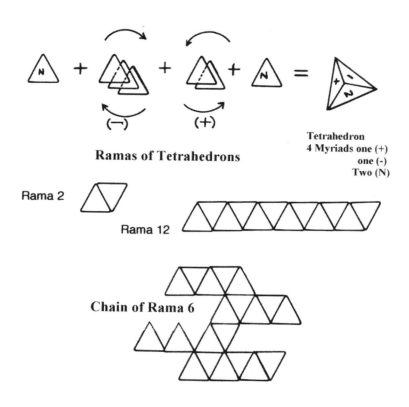

Ramas of Tetrahedrons

Tetrahedron
4 Myriads one (+)
one (-)
Two (N)

Rama 2

Rama 12

Chain of Rama 6

These spheres are PARTONS, formed exlusively by chains of an equal number of alternate ramas. Partons are, what we'll call, THE ESSENTIAL PARTICLE IN THE INTEGRATION OF MATTER. (Figure 35)

196

FIGURE 35

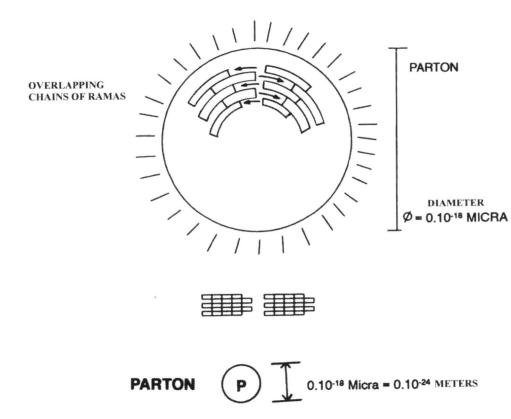

The particle, PARTON, grew into a brilliant blue sphere. Very minute overlapping bricks on the surface were the facets of the union of tetrahedrons in ramas and chains that integrated the surface of PARTON.

Once again Yunner Krinnell stopped the animation and went to the computer, where another table appeared.

Up to now, you have seen the essential particle of matter being born. It is the accumulated condensation of cosmic energy, but it already has a size within the micro-Universe to which it belongs; but it is REAL, and its diameter is:

0.10_{-18} of Micra

That is:

$0.000\ 000\ 000\ 000\ 000\ 000\ 000\ 001$ of a meter

or, $1 \times 10_{-24}$ of a meter (of planet Earth).

Just as you saw the CESNA DOTS being grouped, in small concentrations of energy, so later CARPINS, MEGACARPINS, SYSTEMS, MYRIADS, TETRAHEDRONS, RAMAS and CHAINS, to arrive to the integration of PARTON.

Now, using the PARTON as a starting point, subatomic particles will be formed, and finally atoms and the elements to integrate the molecules of matter.

The chart that appeared on the screen was the same one that Eric had seen in his quantum mechanics course, which confirmed, without doubt, they had left it on Earth. (Chart 2).

Yunner Krinnell went to his omnipresent tea dispenser, and Kunn and Shem very courteously offered him a cup.

Eric tasted it and was surprised at its delicious fresh flavor, and soft aroma of wild flowers. It was stimulating, comforting, and produced a feeling of general well being.

"Ever since I arrived, I have seen tea dispensers everywhere, and looked forward to taste it. It´s really delicious, what is it made of?" asked Eric.

Shem translated, "The equivalent on your planet would be, an infusion of leaves of different fruit trees. This tea is the product of deep analysis, so it is completely harmless, but at the same time, comforting and pleasing to the palate. It acts as a spiritual tranquilizer and a balm for nerves for the physical body."

"I supposed you had studied it in length, and the result is a small pleasure," commented Eric.

"And, the great advantage is that it substitutes cigarettes, candy and harmful junk food. You seem to be your own executioners. A very good wine would be closest to our tea;

although tea would be better in that it does not contain alcohol, that causes much harm."

CHART 2

No OF RAMAS	ESSENCE	SYMBOL	NAME	TYPE OF ACTION	No OF INTEGRATION	VALUE	VOLTAGE IMV	ATOMIC RATIO
4 - 2	YAL	N	Neutro	INSULATION	9×10^6	3	0.25	Ca. (CALSIUM)
6 - 3	CAT		Dum(+) Kual	THERMAL	12×10^6	4	1.5	C. (CARBON)
5 - 10	DAT		Dum(-) Duar	LUMINESCENT	15×10^6	5	3.0	Cl. (CHLORINE)
3 - 6	SEI	E	Electrón	KINETIC	18×10^6	6	6.0	Na. (SODIUM)
8 - 6	NAT		Kum	COHERSIV	21×10^6	7	12.0	N. (NITROGEN)
8 - 6	TOR		Kemio	DIFUSE	24×10^6	8	24.0	K. (POTASSIUM)

A   B   C   D   E

Column A = Combination of ramas of the pattern
Column B = Main feature to the energy result
Column C = Number of miriades
Column D = Tension in infra microvolts
Column E = Typical elements

   Eric smiled while thinking about his planet. Commercial interests are certainly a distant second, to be involved so much in preparing a beverage such as this!
   The professor activated the computer and the monitor showed a short video about tea. Papayas, mangoes, peaches, oranges and grapes resembled the fruits from the trees whose leaves were used to make tea. What especially caught Eric´s attention was the thorough biochemical analysis where they had studied the protein structures of the tea. There was no doubt it had been pondered in depth!

199

"Before continuing with the integration of matter," said Yunner Krin, "I want to call your attention to a detail as physical proof of what we have seen which can be easily checked."

"For some physical reason and, always obeying the Laws of the Universe, phenomena do occur, which can be used if we know what they are; although the explanation might be a paradox in physics for your brothers. Everything that happens has a cause and effect. But this is an effect whose cause they cannot decipher as the behavior of an element called analfa, and of the partons, is unknown to them. Also, the following questions would arise:

- Why is it that 12 partons integrate a leg of the analfa?
- Why does the combination of valencies originate subatomic particles of a different dimension?
- What is the effect of the angle between the legs of the analfa and of the elements trapped in its magnetic field?

There is knowledge we use coming from our Superior Brothers which, at times, goes beyond our comprehension, so don´t be surprised when scientific progress reveals things you can´t understand. You are just at the threshold of true technology and as this advances, you will encounter aspects you couldn´t even imagine before."

"Let's look at the subatomic particle with a valency of four. It is a pyramid whose square base represents affinity to physical bodies that have megamultiple edges of analfas, and at a similar angle, can cause the phenomenum I mentioned. There is a concentration of positive particles on the sides of the pyramid, as the edges act as gigantic legs of the analfas."

"As a result of the magnetic fields, there is a concentration of energy inside the pyramid. It is ovoid shaped and its center is located at one third of the height from the base. The pyramid has the effect of a lens concentrating the cosmic energy inside. It´s positive energy, rich in particles which can be incorporated into live cells and tissues. It destroys malformed cells, neutralizing processes not in harmony with life or replacing the regularity of microstructures or inorganic elements, such as metals with kinetic energy."

"An experiment of this manifestation can be done by building a pyramid out of cardboard. The angle of the triangles of the sides at the vertex must be 62 degrees; thus, there is a proper proportion between the sides of the base and the height. The base is removed to be able to put the pyramid on top of the experiment. The sides of the pyramid prevent the passage of air, but in fact, this could be done by simply using the edges of the pyramid." (Figure 36)

FIGURE 36

CARDBOARD PYRAMID FOR EXPERIMENTS

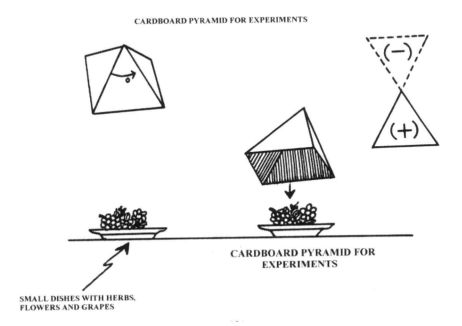

CARDBOARD PYRAMID FOR EXPERIMENTS

CARDBOARD PYRAMID FOR EXPERIMENTS

SMALL DISHES WITH HERBS, FLOWERS AND GRAPES

"Place   equal samples in two dishes; for example, some herbs, a flower and some grapes. In one of the dishes, put a used razor blade with the edge facing north-south.   Cover the dish containing the herbs and razor blade with the cardboard pyramid oriented towards the north-south magnetic line of the planet. Compare the samples after four weeks. The organic matter, under the pyramid, will be in much better shape and the razor blade will be sharper, because the energy has reconditioned its surface structure. This effect is more noticeable in animal cells."

Then, the professor returned to the subject of matter. When he turned on the hologram projector, a PARTON could be seen, looking like a sphere the size of a softball, rotating slowly in the center of the stage.

Professor Krinnell communicated by telepathy as the images appeared, and Shem translated for Eric, "The PARTONS form groups which bind with each other. These groups can be made up of two, four, six or eight PARTONS.

A) **SOLEN** means   two partons bound together by gravity. They join through electromagnetic attraction. (Figure 37-A)

FIGURE 37-A

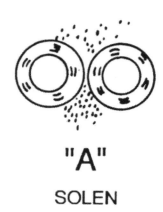

"A"

SOLEN

B) **MERTANER**: Four interlinked partons. The force of their fields is exponentially multiplied in a combined form, in such a way that the value of the magnetic field of this union is 256 times larger than one of a single parton. (Figure No. 37-B)

FIGURE 37-B

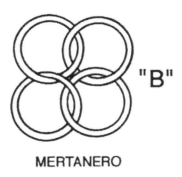

MERTANERO

C) **BEAM**: Six partons united by their magnetic fields. This is a semi-stable organization, but it´s useful to integrate other more complex organizations that are stable, called PARALFICS. (Figure No. 37-C)

FIGURE 37-C

"C"   BEAM

MARSIN: 8 Partons in the same Space-Time
   D) **MARSIN**: Eight intersected partons. (Figure No. 37-D)

FIGURE 37

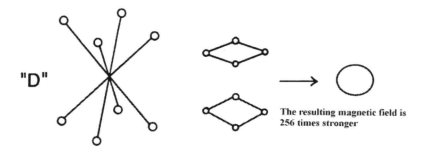

"D"

The resulting magnetic field is
256 times stronger

   E) **PARALFIC CHAIN**: Four BEAMS forming a chain
   folded in two. (Figure No. 37-E)

FIGURE 37-E

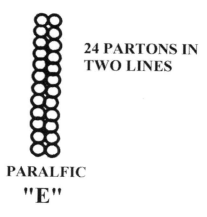

**24 PARTONS IN
TWO LINES**

**PARALFIC
"E"**

F) **ANALFA**: This organization corresponds to an open paralfic one, when the analfa is stabilized at an angle; the action of the magnetic fields of the ramas is in keeping with the angle. (Figure No. 37-F)

FIGURE 37-F

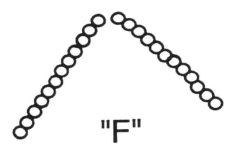

"F"

ANALFA (OPEN PARALFIC)

An analfa can trap lone PARTONS, groups of SOLEN, MERTANERS, and MARSINS in its magnetic field that forms a film in its internal area, where the different types of analfas are determined. These can also trap only PARTONS in its interior. (Figure No. 38).

G) **FASTEN**: This particle is a true cylinder formed by PARTONS. These cylinders organize themselves by linking the extremes in groups of up to 12, and they trap exclusively MERTANERS and MARSINS in their interior. (Figure No. 37-G)

205

FIGURE 37-G

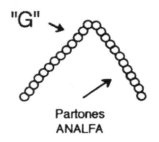

"G" →

Partones
ANALFA

FIGURE 38

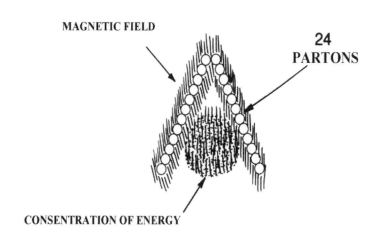

MAGNETIC FIELD

24
PARTONS

CONSENTRATION OF ENERGY

ANALFA

All the subatomic particles were being integrated by PARTONS, and had different colors in the animation. The partons were brilliant blue spheres that joined in pairs forming a SOLEN, thus, automatically, changed to the indicative coloring of the SOLEN. Then two SOLEN united intersecting and forming a MERTANER, these also took on a different color. In that universe of particles, two MERTANERS trapped each other and formed MARSIN, that instantly took a different color to distinguish the new element. The spheres of the BEAMS united to integrate PARALFICS, and these in turn opened in diverse angles trapping PARTONS. It appeared to be a bright multicolored rain of confetti with different shapes. (Figure No. 39)

FIGURE 39

The "observation vessel" of the animation backed up sufficiently to see only little colored dots, although the little cylinders of the FASTENS were clearly distinguished by their forms and brilliant violet color. Then the FASTENS started to unite one after another. When the number of elements of the group was an even number, they formed a broken line, each little cylinder remained straight, since their magnetic fields were in equilibrium. (Figure No. 40)

FIGURE 40

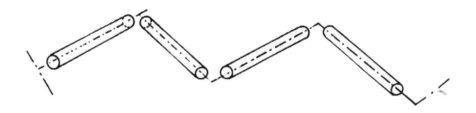

When they united in an odd number, the cylinders formed a helicoidal curve, due to the effect of the sum of the magnetic fields of the internal particles of the FASTEN. (Figure No. 41)

FIGURE 41

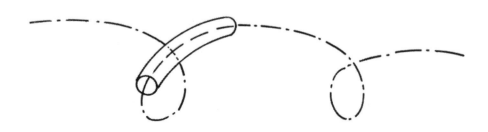

"The FASTENS are the integrating particles of energy, depending on their polarities and group formations. Different combinations of ENERGETIC FASTENS result in different types of electricity."

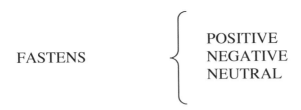

FASTENS {
POSITIVE
NEGATIVE
NEUTRAL
}

Once again, the professor interrupted the hologram and turned on the computer. The screen illustrated the table of resulting energies, according to the combinations of the ENERGETIC FASTENS.

CHART NO. 3

NAME	SYMBOL	MNIFESTATION	TYPE OF ACTINON
DUM KUALI		In Resonance	Thermal
DUM KUAR		In Resonance	Luminescent
ELECTRÓN	E	Direct Current	Kinetic
KUM		In Harmony	Magnetic
KEMIO		In Harmony	Static
NEUTRÓN	N	In Equilibrium	Neutral
KOR		In Equilibrium	Pulsating

ELECTRIC ENERGY groups ENERGETIC FASTENS.
ELECTRONIC ENERGY groups ELECTRIC FASTENS.
PLASMATIC ENERGY groups ELECTRONIC FASTENS.

QUANTA: One ENERGETIC QUANTA is the spheroidal grouping of:

$$12 \times 10^9 \text{ PARTONS}$$

One ELECTRIC QUANTUM are two ENERGETIC QUANTA.
One ELECTRONIC QUANTUM are two ELECTRIC QUANTA.
One RADIAL or PLASMATIC QUANTUM are two ELECTRONIC QUANTA.

209

The professor illustrated in the computer, how also the union of three up to twelve ANALFAS, the valence depended on the number of sides to the base.

SUBATOMIC PARTICLES: According to their valence and their polarity, the analfas gave origin to different types of particles. (Figure No. 42)

FIGURE 42

THE NUMBER OF ANALFAS DETERMINES THE VALENCE

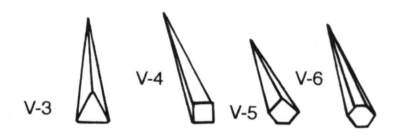

CHART NO. 4

VALENCE	NAME	POLARITY
V3 – V4	PHOTON	(-)
V5 – V6	PION	(-)
V3 – V4	MESON	(+)
V5 – V6	ALPHA-MESON	(+)
V3 – V4	ION	(N)
V5 – V6	DION	(N)

ATOMIC PARTICLES are formed with the grouping of subatomic particles in clusters of two to twelve units.

CHART NO. 5

NAME	INTEGRATION	DIMENSION
ELECTRON	From 2 to 12 PHOTONS	Third
NEGATRON	From 2 to 12 PIONS	Fourth
PROTON	From 2 to 12 MESONS	Third
POSITRON	From 2 to 12 ALPHA-MESONS	Fourth
NEUTRON	From 2 to 12 IONS	Third
NEUTRINIUM	From 2 to 12 DIONS	Fourth

FIGURE 43

The subatomic particles with a valence of 11 are unstable and of short duration.
Only those of a valence of 12 are stable and long lasting.

SYMBOL

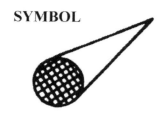

DIMENSIONS. The particles of different valences are those that integrate matter in different dimensions.

FIGURE 44

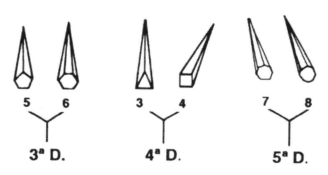

| 5 | 6 | 3 | 4 | 7 | 8 |

3ª D. 4ª D. 5ª D.

Third Dimension   **Fourth Dimension**   **Fifth Dimension**

After this last image appeared on the monitor, the professor pointed out.

"These images were especially prepared in your language and this recording was used in your planet to share our knowledge, and should be an objective to be attained by your brother scientists. Now let's to back to the beginning of the holographic animation."

The stage lit up with an image where energy was represented by blue steam invading the spaces and finding the concentrations of energy that had been previously emitted.

In a close up, it was clearly seen how the wind of cosmic energy, upon impact, formed whirlwinds and these promoted the concentrations where brilliant dots were generated, initiating the formation of matter. The intensity of the brilliant dots formed belts as they advanced. They looked like red lights, but kept an intensity of homogeneous luminosity as they spread out.

The animation changed: as it got closer, it gave the impression that the lights exploded into thousands of smaller lights which separated from each other, but new lights kept appearing to fill in the spaces.

Yunner Krinn again stopped the projection. He got close to the table and continued his explanations which were translated by Shem.

"The blue steam in the animation is a visual allegoric representation of primitive energy, that we call cosmic, because it invades all the Universe of creation. When it reached previously energized zones, the impact when combined, promoted concentrations of energetic formations that integrate matter."

"In large quantities, we go from microcosms to macrocosms and in both the human mind is far too small to completely understand reality, since it is far more complex than it seems, because we will simultaneously have the coexisting integration of several dimensions."

"Just to illustrate my words, let us try to rationalize in our mind the size of the essential particle called PARTON."

"Let's take, for example, a PHOTON, this sub particle belongs to the DUM-KUAR energy and is manifested in the form of light. Each photon is formed by PARTONS which are integrated by chains of ramas of five to ten tetrahedrons.

The number of integers is $15 \times 10_6 = 15,000,000$ (fifteen million) of myriads. Every four myriads form a tetrahedron, thus each rama of five tetrahedrons will have 20 myriads and those of ten tetrahedrons, 40 myriads. As they have an equal number of chains, if each pair has 60 myriads, then each PARTON is formed by 250,000 chains. And all this structure forms a sphere of:

Diameter of parton = 10_{-18} of a micron = 10_{-24} of a meter

"Now that we have in mind how a parton integrating a photon is formed, we will see an example that will allow us to rationalize its size:
The size of a bacteria on Earth is approximately one MICRON and one ANGSTROM, which is the theoretical limit of the capacity of an electronic microscope, which is almost the size of the diameter of an hydrogen atom." (Chart No. 6).

"We know that the ANGSTROM is one ten-thousandth part of one micron. Let us suppose that we increase one ANGSTROM to the size of a planet like the Earth, 10,000 kilometers in diameter. One proton, which is ten thousand times smaller, would be a sphere one kilometer in diameter and the PARTON would be only one tenth of a micron. This means that a being living in that planet of one ANGSTROM in diameter and even though he had the same technology that exists on Earth, he couldn't see it either!"
"The microcosm is a complete universe you cannot see, but in the macrocosm you are equally defenseless. Your galaxy, your own home, is also unknown to you. What could we say about the galaxies that you and your brothers can hardly see?"

CART NO. 6

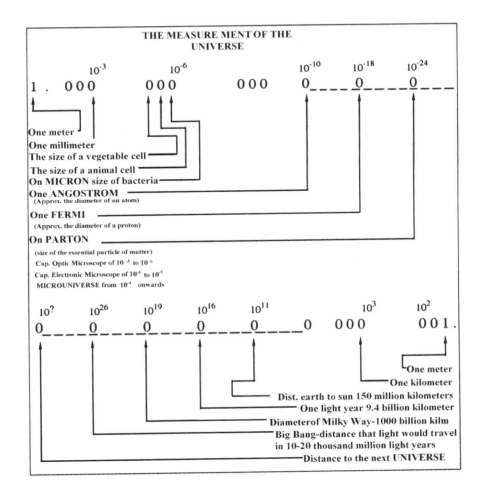

THE MEASURE MENT OF THE UNIVERSE

"You consider that the largest distance in the Universe is of approximately 18 thousand million light years, since you believe that was when the BIG BANG originated the universe."

"What would you think if I told you that the Big Bang was only one of the red lights you saw light up in the animation when the cosmic energy in one of the clouds of impact originated this universe. Besides it wasn´t only one Big Bang, but many more that formed this local universe, of which you don´t know even one tenth!"

"The creating process of partons in the microcosm is similar to the formation of stars in the macrocosm. Everything began when cosmic energy reached previously energized zones, as a preparation to generate matter."

"The sudden generation of stars and your known universe, is what your brother scientists call the Big Bang. As you have noticed, it isn´t one but many Big Bangs that form a universe; in fact, many local universes are formed that, little by little, will constitute what we call a super-universe."

"In order not to be too confusing, allow me to clarify the terminology. The word Universe really should cover all creation, but it is so large we call it the MASTER UNIVERSE."

"This MASTER UNIVERSE, to the extent of our knowledge, is integrated by the CENTRAL UNIVERSE or ISLAND OF LIGHT, where our Father dwells, and there are seven SUPER UNIVERSES surrounding it. The last one, which is just in the process of being formed is the one to which we belong. (Figure 45).

FIGURE 45

MASTER UNIVERSE

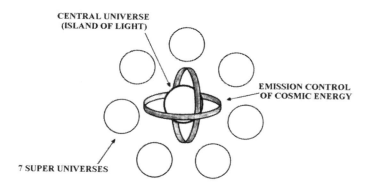

"Each super- universe is composed of ten circles of universes, we call it big wheels, each big wheel has 100 small

216

wheels and in each small wheel exist 100 local universes, account as local universe the space that contain 100 galactic constellations." (Figure No. 46)

FIGURE 46

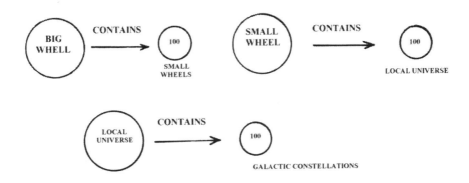

"These diagrams are only intended to help you understand the concept. We´ll return to this subject, further on. For now, just keep in mind what we told you, and remember it is a diagram without graduated scales."

"Our local universe is called NEVADON and at its head is a MICAEL. This is not a name but a rank within the organization of the master universe. There are a total of 700,000 Micaels, one for each local universe in creation. Our Micael incarnated in your planet as Jesus of Nazareth. He wanted to visit you personally to leave his teachings when he considered you were ready for them."

"Allow me to ask a question," Eric dared to interrupt. "You mentioned Jesus of Nazareth, the one called Christ, who is the origin and center of several religions and is considered on Earth as the Son of God, the Father of the Universe. I suppose that he is the one you are talking about, is this correct?"

"That is so, he is a son of our Father."

217

"Then, how can you include him in the same hierarchy as the other 700,000 Micaels?"

Professor Krinnell gave him a long look, trying to penetrate his mind and assess his capacity of comprehension, and after began to explain with his usual gentle patience.

"Look, Eric, we are all sons of God, because we believe He is our Creator Father, as we have spirits and exist in or around evolving worlds, thanks to his love. Since that is his wish, because he considers it convenient and proper, and in his wisdom, he had determined this is the best way to reach Him. But the path is long and the trials to be overcome are many. He, in His divine kindness and generosity, has foreseen everything; not only the way but also the means through which the necessary merits can be attained and all the opportunities we need to be able to learn. Learning is the evolution of the spirit, for it to acquire the necessary characteristics to rise to each level."

"Please accept your limited capacity of comprehension with humility. Both of us are still small, we have just started to be aware of our being and we must act with patience and respect. It is as if a child who has just learnt about numbers be expected to understand what can be calculated with them. For now, only listen, the time will come when you will be able to understand with a broader and deeper perception."

"All of us were created as pure and perfect spirits, but without merits of our own. We can build machines and robots, whose behavior is perfect in accordance to their programming. But after the task has been done, there is nothing else they can do. The success or the failure of their performance is only the result of cause and effect, but there is no personal involvement. It depends totally on the material and the technology."

"The human being is special within creation because he does have FREE WILL. Besides he has an independent body, intelligence, memory and mind. The mind is his contact with his Creator and from Him he receives direct guidance through the CONSCIENCE."

"The generosity of our Heavenly Father with His children is enormous. He sends His help to us through more evolved spirits, who are our brothers with a higher degree of evolution, to guide us

218

in ours. When a humanity has not reached the necessary spiritual development to receive spiritual help, those spirits incarnate and live among them to serve as examples and guides."

"In the case of your planet, since that wasn't enough, a superior spirit was authorized to incarnate to give you teachings and examples. For this, He was born and lived in a material body as a human to fulfill his mission as a teacher. It was determined that the best way for you to learn, was through actions, words and examples within your comprehension."

"Maybe to many of your brothers it will be hard to accept that Jesus wasn't God Himself, but His child as we are, although far more evolved. Above all, since the opposite has been declared and accepted for generations. It is not that our Father doesn't come to give you his message of love personally, but He is doing it in the way He considers the most appropriate. As our Father, he gets close to each of his children, be they as small as we are or more evolved as those already carrying on other activities according to their evolution."

"We are all progressing, each one at his own level, but equally as brothers, because we are all His children. He gives each one, as part of his evolution, the opportunity to serve by helping his smaller brothers, as we are helping you and you should be helping each other."

"In an effort to aid poor human comprehension, the Father manifested Himself as three different persons, although He is only one. God Father is the Creator, God Son is the Teacher and Guide, and God Holy Spirit is the Wisdom and Knowledge of all Creation."

"He is omnipotent and omnipresent and his immensity is beyond our capacity of comprehension. God, the presence of our Father, is everywhere, including in the spirits He created to His image and likeness. Regarding the evolving levels we have been talking about, we are not yet able to understand up to what point the Father is in them or they are in Him."

"Remember that Jesus himself told them, in his teachings, that there was matter and spirit. Word was for matter--your human body, and the essence was for your soul, for your spirit. The existence of your spirit, is precisely what I am trying to help you understand. Spiritual life must stop being an enigma for human beings on your planet. It is absurd to consider your own spirit a mystery when intelligence, will power, free will and conscience is manifested through it."

"Surely Rahel will talk to you in more detail regarding the different evolving levels and about the missions we must fulfill in each one. The fact our elder brothers, who are already at those levels, do things that may now be difficult for you to understand, does not mean, they are not real."

"Earth is not the only place where that Spirit has gone in person to help his smaller brothers," Shem added. "On occasions, as in the case of Earth´s humanity, he will return in spirit to guide them when they have a change in era."

"Precisely because of his second visit has allowed us to have this type of contact with you-to help you-as time is running out and you have not evolved enough."

"There is a time for everything in the Universe. Everything is programmed and nothing is left to chance. The time for you to reach the necessary evolution and attain the next step is practically ending and you are still not prepared."

"But, then what is going to happen?" asked Eric.

"Your own planet will do whatever is needed to make you react. It will be renovated to become the home of those who reach the necessary evolution for the next level."

"Do you mean to tell me that there are those who will not reach it?" Eric interrupted again.

"That is so, and those rebellious spirits will have to start over in another time, and in another planet, which must already be ready to receive a humanity in evolution, to give them shelter for another 75,000 years, in the hope that, maybe then, they can attain it."

"The local universe where we live is very large. Let´s say that it is a small handful of almost simultaneous Big Bangs, but there are many more in the space of our super-universe. It is as difficult to understand the size of the Universe, as it is to understand the microuniverse that forms part of our material life."

"You also saw the animated representation of the concentration of energy that goes on grouping itself in ever more complex and powerful concentrations, but always in a set pattern where everything has been foreseen."

The energies that have been formed will interact and, little by little, the sublimation of cosmic energy, that is God´s LOVE, will originate the subatomic particles from which matter is formed, simultaneously, in several dimensions. Each dimension is independent and can coexist and interact with the rest following the same marvelous pattern of the Laws of the Universe. The human being tries to understand these laws and one day will, in accordance with what is allowed within the capabilities he is given in each dimension."

After a short pause, Yunner Krinn stood up and smiling to Eric, said: "Now you have to go, but you will have the opportunity to return and acquire more knowledge."

Eric was fascinated, and would have preferred not to end the interview, but it was obvious Yunner Krinnell had other matters to attend to. Shem and Kunn stood up and the three said their goodbyes to the Professor. First, as it was their custom, but then Eric could not restrain his emotions and profusely thanked Krinnells´s hospitality with a handshake. At the same time, he transmitted through mental telepathy: "Thank you very much, Professor, I hope to see you again to learn more from you."

Yunner Krinn nodded with a smile. They took the elevator and quickly arrived at the level of the belts and from there, it only took them seconds to leave the building, guided by Kunn.

Eric took his place on board the vessel and watched Kunn do the flight´s checklist. After a few minutes, they were descending in the Golemisbeck of Parthelia. When they were on the platform, Eric watched the screens of the television and computer monitors, while Kunn did the final inspection and then turned them off. As Shem and Kunn talked, Eric felt the need to rest after such an exciting day—so productive and full of excitement. He closed his eyes and fell fast asleep.

CHAPTER XII

The Planet Earth is at the end of an era
and at the beginning of another.
It will be the same planet, the same nature,
the same Sun, but with a different humanity;
and new ideals where there will be justice,
harmony, wisdom, truth and love.
That will be the New Era.

Pablo E. Hawnser

ENCOUNTER IN MERIDA

Eric had several days of hard work. He was glad he had had the opportunity to rest mentally and have practiced mediations in the "Ashram" of his friend, Oscar before having another encounter with his friends.

Memories of Shem, Yunner Krinn and Kunn appeared constantly in his mind. He smiled thinking that they could have been Misha´s, Elim´s and even Mirza´s brothers, their physical characteristics were so similar. Now, besides, he completely understood what Rahel meant when he assured him that they would talk about his "dreams".

He expected to get a telephone call from Mirza at any time, since he hadn´t heard from her since she had arranged his appointment with Rahel in Culiacán. But several days passed and he thought that if by the following weekend she hadn´t called him, he would try to get in touch through mental telepathy.

However, on Tuesday he decided that if she didn´t call him during that day, he would initiate contact on Wednesday, as he was leaving for a trip to Merida on Thursday. It would be timely to see Rahel, since they could have a confidential talk over there more easily. On Wednesday, however, the phone rang and Mirza´s familiar voice made his heart do flip flops. Again he was sure it was her, even before answering the phone!

"Mirza! I am so glad to hear you! Tell me, are you calling me on your own or did you perceive I wanted to communicate with you?"

"Both, Eric, the detector showed emission signals on your frequency, but besides I had to call you. Are you worried?"

"No. Mirza, on the contrary, excited and baffled. The last time I talked to Rahel, he told me we would talk about my dreams. Of course, at the time, I thought it would be about what I had mentioned to you. But let me tell you, I had a "dream" that seemed to be a movie. Just imagine, I traveled to different planets in outer space!!"

Mirza´s crystalline laughter made him stop. "Don´t you believe me?" Eric asked, slightly puzzled.

"Of course I do, I am sorry. I am laughing because I am happy for your excitement. I want to hear all about your adventure, but when we are together with Rahel. Also, we are going to introduce a visitor to you. How do you like that?"

"That´s great. But who is he? Where does he come from?"

"Calm down, everything in it´s own time. Now, tell me, is Saturday all right?"

"Yes, but I have to be in Merida and Campeche on Thursday and Friday. I can hurry back or we can meet over there. Where would it be better?"

"Yes, it could be over there," Mirza replied, after a brief pause.

"Then I´ll sleep in Campeche, that way I´ll be back in Merida early."

"Very well, just remember that we can not interfere with your obligations in any way. It must be when you are completely free."

"All right, Mirza, please call me at the Baluarte Hotel in Campeche around one or one thirty on Friday afternoon. Will you?"

223

"Yes, but don't worry, if you can't be there at that time, we'll see each other on Saturday."

"Yes, of course, Mirza." After hanging up, Eric felt glad, and willing to get to work. That night he remembered "the trip" in which even Rahel appeared, the places, the teachings...until he fell asleep.

On Thursday, on the plane to Merida, he was excited and wished he were already meeting with them. He remembered Mirza's words. Who was he going to meet this time? It was incredible! How could he live something like this and keep it to himself? Sometimes he felt desperate, wanting to have someone he could talk to, someone who could accompany him. That was it! He would ask Rahel if he could. But, who could be the ideal person?

The flight attendant brought him out of his reverie, offering him some breakfast. He accepted with a thankful smile and as he got ready to eat, tried to imagine the adventures Mirza and Rahel had planned for this new encounter. It would be the fourth time they met and there was already an impressive amount of information. Besides, he felt they hadn't answered all his questions yet.

All his business in Merida and Campeche turned out better than he had expected, and by 12 o'clock Friday he was ready to return to Merida to take the 7:00 P.M. flight to Mexico City if need be.

At 12:15, after paying his bill, he went to the dining room. He had had a light very early breakfast, so he would have a snack while he waited. If he didn't hear from Mirza, he would return calmly to Merida. While he was being served, he decided to let the front desk know that he was waiting for a phone call. As he left the message on the counter, the expected call came in.

"Mirza?"

"Yes, Eric, how are your business meetings going?"

"Everything is fine, thank you. In fact, I am ready to return to Merida. I expect to leave in about 40 minutes."

"How long will it take you to get there?"

"If I hurry, approximately two hours."

"Try to make it three and a half hours, we'll wait for you at the airport's restaurant. Drive carefully."

"All right, we´ll see each other there…valim alek!" Eric was surprised at the words he had pronounced so spontaneously. Where had he gotten them from? He remembered then that at the end of his "journey", when he had fallen asleep in the vessel as they were returning, he had a mental image of Shem and Kunn smiling while they said "See you later" raising an arm. He clearly perceived they were saying "Valim alek!" and he had understood it as an expression of farewell.

He ate something light at the hotel´s restaurant and then left so as not rush on the road. It was 3:45 p.m. when, after delivering the rental car, he entered the terminal. Mirza was awaiting him at the restaurant. She looked radiant, wearing white pants, a blue blouse and blue shoes. Eric smiled to himself when he saw how she took care of her color combinations—a woman´s privilege, no doubt!

"Hello, Mirza, glad to see you."

"Same to you, Eric. Go ahead, we have been waiting for you."

Rahel and a young lady were at the table by the entrance. Both stood up and watched Eric, while Mirza attended to the introductions.

"Eric, she is Vanny, she comes from a brother planet of ours. Its system is known as number 25, the planet number is 610 and its sun is called Splendon. They already live fully in the era of SUPER-MEN, their NEW ERA was reached with love, thanks to their degree of evolution, about 200 years ago in Earth´s time."

Eric smiled, at the time he bowed slightly in the Japanese fashion. He always felt natural with this greeting that, being courteous, left the other person free to extend a more effusive greeting or not.

Vanny, in turn, got close to him and with a kind smile offered her hand as we do. "It is an honor to be with you," she told him, with a voice resembling Mirza´s. It sounded like that of a young lady.

Eric hesitated to ask her age; he held back since you don´t generally ask that of the ladies. He didn´t know if she would think it was incorrect. To his surprise, she answered mentally: *"I am 55 years of age in Earth´s time, approximately."*

Eric answered, "*I'm sorry, thank you.*"

"We greet the same way you do, don´t we?" added Vanny, while they shook hands.

Eric agreed and then turned to Rahel. They greeted and the four sat down at the table.

"Take note, Eric," Mirza started the conversation. "When they started their era as men, Earth was already 10,000 years into that stage. They destroyed themselves and had to start again and it wasn´t until later when they were able to advance without setbacks. Now they have been living, in the equivalence of 200 years on Earth, in their era of super-men. Whatsmore, they attained it in a natural way. Pain or tribulation, the kind we are trying to avoid here, was unnecessary, that is why your mission is so important."

"Vanny came with her group to visit this planet, as they have visited many others. They are also on their way to help another planet with similar problems to yours."

"Rahel, are there visitors from other planets besides you?" Eric asked.

"Yes, the ones that are in their era of super-men do biochemical and genetic studies, and some others travel to different places for diverse reasons, but always under our control. Not only here, but in all the planetary system of this Sun and in other similar systems. The same thing happens in other areas of the galaxy."

"There are 619 planets in our galaxy inhabited by humanities in evolution. Earth is member 606 and its solar system is number 24."

"I understand you perfectly. Does she know our language?" Eric asked.

"No," Rahel answered, "but she does understand ours, and what you received from her are ideas, not words."

"Why don´t you teach me your language? I don´t think I will have any problem in learning it."

"Of course you could, but that is not what I came to teach you, it´s not the proper moment. Right now, the main thing is for you to carry out your mission. It is urgent, you certainly don´t have much time. We want to avoid, or at least soften the physical suffering, as much as possible, that will force you to recover lost time, as you have to start the new era, the one of super-men and continue your evolution."

"Isn´t it natural for that era to occur progressively? Why the physical suffering?"

"Because at a certain pre-established date, all your brothers on Earth must have evolved spirits that correspond to that stage. Whoever doesn´t attain it will be taken (in spirit, of course) to new planet, where they will have to start the process again from the first stage until reaching the necessary evolution to allow them to go on to the next level of men, that of super-men-- the last step in evolution."

"When that moment comes, they must leave the body they dwell in, maybe even with violence. In those cases, many that already have the proper spiritual evolution will leave them also. But that doesn´t matter. As they will return, little by little, to this planet, reincarnating, to revitalize it and continue with their evolution. Then we will be able to communicate with you openly or "officially", as you call it, and help you rebuild what is necessary."

Eric didn´t know what to say, he was struck dumb by the impact of Rahel´s words. Mirza noticed his anxiety and intervened to continue with the purpose of this new encounter.

"Eric, tell us about your dreams."

Eric was still stunned, but he took a deep breath and said, "You have already given me an explanation for my "changes" with my twin soul; but I would like to include something more."

"Yes, tell us," Rahel urged.

"Several years ago, when I had the last change, some very close friends, who I saw on a daily basis, told me that they had seen me in places I had never been to. They hadn´t spoken to me, but there was no doubt it was I. There were two instances, and in both they didn´t know how I had disappeared so suddenly. Do you believe that this is included in the same explanation, or do you think they made a mistake?"

"In your case, it´s very possible," Rahel answered. "I dare say that your friends weren´t confused, and that it really was you. But it wasn´t precisely a case of ubiquity, that is reserved only to very elevated spirits. In reality, it has to do with the phenomenon of consubstantiation of plasmatic energy in a spirit during a "passing".

227

Remember that a spirit can get "prana" type energy. You know it as ectoplasm, which reveals spiritual presence in a material form."

"I will give you an example. If you have a magnetic field and metallic dust. This will reveal the contours and shapes of the magnetic lines. "Prana" energy can condense itself and form a coating dense enough to reflect rays of light. When it covers the spirit, it takes on the form of the body in which it lives, like a holographic image in third dimension."

"If you are in deep sleep and have a "detachment", your soul can go, among other places, to see someone in whom you have thought a lot of or return to some place, that for some reason is on your mind."

"It is the same phenomenon that occurs when "spirits" or "ghosts" are seen. Ghosts are like holographic images of souls that almost always belong to people already dead. These souls needed to leave their material body due to the passing away of the one they had, regardless of the cause of death."

"When that happened, they probably had a large negative karma. When their material body that supplied their energy died, their soul was suddenly released and the negative charges do not allow its spiritual brain to properly interpret their situation."

"When the spiritual brain is suddenly not allowed access to its own knowledge, it is not fully conscious of its situation, the soul will try to hold on to material life and continue to worry about its possessions and loved ones in this life of the third dimension."

"A soul in such a trance will desperately try to hold on to the useless body that was its home. The dense energy of karma doesn´t permit the spiritual brain to work properly. For this reason, it searches for "prana" to reincorporate itself to material life. Eventually it receives small quantities of energy taken from the living beings that release it unconsciously when they are under strong emotional stress. When the soul notices that it can be obtained from a frightened person, it will try by all means to provoke that fear, only to prolong its stay at the level as closest as possible to material beings."

"Nevertheless, in spite of its grief, the soul suffering because of its mental darkness, will go on trying to rise. This rising is really the physical departure from the planet until, due to effects of cosmic energy, it can free itself of negative charges and return to the mental clarity as the circuits of its spiritual brain have been reestablished, returning with proper energy to the fifth dimension."

"When you have a "detachment", your soul can carry out astral projections, and keep all its experiences and knowledge in its spiritual brain. When it returns to its physical body, these memories can filter to the physical brain and the person will think of them as "dreams". Now, if that body has not been able to live that experience, there is only one explanation left and that is a spiritual memory."

"A person can consciously identify the memories of its physical experiences and the rest as "dreams". These can be of different origin:"

a) Spiritual. This is a memory that comes from its spiritual brain where past lives in other physical bodies of the third dimension are recorded including all the experiences of its twin soul.

b) The recording is a "memory" that comes from a spiritual experience of the fourth dimension.

c) More or less coordinated happenings emerge from the imagination in the physical brain. These are provoked by mental impulses generating images in different stages of consciousness during sleep, originating in the brain. The result is a fictitious story we sometimes remember as we awake, these are the true "dreams".

During the night, under normal conditions, a human being can have up to five mental activities that generate dreams during periods of eight to thirty minutes, with intermediate periods of deep relaxation between the levels of ALPHA and THETA. Cerebral activity when dreaming varies from eight to twelve cycles per second. Spiritual communication happens at DELTA level at four cycles, and then rises to BETA so the "memory" of the dream is registered by the physical brain coming from a spiritual origin.

"During their lives, human beings are influenced by spiritual knowledge of their evolution that filters to the physical brain, subconsciously modifying their way of thinking and acting."

CHART NO. 7

STATES OF CONSCIENCE	CYCLES PER SECOND	REPRESENTATIVE ACTION	LEVEL	MANIFESTATION
Vigil	60-13	Study, work, sports	BETA	Communication through Physical Senses
Subconscious	13-7	Step between Vigil	ALFA	Mental Communication
Unconscious	7-4	Deep sleep	TETA	State of contemplation, Nirvana
Transdimensional	4-1	Intercommunicator	DELTA	Spiritual
In Coma	1	Inert	------	None
Lifeless	0	Lack of life	------	None

"The behavior of people that possess evolutionary spirits stands out due to their high moral values and their intellectual capacity. They will be the new guides for humanity and will find the path that leads to other dwellings in the Universe where we will be received as their brothers."

Vanny, who had only been a spectator, stepped in to transmit: *"Eric, I am happy to know you. Soon I will have to meet someone like you, and I hope he can understand me as you do."*

Eric looked at her and smiled in agreement, but his mind was still trying to grasp Rahel´s and Mirza´s concepts.

230

"The behavior of human beings in a planet such as this," continued Mirza, "is the result of many factors; some of them are understandable. Some are external, which are the more material ones, such as the influence of the natural environment, climate and all the physical conditions where they are forced to live, as the temperature, humidity, oceans, rivers, deserts, forests, etc. and consequently the type of food. Societies are also an influence, considered external because of the effect of their moral values and customs."

"After this we have the internal ones, which are of genetic origin. Here we find the influences that affect physical and mental states, as revealed through their physical and intellectual capabilities."

"The factor that up to now has not been accepted, and that is why you do not consider it important, is the spiritual one. You do not want to take into consideration what you cannot measure or whose existence you do not understand since you can´t see it. However, the time has come when you have to understand the spiritual factor to be able to accept and learn, in addition to correct your attitudes and behavior."

"If the spirit already has a certain degree of evolution, the body where it lives will serve as a vehicle to perfect itself and so naturally take advantage of it to try to improve. Its mental and moral capacities will develop very easily, and even in the most adverse physical and social environments, its performance will be positive. Soon it will stand out as a guide and as an example to follow in life. Its moral and mental qualities will clearly influence material life. They are the men that inspire and stimulate our development with the technological and moral help of all concerned."

"When a spirit has reincarnated, its mission can be its own restitution to accumulate merits through the physical body and eliminate his karmas for not having lived harmoniously in his past lives."

"A human being who did not listen to the spiritual guidance of his conscience, could have achieved success on Earth supported one hundred percent by material interests, and not developing his spiritual gifts. He preferred ambition, lies and pride and didn't practice charity nor love, that are positive."

"If his physical life ends when his soul is under such imbalance, the soul will have to suffer the law of cause and effect in the process needed to restore spiritual equilibrium. This is called restitution."

"This equilibrium will come, without a doubt, being bound by the universal laws, and more so, if it is the case of a spirit with material life. He will have to make up for his bad behavior to be able to fulfill his own process of living in harmony with the Universe."

"When the material elements do not affect a spirit, it can clearly understand its situation and recognize the actions it needs to eliminate karma and be in equilibrium and harmony to continue its path of evolution."

"When this is the case, it will also reflect clearly on the behavior of the human being."

"Do you notice the most important influence on the human being is its own spiritual life? The spirit and the soul do not have substance, they don't belong to the third dimension, but to higher dimensions. Here you could ask, what is another dimension? Another dimension is another level of existence. Human beings belong to two dimensions, a material one with its physical body and a spiritual one that begins with his mind."

"Scientific knowledge in your brothers´ technology gets lost when the dimensional change begins. The most modern scientific advances, due to the lack of applied knowledge, become blurred as much cosmogonically as in the quanta, as much in space as in time, in the genesis of the Universe and its boundaries, as the small subatomic particles and the energetic charges that are the origin of matter and energies."

"This happens to human beings when nature limits their own minds when trying to apply science in their material frontiers. In this way, nature itself forces them to begin to perceive the existence of other dimensional levels that can explain physical phenomena."

"When cause and effect provoked by cosmic energies lead to a visualization of divine existence—apart from the fact that ALL is divine because it comes from God—that is when they begin to understand that physics has a wider scope in higher dimensions where, what is spiritual is real."

232

"The most modern and advanced knowledge of man leads him to the threshold of other dimensions, and there is the paradox. They are not contradictions of science, but rather voids in knowledge, because without a doubt they have a natural explanation under the interpretation of "natural" in other dimensional levels."

"The theory of the Big Bang, for example, becomes swamped in a morass, when asked what came before, and as there is no answer, the premise is no longer valid. That great moment that scientists consider unique happens to be not unique nor the beginning, it is only a moment where cause and effect give origin to the local Universe."

"In an undetermined more or less brief period of time, when cosmic energy began the creation of this local universe, a small part of the master Universe. In fact, it was not a Big Bang, there were many similar ones and on a smaller scale, and they continue to occur as energy condenses into matter to maintain the balance between the intergalactic cosmic spaces of the new universes. Precisely, because of this, they will find themselves at some time with a paradox, an apparent contradiction in measuring the age of the Universe."

"On one side, they use the measurement of the quantity of matter in the universe they can observe; and on the other, their calculations are based on a cosmological constant. In the near future, scientists will discover stars older than the age of the universe. This is not possible. Unless, of course, these are stars whose origin wasn't the same Big Bang of what we consider our universe, but a manifestation of the existence of other parallel universes. As each Big Bang is the point of origin for the generation of matter in space-time, a consequence of the condensation of cosmic energy."

Rahel was watching Eric and noticed his interest in the subject, so he continued:

"To sum up everything that Mirza said, your spirit can communicate with you. Spirits of all men want to communicate with their own beings in the third dimension, although only few attain the comprehension and integration that emerges when we human beings are willing to rise and live life in that spiritual dimension."

"Scientists find, as their knowledge increases, a convincing entrance to spatial dimensions and the relativity of temporary ideas. When cosmic energy, in its different presentations (gravitational, electromagnetic and nuclear) is better known, they encounter the paradoxes, they call the singularities, that are physical manifestations of a new light to understand the existence of other dimensions."

"Man will accept this reality, very slowly at first and more easily later, as he becomes conscious of his own physical-spiritual duality."

"Faith must be light, not dogmatic fanatism. God is life itself and His manifestation is the Universe. These are the concepts that you must reason with your intellect and the mind, to comprehend your own spiritual being."

"Once the human being is able to comprehend this, he will also understand the multidimensional cosmic reality. Unexplainable mysteries will become part of his Universe, his mind will extend its dominions and he will comprehend the correlation that exists between the phenomena lost in the fog of metaphysics."

"As mankind acquires this knowledge, it will become more humble. When wisdom and perfection are attained, his spirit will be raised and will contemplate the love, the greatness and the immense generosity of the Father Creator."

"When mankind reaches this step in his evolution, it will be ecstasy, and will then continue human life under a new perspective."

"Once he becomes more spiritual, he will stress his moral values, listen to the voice of his conscience to guide him and will experience a happiness, unknown until that time. His life will have a new meaning, he will no longer fear the dimensional change called death, as he will know that his soul doesn't die. But returns to the dimension where his true life goes on in search of his evolution."

"He will understand the existence of the spirits as they try to communicate from their dimension to the material world. He will understand the immensity of the Material Universe where he lives and the interrelation between the different dimensions that begin in him, for his creation, for his transformation and to serve the end for which he was, is and will continue to be created."

"Everything is perfectly planned and interrelated, humanity has had the time of three complete turns of the Earth's axis. Each turn takes approximately 25,000 years to complete. It's time for the last stage, which must be one of spiritual light and of the light of knowledge of the Universe to accelerate his evolution."

"Change is mandatory. If mankind refuses to change for the love of his creator and his brothers, it will be necessary for the planet itself, reacting to the damage it has endured, to subject you through natural elements, to eliminate the largest part of humanity, to begin a New Era with properly evolved spirits. It doesn't matter that many men with that degree of evolution will also perish. They, as we have previously mentioned, will return to have a new life, but in the New Era, where they will have the civilization and the technology that today is just beginning to be visualized. At that moment, we will officially be with you to help you."

"However, there is still time to achieve this change without violence, by yourselves, with love. Yes, Eric, with the simple rule that the Creator Father sent to you with the Spirit of the Maitreya incarnated in Jesus of Nazareth: "Love one another.""

"The religion that the Father asks of you is one of living with love and charity, with humility, justice and patience. All the rituals and traditions are not necessary, as they spring from ignorance and pride, and in which you believe to erase your selfishness and materialism. The doctrine of the Father is one of love in order to have greatness of spirit and understanding."

"Of course it will be difficult, as men are divided, not only by their material and political views, but also by their religious and spiritual guides, who separate rather than unify. All are spiritual children of the same Father, and although having all the same beginnings, are confronted by ignorance and fanatism that blinds and enslaves."

Eric, just as Mirza and Vanny, were utterly absorbed by Rahel's words, while he paused for a drink of water. He then continued:

"Eric, as you already know, part of the teaching is provided mentally to you, another is illustrated by astral travels, and by other means, as the one of teletransportation, the same as you had at Milburbek, that you remember as a "dream". In another

235

conversation we will again talk about this system, which is so advanced we only have it through the intervention of our superior brothers, since it surpasses our technology. Just to give you a brief description. Two systems that are commonly used by us are by levitation through a halo of vibrations for short distances, and transmigration of matter to another dimension for long distances.

Energy being transmitted to another site and then reintegrated with the body at its destination where the spirit joins it to travel in its own dimension. Another similar transmission is carried out to return and all the experiences come from your spiritual mind. Simple, isn´t it?"

Everyone had a good laugh!

The loudspeaker announced the departure of the flight to Mexico City and all stood up to say goodbye to Eric.

"After the last comments from Rahel, I have the impression I am returning to my house in a horse buggy!" Eric commented, addressing Mirza and Vanny.

All of them received the message and understood the expression, which made them laugh again. Vanny looked at Eric and transmitted: "It was certainly a pleasure to meet you, I hope we´ll see each other again. I wish you every success and happiness in your mission."

Eric looked at Vanny, since his arrival everyone had been involved in the conversation and he hadn´t had time to see her. She was a beautiful woman, intelligent and young looking. She had said she was 55 years of age, but she did not look older than 23! Her body was well built, her face was oval, regular, with harmonious features, deep-green eyes, well-formed eyebrows, a small mouth and perfect teeth. She was smaller than Mirza, and Eric felt she was more emotionally accessible. He turned to Rahel: "Is it a requirement to be a beautiful woman to be able to be an astronaut?"

Mirza translated the compliment to Vanny, and both thanked him with the same sincerity that made Eric think they weren´t very different to the human beings of his own planet.

Then he tried to be friendly and got close to Mirza to kiss her goodbye on the cheek, she reacted accepting it naturally, Vanny did the same. Then he took Rahel´s left hand over his shoulder, and said: "Thank you, Rahel, truly thank you very much. I hope we´ll soon see each other again to continue."

"As usual, Mirza and you will be in touch, take care and I promise we´ll see each other soon," answered Rahel.

Eric smiled to everyone and went to the boarding gate. At the door, he turned back to wave goodbye and they did the same. Mentally he transmitted: "Valim alek." He had the satisfaction of watching them react favorably and received the same farewell from them.

When the plane took off, it was getting dark outside, but he couldn't avoid searching for some sign of the space ship. Then he felt a great peace and tranquility come over him. He closed his eyes and remembered his boldness in giving Mirza and Vanny a goodbye kiss. In fact, he had thought of doing this before with Mirza to feel her closeness and see if he received some sign of surprise, of friendship and acceptance or rejection....but nothing!!

The truth is that it was nice, both had accepted his kiss in good faith, and had reacted as earthlings. He had smelled a pleasant aroma when close to both of them, although he didn't know if it was lotion or perfume, it seemed more likely to be from scented soap. The texture of their cheeks was similar to that of a young girl's, without make-up, except maybe for a little color on the lips...interplanetary feminine flirtation!!

CHAPTER XIII

Love is the immutable power
that moves the Universe.
It is the beginning and essence of life

B.T.L

When a person does not feel
shocked by the quantum theory,
it is because it is not understood.

Niels Bohr

QUANTUM BIOGENETICS

Two weeks went by since the trip to Merida for Mirza to communicate again with Eric. The appointment was to take place at the University Center, south of Mexico City, in front of the Concert Hall of Netzahualcoyotl; once there, they would look for an appropriate place to talk. Eric suggested the spot, because besides being peaceful, in a certain way it made him feel at home. Mirza offered to bring breakfast again.

Eric arrived early, at 7:30 a.m., he entered the parking lot thinking he would have to wait for them...but Mirza´s unmistakable pick-up truck was already there, although he couldn´t see them.

He walked calmly and started going around the hall to meet them, when he heard the telepathic transmission of Mirza´s voice saying: "Look for us at the sports field." He headed in that direction and soon found the place where they were waiting for him.

The scene was already familiar, Rahel carried a cart for luggage like the kind pilots use. Their meal was inside.

When Eric caught up with them, they greeted affectionately. Mirza got close to him, took him by the shoulders and staring deeply into his eyes, told him:

"Eric, I want to congratulate you on the way that, up to now, you have managed our relationship. Vanny sends her greetings and says she wishes to find someone like you on her mission. Rahel is also very pleased, isn´t that so?" Rahel agreed.

"I am glad you are already here," Rahel said. "Today I want to explain the material part of humanity and of the inhabitants of your planet including animals and plants a little more." The three of them walked slowly looking for a place to sit down. Rahel continued:

"We have already discussed that all animals and plants, have genetic pre-recordings that determine the physical characteristics of each. This you know already, but now the question is: How is it done? Who does it?"

"The genetic action is done through biochemical and biophysical phenomena. These are the actions and reactions, the cause and effect. The living cell is developed and reproduced following a certain pattern, but ever since the beginning, it has all the information required for the morph genesis."

"Cellular transformation is very complex and it all happens in that micro universe, from the preparation of the form for the development of an embryo, up to the complete development of the living being. "

"Think of the size of a cell and imagine you are small enough for the cell to have 100 kilometers in diameter. In that space, there is place for a large city like this one, the capital of your country and more; that is to say, for an enormous amount of factories, workshops, laboratories and big buildings where hundreds of engineers can draw up blueprints, in addition to sites where to produce the necessary materials and parts for a great project that would be the manufacture of a plant, an animal or a human being."

"The marvelous combinations of protein structures and nucleic acids will be the tools and components capable of reproduction."

239

"Morphological control is a biological characteristic mainly of a genetic origin. The morphogenesis of a living being implies the form and development of the organs and systems of the body and it begins with the fertilized ovule, the first cell."

"When it is time, more than 350 types of cells with different structures will be generated. Many of them will be programmed to appear at a future time, during development, but they are already part of the original
genetic program, where their functions and destination in the new body are defined."

"The process of interpretation of the genetic orders are in charge of the DNA, and go to the RNA to define the course of the morphogenesis."

"From the first cell, the blueprints, specifications and instructions are readied, to the most insignificant of details, including the faults that will appear in adulthood, causing illnesses that come from their initial genetic pattern."

"The structured proteins of the RNA will integrate another complete cellular unit, having the same information and the elements to operate independently and automatically, in combination with the original cell, and so on successively. Each one will generate other cells without stopping, providing them all with a copy of the information regarding the complete project and the geometric order of proliferation."

"A first axis will be formed in the embryo and from then on, the development of the being will continue, through complementary sub-axes."

"The cells will reproduce under a predetermined pattern, always passing along all the complete information to their descendants, that will indicate what their function is and when it will be carried out, within that harmonious concert."

"New axes, sub-axes, and ramifications will locate and generate organs and parts with different organic tissue and functions."

"Through the DNA and RNA, the cellular ribosomes will manufacture the proteins in their infinite combinations of structures."

"Your scientists have already determined all this. They know how it happens, but can see what is happening now, because they do not have the elements to know how it was programmed, nor where, nor when, nor why all this orderly perfection was made."

"For example, regarding the nucleic acids, what makes them appear at the right moment, and how was the program recorded so they generate protein structures at the precise time they are required? The body of a living being is a universe of cells; the life of each is integrated with the rest. It begins and forms more complex units to fulfill more complete functions."

"In the case of plants, trees for example. Even the color and the size of the fruit they will produce is carried in their genes. They have biological systems and mechanisms capable of making contact with other plants and to interchange information regarding external agents that affect their own existence. They can even exchange acquired knowledge and react by expressing their satisfaction or affectation by the effects of energy they receive from the environment."

"In plants, besides the morphology of genetic origin, mutations will be caused by external influences in order to adapt to their environment."

"In animals, the change is more noticeable in order to adapt to the environment. All this is considered before the embryo is formed. There are room and necessary provisions in the original cell to foresee everything. Before the formation of a new being is begun, the necessary information will go from cell to cell and the instructions will be carried out completely. The language is based on biophysical and biochemical action and reactions. Proteins and nucleic acids are the participating elements."

"Your scientists still don't know the molecular mechanism of morphogenesis; how the exchange of cellular information takes place, how the patterns of development of the embryo are established and how the different cellular behaviors are defined for the formation of tissues and organs, nor how neurological intercommunications are established and, specifically, what relation there is between the material organic development and evolution."

"It is true that, little by little, they increase their knowledge. But they will not be able to surpass certain limitations without knowing the origin and the formation of subatomic physics first. Then learn to identify new energies and means of interaction that actively participate in the complex web of changes and transformations that take place during the development of a living being."

"Imagine how complex the formation of webs of nerve conduits are throughout the muscles. Their anchorage to the bone structure, the arteries and capillary vessels for the irrigation of blood. They are as complex as the organs themselves have different organic tissues."

"The same thing happens with all the endocrine system, all the nervous system beginning with the brain, the central and peripheral system; muscles and organs have an immense variety of tissues; also the glands and blood and, besides, the automatic and independent functioning of each system."

"During the gastrulation, when the original cell begins to split and start the formation of the embryo, the cells suffer internal transformations to form the egg, which is already a super-cell containing the asymmetries which will originate the axes for development and growth."

"The development and transformations of cells, the egg, the embryo and the complete being are beyond the actual capabilities of mankind on Earth."

"The effort to understand the origin of life must lead man to acknowledge this. Just the fact of accepting it, consciously, will be a big step. Everything being discovered will make him see the similarity between the microcosm and the macrocosm, and will understand that the natural laws are divine, perfect and invariable."

"For the moment, they can not go much further within the sciences of all fields. But the limit of what they can understand will convince your brothers of my words. Scientists are like babies, each one is crawling and absorbed in following a line of light on the ground. As the lines they follow converge at a certain point, the time will come when, after this occurs, they will stop and look up to see where the light of truth, knowledge and creation comes from. Then, they will be able to see God with a vision of comprehension."

"God is not a person. He is in the Universe of His creation, and He is in heaven and in all of us, because we are part of Him. He is the creation of our reality; the fourth dimension is only one of the dimensions we will have to understand and know as we go forward through evolution."

"I hope that you understand that the fourth dimension is intimately linked to our third dimension, by interacting they complement each other, how? Through the energies our soul and our mental spheres provide."

Mirza had breakfast ready and Rahel stopped to give Eric a break.

"I hope you like it, Eric, look," Mirza said as she offered him the special plate with divisions and an adjoining glass, containing some liquid.

They got comfortable and started eating. Eric took the glass and had a drink. He raised his eyebrows in surprise, and said, "It's delicious! Is it water?"

Rahel smiled and transmitted: "Water, pure and crystalline water, as the water you should always drink!"

Eric confirmed it was so. He would have never imagined pure water could have such a wonderful flavor. After tasting the cream of vegetables, he had to admit it also had a delicate flavor. Remembering what he had seen on his "trip", he asked Rahel if they had brought the food from there.

"No, we don't bring food so far. This was prepared on the spaceship, which is our base, in orbit around the Earth. All the vegetables and fruit come from Earth."

Eric quickly tasted the other color. There was a complete change in flavor. Sips of water between each bite took away the taste, so each one could be enjoyed thoroughly. "How delightfully soft!" he exclaimed.

After they finished their meal, Mirza took a little stick and drew an imaginary figure on the ground. She showed Eric the position of the mental spheres in order to completely cover the physical brain.

"As Rahel explained to you, mental spheres are elements of the fourth dimension. They control the neuronal activity to obtain the required interaction."

243

"Look, energy for the soul in the human body is received from three different sources, which are:

Cosmic energy. That is the presence of the Creator in the love of God.

Solar energy. That implies light, thermal energy and all the vibrations, identified as rays (infrared, ultraviolet, gamma, "x", etc.) outside the range of sunlight.

Serpentine energy. The energy that is received from the planet itself, as a reaction to those the celestial body receives from the cosmos and from the sun."

"Each of these energies is received by one of the spiritual senses in the same way the body is aware of different vibration ranges through the physical senses, as light comes through the eyes, sound through the ears, temperature through touch, etc."

"All the mentioned perceptions are transformed into electronic signals transmitted to the brain for their identification."

"The soul received vibrations detected through the charkas that, as you may remember, are its senses."

"There are seven spiritual senses, and we will broach them, as it becomes timely and necessary, for you to know what type of energy the mental spheres will work with. We are going to broaden the concepts you learned from Yunner Krinnell on your trip."

"In the course of quantum mechanics, you were taught that the parton is the essential particle, the origin of the combinations that lead to the formation of the subatomic particles. You will remember this integration is shaped like a spheroid by a system of chains formed by ramas, each with a different number of tetrahedrons."

"The parton, at the same time, will integrate with other partons to form other particles. This unit has a diameter of 10^{-18} of a micron, that is, one trillionth of a micron, in such a way that we wanted to make a parton visible the size of a millimeter, the millimeter would grow in proportion and be the size a ray of light would travel in 105.7 years: 1,000 billion kilometers!!"

"The diameter of the Milky Way is approximately 100,000 light years, so that we would be talking about one thousandth the diameter of our galaxy!"

The size of a parton, compared to the micro cosmos, is similar to Earth´s size in the macro cosmos of the Universe. (Figure No.47).

FIGURE 47

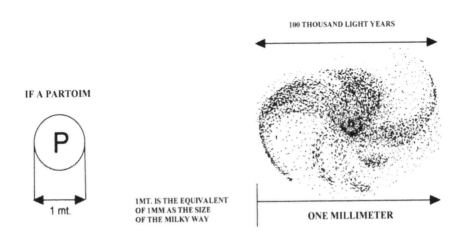

100 THOUSAND LIGHT YEARS

IF A PARTOIM

P

1 mt.

1MT. IS THE EQUIVALENT
OF 1MM AS THE SIZE
OF THE MILKY WAY

ONE MILLIMETER

"Depending on the ramas that integrate the chains constituting the parton, the energies will be determined to manifest the characteristics of their polarity, the number of partons that will integrate each particle and the characteristics of each energy."

"As we have seen when the partons unite, they form groups of two, four, six, eight and twelve partons. These groups have specific characteristics and are the basis for the formation of the so-called paralfic chains and analfas, that are the filing units that work in the cerebral neurons, and in a certain way are the equivalent to the "bytes" of a computer."

"One of the systems, product of the grouping of partons, are the fastens, that as they group, originate different types of manifestations of energy, we call electricity."

"Electricity is the result of the union of energetic fastens and, depending on the type of fastens, the types of energies such as, thermal, luminescent, kinetic, magnetic, static, neutral, pulsating or alternating current will also be integrated." (Chart No. 8)

"We will obtain electronic fastens from the electric ones; and radial or plasmatic energy from the electronic ones."

CHART NO. 8

DIFFERENT TYPES OF ELECTICITY

NAME	SYMBOL	ACTION	UNION
DUM-KUALI		THERMAL	IN RESONANCE
DUM-KUAR		LUNINESCENT	IN RESONANCE
ELECTRÓN	E	KINETIC	DIRECT CURRENT
KUM		MAGNETIC	IN HARMONY
KEMIO		STATIC	IN HARMONY
NEUTRÓN	N	NEUTRAL OR INERT	PARALLEL IN HARMONY
KOR	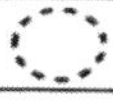	PULSATING OR ALTERNATING	PARALLEL IN HARMONY

"The units of energy, starting from the spheroid groupings, are called QUANTA, and according to the way they group, we will have electric, electronic or plasmatic quanta. Each of these quanta is formed by integrating two of the previous quanta."

Two energetic quanta = one electric quantum.
Two electric quanta = one electronic quantum.
Two electronic quanta = one plasmatic quantum.

"Similarly, the analfas united in the form of pyramids. The valence of the resulting particles that will be formed will depend on the number of sides to the base."

246

"You have already seen all this in detail during your visit of Professor Krinnell. As you will notice, there is a complete Universe in the micro cosmos, similar to the one in the sky, in shapes, sizes and distances, and they are both ruled by the same natural laws."

"Do you understand now why we told you that the law that unifies quantum mechanics and cosmology is God? These are the representations of his almighty divinity. Please also notice how other dimensions that materially and spiritually affect us directly have the same energetic origin as those which are integrated to our physical and spiritual body."

"Do you now understand the purpose of this explanation? All this is the rationalization of our being, our true ID is spiritual in the fifth dimension and this material body, which is our means for evolution, is in the fragile third dimension."

While Mirza spoke, Rahel showed Eric tables and charts so the images would be clear in his mind. Now Rahel took over:

"You must analyze and digest the integral process of the formation of matter as it is basic. The rest of knowledge starts with this. They are the building blocks for all you see and, besides, are the elements with which you live. You transform energy and understand how our universe in the third dimension is made. That is only one part of the energy and matter it is made up of."

Mirza packed everything and they returned slowly while Eric tried to put his doubts in order.

"Don't worry, everything will come together in your mind and you will have no trouble remembering it. This is the basis of what we'll be seeing later," Rahel told him as he said goodbye.

After Mirza and Rahel had left in their pick-up truck, Eric stayed in his car, trying to arrange his thoughts and these new concepts in his mind. It was not easy to comprehend all that information in such a short time, but he realized he had to make an effort before a new encounter could be sought.

CHAPTER XIV

Higher life exists and vibrates above man,
but man does not know how to question it.
I ask men of science, but they only understand
that which is made of matter, not of the spirit,
as they will first need to discover their own spirit.

Pablo E. Hawnser

The fourth dimension has become a familiar word...
beginning with the ideal realism of Kant and Plato,
to the solution of problems of modern science,
the fourth dimension can become everything to everyone.

Stephen Weinberg

ENCOUNTER IN LA MARQUESA

The next meeting was set for the first Saturday in March to take place in the National Park of La Marquesa, on the road between Mexico City and Toluca. This location was chosen because Rahel needed to be near his space ship to be able to go to another meeting far away, as soon as this encounter had taken place.

Eric arrived on time and was ready to wait patiently when he saw his friends walking towards him. They looked like two tourists on a morning stroll in the woods. They had landed five kilometers away, near a lake at the edge of the village of Salazar. He went to meet them and their greeting was as friendly as always. They got comfortable near his car and the setting was just right for their talks. The morning sun was casting its warmth on the fresh dew on the trees.

Mirza decided to start the conversation this time and she transmitted: *"Do you have any questions regarding what we have covered up to today?"*

"Not only one....many!" remarked Eric. "But I don´t want to delay or change what may be your program for today. I know you don´t have much time. I can leave the questions for a later date. What is on the agenda for today?"

"For you to understand what was put forth last time, and to take a look at the participation of energy between the spirit and the charkas," Rahel answered.

"Fine," Eric got ready. "You were explaining the energy they use."

"Yes, I told you about the integration of quanta, but now let's deal with the spirit, the soul in the physical body and the senses. CHAKRAS are called the senses of the spirit, but in reality they are the centers of energy that capture cosmic energy in the form of quanta."

"The charkas transform these quanta in two types of rays which are the origin of light and heat."

"When two subatomic particles, the equivalent of second and third dimensions, unite, this is an electron and a negatron. When they intersect, they form a semi-stable union, due to an energy generated at this time called BULTIC RAYS, that are positive and the union is called ELECTRO-NEGATRON. (Figure No. 48)

249

FIGURE 48

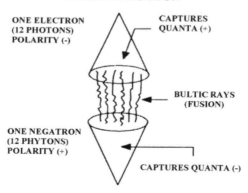

ELECTONEGATON

ONE ELECTRON
(12 PHOTONS)
POLARITY (-)

CAPTURES
QUANTA (+)

BULTIC RAYS
(FUSION)

ONE NEGATRON
(12 PHYTONS)
POLARITY (+)

CAPTURES QUANTA (-)

"On the other hand, combining equivalent particles of the third and fourth dimension results in another duo susceptible to be united and complement the previous one to maintain electronic equilibrium. This other duo is formed by PROTON and POSITRON particles generating energetic rays called STRANG RAYS having negative energy and the group is known as PROPOSITRON. (Figure No. 49)

FIGURE 49

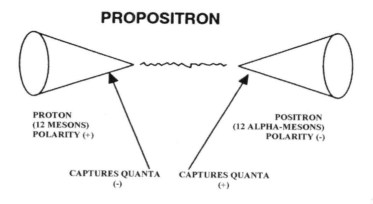

PROPOSITRON

PROTON
(12 MESONS)
POLARITY (+)

POSITRON
(12 ALPHA-MESONS)
POLARITY (-)

CAPTURES QUANTA
(-)

CAPTURES QUANTA
(+)

THE CHAKRAS

"Chakras are whirlpools of energy that operate in the fourth dimension; each one is a CYTOBARIC QUANTIMONIUM. The difference between each lies in how they are integrated. Remember the number of integers refers to the quantity of elemental particles that characterize the subatomic particles, with which we formed "duos" between the third and fourth dimensions."

"Let's also remember that the electronegatron duo is made up of one ELECTRON (a subatomic particle of the third dimension) and one NEGATRON (a subatomic particle of the fourth dimension). The ELECTRON is formed by photons and the NEGATRON is formed by pions."

"The quantity of photons and pions must be the same and these, also, should have an INTEGRATION NUMBER of between 3 and 12 to be stable. This means the "duo" must have the same amount of photons and pions to be in balance."

"When these two "duos" of subatomic particles (electro negatrons and propositrons), made up of the combination of particles of the third and fourth dimension are intersected, they form a balanced group called NEUTRONIUM." (Figure No. 50)

FIGURE 50

NEUTRONIUM

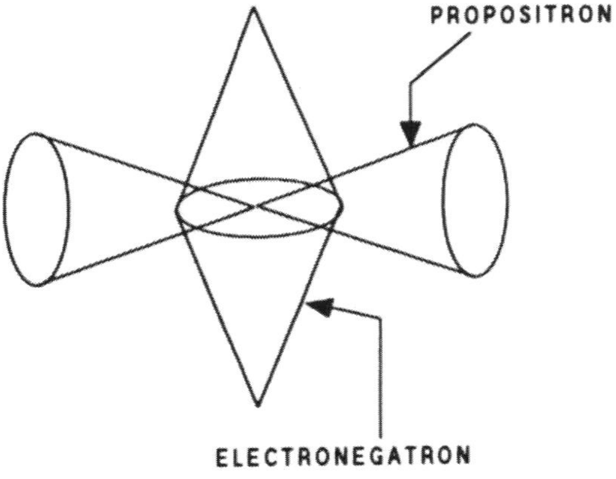

PROPOSITRON

ELECTRONEGATRON

251

"This group formed by four NEUTRONIA is called CYTOBARIC QUANTIMONIUM. Both the electro negatron and the propositron that integrate a NEUTRONIUM must have the same number of integers. The neutronia that unite to form the CYTOBARIC must also have the same number of integers in order to be stable. If the numbers are different they do not unite. To form a harmonious and balanced group, the NEUTRONIUM must have the same numbers of integers in all its particles."

"Are you following me, Eric?"

Yes, Rahel, I understand. They are the elements of quantum mechanics."

"Good. Let's continue. There are two energies that generate in the QUANTINOMIUM: KUM, the magnetic energy and KEMIUM, the static energy."

"The NEUTRONIUM is, then, a generator of energy formed by a combination of particles in balance of the third and fourth dimension."

"Now look at these illustrations. The electronic arch comes together through a magnetic field with static electricity integrated by the Kum and Kemium lines. This group of energy has emissions of luminescent and thermal radiations." (Figure No. 51)

FIGURE 51

CYTOBARIC QUANTINOMIUM

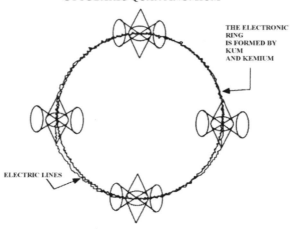

THE ELECTRONIC
RING
IS FORMED BY
KUM
AND KEMIUM

ELECTRIC LINES

"This is a CHAKRA. A real whirlpool of energy; and there are seven, whose performances depend on the intensity of the neutronium and quantum charges caught in the center of the cytobaric ring. You can see the positions of the charkas in relation to the physical body and the energies they work with in the following chart." (Chart No. 9)

The names of the charkas mentioned here are those you know, as this topic has been widely discussed on Earth, especially by people from the East, who have always given them characteristics of parapsychological phenomena, magic, esoteric or, in the best of cases, of metaphysical mystery. All this is not so. It´s just the physical anatomy of a spiritual body."

CHART NO. 9

THE CHACRAS

	NAME	MANIFESTATION	INTENSITY NO. OF PETALS	LOCATION	PLEXUS	COLOR
1	MULHADARA	SEXUAL	4	LOWER PART OF BODY SEXUAL	SEXUAL	RED
2	MANIPURA	EMOTIONAL	8	NAVEL	SOLAR	GREEN
3	SWADHISTANA	TEMPERAMENTAL	6	BETWEEN LIVER & SPLEEN	SPLENIC	YELLOW
4	ANAHATA	DEPRESSION & FEAR	16	NODULE OF ASHOW TAWARA	CARDIAC	WHITE
5	VISHUDA	AMBITION	12	THYROID	THYROIDAL	BLUE
6	ACKNACHACKRA	INTELLECTUAL	2	HYPOPHYSIS	CEREBRAL	ORANGE
7	SHAHASRARA	SPIRITUAL	1000	PINEAL GLAND	MENTAL	VIOLET

"In the diagram, you can see that their positions are also near the important physical organs, as these are located within the plexus of energetic influence of the chakras. (Figure No. 52).

253

FIGURE 52

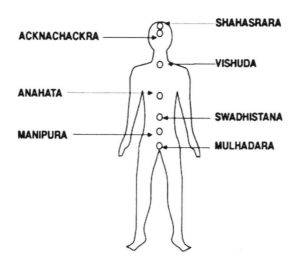

"The aural cocoon is the magnetic field of the soul, and it is formed by the energetic fields of the chakras. The cartic body is nothing more than a magnetic field formed by electrical and electronic currents of the physical body in the third dimension." (Figure No. 53)

FIGURE 53

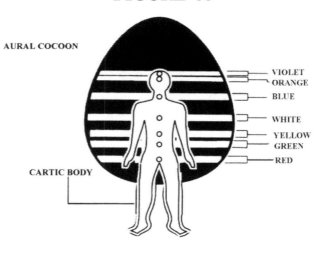

"Important things should be explained in a simple way. It is easier and the mind can understand them better. I will try to be more graphic."

"A chakra is a whirlpool of energy, as I have said, but if you could see it, it would be shaped like a flower; like a bellflower with a carnation in the center, whose petals resemble those of a daisy. The cone would be as long as your index finger and the corolla of petals would open up to be the size of your hand. At the base, there is a stem to its point of origin. All the petals act as antennas to capture and emit energy. (Figure 54 and 55)

FIGURE 54

**APPROXIMATE SHAPE
LONGITUDINAL CUT**

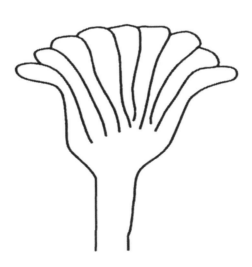

FIGURE 55

TYPICAL ASPECTS OF THE CHAKRAS

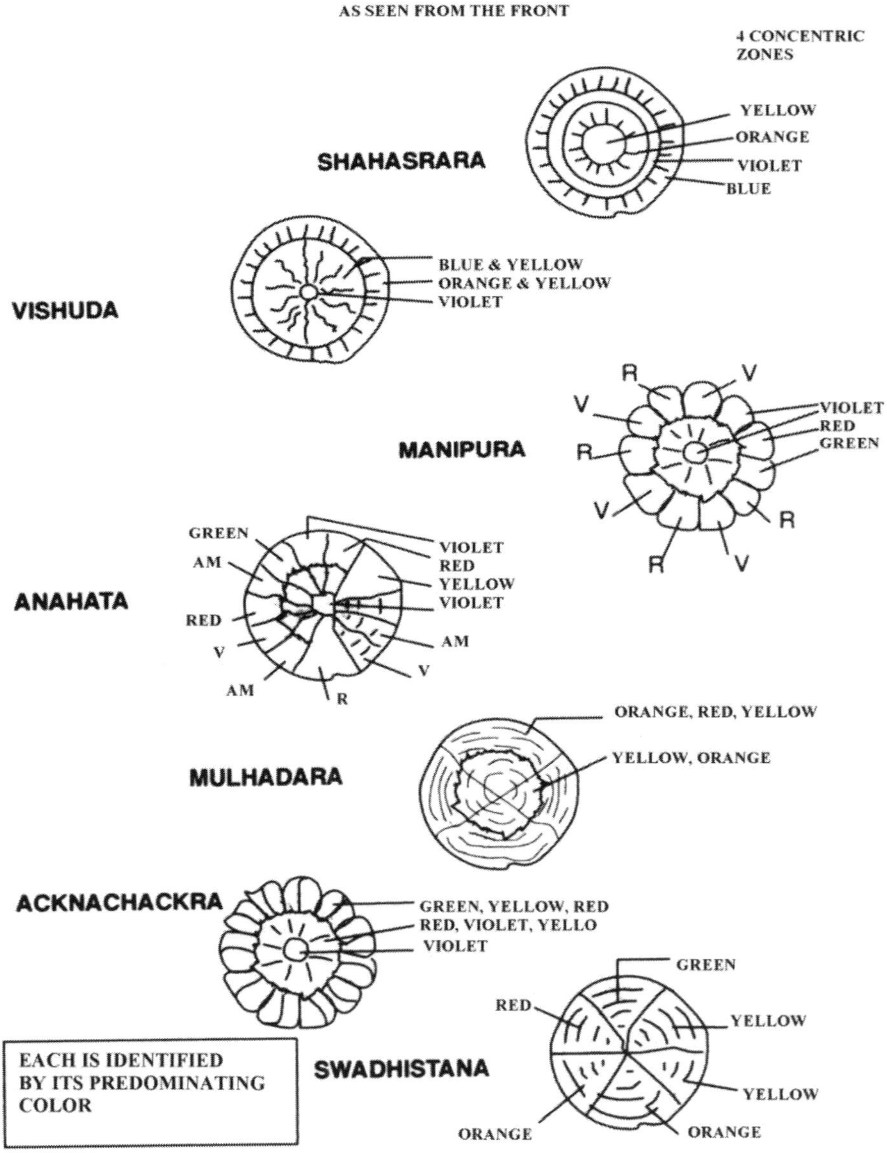

AS SEEN FROM THE FRONT

4 CONCENTRIC ZONES

SHAHASRARA
- YELLOW
- ORANGE
- VIOLET
- BLUE

VISHUDA
- BLUE & YELLOW
- ORANGE & YELLOW
- VIOLET

MANIPURA
- VIOLET
- RED
- GREEN

R V
V R
R V

ANAHATA
GREEN
AM
RED
V
AM   R
- VIOLET
- RED
- YELLOW
- VIOLET
- AM

MULHADARA
- ORANGE, RED, YELLOW
- YELLOW, ORANGE

ACKNACHACKRA
- GREEN, YELLOW, RED
- RED, VIOLET, YELLO
- VIOLET

SWADHISTANA
- GREEN
- RED
- YELLOW
- YELLOW
- ORANGE
- ORANGE

EACH IS IDENTIFIED
BY ITS PREDOMINATING
COLOR

256

"Each chakra uses a different energy, but they are all linked through one, or up to four electronic channels, where they interact. (Figure No. 56)

FIGURE 56

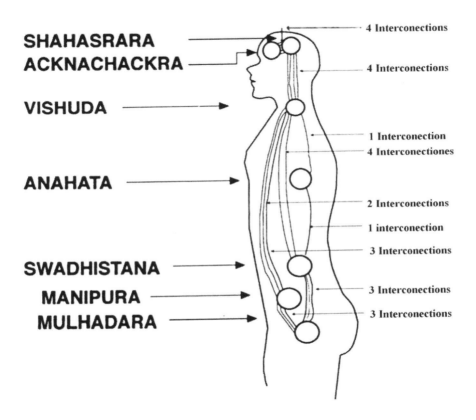

"The external function of the chakras is to capture vibrations and energy, transform them and energetically feed the plexus in their area of influence. The sum of their energetic radiations form a sort of magnetic field around the body that concentrates into an ovoid and becomes a protective cocoon for the physical body and a multiple antenna for the spiritual body.

The normal size of the cocoon, when it is at its smallest, could be described as covering the area within the extended length of your arms, from your legs up to above your head. This luminous and energetic field constitutes the AURA."

"The aura must not be confused with the cartic body. This is the magnetic field of the physical body which is the result of the sum of all the magnetic fields of all the internal conducts."

"We know the physical body moves through the electric impulses of the motor nerves and, when acting in the packs of muscular fibers provoke the muscle to shrink, and thereby transform electric energy into mechanic energy to start up all our voluntary or automatic movements."

"Also, all the organs of the body, activated by electric energy, are real chemical laboratories. As well as to move liquids internally through electro-osmosis and electro-dialysis, in chemical reactions through electrolysis and the transformations of electric to thermal energy, etc. All this is monitored electronically and generates the cartic body, the magnetic field that covers the physical body." (Figure No. 57)

FIGURE 57

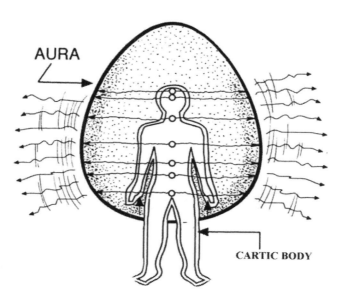

AURA

CARTIC BODY

"The spirit attracts 3 basic energies for its nourishment and transformation:

COSMIC Energy. It is received through the crowning chakra called SHAHASRARA, found at the top of the head. The flower is approximately 10 to 15 cms. above the cranium, and is placed facing up as an antenna.

SOLAR Energy. It is received by MANIPURA, in the center of the body. The flower is on the skin, at the level of the navel and it opens out toward the front.

SERPENTINE Energy. This is the energy radiated by the planet. It is received by the MULHADAKA chakra, found in the lower part of the body. The flower is facing the ground. (Figure No. 58)

FIGURE 58

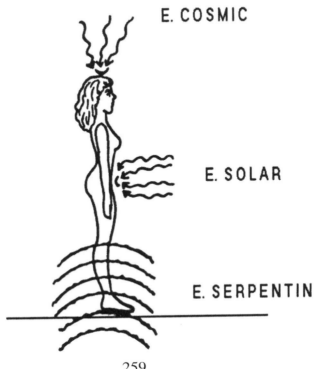

E. COSMIC

E. SOLAR

E. SERPENTIN

"The three energies are transformed and interact all along the axis, from Mulhadara to Shahasrara and they stimulate the other chakras. The current established between these chakras is represented in the symbol found in the following figure. (Figure 59)

FIGURE 59

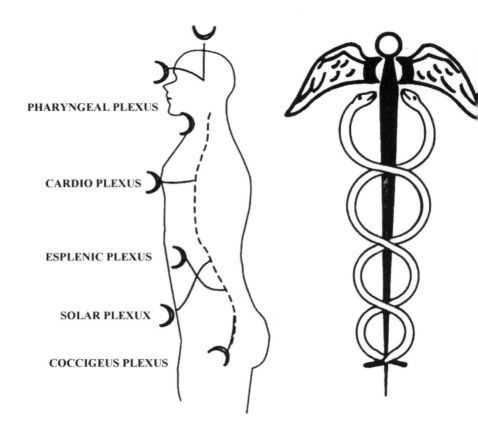

"Now let's analyze each of them:

SHAHASRARA. This chakra, also called pineal, is located precisely over the pineal gland in the center of the brain. It extends its flower to 10 or 15 centimeters above the cranium, attracts cosmic energy and has a spiritual essence.

ACKNACHACKRA. This is the mental chakra, located on the forehead in front of the brain, between the frontal lobes. The cone comes out between the eyebrows and opens up 3 cms. from the forehead. It was baptized as "The Third Eye" by Orientals, but this is not exact; as it does not see nor attract clairvoyant images. It is a sender and receiver of mental energy. It got this name, as in the end, images are captured in the brain. Its influence is mental.

VISHUDA. This chakra is located between the spinal column and the thyroid gland. The cone or flower is in the throat, the stem penetrates all the way to the third cervical vertebra. It influences the glands and is thyroidal and pharyngeal plexus.

ANAHATA. This chakra begins near the spinal column, at the eighth cervical vertebra. The stem goes to the front and the flower stays on the chest over the heart. This is why it is called the cardiac plexus. It influences the heart, lungs and arms. The flower faces the front.

MANIPURA. This chakra begins at the eighth thoracic vertebra. The flower, however, is presented on the navel as the stem curves down to exit the skin further down. This is the solar plexus as it attracts energy from the sun.

SWADHISTANA. This chakra begins in front of the spinal column at the first lumbar vertebra. The stem is short and the flower faces the front, inside the body, between the sternum and the navel. It influences the internal organs and is known as the splenic plexus.

MULHADARA. This chakra begins at eh fourth lumbar vertebra. The stem is short, and the flower faces downwards and remains outside the body between the excreting and sexual organs. It attracts serpentine energy from the planet. Its influence is sexual and the lower extremities. It is the coccygeal or sexual plexus."

"As the being evolves, the spirit develops its gifts and these are manifested through the chakras´ performance, that influence the physical body. Telepathic capacity for emission or reception is

261

acquired or increased, as is the gift of healing, clairvoyance, etc. We'll talk about this later, as it is especially important and illustrative."

"The energetic whirlpools, which are the chakras, will be manifested more clearly in the physical body, as another proof of spiritual coexistence."

"The aural cocoon can be defined as the magnetic field formed by the conduits between the chakras."

"Feelings and emotions, in the spiritual mind, produce alterations that are manifested by emissions of energy from the chakras. The characteristics and intensity depend on the feeling that generates them--from love to hate, going through hope, illusion, sadness, fear, etc.

"The emissions radiate from the chakras as a reaction of cause and effect. These energetic emissions act in the cells at the third dimension through the ribosomes and, provoke the generation of biochemical elements. These result from special sequences of amino acids, such as the protein polymers, enzymes and chains of polypeptides synthesized by RNA. Acting within certain selected circuits of the components, they take the protein signal to a prefixed destination."

"There they cause a physically detectable reaction that the human being can identify with feelings he is spiritually experiencing. In other words, the chakras manifest themselves physically making us "feel" emotions."

"The cocoon presents colored horizontal bands named "khans". These are the result of the direct emission of each chakra. The bands also show the characteristic color and vibrations of each chakra, the influence of the magnetic fields in the energized organs, in such a way they can be detected as a group. Manifestations of any electromagnetic dysfunction in the organs can also be identified through the aura."

"The dysfunctions are shown when continuity, color and homogeneity are altered. The bands of color of the chakras can show the presence of non-harmonious vibrations which alter their appearance in the plexus under their influence."

"The bands or khans will be influenced by the energized organs of the chakra. Alterations induced by the dysfunction of these physical organs will appear within the bands affecting the cartic body which, in turn will impact the aura electro-magnetically."

"In a not too distant future, the aura will, this way, help to determine medical diagnoses of the dysfunctional organs. A computer, after identifying intensities, colors and vibrations of the aura, will not only diagnose, but also propose a treatment and/or the proper medication for healing."

"When a band or khan is affected by the electromagnetic influence of the dysfunctional organ, the corresponding chakra detects the variation in the polarity and voltage in the aura. To counterbalance this, it increases the intensity of its emission and stimulates a similar phenomenon in the other chakras. The result is as follows: when reaching the limit of the aural cocoon, the energetic emissions breakdown into subatomic particles at the second level, which is from partons to energetic fastens and quanta. (Figure 60)

FIGURE 60

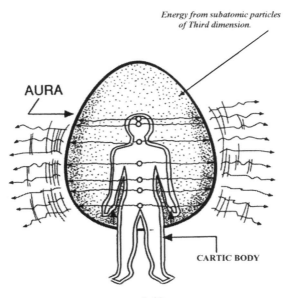

Energy from subatomic particles
of Third dimension.

AURA

CARTIC BODY

263

"These subatomic particles are attracted and absorbed by the physical body through the nerve endings of the hands and feet. This is why a sick person unconsciously tends to lie in a fetal position to remain within his aural cocoon and thereby absorb more energy. These nerve endings are located at the tip of the fingers and palm of the hands, and to a lesser degree, on the soles of the feet."

"Healing by self-energetization is similar to acupuncture. The subatomic particles are the raw material for cellular reproduction and energy tends to balance and harmonize the dysfunctional organ. The energy attracted by the britis reaches the mental spheres and closes the circuit so the chakras can be activated from there to correct the dysfunction."

"The acupuncture treatments you use are taking advantage of the interaction between electric energy and biochemical reactions of the same organism to recover the bioelectronic equilibrium and thereby, health, as the dysfunction is corrected.

"The energetic emissions of ACKNACHACKRA can be directed by the mind and through the eyes, either unconsciously or consciously. This energetic emission of vibrations can penetrate the aural cocoon and are caught by the aura."

"Anyone can determine if the vibrations he receives are good or bad by measuring them spiritually."

"The aura acts like an antenna attracting vibrations that are emitted subconsciously by the ACKNACHACKRA of someone else. If this person has bad intentions, the vibrations are contaminated as he cannot avoid producing unharmonious parasitic vibrations that use the energetic emission of acknachackra as the bearer wave."

"When these are received and analyzed in the spiritual brain, they are sent to the mind of the receiver with an instinctive rejection toward the sender, even before having physical proof to form a reasonable judgment regarding these unharmonious vibrations."

"You call it a "sixth sense"—based on intuition-- acceptance or rejection of a person is a very common and highly developed skill on Earth. Normally, this information is revealed unconsciously. The result is well known, judgments made based on this spiritual instinct are more on target."

"When we stare at a person, we are unconsciously sending an energetic emission of varying intensity, depending on our interest in that person. The receiver will "feel" someone watching him and will usually look around to find out who it is. This reaction is done unconsciously through the aura. (Figure. 61)

"I will repeat: the aura is an antenna that attracts waves and vibrations within a scope and range that are beyond man´s physical capacity in the third dimension."

FIGURE 61

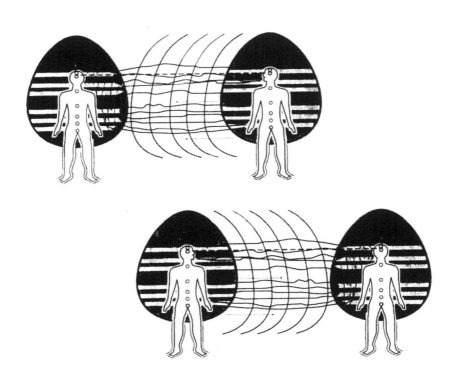

"A karmic vibration occurs when negative feelings such as hate, envy, jealously or greed exist. These can increase due to anger or if uncontrolled sexual excitement is present. This vibration is not in harmony with the Universe, but can be for the souls who do not have physical bodies and are under the gravitational effects of their karma."

"This vibration unbalances the human being's will in a natural reaction to seek justification for his attitude that can become psychopathologic, and is usually found in aggression. This behavior provokes depression, anxiety, headaches and neurasthenia."

"When human behavior goes against laws that regulate life, a karmic vibration is also generated that will leave a magnetic print on the mental spheres. For example, stealing provokes the feelings of fear and risk, which produce an activation of unharmonious energy that is physically "felt". Adrenalin flows in the blood and a feeling of excitement, similar to that provoked by drugs occurs. The human being is conscious of his actions, but his free will welcomes the sensations of vile pleasure."

"Souls having karmic charges or "disturbed souls", upon perceiving that vibration, may go to that person and increase the intensity of these feelings causing greater mental imbalance."

"A person who generates karma in this way will need help to correct his attitude toward positive and harmonious energy of DARMA, that must be born out of love after reflection and repentance. If not, physical pain will be necessary to aid him to attain equilibrium and not become a disturbed spirit if he dies while under unbalanced spirituality."

"If a person lives in harmony, the DARMA keeps clear intercommunications between the spiritual brain and the mind, and the mental spheres function perfectly, inciting the chakras to keep the aura saturated with positive energy. The aura can grow and its magnetic influence can be detected by the auras of those close to it, even several meters away, as they perceive the positive energy and want to get closer. Positive energy is love, light and spiritual sustenance."

"Clairvoyance and clairaudience are spiritual gifts; they attract vibrations, through the aura, that transmit images and sounds. Vibrations of very high frequency attracted by the chakras go to the spiritual brain to be identified, and in special circumstances can be transmitted to the physical brain to be identified by the mind."

"A human being can receive information in his physical brain, not necessarily coming from the senses. For example, if a person suddenly is risking his life, the impact is dramatic, and the images coming from his senses to his physical brain plus his thoughts at that moment, are simultaneously received by his spiritual brain. These vibrations can be retransmitted at the speed of light."

"These waves had a destination, which can be reached instantly, no matter at what distance. The recipient may be the person remembered during this emergency, but can also be someone close (mother-child) and not necessarily called upon."

"They can also impact matter located at the scene and remain vibrating for some time. In this case, if someone having these highly developed spiritual gifts passes by, he too may also attract them."

"When these vibrations are received by that person's aura, these are transmitted by the chakras to the spiritual brain and from there, sent to the physical brain transdimensionally as occurs with messages from our conscience."

"The recipient considers these images as a "vision", similar to the sudden remembrance of a dream, having the impact and clarity that the emotional strength of the transmission can convey. The brain immediately analyzes and links them together."

"In this phenomenon, the transmission is from spirit to spirit. It is manifested interdimensionally, where up to 3 can participate: the physical body, the spiritual soul, in the third and fourth dimensions; but also there is an element that participates from the fifth dimension as it is in constant contact with the other two, through the conscience."

"When the physical being receives the information and is instantly conscious of it, it will act; and independently from the physical reaction provoked by adrenalin, his spiritual being will act through the plexus stimulating all the organs and systems of the body fully."

"All these metaphysical and parapsychological phenomena, are proof at the physical level in the third dimension of the coexistence of the fourth and fifth spiritual dimensions."

"That is the essence, Eric. The lesson consists in your being conscious of your spiritual reality. I repeat this so you can absorb it and see it as clearly as you see physical images with your own eyes."

"The spirit being manifested through the soul in the third and fourth dimensions occupies the same time-space as the physical body and it adapts to it as a liquid to its container, including clothes and objects used by the physical person, such as a watch, hat, boots, necklaces, earrings, etc. It is all kept within the cartic body, which is its magnetic field in the third dimension. This is why when a spirit absorbs ectoplasmic energy (prana), if this is able to form a superficial film, only a few microns thick, but enough to reflect light, it can be seen and will usually take the shape the physical being the soul lived in, even down to the attire they preferred in life or were buried in."

"When the soul is freed upon the death of the physical body, it must leave the planet´s surface, beyond the force of gravity and get to the stratosphere—the last physical place of the planet—to continue to its destination to join its spirit in the fifth dimension. When this cannot happen due to its karmic charges, it becomes trapped in a state of physical flotation and mental darkness."

"The soul charged with plasmatic energy, when it leaves the lifeless physical body, does have weight and this is not more than gravity caused by the ectoplasm it contains and belongs to the third dimension. The body looses weight, if only a few grams, when the soul leaves the body—this is physically palpable, which constitutes further proof of what we are analyzing."

"The soul will only be able to reach the fifth dimension when it has been freed of all karmas. This is state is known to religions as "Purgatory", "Limbo", or any other name given to the transit zone between Earth and Heaven, where restitution for sins is carried out, while being freed of karmic burdens."

"These regions are referred to in the different religions, but are never given an exact location. Even if it were known, it would be difficult to explain. Therefore, heaven, purgatory and hell were created, where rewards and punishments exist and these can only be given to physical beings."

"How can you define "heaven" and "hell" then?" asked Eric.

"We could say heaven is a beautiful place, the whole Universe. Heaven is where God is and the Universe is part of Him. Heaven is not a specific place, it is a spiritual state in a higher dimension to that of space-time, where perfection, kindness, purity and light exist. It is another dwelling different to the dimensions for evolution that were created for the life of the physical bodies of the third dimension in space-time."

"And we could define "hell" as the spiritual torment of a disturbed soul. A state of darkness, mental emptiness, horrible confusion, uncertainty, bewilderment of spiritual pain and suffering. Hell and death do not exist for the spirit, only transitory states of the soul during its evolution to acquire experience and wisdom."

"When souls are incarnated in a human being, they live a normal existence in a planet in evolution like this, and they can choose between:

a) Taking a path toward evolution through love. That is, living in harmony with the Universe around them according to their conscience, using their free will in such a way as to ascertain inner peace, giving and receiving love, or

b) Forgetting their conscience, acting selfishly for material gain, denying themselves the opportunity to conceive and comprehend their spiritual being.

"In this second option, maybe material success can be momentarily achieved, without honor and not caring about the cost of accumulated karma. Then, they choose pain and suffering to guide them to the same objective, which is spiritual evolution."

"Spirits who live in bodies, deaf to the conscience, see their human being taking advantage of evil, lies, greed and egotism. In their pride, they believe the end justifies the means, whichever these may be. Their goal is exclusively human, their greed is power and wealth with which they will have happiness on earth. The only thing they care about as they do not take their spiritual existence into consideration."

"These human beings have no scruples and walk over everyone else. Except in those rare instances when the spirit rebels and forces them back to sanity. What can be considered as their successes, if at the end of their life they are full of karma and the physical battle to free themselves of it will be their own hell?"

"They become disturbed spirits unable to rise above and spiritual pain is far greater than physical pain. When, at last, they are able to be conscious of their physical being, they want to comply with the laws of atonement. Every injustice and bitterness they have caused will be inflicted upon them."

"It will be a judgment based on self-analysis. Each spirit will be free of karma, when its own soul, no longer mentally confused, will identify its conscience and be able to exercise free will. Then, once again, it will have the opportunity to evolve. You can be sure, this time, it will be through love, and that divine energy will be the guide to continue the next steps to higher evolution."

"Do you understand now, why there is so much insistence in explaining the spirit? The New Era you are about to enter is that of spiritual conscience, even though you continue to be human beings in the third dimension on this planet of space-time evolution."

"Matter was created, in the Universe, to provide a temporary dwelling for the spirit that is part of God. We are His children. He is our Father Creator, of the real being who is spiritual and also creator of the material world that provides the means for evolution."

"Planets were created with infinite patience and wisdom. Human life is the hearth for the spirit, where it can experience needs, pain and satisfaction, all the result of thoughts and actions."

"Evolutionary spirits received the gift of free will. Acting freedly generates positive or negative vibrations in the fourth dimension which belongs to the souls."

"Positive vibrations are characteristic of the energetic emissions of the chakras, when actions taken with free will are in harmony with Universal Laws. This happens if the spirit´s performance, through the human soul, follows the voice of his conscience."

"Negative vibrations are generated when the actions of the human being are for material gain and against the recommendations of the conscience, and naturally, also the laws of the Universe."

270

"In these cases, the human being is dominated by interests that demand satisfaction for physical needs. Negative energy is very strong and can easily impose itself on human frailty."

Those who decide on traveling the right path, with honesty, justice, and love for fellow man, create positive vibrations. Those who prefer to turn a deaf ear to their conscience and are inclined, through selfishness, to material gain create negative forces."

"The positive and negative vibrations they have and are emitted by those spirits are perceived through the aura by human beings, whose lives are affected by them."

"When these are negative, they incite humans, who already have negative tendencies, to evil, abuse and injustice to support their natural greed. They believe they deserve their personal achievements and thus go on searching for more victories and eventually, join the ranks of fanatics, with selfishness and pride. These humans are easy prey to vice and base instincts. Since they have many ideas in common, they attract disturbed spirits, who are also under heavy burdens of negativity and unconsciously spur them on to continue those vibrations."

"The light of our Heavenly Father is love, but human beings must choose their paths through their free will. Do they want happiness? All they have to do is love, be understanding and have mercy for their fellow men. Do they want tears, bitterness and desolation? Well, let them continue in egotism, hypocrisy and material vanity."

"Spiritual greatness is living within the laws of love, loving truth and justice. Human beings radiate those energies through their aura, whether they live positive or negative lives."

"When the human being they inhabit dies, these souls with negative burdens become dwellers of darkness. In their confusion, their spiritual mind is blocked and no longer knows what life or death is. They take advantage of the desperation of those beings who, having a physical body, can provide a means of expression. When they can do this, they can perturb the peace and cloud the mind of the being they have approached."

"For all this, your brothers need to connect to their own spirit and become conscious of real life. With this in mind, I am trying to explain your own spiritual existence in the easiest and most human way possible."

"The main factor that hinders an adequate evolution in order to enter the New Era is the mistaken concept between giving and taking. This is why your brothers always think materialistically. They want to give or receive material goods or the equivalent: money. This is not the way. Love must given in friendship, company, knowledge, understanding, consolation.....and this does not cost money, but it will help them and those around them."

"Look, everybody wants everything, to have and get more each time, because they want happiness for themselves and their loved ones, believing happiness is wealth. They understand wealth as the accumulation of material goods."

"That is the mistake. Happiness cannot be bought. It is a spiritual state. It is transmitted to the physical body as health, tranquility and harmony. There can be joy and excitement or peace and physical rest. Both are compatible with spiritual peace and the feeling of happiness comes from harmonious spiritual vibrations. There is only one coin that can buy happiness, and that is LOVE."

"The problem is happiness does not depend on how much one has, but how much to give and give more each time. HAPPINESS is not receiving. IT IS GIVING, and the only thing one can offer without restraint, is love. Whoever gives love, whether in the form of help, company or consolation will receive as a natural consequence. Whatever it receives will be sincere gratitude in all its manifestations: love. That is the secret, Eric. First you must give, but spontaneously, unconditionally, without expecting anything in return. To give for the pleasure of giving. Natural law will return love in the form of gratitude from whoever was benefited or simply for the intimate satisfaction of having had the privilege of giving love. Also, that love never ends, the more you give, the more you will have."

"Do you want a physical explanation for this? Love is pure energy. You receive it directly through your spiritual chakra from the cosmos. It is transformed by your spirit: one part you spend on the wear and tear you may exert they your physical body to give help; and the other, you pass on directly as energy projected mentally from Acknachackra. You emit spiritual energy with your words and good wishes. Physically, you can transmit through your britis as comforting energy for healing."

"When you learn to attract cosmic energy, you stimulate the general process of interaction between the chakras through their lines of communication and you can, at will, obtain energetic projection through Acknachadkra and through britis."

"The projected energy is perceived as thermal radiation and contains healing properties. It is the result of the combination of cosmic, solar and serpentine energy, interacting and being transformed in the chakras. This causes a vibration frequency that can be beneficial to the physical body, as transmitted through the plexus."

"Tell me, Eric, when you read that Jesus cured the sick and even brought Lazarus back to life. Did you believe it? Or, did you think they were just historical allegories of a legend, distorted through 2,000 years of human intervention?"

"Well, let me confirm it. It is true. This can be done by you and your brothers, although on a different scale. Jesus attracted such an amount of cosmic energy, his aura was saturated. Just by wishing it, with a look, he could project, through Acknachackra, so much energy, those beings were overwhelmed. Also, if in addition, he touched them, an avalanche of energy burst forth from his britis."

"But, let's see how the "miracle" physically occurs: Remember how cosmic energy is transformed as simple elements accumulate to form matter?"

"Matter is integrated by molecules of specific atoms of one element. But atoms are made up of subatomic particles that are not of any particular element, like bricks that can be used in any building. Likewise, subatomic particles, depending on their polarity, can integrate atoms of the third or fourth dimension."

"Remember partons are an essential unit. They integrate a basic energy other energies can join. They are made up of elements to build cells, which are the essential units of organic life."

"Healthy cells are in harmony, the union of the electronic charges and all their vibrations are balanced and cohesive."

"Sick cells are dysfunctional, they do not have electronic balance, they are not stable, their vibrations are unharmonious, they tend to self-destruct or grow and reproduce defectively, like tumors do not have complete and correct genetic information. There is no order in these cells and, therefore their life vibrations are not in harmony with the Universe."

"When a sick cell is found in an energy vibrating in harmony and life, it tends to disintegrate. An involuntary process if caused. The atoms disintegrate because there is no exothermal reaction as there is no sudden desegregation. The "anti-matter" of the fourth dimension neutralizes and annuls with equal force and different polarity to the subatomic elements, and the atoms dissolve easily."

"This involuntary process transforms matter in subatomic elements that if each were in equilibrium would tend to reintegrate to form matter once again. The elements of the third dimension are attracted by healthy cells for nourishment and these multiply harmoniously to substitute missing tissue, integrated by dysfunctional cells. Acids and proteins are then generated to serve the new matter."

"In the previous process, dysfunctional cells, without witchcraft, magic or tricks can be transformed within universal laws of physics, to provide the elements to generate new healthy cells."

"This physical phenomenon, apparently so incredible, is natural. It is a biophysical reaction provoked psychokinetically at a quantum level. It was not possible to understand, although observed by many and felt by the sick."

"When a psychotronic phenomenon occurs, it is the dimensional interaction between your physical and spiritual body. A cosmo-electro-chemical-biological reaction takes place, when the chakras, aura, plexus and your mind intervene with the physic-biologic-glandular and neurons of the physical body. The phenomenon is also psychokinetic at a human level, but 2,000 years ago it wasn't even parapsychological nor metaphysical. It was simply a "miracle".

"You would think Jesus' magic would go against the laws of nature, wouldn't you? He took advantage of them. Remember, these were not laws made up in a hurry to solve an immediate problem or to make his mission easier. They are laws that exist as does the Universe around us and were created by our Heavenly Father."

"The same logic applies to concerns of the spirit. There are no miracles. Everything has a rational explanation and the fact you don't know it, does not change the result."

Rahel stopped for a moment so Eric could catch his breath and have a few seconds for reflection. Then Mirza added, her lovely voice and her participation were a welcome rest.

"Remember, Eric, when we spoke of miracles in relation to civilization and the technological advances of mankind? Well, this is another of those "natural miracles". When a mother caresses a weeping child, even without being aware of it, she is passing on healing energy. The energy will do its job and at the same time will calm the pain. The body will heal as it recuperates harmony to carry out its endeavors."

"When you hurt yourself, automatically, even without rational thoughts, you apply healing energy with your hands. It works as you massage or caress the body part and feel the beneficial effect. The same thing happens if someone else does it. Wanting you to heal is projecting love, energy through the Acknachackra. The physically healing energy of your hands called psychokinesis."

"Well, even though it seems magical, it is really only natural physics. But Rahel was referring to spiritual physics when talking about love. Let me add something regarding your brothers' attitude towards wealth, understanding by wealth, the accumulation of goods that provide them with safety and power."

"Rahel told you to give. The rich have, but do not give, preferring to invest to obtain more. You well know that true wealth is not measured by gold. It can be stolen or lost; but, let's say you have it safe and sound, it will not help you spiritually."

"The love you receive from those beings around you cannot be bought with gold. Love begets love. You cannot take your gold with you when your body and soul separate. Which would your wealth be then?"

'Spiritual wealth will be the love you have amassed. It will be the capital to pay your spiritual debts or karma. The accumulated darma is positive energy and it will neutralize the negative energy you may have due to your human behavior and negative actions carried out with your free will."

"Your body's death will cause the judgment of your soul. It is facing your conscience to analyze your life. At that moment you will be alone, your spirit before its karmas and its own judgment of conscience. And, I can assure you, you will want to change all your fortune for the love you could have received from the most insignificant beings you met in your world. That love, the divine energy, will be your spiritual treasure to help you overcome the transition."

"Remember well, Eric, that is the wealth you must treasure and increase; this will be what helps your spirit, when nobody else can."

"Eric, tell me," asked Rahel. "How is it possible that such simple things be so incredible and practically impossible for you? All your mankind is on the verge of an apocalypse and there is no change. On the contrary, you are all perfectly ready and willing to fight among yourselves, even to the point of destruction, in order to take away what others have and thereby obtain more power."

"When you come together as groups, it is even worse. All proportion is lost when racial, religious or political issues are at stake. Charged with negative energy and incited by disturbed spirits, they become savage beasts, renouncing all spiritual feelings which are the difference between animals and man."

"The greater part of mankind is manipulated and subjected through ignorance. Religions pretend to show the way, but human fanatics spoil any good intentions there may be. Humans will happily go to their deaths for causes, supposedly in the name of justice, and they will never know who benefited from their sacrifices."

"Well, enough for now. As always, please try to analyze and understand what we have taught you today. In our next meeting we will discuss the workings of the mind, which you will see, is another proof of the existence of the spirit."

Mirza was ready to leave, as the conversation had been longer than planned and Rahel had another appointment. Both bid their farewells and Eric, though mental telepathy, requested permission to accompany them to their space ship.

Rahel quickly pondered the situation and transmitted: "Everything seems very peaceful here, however, you are very valuable to us and would not like anything to happen to you. I would prefer you to go first. You will have a chance to see the space ship later, as I know this is what you want."

Eric agreed, but replied, "If anyone were watching us and had bad intentions, both you and Mirza would also be vulnerable. Mirza is very attractive, and this area is very isolated. Don´t you think she is safer having two men at her side?"

"Thank you, Eric, you are very kind," Mirza said. "But you forget who we are. We would never hurt anyone, evern if it were deserved. Stay calm, you can be sure we are protected. You do believe me, don´t you?"

"Yes, Mirza, I do. I know you are in a hurry. Maybe next time you can explain to me how that protection comes about. Would you, please?"

"I promise, Eric, just as I promise we´ll meet again in less than 30 days. Is this all right?"

Mirza and Rahel left calmly. Eric watched them until they disappeared from sight, and started his car. As he got on the highway, he received a message, through mental telepathy: "Thank you, Eric. See you next time!"

CHAPTER XV

There is progress as people increase
their scientific knowledge,
but what knowledge is this,
that the more men learn, the further they are
from spiritual truth, the source of life?

B.T.L

Science is light, and light is life,
health and peace.
If we not enjoy these benefits;
if instead of light there is darkness,
instead of peace there is chaos.
Then it becomes imperative
to let our conscience be our guide.

Pablo E. Hawnser

OUR SCIENCE

It had become quite natural for Eric to live and think in accordance with Rahel´s teachings. He was thrilled to learn and understand everything he was being taught; to be prepared and better comprehend the knowledge transmitted to him. In his free time, he read about scientific progress that would help to adjust his knowledge of advanced terrestrial physics to that of extra-terrestrial origin taught by Rahel, Mirza and Professor Krinnell.

278

It was comforting to notice how scientists like Einstein seemed to go in the same direction, but kept their eyes on the larger picture. Not only did they concentrate on solving specific details of their theories, but also explored the whole system to understand creation and the truth of our existence.

Other scientists, however, looked for the satisfaction of solving the details by themselves, as they were more concerned in investigating the "what" and "how", rather than searching for the "why".

In his research on the different areas and theories of "terrestrial" physics and cosmology, he began to understand that they all seem to go in the same direction, and never contradicted the teachings he received, at any time. On the contrary, they complemented each other. From this perspective, he seemed to better comprehend that phenomenon that, many times scientists of different disciplines are struggling to understand and explain.

The Nemesis Theory of Richard Muller was very much on his mind. It coincided with what Professor Krinnell had mentioned about the comets. Richard Muller is a professor at the University of California and was a disciple of Louis Alvarez (who, in 1977, put forth the theory that dinosaurs disappeared due to an asteroid colliding with Earth). Muller wrote a book about the theory that there is a star associated to the Sun and that both rotate interconnecting orbits.

He named that star, Nemesis, and estimated it was one twentieth the size of the Sun and believed it to be the cause of a true rainfall of meteorites and asteroids on our solar system in approximate periods of 26 million years. Obviously, some of them can reach Earth with fatal consequences for living beings. David Ramp and John Sepkoski were the paleontologists who discovered that there were signs on Earth of catastrophes approximately every 26 million years, supported by Dave Russell and Stephen J. Gould.

The orbit of Nemesis would have a trajectory of some 176,000 astronomical units, according to Keppler´s Law of Gravity. These are equivalent to the distance light would travel in 2.8 years. In astronomy, this means the distance of 176,000 AV is the length of an orbit where this star can accompany the Sun without being captured by other stars.

Massive destructions of life, in the history of our planet, have occurred caused by a similar phenomenon. No less than eight times in the last, more or less, 250 million years. Iridium layers found in several strata of terrestrial cortex indicate these were caused by Nemesis and its asteroids. This star must have the same isotopes there are on the surface of the Earth, as it has been a part of our Sun for 4,500 million years.

Geologists, Digby McLaren and Carl Orth, found signs of iridium on the cortex of the Earth at the end of the Cretasic Period (65 million years ago), at the end of the Eocene Period (35 million years ago), at the end of the Devonian Period (365 million years ago) and another layer, 90 million years ago. Studies of the effects of the dust provoked by cataclysms have been called Nuclear Winters. They are considered to be the cause of the massive disappearance of life on this planet.

Eric smiled to himself at the coincidence; after all, if Muller´s theory was correct, what could we do when the cycle came round again?

He also researched the Werner Heisenberg quantum theory, and The World of Elemental Particles by Kenneth W. Hord, a nuclear physicist from Brandeis University, where the size, mass and timing of the micro universe is discussed. Also, he studied Dr. Ernest Rutherford´s experiments and those of Cook and McLennan regarding the radioactive elements and the groupings of electrified particles that already foresee profound modifications of the principles of physics.

He also thought about the quarks of our scientists and the partons of Professor Krinnell, on the theory of the electrons and positrons of Dirac, on the distinction of the past and the future of Richard Feyman of Cornell University and the anti-matter particles.

He pondered the theory of Nobel prize winner, Francois Jacob, on his book The Possible and The Actual; on the experiences of Dr. Rubbia and Van Der Meere of SCRN (Switzerland´s Center for Nuclear Research); where the efforts of 120 physicists of 20 universities and many engineers, in the summer of 1983, were successful in producing anti-matter with the collisions provoked in the Cyclotron (accelerator of particles) of Switzerland´s Center for Nuclear Studies; and on The First Three Minutes of Creation, by the

Nobel prize in Physics, Stephen Weinberg and his work on nuclear interactions.

He meditated on Ernest Rutherford´s extraordinary inspiration when conceiving the Theory of the Atom and the contribution of George Danov regarding electrons. In addition, Max Planck´s large contributions, particularly his second Law of Thermodynamics. And of course, Einstein´s magnificent ability to prove the existence of space-time and of his sublime humility in recognizing that:

"THE DEEPEST SCIENTIFIC KNOWLEDGE MUST ENABLE MANKIND TO ACCEPT GOD, WHEN UNDERSTANDING THE KNOWLEDGE OF TRUTH SURPASSES THE RATIONAL CONCEPT OF OUR EXISTENCE."

He reflected upon some of the most modern theories that scientists still have not proved; as many others that have been, thanks to geniuses like Newton, Keppler, Planck, Russell, Bohr, Eddington, Maxwell and Einstein.

But we have fighters like Stephen Hawking, Jacob Bronowski, Werner Weisenberg, Karl Popper, Penzias, Rubbia, Wilson, Salam, Schwinger, Tenonaya, Watson, Nomoto, Chaidrasekhar, Fermi, Rutherford, Chadwick, Penrose and a large number more of evolved spirits who dedicate their life and efforts in the search for the origin of light. They are geniuses by nature and educators of mankind.

Carl Sagan, the most popular of today´s scientists, for his teachings through his book and television series Cosmos, has awakened the interest of young and old on his favorite subject, the knowledge of our Universe through the science of today.

Mr. Sagan defends cold skepticism and incredulity regarding any theory that is not proven scientifically. He considers the material results as a basis for mathematical and statistical calculations of the most brilliant minds of the planet, including his own. Although, in his book, Contact, his spirit leads him to the most intrepid of theories when he surpasses the limits of proven science and invades hyperspace, although it is a work of fiction.

The Institute of Advanced Studies of Princeton University, where Einstein spent his last years, was the first place to open the door to studies considering other dimensions of hyperspace. The Enrico Fermi Institute, at the University of Chicago, is also a pioneer in the theories of hyperspace.

There is a natural interest in research being carried out today, where we can all easily visualize space of the third dimension where we live. If time is considered as a fourth dimension, we have a clear concept of our world. But other dimensions........how and where are they?

By analogy, we can imagine a man who lived in the semidarkness of a cave and hence could only distinguish silhouettes and touch the forms within his reach. How could his mind imagine that place in broad daylight and in full color? If we lit up the cave surely, upon seeing it so clearly he would radically change his perception. Everything is always simpler when it is perceived completely by the proper senses.

Einstein once said: "Nature shows us only the tail of a lion, but we are unable to see the lion because of its size." What was he referring to? Maybe he already had an intuition of the existence of higher dimensions so enormous we cannot see them.

The principle forces we know today are as follows:

1. ELECTROMAGNETIC FORCE is within everything that surrounds us; it is used in the form of electricity and its applications.
2. GRAVITATIONAL FORCE is the force of gravity which keeps us chained to the planet´s surface, which we have to overcome to be able to walk. We take advantage of gravity in the generation of electricity with water and we detect its manifestation in space interacting between the planets, the Sun and the rest of the celestial bodies.
3. STRONG NUCLEAR FORCE (FISSION) is the energy that animates our Sun and the Universe. It is generated by transforming hydrogen into helium.
4. WEAK NUCLEAR FORCE (FUSION) implies radioactivity and is used by nuclear plants to produce electricity.

If we consider we have "the tail of the lion" only with these four forces of manifestation of energy, who can imagine where the lion is?

The fantasy of the famous movie, Back to the Future, can give us an idea of what the other dimension is like. Another reality could be imagined in a "time machine" if the two dimensions intercepted each other, but all this would imply the invasion of hyperspace with the same frame of mind of man trying to conceive the unknown dimensions. But in any case, although man couldn't imagine them, they already existed.

The same thing happens with all scientific inventions. For example, we didn't know a letter could be sent by fax, or images transmitted on television, because we didn't know how to do it. But the possibility was there and it was the same when man lived in caves. We were only missing the knowledge and the know how.

But where do spirits fit in all these concepts? There's no easy way of understanding this phenomenon and linking it with Einstein's Theory of Relativity in Space, that includes the fourth dimension. Much less when Einstein, using Riemann's Tensor Theory, modified his own theory to be in agreement with concepts of Maxwell's Theory of Light and obtained the General Theory of Relativity.

Where does the fifth dimension come in, then? The curve of space-time could be understood mathematically. But could it the fifth dimension be mentally visualized in the world of physics? Would the so-called Einstein-Rosen bridge a mathematical concept of intercommunication between two universes? And, could the electromagnetic force be the key to understanding?

Thomas Huxley once said: "The known is finite; the unknown, infinite." We are in the middle of an ocean of the unexplainable, but each generation is able to advance a little further.

Patient and constant study of all these concepts and theories led Eric to the conclusion that the knowledge of terrestrial science doesn't have the level to verify Professor Krinnell's teachings. Although, he didn't find anything that contradicted the concepts that he was taught. On the contrary, they complemented perfectly all the loop holes of science on Earth perfectly. There were clear signs it would follow the path, at some point, to verify the knowledge he had acquired.

These and other considerations were at the front of Eric´s mind, when he remembered an anecdote:

A short time after having had the first encounter with Rahel´s vessel, in those first weeks, when it was still difficult to control his emotions, he had to go to arrange some business at the Ministry of Commerce. He had to see a certain officer who, at that moment, was attending to another exporter. They were talking about UFO´s and the exporter maintained it was absolutely impossible for extra-terrestrials to be involved. His reasons were fully accepted by the official.

Eric listened in respectful silence till the end of the discussion, when he intervened: "I agree with you, in the fact that we, the terrestrials are not able to visit planets outside our solar system, but this does not mean, "they" cannot come to us."

The exporter replied with infinite patience. "Allow me to give you a book about this subject, but promise me you will read it; the author will give you full details regarding my point of view. I will leave it here tomorrow with this kind sir. I hope we´ll have a chance to discuss this further."

"Yes, of course," replied Eric. "I will read it with much pleasure and we can talk about this later."

The book was Extra-terrestrial Civilizations, by the distinguished scientist, Isaac Asimov. He explains that a round trip to the closest star, Alpha Centaurus, would take at least nine years. Too long a time. He concludes, therefore, that civilizations in other places in space, if there were any, would stay where they are, as we would stay here.

He explores the possibilities of future travels in space. He mentions "taquions" as particles whose speed is greater than the speed of light and thus accepts the probability we are inheriting an Universe inhabited by other beings and will form a Galactic Federation of Civilizations.

Time has passed and Eric continues to wait for the opportunity to see this gentleman and give him a copy of this story.

CHAPTER XVI

Cosmic energy combines with natural
physical energies to nourish the systems
of the third and fourth dimensions.
The result is the proper physiological
and psychological function of the thermal
and electro-psycho-magnetic systems of energy.

Yunner Krinnell

FROM HERMOSILLO TO GALIMOR

Eric took advantage of the three weeks after his last encounter with Rahel and Mirza to remember their conversations and analyze their content. This raised new questions. He began to look forward to their next meeting with renewed interest. When he felt the mental presence of his friends, he knew that it was only a matter of time for the phone to ring to arrange an appointment. When it did, as in previous occasions, he already "knew" it would be Mirza inviting him to get together again.

This time Eric suggested the beautiful, warm and hospitable city of Hermosillo, where he had some business to attend to the following week. It would be a perfect place for another encounter with Rahel.

Mirza accepted and said farewell reminding him that they would see him after he had finished his business and was able to sit down calmly.

On the fixed date, Eric had a great steak lunch with a customer. People there were always friendly and welcoming. He felt so much at home.

As he paid the bill at the cashier´s, he recognized Shem´s familiar face. Eric introduced him to his customer, "Look, Rogelio, may I introduce a friend from very far away?"

"It´s true, but the trip is worth it. This city is something special," Shem cordially acknowledged.

Rogelio offered to take them wherever they were going, but Shem thanked him, pointing to Mirza´s pick-up truck. Then, they said goodbye and left the restaurant.

Eric asked Shem, "Who else is with you? I am sure you are at least, three. Or, am I wrong?"

"You are not wrong," Shem answered nodding to Mirza, who was in the truck.

"Did you travel in it from Mexico City? It´s a long trip."

"Of course not, Eric" answered Shem.

Mirza got off the truck to greet him and transmitted: "The pick-up has gone to Mexico City at times, but this is its base."

"Rahel will be here soon," Mirza said as they walked down the avenue, over to the shade of an impressively large tree. "Shem wanted to see you again."

"Thank you, Shem. Believe me, it´s great to see you again. I had begun to think you only existed in my mind!"

"Kunn and Professor Krinnell send you their regards. I have a surprise for you. I´m sure you would like to return once more, wouldn´t you?"

"When, Shem?" Eric felt stunned and thrilled at the prospect of another astral voyage.

"Today! You had thought of spending the night here and returning home tomorrow, hadn´t you?"

Eric turned to Mirza, not being able to contain a nervous giggle. "Is it true?"

She also smiled and transmitted: "Rahel thought you would be delighted with the news!"

"Of course! When are we leaving?"

"Have you finished your business here? If you still have something pending, you must do that first. Just tell us at what time you will be free."

"The person I had lunch with was the reason for my trip. We were at his office this morning and took care of everything. So I´m free now."

They got on the pick-up and set out on the highway to Ciudad Obregon. The sun was shining brightly so it was really hot---the air-conditioning in the car was most welcome!

"Mirza, in your opinion, which is the real value of the teachings regarding the existence of the spirit for men on this planet?"

"Look, the entire Universe is like a school for our spirit. From the beginning, man acquires experience and knowledge. His body is his means for evolution and, when need be, also for restitution to obtain equilibrium and harmony. This is real justice. Of course, it implies reincarnation and successive material lives of the same spirit to attain this."

"The first step to begin to understand is to know and accept the existence of the spirit within man´s rational mind. The best way for the material being to do this is to know its manifestations in his own physical body."

"The human being, even though he is matter of the third dimension, should be capable of understanding his feelings and other spiritual aspects of his persona, because of how he has evolved up to now. But while he is not conscious of the fact his own conscience has a spiritual origin, he will not be able to aid his evolution."

"The spirit is the noble and lofty part of his being and man on Earth already has sufficient knowledge to comprehend that everything is vibration and, spiritual vibration and its manifestations can be detected at the material level. Love is the purest manifestation of spiritual energy and the main element for evolution."

"This is why what you are about to learn is so important. It is about the manifestation of spiritual life applied to the mind in order for it to work properly."

"Remember, much of the knowledge we are sharing with you was prepared to be understood at your level of comprehension. Something like the parables used by Jesus, so uneducated people could understand him. You have a much higher cultural level that those men had 2,000 years ago, but don't forget both you and we are barely at kindergarten level in the Universe!"

The car covered the miles smoothly. Eric closed his eyes to better absorb Mirza's words. He didn't realize when he fell fast asleep.

When he woke up, he felt strange and disoriented. "Where am I? What time is it?"

He sat up in a comfortable bed; he looked around and recognized the apartment he had had in Galimor. He relaxed listening to the soft music and opened the window screens. He heard a familiar voice. "Hello, Eric, would you like some tea?"

He turned to the bedroom door where Shem was standing, cup in hand. Eric accepted with a smile. After a few sips, his mind cleared.

"I would have preferred to enjoy the trip. Didn't Mirza come?"

"No, but she'll be waiting for you upon your return. Shall we go?"

Eric quickly finished his tea and they left. He already knew the route to the station, passing the electric belt system towards Golemisbek. He had thought about that path so many times. He looked at his watch and realized it had stopped at 3:28 p.m., a few minutes after falling asleep.

This time they took a different route on the belts and five minutes later, arrived at the airport. They boarded a space ship, approximately 15 meters in diameter. It was ready to leave. Kunn was waiting at the top of the vertical hatch, with a big smile.

"Welcome! I knew I would see you soon!"

"Thank you, Kunn. I'm thrilled to be here and, of course, to see you again!"

Eric stopped for a moment. He felt something was not quite right. Then he remembered that, it was 4:00 p.m. his time, yet it was completely dark outside. Two small moons, with a 30-degree

288

separation, stood out in a sky covered with stars. It was brighter than a clear starlit night on Earth—and no doubt, a marvelous sight! He thought that even without the moonlight, the night would still be clear with the light of the haloed stars.

He noticed a few small differences in the vessel, compared to the one they had used previously. But quite unremarkable; more or less similar to the differences between two makes of cars. The command controls and computer system were the same, however.

They sat at the controls and while Eric oriented his monitors as he had been taught, they departed speedily towards their destination.

Shem began, "Eric, Professor Krinnell is waiting for us especially. You must have realized, it is our time for rest or relaxation. But he is very happy to see you and will explain some points requested by Rahel."

"You know there is a special interest for you to understand the importance of your mission, which is to try to make your brothers become aware of their own spirituality."

"The spirit manifests itself in the physical-biological entity of your material body, through a sensorial identification that provokes energy in the plexus, through the aura and the mind."

"The mind is a mirror of your soul. The spirit connects with your being through the mind. It is the place where the answers, having been processed and judged by your conscience, return. That is how you can detect the presence of your soul in your material being through your senses."

"Feelings and emotions live in the spirit; that is why it is so sensitive and can experience great suffering when its instinctive affectionate bond with family and loved ones is damaged. The suffering of the soul is reflected by jealousy, depression and anguish."

"The pain is physical, neuron interactions can be altered or damaged for several reasons, much like the effects of external chemical elements, or through functional defects, degenerative ones caused by the use of drugs, alcohol and viral illnesses or by genetic malformations."

"In these cases, also, body pain can also be felt, but this is acceptable and even sought by the spirit, as a proper way to help evolution or restitution for the elimination of karma."

"Man needs to elevate himself to be able to enter the era of a super-man or spiritual being. This era, for your mankind, will be in your own planet. But remember, those who do not attain this level, will have to begin in another evolutionary planet, already available elsewhere in the galaxy."

"Successive reincarnations of the spirit for its evolution are proof of the generosity of our Heavenly Father, and they are the best way to learn and evolve. Your brothers need to understand this, but at times, religious fanaticism prevents the use of reason and criteria, which should be possible in the light of their own intelligence."

"If your brothers can accept and understand that intelligence is a gift from God, why do they refuse to use it in the search of their divine origin and in recognizing their own immortal being, which is the spirit?"

"You will never be able to teach deep scientific topics to someone who can barely read and write. How far could he go using only his memory? By the same token, how could a person comprehend other physical knowledge of the micro universe or the cosmos, if he is not capable of believing anything he can´t see nor feel? How can he aspire to understand knowledge regarding energy and spiritual domains? For all this, necessary evolution is required to allow the proper conditions to accept and comprehend the knowledge of his own spiritual conscience."

The vessel landed softly, Shem and Eric went to see Professor Krinnell, while Kunn remained at the site to wait for them.

Even at that hour the University was a hub of activity. Students were in the workshops and labs. The elevators and belt service were working as usual.

"All the work, in this center of studies, after 6:00 p.m., is done voluntarily. All the services are provided on a continuous basis as there are people who work all night, and others come and go if they are part of a group," explained Shem.

The Professor saw them come in and waved them over; he was talking to Rahel through the telecommunication system of the holographic projection.

"Hello, Eric," Rahel greeted as they neared. Eric would have liked to get closer to him and greet him more effusively, but smiled when he realized it was only a projection. He waved a greeting and turned to Yunner Krinn, who welcomed him affectionately.

"Thank you, Rahel, for this new opportunity," said Eric. "I am very happy and ready to listen to the Professor. I hope to be a good student."

"Yes, you are. I congratulate you. This time, the Professor will teach you how the spirit controls the physical functions of the brain. The brain has all the elements needed and will respond to the different activated energetic stimuli to guide the actions and interactions of that wonderful biologic computer. I'll see you when you return to Earth. Until then."

Rahel and the Professor exchanged a few words in their language and then the communication was over.

The Yunner asked them to take a seat, while he turned on the hologram projector and inserted the cassette he had prepared. A human baby appeared on the screen. A newborn seemed to float on the stage; then he became transparent and motionless. The inside of his head could be seen. Then only the brain was floating.

Shem once again was translator for Yunner Krinn.

"After the human baby is born, spiritual beings from the fifth dimension are needed to connect the mental spheres. These are prefabricated groups of energy that will influence the human brain."

"Each sphere is a spiritual organ. Its matter belongs to the fifth dimension and each one (there are six) will be responsible for the management of energy in the area it influences. They contain THINKING ANALFAS and constitute the essence of the mind."

An infinite number of dotted lights appeared on the holographic stage, much like the time the integration of matter was illustrated. These dots joined each other to form more complex systems in rapid succession. Then, turning softly in the center, the image of a PARTON, the essential particle could be seen as a round, luminous, white transparent bubble.

It then shrank and became a dot. The space was then invaded by dots to form a sphere made up of 12 x 109 (twelve

291

thousand million) partons. That sphere represented one ENERGETIC QUANTUM.

Now this ENERGETIC QUANTUM turned slowly and acquired a luminous yellow color. It moved to the right and another appeared. Both combined to the right and another appeared. Both again came together and turned an intense blue. This new element was an ELECTRONIC QUANTUM.

The same thing happened again, and another ELECTRONIC QUANTUM appeared on the stage. When it melded into the first sphere, it turned into an intense violet color and became a RADIAL or PLASMATIC QUANTUM.

They disappeared and now a luminous yellow ENERGETIC QUANTUM showed up. The others appeared and formed a square. Four more appeared and were placed inside. They formed the angles of a cube, which lit up and lines emerged to join in the center as if they were diagonal tensors, known as plasmatic reserves. (Figure 62)

FIGURE 62

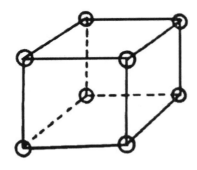 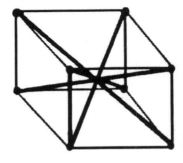

The lines of the plasmatic reserves turned violet and then six more cubes appeared and grouped together in a septicube (7 cubes). (Figure 63)

FIGURE 63

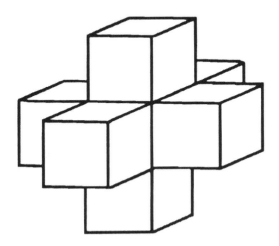

"This form is a QUANTUM made up of 7 cubic quanta", the Professor explained.

Septicube groups soon filled the screen and began to join to form a sphere.

The sphere shone violet and shrank to a brilliant dot, keeping its intense color. Five other dots appeared and formed a structure joined together with fine violet lines. (Figure 64-A)

This strange structure that looked like a spider made up of 6 luminous violet dots joined by the violet lines, slowly turned upside down. (Figure 64-B)

FIGURE 64-A

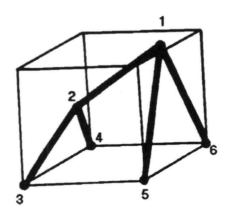

FIGURE 64-B

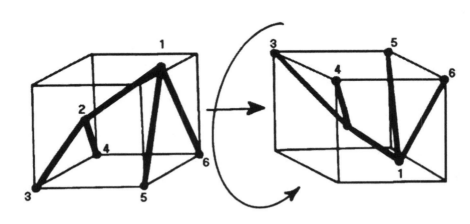

At that moment, the image of the brain appeared at the right advancing toward the center of the stage. The six dotted luminous structure slowly descended until it entered the transparent brain. Four dots remained at the top and two went deep inside; one in the middle and the other a little further behind, under the posterior two. (Figure. 65)

FIGURE 65

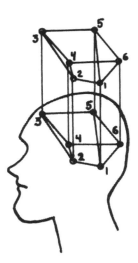

Then, the luminous violet dot of each intensified and began to grow forming bubbles that covered the encephalic mass in seconds.

(Figure No. 66)

FIGURE 66

The spheres lit up their violet color to emphasize their position inside the brain. They arranged themselves in such a way as to perfectly wrap round specific areas, coming forward from the lowest part.

Sphere No.1: Wrapped the cerebellum and medulla oblongata.
Sphere No. 2: The cerebral cortex, the pineal hypophysis an pituitary gland.
Sphere No. 3: Right frontal lobe.
Sphere No. 4: Left frontal lobe.
Sphere No. 5: Left back lobe.
Sphere No. 6: Right back lobe.

The spheres grew in size until gently touching each other and then, little by little, faded and the brain was covered by that faint violet color.

Professor Krinn continued explaining:

"These spheres represent the zone of their influence in controlling the brain, but only in the human. There are, due to their make-up, the symbiosis of two dimensions. We can say the brain is where the body and the spirit join."

"To simplify this, we'll call them Mental Spheres. Let us look at the characteristic influences of each, but first you must understand the way they work."

"The spheres together with their physical mind, are a mental screen that will be integrated by the images seen with the mind. Not only through memory (of things past), but also of actual reality and future projections."

"The IMAGINATION is the mental arrangement of a something you want to happen, more or less like a movie of the future. If you don't imagine anything, you will never be able to carry it out. It is necessary to do this, so that the mind can show the voids. You will not have images of what is unknown to you and you will know what you need to bring the sequence together in order to made it real. Your brain will provide the physical elements and your mind will provide the result of their actions."

"A MENTAL PROCESS is the result of integrating the known elements to "imagine" what can happen when actions are taken to obtain a certain purpose."

"In the knowledge that has already been given to your brothers, there is a simple example: you have a car ready for use, but to go from one place to another you need a driver. The car provides that which is physical, mechanical or material; and the driver, intelligence and knowledge, not only to move it, but also its destination. The result is transferring the car with its passenger toward an objective."

"In a mental process, the driver will represent the SPIRITUAL part that is the mental spheres, the car is the MATERIAL part of moving the physical body."

"In a similar way, the brain and mental spheres are the physical part and spiritual one, respectively. This is a mental process."

Afterwards, he pointed toward the holographic stage and they all observed the following process:

The silhouette of a human being looked at an object. The line of light of the image, when it got to the eyes, became a blue line of vibration that left the eyes and went to the central nervous system. From there, to the cerebellum and divided in two; one went directly to the pineal gland where it lit a bright dot. The other went to the cerebral cortex, multiplying itself to follow several routes that, as vibrating spider webs, connected to different lobes and the flow returned finally to the pineal gland.

After, only the person´s silhouette and the mental spheres, instead of the brain, could be seen. Only the bright dot of the pineal gland remained. Then, a vibrating line left the bright dot, but this time having a violet color, like a small arch that provoked the phosphorescence in the spheres.

The first branch, as the route was shorter, was the first to light the bright dot, before the vibrations returned after their travels throughout the brain.

Once again, there was a change to the fourth dimension and the violet colored impulses could be seen exiting the pineal gland and covering the mental spheres with phosphorescence. (Figure No. 67)

FIGURE 67

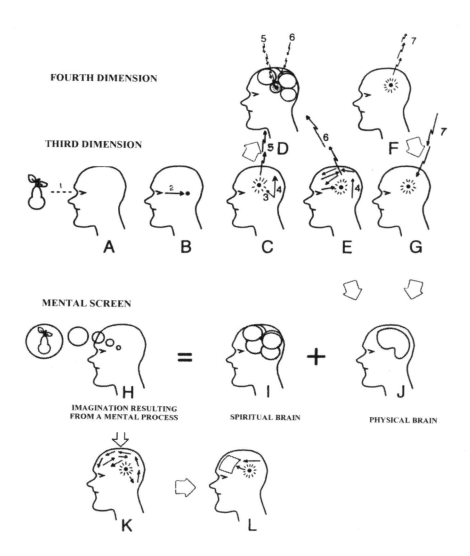

298

1. Figure 67-A
The physical sensorial reception can be through luminous, sound, thermal, etc. energy depending on the physical sense that attracts it.

2.Figure 67-B
Transmission through the nervous system of the physical being (2). It is originated in the sense that perceives it, within the carrier´s energy range of attraction, and transforms it into an electronic signal that goes through the nervous system to the spinal cord and, from there to the cerebral cortex, hippocampus and thalamus.

3.Figure No. 67-C
The signal is divided into two, the short branch (3) goes directly to the pineal gland and transmits the information transdimensionally (5) to the spiritual brain in the fourth dimension.

4.Figure No. 67-D
The spiritual brain (5) receives information of the action transmitted from the third dimension, by the physical being.

5.Figure 67-E
The long stem (4) goes from the thalamus to the cerebral cortex and the action is analyzed in the physical brain. This mental reasoning is based on what the material being knows, his experience, and all the information available in his memory (the cerebral lobes are the files). The result is also sent to the spiritual brain (6) when it reaches the pineal gland, fractions of seconds after the image had been received directly through (3). It may happen that as soon as the person is aware of the sensorial reception (although normally there is no difference), he may be able to differentiate between the two, and register them as being different in time with (3) and (4) stems beginning at (2). It is similar to seeing two slightly different images with your eyes and having the brain turn them into one. By the same token, in this case two images get to the pineal gland, one before and the other after the brain has processed the action mentally.
Under certain circumstances, the person can notice the duplication and believe he has already lived this before—a sense of dejá vu. In reality, it is the same scene he received instants ago. Only the period

of time between the senses having felt something to when the brain, after processing this, turns it into consciousness. This becomes even more noticeable in new visual situations. The person has the feeling it knows the scene although he is aware this could not have happened.

6. Figure 67-D
In the same way, the transdimensional information (6) of the action received, analyzed and processed by the physical brain.

7. Figure 67-F
Now it is the spiritual brain that transmits to the physical brain (7) transdimensionally, its view of the action; which becomes enriched by feelings and emotions from the soul and transmitted by the charkas. When this is the case, the transmission is simply a spiritual evaluation—(the voice of your conscience)—that arrives as a subconscious reaction.

8. Figure 67-G
The physical being receives the transmission (7) that will be registered as intuition to be added to self-reasoning, as a result of the mental process. In addition, depending on the case, it may also receive an evaluation from the conscience that is identified as a subconscious reaction. The hypophysis intervenes to transmit from the physical brain through the endocrine system to the rest of the body, when immediate action is required from the reflex system.

9. Figure 67-H
Finally, it is the result of the interaction between the physical brain (5) and (6) more that the spiritual (7). The human being projects the resulting thoughts on the mental screen of his imagination, that will be the basis of his actions, according to his free will, but in the presence of his conscience.

10. Figure 67-K
The human being rationally evaluates the alternatives in accordance to his interest, his moral principles, etc.

11. Figure 67-L
The human being projects the decision he has taken on the screen of his imagination with his own free will and later proceeds to carry it out.

Professor Krinnell stopped the projector, and asked him, "Is the course of the impulses that are received in the material body through the physical senses clear to you?"

"As you have already noticed, as soon as your physical brain analyzes them, the spiritual brain is doing the same thing, simultaneously. Only, that in the latter, all knowledge and experience acquired in past lives are also part of the process. And, eventually when need be, due to the importance of the result or human reaction, there is a communication to the contrary. Communication with the spirit is also a means of restitution or elimination of karma. Look."

He started up the holographic projector and a person could be seen talking to another person. The vibrations of the visual and audio images followed their course continuously. After the route through the brain, the vibration´s image arrived at the pineal gland again. But, at that moment, a red phosphorescence lit up in the area, at the base of the brain over the cortex, indicating the return of the spiritual brain´s signal and, from there extended itself to the hypophysis gland which activated the endocrine and nervous systems.

Then, all the body was covered with this luminosity, as the luminescence from the peripheral system reached all the cells of the physical body.

In this way, it was shown that the impulses coming from the spiritual brain activate all the vital systems of the physical human body as those the being receives from the corporal senses, and the vibrations of energy coming from a spiritual origin course through all the material body as those coming from the physical brain.

301

Words, converted into ideas, were analyzed and activated the mental process needed to be able to answer the speaker. Including accompanying his words with hand gestures to express and emphasize. This process continued for a few seconds and then changed once again to fourth dimension.

Then, the silhouette was receiving the violet vibration to activate the mental spheres. Suddenly, the image of the softly lit up charkas appeared over the mental spheres.

There was continuous communication from the mental spheres to the mental charka, Acknachackra. The latter simultaneously sent a current of energy to the speaker and received vibrations from him as well, that were directed to the mental spheres. All of a sudden, a short circuit occurred—a vibration lit up that went all the way to the pineal gland.

He returned the image to the third dimension and a brilliant yellow dot lit up in the pineal gland and a bright blue vibration was sent from there to the cerebellum and then to the cerebral cortex, as it did at the beginning.

"What is your interpretation of what you have seen?" Yunner Krinn asked Eric.

"Well, I think the spiritual brain found something it experienced or knew that was not in the physical brain, and is advising or warning the physical being. Also, I see the spiritual brain is offering information through the charkas, but it not perceived by the physical brain. Did I understand this correctly?"

"Excellent!" answered Yunner Krinn. "It is the image of spiritual input."

"But it is not only that, of course. The spiritual brain is taking advantage of its knowledge and tries to influence the MENTAL PROCESS in the human being, by INSPIRING what should be done. Remember, it is received as something the human being itself generates, apparently without getting that information from the outside, and interprets it as an inspiration, a hunch or "sixth sense" and, having already been evaluated by his CONSCIENCE."

"Once all this has been done, in a matter of instants, the human being is able to assess the situation and make a good or bad

302

decision he is completely responsible for, through his own FREE WILL."

"For example, if he is planning to rest or work, his spiritual brain is aware of this, but does not intervene. If the action to be made, is in bad faith (where some damage will occur), the conscience will enter the arena and say, "No, this is not right", "It is a lie", etc. But once the action has been evaluated in the mental process, the conscience has fulfilled its mission and allows the human being to act in accordance with his own free will."

"The human being will accumulate negative or positive loads as a consequence of his actions, for or against, spiritual harmony and these remain in the mental spheres. Now look at this:"

In the image, every time there were sparks of spiritual vibration towards the third dimension, the being would, after receiving the information, make decisions and act upon them. One could see the mind weighing the pros and cons and, simultaneously, sparks of violet-colored energy lit up every time in the mental spheres, leaving behind a sediment that eventually covered the lower part. All these were thoughts and actions producing and accumulating KARMA.

The being lay down inert, meaning it had died. A few instants later, the soul´s silhouette began to float. But, when it got two or three meters above, a magnetic or gravitational force of the third dimension seemed to stop the green-colored negative energy from rising further.

Desperately it tried to free itself, but it was impossible to overcome the force of gravity; it could only travel horizontally, in the space between the surface of the planet and its 3-meter high flotation limit.

Yunner Krinn turned off the set when the projection ended, and said, "I think you have understood all this perfectly. Do you have any questions?"

"Yes, Yunner," said Eric. "The animation explains the interrelationship between the physical and the spiritual brain of a human being who, interacting as well with charkas and mental spheres, explains how a spirit can accumulate karma, the negative life history of the physical being. How can he eliminate this, either during his life or after?"

"It´s probably incredible to you, but the hard part is precisely the accumulation of karma. Positive energy is far more abundant in spiritual life. Look."

He turned on the projector and the person appeared being "covered" by his spirit. The spirit received a continuous current of cosmic energy, serpentine energy from the planet and solar energy through the charkas—all these are positive energies.

The person then walked hand-in-hand with a child; love vibrations left his hand and went to his brain and passed to the fourth dimension. When this person approached someone else in a wheelchair and helped him to bed, he put a hand on his forehead and a great amount of energy was released to comfort the sick. (Figure No. 68)

FIGURE 68

After he kept on walking and then started to pray. Great energy was released from Acknachackra toward the sick person, benefiting both. Then, he extended his arms and hands and large amounts of energy were released. Each time there was an emission of energy interpreting good thoughts and feelings, this information passed on to the fourth dimension through the pineal gland. The positive energy was caught in the aura and sent, through the charkas, to the mental spheres.

The spiritual brain received a yellow spark from the third dimension and a golden, vibrating current flooded the mental spheres. The green sediment of karma evaporated little by little, when the accumulated positive energy through love, made it disintegrate and disappear.

The projector next showed the person on the wheelchair doubled over in pain. A yellow vibration of pain also passed to the fourth dimension and in a similar way, eliminated karma, although the intensity of this energy, produced by pain, was less than that produced by love. (Figure. 69)

FIGURE 69

Yunner Krinn turned off the projector and Shem translated: "I hope you have clearly understood the interrelation between the physical and spiritual body. Mental spheres act in the third and fourth dimension at the corresponding levels of each."

A chart appeared on the computer and the Professor proceeded to explain:

CHART 10

SPHERE NO.	NAME	PERFORMANCE LEVELS	LOCATION	ACTION
1	PRECONSCIOUS	3	Cerebellum	Connects psychological acts conscious and unconsciously. Found in third and fourth dimensions
2	SUBCONSCIOUS	1	Cerebral Cortex Hypophysis Pineal Gland	Files recordings not graded by the conscience in third and fourth dimensions
3	CONSCIOUS	4	Right Frontal Lobe	Alpha-Meditation-Analysis Beta-Vigil-Active Life
4	CONTINUAL CONSCIOUS	4	Left Frontal Lobe	Eta-Sleep-Twilight Delta-Light T=0
5	Supraconsciente	4	Right Back Lobe	Alpha-Hipnosis Beta-Mediumlike
6	Subliminal	4	Left Back Lobe	Eta-Anaesthesia Delta-Light T=0

"The human brain usually works at the beta level of the third dimension,   although through meditation can reach the alpha level to improve mental control."

"Excuse me, Professor, what does the stamp of the data base of the computer mean?" asked Eric.

"It is the cosmic teaching symbol and cosmic elevation. Its origin, according your stellar notations, is in the galactic union of Andromeda-Alpha Centaurus-Orion."   (Figure 70)

FIGURE 70

TEACHINGS

ELEVATION

"What do cosmic elevation and galactic union mean?" asked Eric.

"That´s a question for Rahel," said Shem. "We have already answered your first question, but further details should come from Rahel. Also, let´s not stray from the subject we were on, O. K.?"

"The SPHERE NO. ONE covers the cerebellum, the upper part of the spinal cord and the medulla oblongata. It works on two levels for each dimension—one for interaction between the third and fourth dimension for the human body to perform with knowledge not contained in its physical brain, but at its spiritual brain in memories or caught by the charkas as a telecommunication through clairvoyance and/or clairaudience."

"The physical being is consciously aware of the information, although he doesn´t know how it was acquired. It also works in telekinesis, the human being as the unconscious emitter of energy charges; the action as receptor is involuntary, but the emitter must be voluntary."

"A human being uses energy, even in the least of gestures. Working muscles, organs and other body systems entail energy to keep alive. All voluntary movements and reflexes use energy from the third dimension."

"Even in sleep, a human being consumes energy of its own biochemical transformation to support physical life, but in these conditions, spiritual consumption of energy is higher than physical. This cosmic, solar or serpentine energy is received by the physical body from the spiritual body through the plexus."

"The body can biochemically obtain this energy by transforming carbohydrates into oxides or glucose into lactic acid for thermal and electric energy to "nourish" the muscular fibers of the cells."

"The physical body is an electromechanic machine of such perfection you cannot even begin to comprehend. It´s highly efficient, thereby keeping the cost of energy it uses low, but even then has to economize its strength and work time, selecting and adding other parts of the "equipment" to help in its performance."

"The body is designed to be self-sufficient, but within the mechanisms of interaction and intercommunication for proper control and performance, one part is run and controlled through the spiritual participation from the fourth dimensions. It acts in the body through the charkas that energize the plexus and provide vital energy to the different organs it influences and are elements of third dimension."

"SPHERE NO. TWO covers the pineal gland, cerebral cortex, thalamus, hypothalamus and hypophysis. Its main function is the interaction from third to fourth dimensions and vice versa."

"SPHERE NO. THREE covers the right frontal lobe and normally is at beta level. This is the only mental level that man controls at will and with no effort, although evolution and practice can also function at the alpha level. The other two levels are similar in the fourth dimension."

"SPHERE NO. FOUR covers the left frontal lobe. It is similar to the third sphere, but operated by the fourth dimension for levels eta and delta."

"SPHERE NO. FIVE covers the left back lobe and is similar to sphere number four."

"SPHERE NO. SIX covers the right back lobe. It functions at alpha level for the third dimension, but under hypnosis can go to beta, only through a medium, which is the interpretation of frequencies from fourth dimension in third dimension, and the control is subliminal supraconscious. As these levels are beyond human control, when used (which is dangerous in deep hypnosis), can commit mistakes and cause grave physical harm, even of spiritual origin."

"MENTAL SPHERES are controls that Acknachackra energizes for the interrelationship of the physical body in third dimension and its soul in the fourth dimension."

"Only ONE of the 20 available levels in the spheres is managed by man effortlessly and at will—beta level of Sphere No. Three. It can also manage that sphere at the alpha level by effort and evolution, but all the rest are out of his control and in the fourth dimension."

"The most important dimension, from a cosmic viewpoint, is the spirit. Living isolated from the spirit is the same as being locked in matter."

"The Universe is the home of the spirit. Man with his spirit, even from matter, can conquer space, but must be living in harmony to achieve communication and elevation. Love and respect are needed so the spirit can go to spiritual mansions."

"The third era is precisely to attain this. To live as men, but aware of our spirituality to behave accordingly and aspire to the next evolutionary step of creation."

"Only man´s spirit knows the origin and history of evolution, who he is and who he was, without material limitations and consciously with his Creator."

"Our Father is light, simplicity and truth. Dark mysteries must by substituted by clarity. The spirit acquires wisdom as it goes up the evolutionary ladder and knows it will receive more from the divine spirit of our Creator."

"This explanation should make your brothers shudder because, if they can reasonably comprehend the interaction between matter and spirit, they will understand reincarnation. Many mysteries will be cleared up and they will feel spiritual fortitude as they learn the laws of love."

"There are no systems nor laws to reach harmony between you, unless each of you gets it on his own. It could be done in a general way, but evil and pride, which are human frailties must be overcome by spiritual characteristics, such as love, patience and peace."

Professor Krinnell turned off the set and turned to his visitors. Eric realized the lesson was over, and stood up to thank him for his patience. After Shem had translated his words, Professor Krinnell replied: "Eric, I am well aware of your planet´s problem and know it will be very difficult to make changes, peacefully and lovingly, but it´s worth a try. The secret is for you to change first and set an example."

"We may meet again. Much of what you have learned has already been available to your planet. On this occasion, the focus has not been scientific to be proved when your brothers learn how, but rather a simple and easy explanation of the existence of the spirit and its relationship with the human body, its means for evolution, in the hope they will understand and enter the approaching New Era with love. I wish you the best! Until we meet again!"

Eric and Shem said their goodbyes and left his office for their return trip. As they went down the elevator, they saw a transparent dome covering a swimming pool, full of coeds were enjoying some water fun and games under the extraordinary spectacle of their starry sky and bright moons.

Further away, in the sport fields, several teams played a sort of basketball. As they got to the ground floor, many students were on the move and Eric concluded it was not very different from a university on Earth.

What was remarkable was the fact they were all very well dressed and well behaved in a jovial and happy atmosphere. He stopped to try to understand their jokes and laughter, but he could only catch a few words here and there.

They soon got to the space ship where Kunn awaited them. The procedures for the return flight were the usual: energizing the space ship, freeing it from the pull of gravity, rising, setting the destination and flight plan in the computer system, etc. After having verified the instructions, energy sources and setting on automatic pilot, they sat back to enjoy a great flight and marvelous views.

Kunn asked Eric to make the preparations for the cut off of energy and the landing supports. "When the supports are in position and the ship, at zero altitude, you turn off the energy, OK?"

Eric was thrilled with his task and Shem smiled at his excitement. Kunn carefully watched him carry out his duties. Sudden silence descended on the ship, as the turbines and other machines were turned off. Shem and Kunn were on the computer, so he closed his eyes to rest his mind for a moment….and he fell fast asleep…

"Eric," Mirza's voice made him react. "Welcome to Earth. We have been waiting for you." Her image appeared on the main monitor. Shem finished the landing maneuvers and opened the exit door. At that moment, Eric realized he was not in the same vessel. When and how the change had occurred, he had no idea.

Shem transmitted: "Kunn congratulates you on your landing and hopes to see you again. Mirza and Rahel are waiting for you. It was great to see you again. May the Heavenly Father shine upon you. See you next time!"

They waved goodbye and Eric left the space ship, which was set in the middle of some woodlands.

Rahel was 20 meters away and as always greeted Eric with affection. His friendship made him seem almost human…well, more earthly. "Of course, Eric! I am human!" he said with a smile.

Eric felt embarrassed to be caught with those thoughts. Although there was nothing wrong with them—in fact, Rahel would realize he really liked and admired him.

They slowly followed a path Rahel apparently knew well. He stopped after about 50 meters and they both turned to watch the space ship´s departure.

The ship retracted its supports and remained motionless in the air. Shem opened the hatches and his silhouette could be seen at the window. "See you soon."

When the lights went on inside, Eric noticed a transparent ceiling full of kaleidoscopic sparkles. The ship began to softly float upwards. Then it stopped and disappeared behind a moving cloud….and simply vanished.

Eric turned to Rahel to ask what had happened, and Rahel kindly explained: "We don´t want to be seen here. There are many neighbors and too much light. We open a vibration shield of ultra-high frequency to ward off the light rays. It´s like covering the outside of the vessel so it won´t reflect radar waves. In this case, it is the light waves we avoid. By deflecting rather than reflecting light rays, we obtain a capsule of invisibility."

They finally got to where Mirza waited in the pick-up. "We´ll be right on time for your flight. We have 3 hours to spare, so we can chat in the meantime. Are you tired?"

"Not at all, Shem and Kunn took great care of me after the visit and I slept like a log. So I feel fine, thank you."

"In any case, when you get home, you should try to sleep a few hours longer for two or three nights to get rid of your mental fatigue. What did you think of the Professor?"

"Very interesting. I knew a little about it—but the course was too quick to be able to properly digest it. The images on the holograms are very explicit and I think I got it straight. The parallel function between man´s physical brain and the spiritual one are transdimensional intercommunications, so is the interpretation given by the physical brain regarding information coming from the spiritual one."

"That's right. Human understanding considers the mental-spiritual process as being intuitive. When the result of the analysis of a problem is received, it is considered natural. With the information it possesses, the brain continues to deduce and reason automatically during sleep and arrives at a conclusion thought to be logical."

"But the important thing is that man already ponders the viability of the soul's existence within him. He has a feeling there is something and needs a light to guide him to substantiate his feelings. Your brothers today have, not only scientific knowledge, but also a thirst for learning more regarding evolution and wisdom to satisfy their minds."

"I think this lesson is far more important than the others you got, because those cover the phenomenon of cause and effect. This subject, however, is about the spirit and the dimensions, although complex, make you aware of your real self."

"For example, your brothers have made much progress in neurobiology, a difficult science because it is not easy to see how the neurons function. We have about 1 billion nerve cells in the brain, each can communicate with others, either nearby or faraway. The tentacles, you call axons, end in ramifications or dendrites. To communicate, they use a biochemical process called synapsis."

"This you already know, but a microscopic neuron can be connected to the farthest in the brain by an axon up to one meter in length. Each neuron is a complete cell with a nucleus, and all the organs are systems necessary to produce electric energy by metabolizing glucose with oxygen."

"Neurons also contain sodium, potassium and calcium salts that send messages in a sort of Morse Code. Through the salts, that are controlled by polarization, each cell is covered by a membrane and this includes the axons and dendrites. Also, there are spaces of 0.02 microns between neurons, in reality they are not touching."

"The messages are sent from one to another by a liquid neurotransmitter that exits through the neuron's membrane and the next one absorbs it, so the dendrites will bring it inside. The liquid carrying the message leaves through some microscopic ducts, that are tubular proteins. They form millions of entrance and exit pores of the ionized liquid by impulses controlled electrically by a voltage of 40 to 80 millivolts, at a frequency of 800 to 850 impulses per second of alternating polarities."

"Because there is a difference of potency, the transmitting liquid is really pumped to leave or enter the dendrites or axons through the microchannels and the electric charges take it outside the membrane to be absorbed by the adjacent neighbor's membrane."

"This in itself is marvelous, and it is being studied in the field of neurophysiology. However, they still don't know how to control those millions of ducts, perfectly synchronized by the proteins, that operate with the changes of potency to allow the entrance and exit of sodium, potassium and calcium ions, with the membrane changing polarity and potential in milliseconds."

"This is the way they operate: all the physical senses send enormous amounts of continuous information through the vibrations of electronic impulses that join in the central nervous system and reach the cerebellum through the spinal cord."

"As they reach the brain, they speak in another language— the biochemical one. It covers the brain in all directions. It seeks and stores the related information from all the different cerebral lobes to carry out the mental process of making specific decisions for each set of reasoning and the consequent actions to follow."

"Can you imagine the logistics needed to the simultaneous and continual management of the electro-chemical-biological physical phenomenon to activate systems within each nerve cell and be able for each to transmit and request information, and obtain from all that chaos, a human being who is both healthy and sane?"

"We find controlling the neuron behavior is beyond what man can untangle and comprehend completely, as the spiritual brain, mental spheres and the energy of the plexus all participate. There is a participation of the spirit here, also."

"There can be synaptic intercommunication impulses around one hundred thousand billion per second in all the brain. To regulate and direct the functions, and the electrochemical, biologic, and quantum behavior of the neurons is one more test for the human body. Even if it is perfect, it is not complete in the third dimension; it continues, correlates and complements its own being in the fourth dimension, and this, at the same time, with the fifth dimension, and so on until the seventh, where his spiritual origin is found."

"You have to imagine a multidimensional Universe to be able to fit in the life of a transdimensional evolutionary being that it is the human being. This human being integrates a Universe that is part of the cosmos. If the latter is multidimensional, the human must also be, even though he is part of each dimension—the physical, being in the third and the spiritual one in other higher up and interconnected. This is the COSMIC MAN. "

"When the subject of extra-terrestrials and spirits comes up, the majority of people accept the possibility, based on intuition without really understanding that, both do exist. A different opinion may be expressed due to lack of proof. In addition, many of them are not prepared to argue scientific matters."

"Children, innocent by nature, believe their parents and accept the existence of Santa Claus and the Three Wise Men. As they grow older, experience teaches them not to believe everything they are told. Lies and deceit are discovered, but their intelligence can identify what is true and what isn't."

"Adults are guided by their own criteria, based on knowledge and experience; but, when these are insufficient, prudently reject the unknown. However, when religion is concerned, they become childlike once again."

"It is easier to trust a magical god and unconsciously, enter a world of religious fanatics. Man stops using his mind and joins the majority of the population with low cultural levels, as it is easier to mentally descend to idolatry, than to rise to spirituality, accepting dogmas on faith. Ignorance and mental inertia lead to religious fanatism."

"In the different contemporary religions on your planet, each god is a grand magician whose decisions are interpreted by the leaders, and men accept and even defend with their lives, concepts that would be laughable, were they not blinded by fanatism."

"The spiritual world is real and tangible. Its manifestation in the third dimension increase and is more noticeable every day as an aid to open human minds."

"Each must listen to the voice of his conscience, and use his mind for deep thought to find a satisfying explanation regarding the

314

how and why of the Universe, and above all, of his own physical and spiritual existence."

"Death is feared absolutely and irrationally. Mankind even goes to the extent of causing death or other physical torments to others, to protect his own life."

"Death, in reality, is like going on a trip. The unknown part of death is what causes panic. However, man can change his attitude of extreme terror to that of cold courage based on spiritual peace."

"Don´t you think these opposing attitudes in human beings are due to something stronger than the reasoning of a physical person? Naturally! The spiritual brain dominates the physical brain, precisely when a critical situation arises. The spirit does know that death is only going on a trip, that the physical body is disposable and the soul, obligated to leave his body, only undergoes a dimensional migration."

"It is more or less like moving—to another city, another house leaving friends and neighbors—and taking only his possessions. The soul takes memories, experiences, knowledge and electronic charges of love or karma, depending on his conduct in the third dimension, which it will have to atone, in order to continue its evolution."

"To sum up, we realize then, in grave or abnormal situations, the presence of spiritual conscience is at times the only option a human being has to survive or act. When the storm blows over, then all this must be analyzed. Often, what was considered only intuition, thanks to the physical remembrance of the spiritual manifestation, is now proof of the existence of a spiritual being."

"Death, in reality does not exist. It is the end of the productive life of the physical body. When lifeless, it follows the rules for transformation and disintegration of organic matter to its simplest form, and maybe later, these same elements may again come together and form part of another animal or vegetable body."

"The spirit just leaves that vehicle of evolution that served to gather experience. But, for the human being, it is an extraordinary happening, because the physical body was the vehicle for the spirit to evolve and play an important role in these stages. Its love or pain and suffering obtained merits to evolve spiritually."

315

"You have seen our Creator Father never stops helping man, providing easily understandable guidelines. The actual one is to act with love, to treat one another as brothers, with natural affection, spontaneously, freely and unconditionally. The benefit obtained by giving love is receiving love."

"When you are happy to give, you obtain a spiritual reward that you can take with you. What you can give, without any limit, is love in every way. If the love is projected by your physical body through generosity, courtesy, kindness and understanding, your life will be full of peace and happiness."

"However, this is so simple, apparently for all of you, it is practically impossible. You seek to dominate through power and wealth. If you are successful, you believe it is your strength, and consequently you loose your sense of perspective due to pride and vanity."

"Men, who have evolved little, dedicate body and soul for material gain. Deaf and blind to your conscience, your only objective and religion is material power; and everything is allowed, from thievery to murder, even war. Therefore, this evil affects us all and entices family discord and social disintegration. Moral ethics are put aside. Cynicism and indecency prevail. Honor, decorum, dignity, decency and honesty—characteristics that lead to evolution—are discarded. Whoever is drawn into this whirlwind of evil will provoke this change to be painful and in all probability will not even survive."

"We still have more conversations pending and in them, I will tell you about other subjects your brothers are trying to untangle. Maybe some will believe the truths I am giving you and will try to go down that road, then the rest will also believe."

The plane Eric was taking to Mexico City was ready for departure, so it was time to say goodbye.

Eric was not physically tired, but his head felt leaden and stuffy. "I think I have had enough for today!" He exclaimed to Rahel, while pointing to his head.

"Think about something else to relax. You'll be fine in a couple of days. You'll remember everything clearly. I'll be in touch. Take care," said Mirza.

316

Eric smiled and transmitted: "Thanks for the trip, it was great. I hope to see you soon."

As he entered the airport he couldn´t help thinking that in two and a half hours he would just be arriving home. In that same amount of time, he could go to the planet, Milburbek and return. Amazing!

Also, Isaac Azimov or Carl Sagan would be better candidates for his mission than he was. Why he was chosen, was beyond explanation.

He missed his friends as soon as he took his seat on the flight home. He imagined—they would already BE home!! He smiled to himself. At that moment, the flight attendant walked by and, thinking the smile was for her, offered him a candy!

CHAPTER XVII

It has taken almost 2,500 years, since
Democritus and Leucipius put forth
the Theory of the Atom, for mankind
to attain a scientific family of subatomic particles
such as fermions, hadrons, leptons, quarks and mesons.

And now, when some physicists believe
that soon the physics of matter will soon
be completely mastered, we have been told that:
electron and positron,
positive and negative energy,
matter and antimatter,
mass and energy,
third and fourth dimensions, do exist.
All of these are the first steps of a
new ladder for man to climb.

Pablo E. Hawnser

ENCOUNTER AT TANGAMANGA

On occasions, Eric felt his chest would burst when all his feelings and thoughts got the better of him. He would then meditate for long periods analyzing his conversations with Rahel and Mirza. Whenever he could, he would consult books to understand their teachings more.

He spent many hours at night thinking, making notes and comparing that information with his knowledge on the subject. This was how he confirmed scientific knowledge is the light to our understanding of God.

Mankind is set in the Universe between the micro and macrouniverse, from the world of the smallest, almost unimaginable, to the cosmic distances between galaxies of 10 to 20 thousand million of light years.

The natural phenomena that occur and animate life to those universes, and the transformation of energy into matter, with characteristics of mass and electric charges happen in the microuniverse. That world of particles and antiparticles, that are the origin of all creation, are forcing us to think there are different levels or dimensions.

In the cosmic universe of galaxies similar to ours, those dimensional levels are also present, although they are manifested more openly in science.

The presence of other dimensions is also manifested in particles known as antimatter, in the microuniverse, and black holes in the macrouniverse, to only mention physical phenomena that are common knowledge in quantum physics and in astrophysics.

Science explains the phenomena it studies by identifying the laws that govern them. Knowledge is considered scientific when it has been completely identified and verified. The "how" and "when" have been proven, but only the "why" remains without an answer. Science studies the facts, not the "who", "how", "when" and "why" they were designed, nor the laws of the Universe.

The Theory of the Origin of the Universe, known as the Big Bang, was the basis of Edwin Hubble´s discovery, when he proved the known universe was expanding. Assuming that at a certain moment, some 15 and 20 thousand million years ago, everything that existed could be found in a dot so minute it could fit through the eye of a needle. Then, a tremendous explosion occurred and that dot of unconceivable density blew up and scattered energy in all directions. (As it was an explosion, it would have taken the shape of a sphere.) Its energy has been transformed, little by little, into matter and became the expanding Universe we know, with a radius of approximately 15 thousand million light years.

The Big Crunch or Great Implosion was derived, building on the Big Bang theory. It is said that the force of gravity is slowing down the expansion of matter in the universe, and if it were to stop at any time, the inverse would happen. Matter would start to contract, melt and turn into a "great implosion", where everything would return to the original dot of incalculable density.

The fact that the universe keeps on expanding in an indefinite way (Theory of the Open Universe) or, that it would stop and begin to shrink (Theory of the Closed Universe) depends on an undetermined factor relating the force of expansion with that of gravity.

All this is established by the scientific theory published in 1970, by scientists Roger Penrose and Stephen Hawking, based on Einstein´s Theory of General Relativity. They applied their brilliant minds adding mathematics and physics to reason and calculated the "when", imagining the backward march of the expanding Universe, to estimate the moment creation began.

What really is cosmogony? It could be defined as an explanation of the origin of the cosmos or Universe. Therefore must be related to the beginning of Creation.

All the developed cultures throughout history have generated their own cosmogony and cosmologic concepts. From Taoism and Chinese Buddism, the Egyptians who even tried to enter another dimension in life after death, the Greek universe ruled by gods of nature, the Nordic legends of Valhalla, to the astrology of the Middle Ages based on the influence of celestial beings on people´s lives, but combined with mystical and metaphysical explanations.

Scientific progress changed the cosmologic concept of the Universe of Copernicus and Kepler.

When Edwin Hubble discovered the Cepheids, pulsating stars whose brilliance, aid the calculation of intergalactic distance, new horizons opened up to comprehend the cosmos. The old belief it was all a mass of stars changed, and it was discovered that, in reality, there were great distances between them. Even separate galaxies were conceived, obtaining a more realistic view of the Universe.

Russia´s Alexander Friedman, based on Einstein´s equations and Theory of Relativity, was the first to propose the Theory of the Expanding Universe, and was later supported by Georges Henri Lemaitre and the great British astronomer, Sir Arthur Eddington. Sir

Percival Lowell was the first to calculate the speed of expansion as 2,000 kilometers per second correlating the Doppler Effect phenomenon in the spectrum of light. The deductible speeds have reached up to 4,000 kilometers per second due to the linear variation (the farther away, the greater the speed). A speed of 60,000 kilometers per second was taken to calculate going backwards to the moment of the Big Bang and the number from 15 to 20 thousand million years was reached.

Supernovas are stars which don´t last long and show up suddenly some place in space. Let us remember that a supernova is just a phase in a star´s life cycle like our sun, that is ignited continuously by a nuclear chain reaction, where hydrogen is being converted into helium, and the light emitted by the sun is the energy liberated by atomic fusion. When hydrogen is exhausted, a transformation process increases its size considerably, becoming a red giant. The star grows so much that when our sun reaches that stage, the Earth´s orbit will be inside that gigantic red sun, whose size would be more than 300 million kilometers in diameter.

The next step is the collapse of gravity or implosion. When all the hydrogen has been converted into helium, then the helium that is in the star´s nucleus starts to fuse into carbon. The nucleus contracts and the red giant´s implosion is provoked. If the mass is smaller than four times that of our sun, it will most probably become a new and brilliant small star called a white dwarf. But if the mass size is between four and eight times that of the sun, at the moment it contracts, the carbon atoms, by fusion, will become iron. The pressure conditions and temperature are of such a magnitude that as it explodes as a small Big Bang and scatters 90 percent of its matter into space, will form heavy atoms like iron. The explosion produces an approximate brilliance 200 million times the actual light of the sun. This is a supernova.

What ever remains afterwards is compressed matter, the electrons join the protons of their nuclei forming neutrons; one next to the other, and the resulting density of its mass is such, that a sphere the size of a ping-pong ball would weigh, more or less, 1,100 million tons. This is called a neutron star.

When the mass the larger than eight times that of our sun, the result of the implosion could be the creation of a black hole, which is a whirlwind of suction towards....another dimension?

We know that a supernova appears approximately every 100 years in each galactic system. If we take only 100 systems, we would have an average of one every year. This means that throughout the millions of years of age of the Universe, millions of neutron stars would have been formed, already compressed under the laws of the force of gravity. In addition, already 90 per cent of the mass that each sent by the explosion would be found in the cosmos.

If the white dwarfs and the neutron stars are the result of COSMIC IMPLOSIONS, it is logical to deduct that, when the compression reaches a certain limit, compressed energy overcomes the force of the implosion, causing a new explosion.

By logic also, how is it possible according to the Big Crunch that, all existing matter could return to the hypothetical dot of infinite density? It sounds as absurd as the belief that Earth was flat and supported by two elephants standing on a giant turtle.

It is difficult to understand and accept that our Universe could be reduced to a single dot, by inverted reasoning, it is difficult to accept that everything was in that dot to begin with.

Stephen Hawking said once: "We know, by this calculation, when it began, but if we suppose that the Universe had a beginning, we must also suppose that it had a Creator. The laws we know do not tell us how the Universe was when it began." Stephen Hawking also had doubts regarding this origin of the Universe.

But, coming back to theories, we then had that the first was to consider the Universe as an island, everything as we see it, without trying to know who, how or when it began. This is known as the Theory of the Solid State.

Later, as science progressed, it was discovered: THE UNIVERSE IS EXPANDING! But how was this determined?

The explanation is not very difficult. After scientifically proving that when light and sound waves are emitted by a moving body going in the same direction, the frequency is increased and its wave length is diminished. It could be said that they push and shove each other and even pile up. If these waves move against the flow, the opposite occurs—the frequency is lowered and the wave length is "lengthened". We can determine, by this phenomenon, when we hear an alarm or a train whistle, if it is approaching or leaving. A similar phenomenon occurs in the light spectrum, if it flows toward the ultraviolet blue, it means it is getting nearer and, if it flows toward the red or infra red, it means that the source of light is moving away. This is known as the Doppler Effect.

Therefore, watching a starry sky, ALL the lights indicated they were moving away from Earth, because their spectrum was flowing towards red, so it could be that the Earth was in the center of the Universe (illogical!!), or that our solar system moved with the galaxy in the same direction, the stars ahead of us go faster than we do, and we go faster that the ones behind.

Edwin Hubble calculated that the separation speed between two celestial bodies (two galaxies) is in proportion to their distance, 15 kilometers per second for each million light years between them. This is called the "Hubble Constant". Using this constant, calculations were made backwards and this was how it was determined all the galaxies were in the same place, at the time the Big Bang occurred, starting the Universe, approximately 16,000 million light years ago.

We must not get confused talking about distances in units of time. What happens is that the distances are so immense, that we would have far too many zeros to confuse us! "A light year" is the distance traveled by a ray of light at a speed of 300 thousand kilometers per second in one year. If there are 60 seconds in one minute, there are 3,600 in one hour, 86,400 in one day and in one 365-day year, there are 31,536,000 (thirty one million five hundred and thirty six thousand) seconds!!

So, at the speed of light, one LIGHT YEAR is equal in distance to:

$$31,536,000 \times 300,000 = 9,460,800,000,000$$

(nine billion, four hundred and sixty thousand eight hundred millions) of kilometers. This equals 63,972 AU (Astronomic Units), each one measure 150 millions of kilometers, which is the distance from Earth to the Sun.

We can now understand that if the Big Bang explosion took place 16 thousand million years ago, the galaxy farthest away was formed by energy ahead of the explosion, and is located 16 thousand million times the distance that light travels in one year, from the place where the explosion occurred.

During the course of the history of mankind, science has advanced, important contributions by geniuses, the likes of Copernicus and Newton to Einstein and Hawking, have shed light to keep on discovering the Universe.

Stellar phenomena were discovered and this brought about more questions. For example, how to explain the presence of iron, uranium and thorium atoms on Earth, (supposedly these can only be formed under the conditions of a supernova), or the discovery of quasars, that are the most powerful and distant sources of energy (one quasar alone equals the energy of one thousand galaxies which equal to thousands of millions of stars like our Sun).

By analyzing these phenomena and pondering the implications, it is easy for us to deduct the great difference there is between the universe we see, and how it used to be, say, five million years ago.

Einstein´s genius and his famous equation of E=mc2 led to the discovery that energy becomes matter and vice versa. With the General Theory of Relativity, mankind realized the existence of the space-time dimension. Then, the Theory of the Big Bang came about, and a little later, the existence of anti-matter was detected.

To sum up, little by little, science has kept on discovering the "how" and the "when", but the "who" and the "why", up to now, has only been answered by Genesis.

When Hoyle and William Fowler were studying nuclear resonance between carbon and oxygen, they published the following in the Caltec magazine: "A super intellect must have calculated the properties of the carbon atoms." They were right, but it was not only that, such a super intellect also took part in physics, chemistry, biology and in all that surrounds us in nature.

Keppler stated: "There is nothing I want to find more urgently that this: TO FIND GOD, because I feel that I have Him in my hands when I watch the Universe and myself."

Sir Arthur Eddington, wrote in the book, "The Cosmologic Evolution of Intelligent Life": "God gave us something more than his poetry and justice, he also gave us love."

When scientists have managed to understand a little of the greatness of the Universe, they are inspired to contemplate their spirit and thereby, take us to the thresholds of a new science, where the spirit and the new dimensions will integrate to light our entrance to this New Era.

Eric spent his time, "resting between the encounters", studying cosmology to be able to ask Rahel for more information.

After three weeks, Eric began to nervously await Mirza´s call for another encounter. One day, "Hello Eric! How have you been? I know you were waiting for my call, so here I am."

"Thanks for calling, Mirza! You know I get impatient when I wait for your call, when will we see each other?"

"Are you planning a trip soon?"

"Yes, I need to go to San Luis Potosi. I can program it for Friday, if this is OK with you."

"Very well, I´ll call you early Thursday, you select the place and the time. OK?"

"Great! I´ll expect your call, Mirza. Please give my regards to Rahel."

The meeting was set for early Saturday, in the Tangamanga Park in the city of San Luis Potosi. Eric finished his work on Friday, about 6:00 p.m., so he went to the hotel to check-in and rest.

He didn´t feel like going out, so he decided to take a bath, have a light supper and go to bed. He wanted to be on time at his appointment and he knew that Rahel and Mirza always got up very early.

He went over some notes about doubts that he wanted to clarify with Rahel. He wondered just exactly what the mission Rahel was entrusting him with, was all about.

According to Mirza, it was to alert all the inhabitants on Earth, as children of the Heavenly Father , we must follow the teachings of Jesus of Nazareth and live with love for all, showing it in our behavior, to be honest, just, and truthful, which would be easy just by following the voice of our conscience.

It was all clear and easy, but......what about all the lessons about the microcosmos and macrocosmos? Rahel had told him that they were "signals" to get the attention of unbelievers, but Eric could feel that, for many, all this would just be science fictional trash.

It was also true that most of the lessons, in some way did get man´s attention, pointing out his doubts regarding the spirit. It´s true that area has been exclusively dealt with by religions, but now they had to correlate the spiritual phenomenon with their own existence to convince themselves that spiritual existence is not fiction, but absolutely real. It is proof of the existence of other special dimensions, considered up to now as "magic" to explain where your spirit, your heaven and your god, live.

This understanding could help human beings to comprehend the dimension or space where his own spirit lives.

Eric continued pondering Rahel and Mirza´s concepts. True, only when one has the opportunity to learn more about science, leads are discovered as guides to those shady, dark and difficult-to-understand areas that are the manifestation of the presence of other dimensions in space.

Seeing these extra-sensorial manifestations, from the view point of human perception, even having been detected, still have not been identified; and most of all, even recognized as such. He daydreamed a little, thinking which those perceptions would be--of course, the famous spirits or "ghosts" that frequently had contact with human beings. This he knew through his own experience.

Other "unexplainable" phenomena could be the memories and experiences of those who have been clinically dead and have returned to life, and also, all those mysteries of the micro and macrouniverse that man is just discovering.

Eric felt he was falling asleep. He closed his eyes with all these thoughts on his mind, determined to get up early the following day

On Saturday, at 7:00 a.m., he took the car and went to Tangamanga Park. It was gorgeous that morning, and of course, Rahel and Mirza had already arrived.

"We knew you would get here before 7:30 a.m., so here we are," Mirza said greeting him, and as old friends, walked slowly toward the shade of some trees.

Eric decided to begin the conversation and started his questionnaire.

"I have been trying to put all the knowledge I have acquired thanks to you and all the wonderful experiences I have enjoyed. There is something I want to ask you very specially."

Rahel nodded, encouraging him to continue. "For many years, philosophers on Earth have had their questions regarding the spirit. For example, Descartes once said: Only bodies with mass and dimension have physical reality. This, in itself, defines what should be considered as existent.

Concepts have been evolving ever since Plato, Aristotle, Marcus Aurelius, Descartes, Locke, Liebnitz, Kant and Hegel. They have all tried to stay fundamentally within reason, intellect and comprehension. After Saint Augustine, Saint Thomas Aquinas and John Jacob Rousseau declared there was "something in the body" that was not matter or energy, and existed in man, but were never able to prove what "that something" was.

J. Gaylor Simpson added that in "that" lies the difference between man and the animals, since "that" makes men behave ethically, morally and can also have the capacity to manifest ideology.

Henry Bergson, famous for his work, "Revision Against Reason", identified that "something" as the vital impulse. Rene Descartes defined "Thinking of the Mind", the difference between man and beast.

My question is: "Which of the concepts has man been unable to develop to reach the truth of knowledge?

"We could examine each opinion and evaluate it, but it would be worthless and futile. It is not a philosophical concept which will wake you up, but reality."

"I agree, but wouldn't it be better to give a good reason so everyone can understand and comprehend the presence of the spirit?"

"Of course! Just remember that you had the chance to understand on your own, and in fact, could have long ago overcome that stumbling block for spiritual identification. Unfortunately, you are very rebellious by nature and have little faith."

"Faith must be the result of a mental analysis that processes knowledge inspired by intuition. When faith is blind, it becomes fanatism. Man refuses to use his intelligence, which a Divine gift."

Eric agreed, but added, "If we are trying to encourage mankind to be interested in comprehending something totally outside the physical world, it is necessary to help them understand that other place or dimension is accessible to their mind, not only by faith, but also through science. Human science has precisely those contact points in Einstein's Theory of Relativity."

"I think that, for many educated people, it would be a great help to have the opportunity of understanding the spark that opens the doors of scientific knowledge for us, and participate in the comprehension of what a new dimension is. Mirza recommended something like this, do you remember, Rahel?"

"It is possible, but there would be very few who will be interested in understanding. However, do it if you want, and whatever you are able to accomplish will be one more reason to guide man towards comprehending the existence of other dimensional levels within his own physical existence and accept spiritually."

"What would be an easy way to say this?"

Rahel thought for a few seconds, to emphasize his words, he looked directly at Eric. "Would you agree that you can't teach integral calculus to someone who hasn't studied algebra, trigonometry and differential calculus. In the same way, you can't expect the majority to understand concepts without elemental knowledge of physics and mathematics."

"All right. Please help me with a simple explanation."

After a few seconds of deep thought, Rahel continued, "The THEORY OF RELATIVITY is a reasonable explanation of a mind focused on the real perspective of what happens in the Universe."

"Human beings in this and other evolutionary planets are reaching a stage in the development of their civilizations that allows them to unveil the mysteries of science, as is the case of man on Earth. They begin to look for the "how" and the "why", of all the physical, chemical and biological phenomena of their own bodies and of the planet in which they live."

"They already know their own bodies, they know they are made up of energy that is condensed and transformed into a mass, which is matter."

328

"These small groups of energy with definite physical characteristics are what you call subatomic particles, so minute, it is difficult to be able to understand them. When they group together, they integrate atoms and these become molecules of matter as you know them."

"This occurs in obedience to Universal Laws which rule everything. In the same way, once matter and its characteristics are formed, gravitation appears. This is the interacting force between particles. It is the manifestation of the mass obeying Universal Laws."

"A group of particles establish a system, which can be microscopic or a galaxy. These are all groups of matter and they obey the same laws."

"Gravity is the best known form of gravitational force. Each person´s weight is the force with which his matter interacts with matter on the planet. Gravitational force is the one you know as the first of Newton´s Laws, that states: "bodies attract each other with a force equal to the sum of its mass and inversely in proportion to the square root of the distance that separates them.""

"But, allow me to give you a new version of this law, that is more complete, although more difficult to understand:

"GRAVITATION IS THE MANIFESTED CONSEQUENCE BY THE CURVATURE INDUCED IN SPACE BY A BODY MASS."

Eric tried to understand the definition and, after a while, said: "Does GRAVITATION specifically belong to space, as a result of the presence of matter?"

"That is so, gravity is a consequence of that special curve. By this definition, gravitation and inertia are equal. A system of inertia (inertia is one of the physical characteristics of mass) implies the existence of a gravitational system. That is why I told you that if we have matter, gravitation is present, just the same as, if we have mass so is the force of inertia."

SPACE

Rahel continued, "Space is defined as the dimension of an occupied space by a body mass. For example, in daily life, everything has a size; a water tank has length, width and height, as does a car, house and mountain. These measurements of size are the SPACE they occupy on a planet´s surface, just as the planet itself occupies a place in cosmic space."

"We know that if we build a house on a lot, we will not be able to build another one in the same place, at least until the first one is removed, maybe after 100 or 500 years."

"If a car is parked in front of the entrance of your garage, you will not be able to go in or out with your car, because the other one is taking up a "space" through which you would have to pass, and two physical bodies having mass as both cars do, can not take up the same "space" at the same time."

"We are also introducing the concept of "time". When the car parked in front of the door is taken away, then you can pass, as the "space" is free, and it is another "time". With this, we can see that "space" and "time" are linked."

"Now let us think that normally, the planet is a MOTIONLESS PLACE. It doesn´t move, moreover, humans seem to think that the sun revolves around the Earth and even say, "the sun has come out" or "the sun has set". They consider the planet as motionless, stable and still."

"Of course, they are aware that day and night are due to the rotation of the planet on its own axis. Seasons come about due to the inclination of the Earth´s axis, that the planet goes around the sun, and all the solar system moves around the center of the galaxy, which also moves in the Universe."

"Inspite of all this, man still feels he is in a "motionless" place—not upside down, not sideways, nor traveling by car at a speed of 300 kilometers an hour. He is still and calm in his garden and only feels movement if he is in a rocking chair."

"Why doesn't man feel motion or movement? Because he himself forms part of a gravitational system and all he feels is the force of the planet's attraction. Gravity is the attracting force toward the planet and he only notices it physically when he stumbles and falls to the floor by "that force" he believes is his own weight."

TIME

"On Earth, the "time" is defined by a perfectly synchronized conventional system as to know its interrelationship. For example, when something happens in a place, at what time did it happen? Since it depends on the point of reference, a certain moment can mean different times in the world. Mexico time is 12:00 p.m., in London, it is 7:00 p.m., and in Tokyo, it is 4:00 a.m., but of the following day! I'll repeat, although it is a different hour in each place, it is the "same moment" for all.

"The same occurs in space in the Universe. To determine the position of a certain point, it is necessary to refer to a framework of comparison and establish the coordinates for place and speed between both. Time here is of no essence."

"If you try to determine if something was "before" or "after", a point of comparison is needed. Two persons in different places will have different concepts of the same act, as for each, an act occurs when it is known."

"For example, let's us there are four train stations, each a day apart, and the train delivers newspapers published in station "A". When is the news known?" (Figure 71)

FIGURE 71

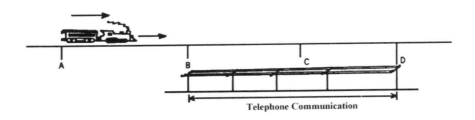

Telephone Communication

In "A", the first day, (where it happened)
In "B", the second day, (when the train brought the news)
In "C", the third day, (when the train arrived with the news)
In "D", the second day by phone (the train arrives on the fourth day).

"Each person will react when he learns the news, and that depends on when it reaches him. For those who don't know, it is as if nothing has happened."

"Let's consider the following basic elements to make an analysis: space, time and an inertia-gravitational system (which is the solar system) containing everything on the planet."

"Let's take Earth as a base INERTIAL-GRAVITATIONAL system, and let´s select a system of coordinates to allow us to locate a certain point, at a certain time, on its surface." (Figure No. 72)

FIGURE   72

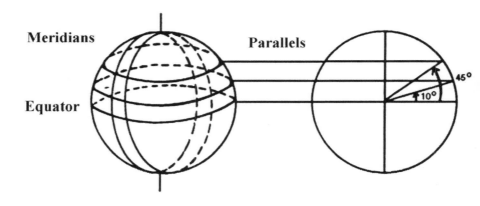

Parallels are the horizontal circles whose number is according to its angle from the center of the Earth on a meridian starting at the equator.

Meridians are the circles that pass by the poles. Zero meridian passes by Greenwich (England). If the 360 degrees of the circle are divided between the 24 hours of the day, there are meridians at every 15 degrees. (360/24 = 15).

"Therefore, using land coordinates, we can locate, for example, a plane flying over Mexico City. These would be:

X = 19 degrees Northern latitude
Y = 99 degrees Longitude
Z = 24 000 feet (8 kilometers approx.) Height

We can place that same point anywhere on Earth. For example, Honolulu, Hawaii is:

X = 6 522 kilometers to the East
Y = 174 kilometers to the South
Z = 8 000 meters high
T = at 12:00 hours on the 25ᵗʰ of December of 1990.

In both systems of coordinates, the point remains the same.

"But don´t forget that, one thing is to ponder a system at rest within the planet, and another, quite different when we are talking about the Universe, where the solar system is a small inertial-gravitational system forming part and interacting with all the galactic system."

The Theory of Relativity provides the solution as it does not depend on the position and characteristics of an observer, but understanding that everything is relative, and seeks to study the phenomenon by itself and independently."

"When studying the interrelationship of bodies in different stages of motion, it was found that the coordinate of "time" varies in intimate relation to the space it covers. Therefore, the relative speed between two bodies WILL DETERMINE the variation of time of one and the other."

"When the relative speed between two observers is high and gets close to the speed of light, there are two important phenomena that occur and are intimately related: spatial deformation and the lapse of time."

"If a mass reaches close to the speed of light, its inertia will increase in direct proportion to its speed, in such a way that it "tends" to arrive at an infinite value, which theoretically, a body with mass and inertia will never surpass the speed of light. Let's remember that the speed of light (300,000 kilometers per second) is a universal constant, that never varies, is independent and absolute.

Let's say we can be in a station in space and we see a special train which will pass in front of us. We get ready to see it pass, measure its length and take its time to pass us.

The train has a twenty-meter long engine and 99 wagons, also twenty meters in length. So, we know there are 100 units with a total length of 2,000 meters.

1.   If the train is traveling at a speed, whose interval is 0.5 (which is the relation between its speed and the speed of light):

     a) We will see: a total length = 1,000 meters.
         Length of each car = 10 meters.
     b) Twenty seconds have elapsed between the time we observed the latter and consulted our chronometer.
     c) El conductor also did the same as we did, but the reading on his chronometer will only be 10 seconds.

The result of case 1.

We realized that between the information we had regarding the train and our observations, this is reduced by HALF, because we measured each car at 10 meters instead of 20, and logically, the total length was 1,000 meters, not the 2,000 we were told.

Also, according to us, the conductor's chronometer is out of order, because it only read 10 meters, when we had measured 20.

To sum up:

The length and time of a speed close to the speed of light is detected approximately at half its value. In other words, apparently matter was reduced in the same direction of the movement, in direct proportion between the speed of light and the speed of the space train. Time, apparently, had the same luck.

Now let's see what happens if the train goes faster:

2. Let us consider that it travels at a speed nine tenths of the speed of light, equal to 270 thousand kilometers per second approximately.

   a) We will observe: train length = 200 meters approx.
      Wagon length = 2 meters approx.
   b) We use 20 seconds observing.
   c) Only 2 seconds transpired on the conductor's chronometer.

Result of case 2.
The time and space appear to be approximately one tenth the value they would have if motionless.

Now let's see what would happen if the train traveled at the speed of light:

3. The train's speed is 300 thousand kilometers a second.

   a) We observe the total length of the train = 0.0 meters.
   b) We know the train is passing, but we can't see it, so we can not measure time with any degree of precision, but we turn on our chronometer and we again get 20 seconds.
   c) When we saw the conductor's chronometer, it read 0.0 seconds.

Time elapsed for the train conductor is zero, "his time" has stopped.

Mathematically, the following can be established:
When speed "S" tends to the speed of light (S = 300,000 kilometers per second),
Then, time "T" tends to zero (T = 0)
And the inertia "I" tends to infinity .

When the space train, with its conductor, reaches the speed of light, it disappears for us, but that does not mean it ceases to exist. As it is a REAL phenomenon, we deduct that space and time are intimately linked together, and that the place where we live plus what we see, is in a Universe that also exists in SPACE-TIME.

This is not a metaphysical paradox nor science fiction. These are physical phenomena, the reality in which we live. This space-time we call THIRD DIMENSION, is the reality of an inertial-gravitational system where we exist in the SPACE-TIME dimension.

Eric requested a pause to digest the famous "simple explanation" Rahel was giving. Then, Mirza began:

"Eric, let's go back to the scientific knowledge of your brothers, who established the bases to understand far more complex applications. Do you know which are the basic principles to develop this theory ?"

"I think so, our science was based on the Laws of Newton until Einstein interrelated space, time, mass and speed."

"OK, let's proceed little by little. First, let's look at the basic principles."

FIRST PRINCIPLE. That is the speed of light, that does not vary in the Universe, and is therefore taken as a constant. Light moves in space at a speed of 300 thousand kilometers a second.

So you can get an idea of its movement, the average distance between Earth and the Sun is approximately 150 million kilometers, that are covered at the speed of light in 8 minutes.

SECOND PRINCIPLE. It is the equivalent between mass and energy represented by the equation $E=mc^2$, where
E is the energy
m is the mass
c^2 is the speed of light, squared.

The speed of light is a parameter that will help us to detect the effects of TIME and MATTER in the third dimension.

This affectation would not have been discovered by man in his civilization, but rather when the time came in his technological progress to be able to understand and measure it.

In order to understand the theory, which is the key to the understanding of natural phenomena we have been trying to teach everyone, let´s slowly go over the factors involved:

TIME. We must understand it as the lapse between two events. It is intangible but measurable.

SPEED. It is the relation that exists between the distance covered and the time it took to cover it. Light, as we said, covers 300 thousand kilometers in one second.

MASS. It is the amount of mass that exists in our third dimension. A body has certain measurements, length, width, height, and weight. These measurements determine the space it occupies and the weight will indicate how much mass it contains.

INTERVAL. It is an abstract concept that relates distance, speed and time.

Light is only an element for life, to animals and plants; but for man, for human technology in search of the truth, it is an enigma and the key to learning at the next level.

Time, as we normally know it, is not absolute and depends on many factors to be measured. It depends on the observer, his position regarding the event to be measured, and its relative speed. The real lapse between two events, in space, must be called INTERVAL.

This INTERVAL can vary from a value equal to time, to zero.

When the speed of the body being observed is zero, which means it is at rest with regard to the observer, the INTERVAL has the same value as time. But if the body is moving at the speed of light, the INTERVAL value is zero.

337

So, we can conclude:

a) When a body mass accelerates, its own time will be delayed inversely to the speed; in such a way, that when the latter reaches the speed of light (300 thousand kilometers per second), its time stops completely.

b) As the speed of its body increases, its mass seems to also increase because its inertia increases in direct proportion to the speed.

c) To an observer, the bodies become deformed as the speed increases in the opposite direction to the moving object, and as they reach the speed of light, theoretically, the physical dimension would be zero, that means, they disappear.

Then, what happens to the mass? Does it evaporate or disintegrate?, or simply, does it go to another dimension?*

----

*AUTHOR'S NOTE: For those readers who wish to learn more regarding the concept of the interval, as well as the difference between the temporal and the spatial, at the end of this chapter there is an Addendum with diagrams and simple notes on calculus and geometry.

Rahel had been enjoying a cup of tea while Mirza was desperately trying to explain these concepts to Eric, who to tell the truth, was really making great efforts to understand how time could stay still in a zero interval and the Universe could continue its on its way as if nothing had happened. Rahel offered them a cup of tea, which they greatly appreciated.

Rahel looked for examples to clarify these concepts, and help Eric to understand more about them.

"Look, Eric, see that little bird on that tree. It is looking at you. Your image reached his eyes and continued its path at a speed of 300 thousand kilometers a second. The images of what you did before are in front, and whatever you do after, will go behind. If you could go in one of them with your mind, you would see everything motionless. The images of what happened around you would also go with you, and nothing would change, unless you increase your speed, then you would begin to see past images as you caught up with them, thus you would be "traveling" in time."

"If you reach the speed of light, your time would stop because the Interval = 0, but if you pass it, you begin to "go back" in time."

"When a system with inertial and gravitational mass accelerates to the speed of light, the mass transforms into energy, and if it is a body structure, it passes to one of wave vibration that is not detectable in the third dimension."

"Matter deforms and is transformed upon acceleration transmigrating to enter another dimension where time of the third dimension does not enter, whose value is zero, is stopped. Remember, time = 0 at the speed of light."

"In this dimension, the laws of nature are equally in force, but their application is different, since they are transformed to take part in that universe which is parallel to ours, and that, to be better understood, we identify it as another dimension."

"Maybe it would be more understandable if we explain it another way."

"Space, without gravitational influences is flat and straight. It becomes deformed in the presence of gravitational masses that act simultaneously in it. This deformation is called SPACIAL CURVATURE."

"The GRAVITATION of the SPACIAL CURVATURE affects mass and time, and is the result of the sum of the curves which deform the space that makes up the masses."

"The routes of bodies in space, from a planet to a galaxy, could be said to be "obligatory", in the same way that the slope and the contour of the land mark the course to be followed by a thread of water or a river."

"When the gravitational fields are very strong, the special accelerations can be produced that lead to other dimensions, what you call hyperspace."

"Hyperspace is also part of the Master Universe and different spaces are parallel universes that interact between themselves."

"After space-time, we could call "fourth dimension" to that state we mentioned, without visible matter nor time, the way the third dimension is conceived."

"Natural laws are simpler and come together to be applied in the quantic and in the cosmic. The main forces of physics that you know are electro mechanic, gravitational and nuclear of fusion and fission."

"They all represent the tip of the iceberg; the main part of the iceberg cannot be seen because it is under water; so the larger part of the natural laws is unknown because they appear outside the third dimension."

"Subatomic particles are made up of elements that are also groups of even simpler ones, but are energy that vibrates in certain ranges. Particles have different "valences" which determine their integration in a certain dimension, which contains others in the same range. As they unite, they will form atoms and molecules that integrate the "mass" of matter in that direction."

"Therefore, there will be specific matter for the different dimensions in which they will appear."

"In hyperspace, we find the true unifying theory to understand natural laws that are the Divine Laws of Creation."

Eric still continued to be confused. Rahel´s concepts, after all, were not simple. There really isn't an easy way to explain relativity.

"The general idea is not difficult," Mirza continued. "The brain can understand it because it is familiar to knowledge within

340

you. Remember that your spirit belongs to hyperspace; it is happy there and you are talking about his place of origin. It is like taking away a blindfold from the mind´s eyes that, because it is in the physical brain, it is knowledge it must learn."

"It´s true that many of your brothers will get tired of hearing this information, not because it is difficult, but because it is new and revolutionary. But surely, they will understand it, little by little, even without a scientific background."

"You will find that those who are knowledgeable, will try to enter discussions regarding the physic-mathematical aspects, but don´t worry. You are talking about general concepts of consciousness, and you are enticing that desire to learn to come from them to stimulate their own spiritual knowledge."

While Mirza was talking, she took out a delicious breakfast of succulent fruit.

While they ate, sitting on the grass, a flock of birds sang in the background. Eric lay down on his back to look at the clouds, and transmitted telepathically: "I really thank you so much for your friendship and for everything you have taught me. I only wish that, it was not just me, but a large group of people. That way, all of them could help me accomplish this mission."

"Don´t worry, you will see that everything will turn out fine, and then you will be surprised so many people will help you. You will find you are not alone, and that many more have to carry out complementary missions to reach our goal," Mirza said as she patted him on the back.

After a short break, Mirza continued. Her lovely voice was always a joy to hear. Eric was happy to listen to her explanations, they were so clear.

"It is the right time to mention the knowledge your scientists work with, so you will know what parts of the bridge you must cover. For example, let´s start with the smallest. What are the basic particles?"

"Well, according to man's knowledge, a classification of the particles and their characteristics has already been made:

SUBATOMIC ⎰ FERMIONS. Particles that constitute matter (mass)

PARTICLES ⎱ BOSONS.　Particles bearers of energy (force)

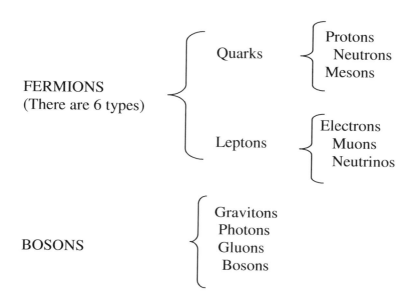

FERMIONS
(There are 6 types)

Quarks { Protons / Neutrons / Mesons

Leptons { Electrons / Muons / Neutrinos

BOSONS { Gravitons / Photons / Gluons / Bosons

Different physical forces are manifested with the following particles:

GRAVITATION	with	GRAVITONS
ELECTROMAGNETIC	with	PHOTONS
NUCLEAR (strong)	with	GLUONS
NUCLEAR (weak)	with	BOSONS

"Well," continued Mirza.　"As there are generic representations of the subatomic particles to integrate matter, there is no problem; it is useful, but if you want to dig deeper, there is no continuity. If you notice, everything in the Universe forms repetitive cycles of similar behavior and human science looses that in the subatomic particles."

"The quark classification is not the most adequate, and the subatomic particles do not explain the participation in the so-called antimatter that floods the Universe. It is atomic physics in the third dimension, but it is necessary to integrate the fourth dimension and also higher ones that are not affected by time."

"The subtle matter which makes up your spirit is stable, its origin is not the same, but similar to that of other dimensions, and is outside the action of space-time. It is there, in that bridge of quantum mechanics that you do not know yet, where the dimension separation begins."

"After going over the scope of matter and energy presentations, and trying to understand space-time, that is when dimensional separation presents itself again."

"You must have, at the tip of your fingers, the explanation of what that "bridge" we were talking about previously, to be able to have a better understanding of this subject. Albert Einstein established in his Theory of Relativity, the specific science of the third dimension."

"Your science based their knowledge about gravitation on Newton´s Laws. In his theory, Einstein gave a rational explication regarding the nature of the interrelation that exists between space, time, mass and gravitation."

"Quantum mechanics considers the small particles of matter as capsules of energy. These particles, many times smaller than atoms, are the elements which will integrate subatomic particles, and are called quantum (plural: quanta).

"One quantum of energy equals the tiniest quantity of matter that could produce it."

"The interrelation between matter and energy was established by Newton. Do you remember the formula?"

"Yes, Mirza, it is the second of Newton´s Laws, where force is equal to mass multiplied by acceleration."

$$F = M\,a$$

"That's right, a photon is a bundle of electromagnetic energy. A group of bundles forms a body of vibrating particles, which has as in all vibrations, frequency and width. Natural vibrating photons generate light, and the latter does not contain mass that can be deformed."

"Tell me, do you remember in what other part of physics do vibrations interrelate?"

"Yes, in the Laws of Thermodynamics. The first establishes that: "Energy cannot be generated nor destroyed, it simply transforms." I understand that it just changes its vibration."

"The second law establishes that: "Entropy (particles of matter in disarray) tends to chaos in the Universe." Which means, it tends to expand in total disorder. In this case, I understand that particles in a relative state of disarray, are disordered through complex behavior, but always tend to go to places with a lower temperature."

"You are right, in a certain way, such is precisely the behavior of the Universe. The Big-Bang Theory itself behaves that way. Vibrations are the life of the Universe, your senses in the third dimension depend on them to detect the presence of matter and energy in a solid, liquid or gas state, their color, temperature, etc."

"Through vibrations, your spirit also attracts, through its senses, the charkas, the manifestations and communications in its dimension."

"Also, mental spheres work through vibrations; cells communicate through vibrations, dimensions in space are detected through vibrations, and your emotions are felt in your physical being through vibrations. Do you see how important they are? They are the characteristic of the Universe that generates our existence."

"Light is vibration, and when matter accelerates toward the speed of light, its own vibration is affected and causes apparently inexplicable perceptions like the deformation of matter and the modification of the coordinate, time."

"An increasing vibration will be manifested as a delay in time and, traveling at the speed of light, disappears. It integrates space, which is the border of the dimension SPACE-TIME."

"Now let's go back to the SECOND basic principle of the Theory of Relativity. How do you understand it?"

"Well, it is the equivalence between mass and energy; we can see it in the equation:

$$E = mc^2 \quad \text{where:} \quad \begin{array}{l} E = \text{Energy in ergs} \\ m = \text{Mass in grams} \\ c = \text{Speed of light} \end{array}$$

The ERGS are units of energy defined as the necessary force needed to accelerate a gram of mass at a speed of one centimeter a second: the MASS is matter in grams; and the speed of light is 30 thousand millions of centimeters per second."

"That's right, and the formula shows us that Mass (m) can be transformed into Energy (E) and vice versa."

"If, for example, a body emits energy through radiation, the energy "E" will be decreasing in value due to that loss, and to maintain equilibrium in the equation, then the value of Mass (m), will be decreasing."

"By the same token, we deduce, from the equation, that if a gram of mass is multiplied by c2 (the speed of light to the square), the energy to be obtained, will be:

$$E = 1 \times (30 \text{ thousand millions})_2.$$
$$E = 1 \times (3 \times 10 \,_{10})\,_2.$$
$$E = 9 \times 10 \,_{20}.$$
$$E = 900 \text{ trillion ergs.}$$

"This is the force needed to move the weight of a mountain like the Everest a distance of 10 meters in one second. Thus we see that the energy obtained transforming mass to energy, is enormous!"

"When a nuclear process is carried out, it must be done slowly, with total and absolute control, to be able to take advantage of it."

"There is grave danger if control is lost, not only because of the explosion which could occur, but also the enormous amount of radioactivity that would be released into the atmosphere, and the wind could take it in unimaginable quantities and distances.

345

Radioactive energy destroys living cells, and is fatal for animals and plants."

"You do realize, then, that concepts can vary in distances, speeds and times, and depend on, and are, related to each other. "

"All this is the door to understand all the concepts outside of what has been studied and comprehended by your science. Such as, invisible matter in another dimension, but having its own mass can produce gravitational effects on the Universe."

"Cosmic energy gives birth to the formation of energetic quanta and particles of matter, which originate particles called quarks and electromagnetic, gravitational and nuclear energy, that are also formed by the existence of matter. Once you have the latter, you have nuclear energy represented by particles you call gluons and bosons, and electromagnetic energy where photons are manifested, and gravitons for gravitational energy."

"But then, you still have equivalencies and laws that rule the systems of inertia and gravitation of what is called "antimatter" and "invisible matter". That is constituted by subatomic particles of the fourth dimension, to maintain cosmic equilibrium."

"This knowledge is necessary to perfect applicable theories of quantum physics, astrophysics and cosmology."

"It is imperative then, to go learn more to control the application of energy you handle. For example, laser rays can achieve chemical and biochemical reactions of molecular disassociation that will lead you down new paths of progress. It is necessary to know the behavior of matter and energy, from the beginning, to take advantage of the type of vibration needed to modify it."

"In astrophysics, phenomena very similar to quantics occur. Just as in quantum mechanics you studied the integration of neutrinos, uniting and combining the electronegatron energy with the propositron to generate strang and bultic rays, in regions of the cosmos you cannot even imagine, there are totally different galaxies to the ones you have observed. There are those where germs of plasmatic energy are gestated, to give origin to bodies in space and the transformation of cosmic energy into mass and matter. All this is very complex, and apparently occurs spontaneously but, in reality, everything is guided by higher spiritual entities, which we will refer to later."

A cytohelium, for example, is a generator of energy and is similar to cells. You have seen the marvels a cell can do. In fact, you already can provoke changes and modify certain parts or functions as in the genetic chromosomes, even without knowing exactly how each gene came about. There are particles in the cells so tiny, they are beyond the borders of your known physics. The cytohelium is on the border of the cosmos, it is a spacial cell."

"I would like to get into details regarding the "how", because I got a glimpse in my course of quantum mechanics, and I would like to know if my concepts are correct," Eric interrupted.

"I promise we will go into that at a later date;   I just mentioned it right now, because it does have to do with relativity."

"The bodies with mass in nature are identified in the dimension space-time according to their physical characteristics. These bodies are ruled by the universal laws of gravitation and electromagnetism. However, when forces take them to the borders of transformation (that is, at speeds close to the speed of light), changes or deformations occur to adapt matter to the change in dimension."

"Electromagnetic energy also causes changes in matter at a structural level, and also at the borders (a physical body in a high-density electromagnetic field) will also experience the deformations to adapt to the change in dimension."

"To prove the previous principles, for now, are beyond the scope of mankind´s science, but correspond to the transdimensional level you are about to enter, beginning with the comprehension of spiritual existence."

Eric remained silent, in deep thought, trying to impress all this in his mind....he would digest it later...! Rahel waited for some comment, but as nothing was forthwith, he stood up and told Eric, "It´s time to go."

"How did you come? May I take you anywhere?"

"Thanks, Eric!" said Mirza, and winking at Rahel, said, "We didn´t walk far this time, did we?"

"That's true, our spacecraft is right here." He pointed to the center of the lawn.

Eric couldn't see anything, but they walked over there, after saying goodbye. After about 20 meters, parallel to the trees, they went to the center of the lawn. He still couldn't see anything, and enjoyed himself trying to imagine what they would come up with next!

There was ample space, about 80 meters. Some children were playing on the opposite side. Rahel and Mirza were heading toward the center, but as they left the shade of the trees, it seemed as though their heads were covered with fog and then,.... they simply disappeared in the fog! About forty seconds later, Eric heard the humming of the spaceship's rotors. The children also heard the noise and turned trying to see what it was, then a light inside a balloon appeared. The children also saw it and pointed to it. At the same time, Eric received a transmission: *"See you next time!"*

"Thank you very much! See you soon!" Eric answered.

He was happy. He started his car toward the airport. He felt it would really be difficult to remember everything he had been taught on this occasion. He didn't even think he had understood it all, anyway. He needed to clarify some information with Rahel at the next meeting.

However, his sense of well-being was greater. He was very excited, more than being worried, about putting some concepts in order. He felt such mental peace, he was confident regarding the future of his adventure.

ADENDUM

THE INTERVAL

Space, speed and time are intimately related. Time, length and mass are altered in the same proportion as the INTERVAL.

When a body is motionless to the observer, its speed has a value of "zero", and in these conditions, it is possible to take its measurements directly and simultaneously. We can measure the distance between its extremes directly with a measuring tape; but when it is in motion, it will have its own time, its own dimensions and its own mass, that the observer can only measure indirectly and not simultaneously, and will appear to be different.

INTERVAL is the name of a physical act between two events which are related. This act does not depend on the particular circumstances of the observer.

There can be three different types of a physical act, called INTERVAL:

1. TEMPORARY INTERVAL: is that in which the observer can be present in both events.
2. "ZERO" INTERVAL: is that which relates the events though the passage of a ray of light.
3. SPACIAL INTERVAL: is that in which a physical body cannot be present at both events, because to be able to do so, it would have to go from one event to the other at a speed higher than the speed of light.

Examples of TEMPORARY INTERVAL.
When V = 0 and there is simultaneous, everything can be measured without alteration, such as, time, inertia and dimensions. (Figure No. 73)

FIGURE 73

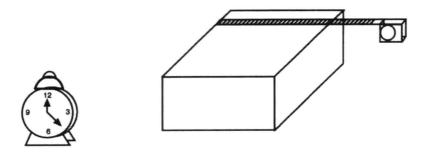

When the body is in motion, we will have the following diagram to relate both events. (Figure No. 74-A)

FIGURE 74-A

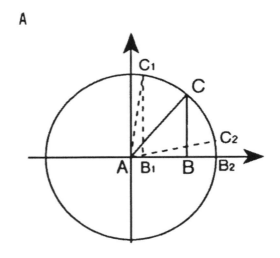

AC = the distance that light covers in space, in the time between both events.
AB = the distance in space between both events.
BC = the value of the INTERVAL between both events.

When AB $\longrightarrow$ 0   If AB = 0   BC = AC
    AB $\longrightarrow$ AC   AB = AC   BC = 0

Points C_1 and C_2 show how B_1C_1 and B_2C_2 vary as the value of AB changes.

We can see that BC varies from a value = 1 when BC = AC, and decreases as AB increases, and when AB = AC, then BC = 0.
Example: Let us suppose a comet travels an arch of 200,000 kilometers in 10 seconds. (Figure No. 74-B and 74-C)

1. On axis "X", we draw the magnitude of AB = 200,000 kilometers (distance between the events, that are the beginning and the end of the arch).

2. With a center in "A", we draw a circle with a radius of AC = z = 3,000,000 kilometers (the distance that light would travel in those same 10 seconds).

FIGURE   74-B and 74-C

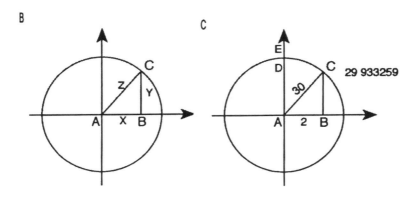

351

3. A perpendicular is drawn from "B" to cut the circumference in "C", BC = the value of the interval.

Calculating using Pitagoras 'Theorem: $x^2 + y^2 = z^2$

Therefore $\qquad\qquad\qquad y = \sqrt{z^2 - x^2}$

Substituting the values: $\quad y = \sqrt{30^2 - 2^2} = \sqrt{900 - 4}$

$$y = \sqrt{896}$$

$$y = \quad 29.93$$

As BC = AD then: DE = magnitude of the deformation of interval.
    BC = 29.93   BC/AC = % of the value of AC
The Interval I = 99.77753 % of AC
If   AC = 10 sec, then I = 9.977753 sec.

This means that the time elapsed for an observer on the comet, his chronometer would only show the value of the interval.

Example of INTERVAL "ZERO".

Supposing an observer on Earth registers an explosion occurring in the Sun:

1. The explosion occurred at 12:00 hours.
2. The observer's watch showed 12.08 hours (the time it took the ray of light to travel the distance between the Earth and the Sun).
3. An observer on Jupiter would see it at 12.42 hours (34 minutes later).

However, an observer traveling in the ray of light, would always be seeing his watch fixed at 12.00 hours, because his time, traveling at the speed of light would stop, and would continue that way, while maintaining that speed.

Example of SPACIAL INTERVAL.

An observer on Earth detects two impacts of meteorites, one on planet "A" and another on planet "B", with a difference of five minutes. The distance between them is 270,000 millions of kilometers. (Figures 74-D and 74-E)

FIGURES 74-D and 74-E

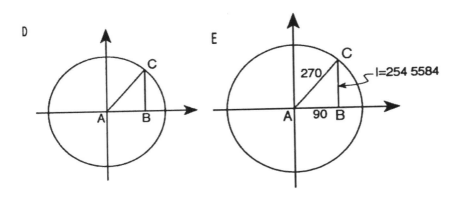

AB = The distance light will travel in time between both events.
AC = The special distance between both events.
BC = The interval between the events.

1. We draw AB = 300 seconds x speed of light = 90 million kms.
2. We draw AC = 270 million kilometers.
3. We draw BC = Interval

Calculating using Pitagoras´Theorem: $BC = \sqrt{270^2} = \sqrt{64,800}$

BC = 254.55844 that is the 94.2809% of AC
T = 5 min. = 300 seconds, therefore:
Interval = 4.714 minutes
This will be the time between both events for any observer in wherever place he is.

353

CHAPTER XVIII

When a civilization has the capacity
to come to us, and we compare
our knowledge with theirs,
it will be the same as if we compared
ourselves to primitive man
at the beginning of time.

That is why it is so difficult
to understand and accept their existence.

Pablo E. Hawnser

THE UNIVERSE

As the weeks past, Eric reviewed his notes, read some scientific articles and tried to prepare his next meeting. The truth was that it was not easy to digest all this knowledge and understand the inertial-gravitational concepts he had received at the last encounter. Although, as Mirza had predicted, little by little, everything was becoming more clear to him.

Two months had gone by since that meeting in San Luis Potosi. He had been tempted, during the last three weeks, to contact them, but an inner voice told him not to. If Mirza had not called, there must be a reason. He did miss them, anyway!

Another two weeks passed, and this time, he did send a message through mental telepathy. Then, he did get a call.

"Is that you, Mirza?"

"Yes, Eric, how have you been?"

"Very well, but missing you. I had thought you would call sooner."

"We have been away, and Rahel has had a lot of work. He may tell you about it when we meet. Are you ready for another lesson?"

"Of course. You probably don't believe me, but I have missed you all very much. I feel as though we have been friends for many years. Also, I have to talk about all this, but as Rahel told me not to breathe a word until he authorized it, I need to get it off my chest and, prove I am not going nuts!"

Mirza laughed. Oh, that pleasant, crystalline laughter!
"You are certainly not, I can guarantee it!"

Eric could not stop thinking Mirza was not a normal woman. She was, literally, out of this world! Of course, her sense of humor was the same as ours, and there were many similarities with people on Earth.

"I have to go to Guadalajara, but I have been postponing the trip. If you want, we can meet there next Friday."

"Yes, that's fine. In any case, it could not be before then, because Rahel has not returned yet. But he should be back by then. If not, we'll be in touch and maybe meet in Mexico City at another date."

"I know that if Rahel would prefer for us to meet elsewhere, away from Mexico City, he certainly has his reasons."

"That's right. Your mental attitude and disposition improve when you are away. Rahel is aware of this."

"I hadn't realized this, is there a reason for it?"

"Yes, it's just psychological."

"Well, I'll get ready as always. I expect to be free after lunch, at around 4:30 p.m. Can you be at the airport at around 5:30 p.m.?"

"Yes, that seems fine. Well, take care and we'll see you then."

"Thank you, Mirza. You take care of yourself, as well."

That day, Eric finished up his business as he had planned, and was on his way to the airport at 4:30 p.m.

There was a lot of traffic, but it was flowing gradually and he thought he would be passing the Hotel Tapatio in about half an hour to get on the highway to the airport. It all worked out and at 5:30 p.m. he had delivered the rented car and was in the terminal. He had thought of meeting his friends in the waiting room, but he saw them outside in the parking lot, and went to them.

They greeted and invited Eric to a parked car, some distance away from the rest. It was a van with dark windows. He couldn´t remember the make of the car, and looked for the logo, out of curiosity. Mirza saw him do this, and said, "It doesn´t have a logo. What do you think it is?

"Well, it looks like a......hum...no, I don´t know."

"It doesn´t have a brand name, we use it in cases like today when we arrive somewhere and we don´t have a car available. The size and design are adapted to fit in the spacecraft."

Eric walked around it, with great interest. The handles and locks on the doors were covered, and emerged when Rahel pressed an ultrasound button. Under the car, there were some spokes linked to the four wheels. When the car was taken to the spaceship, two rails could extend and receive the spokes. The car could then be hauled in, on its own propulsion.

They entered the van. It was ample and comfortable. It operated on electricity, of course. There was air-conditioning, and the indispensable teapot!

"It has some special features for us, as safety measures." Rahel explained. "It cannot be stolen. In the first place, they wouldn´t know how to open it. The windows and siding are bullet proof. It is so resistant, that even if a grenade did go off inside, nothing would be damaged. The glass on the windows equals a steel plate one-fourth of an inch thick. The siding is the same. All the components was equally resistant."

"It´s like a small war tank. It is so resistant and protected. For example, look at this search light. It can emit different types of waves: a conic light beam or a laser ray, depending on the frequency and length of the wave; it can be luminous or invisible, with very varied effects.

Directed to a car engine 500 meters away, we can make the ray cut the electric energy. When this happens, the motor stops. We can, also, control the emission so the effect works according to the voltage. Then, there is no current in the spark plugs, but the radio still works. If we lower the voltage, it can paralyze a person or a group of persons.

At a distance, we can interrupt the passage of current through high tension wires or make a hole in a steel plate. A very intense light can be emitted and, simultaneously, another type of brain paralyzing vibrations—without permanent damage. These are only precautionary safety measures.

Eric was very interested, and since he felt they were on a subject where questions could be asked, inquired: "All this is on your spacecraft as well, isn´t it? This explains a lot of things that have been said regarding extra-terrestrials. Such as when OVNIS appear, car motors stop, there have been blackouts due to interference of high tension wires, blinding lights, and people who claim not to remember what happened while those bright lights were on.

"It´s possible that some crew, during a mission, has had to do this. But you can be sure, and please spread this to your brothers, no one nor no group has ever intentionally been hurt. It isn´t logical. Our missions are to help and protect you. In fact, you can´t even imagine how much we have done to help you all, without your being aware of it."

"Just imagine if a spaceship from NASA would get to a planet inhabited by human beings like you, as we are. Do you think the astronauts would want to hurt them, or help them? I would think, help them. Right? In any case, no one who is not, at least, at the level of super-man could have the opportunity to visit other worlds."

"Operations have been carried out where sightings have been allowed for your awareness, and the authorities have had the most infantile reactions. Children and simple people have more sense, than those who have more education and authority."

"Do you remember our comments regarding our safety, Eric? You wanted to come with us, but we told you we were safe. Well, look at this." Mirza brought out a small object that was hanging from her waist band. It looked like a flashlight the size of a marker pen. She set it, turning a ring and three small radio controls. Then, she handed it to Eric to examine. It looked exactly like a flashlight with an inside radio.

357

"Point it to that man going, with his luggage and the porter, to his car. Don´t worry, nothing will happen to him. Get off the car, press the red button for three seconds, and get in the car again."

Eric turned to look at Rahel, who smiled condescendingly. Eric did what Mirza had instructed.

As soon as he had pressed the button, the man and his porter stopped short, as if they had heard a train´s whistle. The man turned around, as if to go back, but stopped. He seemed to have thought the better of it, and kept going to his car, the porter simply followed him.

"High frequency waves cause slight mental confusion, that is short lived," Mirza explained. "However, we can paralyze them for longer periods, and their minds would be blank during that time. This would cause more confusion. The effect would be in direct response to the physical activity of the person. If he were irate or running, he would feel the effect more strongly, and could loose his balance and fall. But as Rahel told you, these are safety precautions, not weapons for aggression."

"All right," said Rahel. "Let's get to our lesson of today. We have said previously, that nature is our best teacher. If we know how to observe, we will learn and solve problems."

Eric, nodded in agreement. He interrupted, "I am sure everyone understands that we can learn from nature. But to say that I learnt this from you, would certainly not carry much weight."

"That´s true," Rahel answered patiently. "Whatever is obvious and simple, does not impress anyone. You must point to the obvious that they have never tried to understand, because it is not material. It is necessary not only to have knowledge, but also, have the faith and will to try to understand physical phenomena when these are manifestations from another dimension."

"Let me give you an example you all know. When Jesus of Nazareth was alive, he tried to teach people the power of faith. He made "miracles" healing the sick. The people who witnessed these, were marveled. But the rest did not believe."

The healings were miracles to those people and will continue to be for your brothers, until they understand how they can be done again."

"But if you think about it, you will realize Jesus did not want to impress people as being a fortune teller or showman. It was certainly not a show, rather a lesson in awareness, but not even then, did you learn. It´s not surprising for those simple fishermen, but you—today´s mankind—have you learnt it yet?"

"Let's look at another example, man has always been guided by the voice of his conscience. More often than not, they are deaf to the voice, but there is no doubt "something" inside them told them what to do, whether they did it or not, is another matter."

"The same thing happens with "miracles". There are many things to also observe in nature. For example, the electrons rotate around the nucleus of the atom. Why?"

"Galaxies are getting farther away in space and every second, every instant, they are doing so at a greater speed, why?"

"Seeds germinate in the proper medium, why?"

"Why can you remember what you did yesterday, or several years ago, and do it again?"

"All these "miracles" have an explanation that is easier as the intervening elements are known."

"All your brothers have to now is do a "miracle" themselves—reason with their faith and listen to the voice of their conscience. Clearly identifying it in their mind to learn how to get their own spiritual contact."

"Look, Eric, in our conversations and taking advantage of your previous knowledge, it has been easy for us to cover many subjects, but you know, from the beginning, that I cannot, because I should not, give you more information than what was decided initially. Especially information that could be taken advantage of immediately to clear up or solve scientific problems applied to industry, medicine or any other area of your sciences."

"The reason for this is, you must accomplish all this on your own. Of course, there are many things I have told you, and will tell you in future, are crossing an unconquered area, and that you can take advantage knowing what comes after. Anyway, it would not be ethical to give out that information only to a few. Who would be the ideal person to receive such privileged information? You are divided, some are enemies. Who, in justice and in fairness, is right?

359

Precisely because we cannot be the judge, it is not given out to anyone at all."

"The information we are providing can be useful, if everyone makes the effort to obtain it. We cannot interfere directly, as I have explained to you, because other complex problems that would arise. Anyway, it should be your merit to know how to distinguish what you can take advantage of, for your knowledge and your evolution."

"Recapping your history, we find man already has enough knowledge, and has traced the history of his physical evolution. You already know that once the planet was ready, animal and plant life developed to prepare a place where man could evolve."

"Also, I should tell you that this history has been repeated many thousands of times in evolutionary planets. Just in this local universe, there are almost one thousand making their history right now. One planet can serve several evolving humanities, the time to take advantage of in the third dimension can vary, and there could be one or several periods within a several million–year-lapse, depending on diverse factors."

"Let's talk about universal cosmogony. You call "Universe", the space you are able to see around the planet and even further away, considering a tridimensional volume where all the stars you can see now and in the future, can fit. You give it an infinite measurement."

"We call all that the MASTER UNIVERSE, as it is made up of eight elements, which are: a Central Universe (we call Island of Light) and seven Super-Universes surrounding it."

"There are seven Super-Universes that are in operation. The one we are in, is the seventh; where you and we have to cover of first evolutionary phase. It is being formed, and it constitutes the seventh zone of creation. They are all separated by higher than intergalactic spaces."

"Each SUPER UNIVERSE constitutes a gigantic area of Creation and contains 100,000 zones, we'll call LOCAL UNIVERSES."

"Let me explain simply what a SUPER UNIVERSE is. The size in space-time is so immense, it is difficult to understand. So, we will see an allegoric representation, to have a supporting cosmographic image in our mind." (Figure No. 75)

360

FIGURE 75

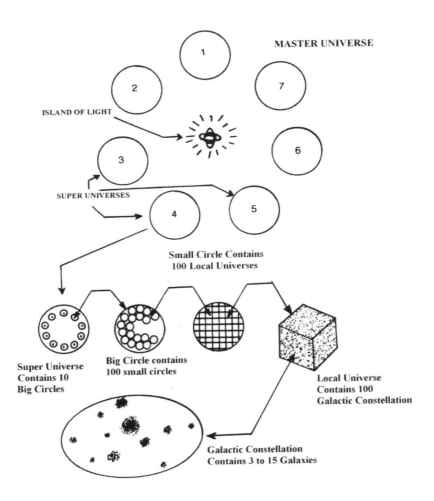

"Within an imaginary circle, we drew 10 circles rotating softly around their center and, at the same time, all did the same clockwise, within the outer circles.

Each of the "big hoops" contains 100 "small hoops", also spinning the same way and also moving clockwise within.

Each "small hoop" is subdivided in 100 areas called "local universes".

LOCAL UNIVERSE is integrated by 100 Galactic Constellations and contains from 10 thousand to 100 thousand "Evolutionary Planets". (Each Constellation has 100 Inhabited Planetary Systems, but can be increased to 1000).

GALACTIC CONSTELLATION groups from 3 to 12 Galaxies around the main one, that is the basis of the Gravitational System. Each Constellation can contain from 100 to 1000 planetary systems that possess an **evolutionary planet,** this means it is inhabited by a humanity in evolution. "Evolutionary Planets" are those that have the proper conditions to allow the existence of intelligent life to develop a technological humanity in evolution.

GALAXY is a group of stars of different sizes, but the smallest can have up to 1 million stars and the largest up to 1 billion (one million millions!).

MILKY WAY is the **Galaxy** we call our cosmic home. It is made up of approximately 200 thousand millions of starts. It is a Galaxy of a young system, but one day will be made up of 1000 evolutionary planets.

STAR is a celestial body having its own light, like our Sun. It can have a Planetary System, although so many conditions are required for it to have an evolutionary planet. It must contain adequate means for life so be able to develop a Technological Humanity in Evolution, it only occurs in one per 200 to 2000 millions of stars.

EVOLUTIONARY PLANET is one which can offer the necessary conditions for life for a technological humanity in evolution. In our Galactic Constellation, there is only one for every 2 thousand million stars!"

"Do you realize what a divine privilege it is to live on one of these planets? All of them started, more or less, the same way. Of course, there are some variations which are natural to imagine given the many diverse conditions."

"You must consider these amounts only as an indication, since the type, variety and the size of the galaxies and constellations are enormous. However, they are all related gravitationally. If we

362

consider the closer groups, we can find some exceptionally large, starting at 12 to 15 galaxies, but even if they are further away, they still have a gravitational interaction between them. For example, the Milky Way has a gravitational interaction with Andromeda, although they are separated by 2,500,000 light years.

"A constellation is a group of galaxies found at a distance of three to five diameters from each other and of the principle galaxy. In the Milky Way, 500 thousand light years would be within that distance. There are galaxies in your group that you know as the Clouds of Magellan, both big and small, Sculptor, Formax, Leo I, Leo II, Osa Minor and Dracus. There are also, other invisible systems acting gravitationally."

"The Clouds of Magellan are the two galaxies of the constellation that are closer to each other, at an average distance of 180 thousand light years." (Figure 76)

FIGURE 76

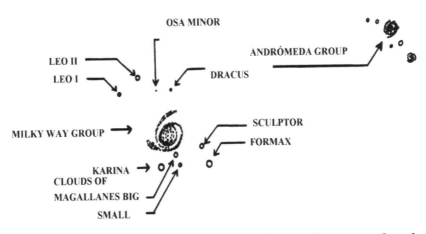

"On Earth, man has the privilege of being the means for the evolution of spirits in a physical world in third dimension in space-time."

"A planet is ready to be inhabited when it possesses the ideal mineral, vegetable and animal elements to permit the development of a technological humanity. The basis, as we have said, will also be a perfected animal primed after thousands of years of study by higher brothers, known as BIOLOGICAL ENGINEERS."

"The irrational being will be transformed by the implant of mental spheres, and assigned to be the physical means of evolution for a spirit, turning him into a "human being". That is how MAN begins."

"Earth, is known in the Universe as Dogue, Dubko or Urania, where a living being like you, was perfected. You call it SIMIAN. It was adapted to the planet and its physical evolution continued to prepare him for the implant of mental spheres. After his brain and all his body systems achieved the necessary development, divine authorization was given. Higher entities proceeded to give that irrational being, intelligence and a mind in his physical world of the third dimension, that would allow him to function in space-time, as the physical body of an evolutionary spirit."

DEVELOPMENT OF EVOLUTIONARY SPIRITS

"When the Father considered it appropriate, babies of irrational beings began to be transformed into human beings by the implant of mental spheres immediately after their physical birth. Simultaneously, a soul was assigned, and came to live in the body of that new born, to experience its life."

"As of that moment, all the descendants will also be human beings with a soul, that is the presence of the spirit in fourth dimension, living in the physical body in third dimension."

"As there are two souls in each spirit, each will be assigned a being of the opposite sex, and all the individuals of that group will begin to form mankind."

"Naturally, due to lack of experience, they begin at "zero", having the expected behavior. In that first phase, when the being reaches an adequate physical development, the electromagnetic identification of twin souls occurs. That is, the souls coming from the same spirit took action so the individuals would have an element to bring them closer through electromagnetic affinity and then, started the prerecording of the sexual instinct to preserve the species."

"These first human beings started their groups on different parts of the planet, at the same time, and constituted the first evolutionary level, that is known as the humanoid."

FIRST EVOLUTIONARY PLANE,
THE HUMANOID

"His immediate ancestor is the SIMIAN. Their appearance was similar even though he had a soul and mental spheres. The influence of their actions and attitudes will bring about the physical changes of the man we know today."

"Twin souls are identified and attracted to each other to form a couple and reproduce instinctively, when the sexual charkas produce energy that is sent to superior planes."

"Their life span is short, an average of only 25 years, due to the dangers and living conditions, but their spiritual brain will store their experiences and influence the physical brains in their next lives."

"As the soul leaves the material body on the planet at the end of each physical life, it will stay in the astral body of the fourth dimension for a short period of time, while eliminating its karmas."

"After it will go to its spirit in the fifth dimension, and there, with the help of higher spirits (its guides and mentors), will prepare for the next lesson. This will be a new opportunity in a new life, accompanying a human being from birth to death. A new cycle for more experiences, to acquire knowledge and enrich the spirit with wisdom."

"During that new phase, the soul lives in the body of the person who has been chosen because of the conditions and characteristics their parents have and their place of residence. This can predict the opportunities it will have to learn, suffer painful experiences and enjoy the fortunate ones, to enrich his treasure chest of knowledge and feelings."

"While the soul is "incarnated" in a body, that is, it is living in symbiosis with its physical body, the spiritual memory is blocked. A free passage of memories from the spiritual memory bank, where the experiences and knowledge are stored from the beginning of its evolution to the physical memory in the material brain of the human it inhabits, are not allowed."

"Only filtrations of knowledge acquired in previous existences are permitted as inspirations coming from the conscience, to take advantage of them as a behavioral guide for that person in the world of the third dimension. The reason is to obligate the physical brain to use the mind and develop an intelligence allowing it to overcome any existential problems."

"The evolutionary plane corresponding to the humanoid lasts approximately 25,000 years. This is the length of an astronomical cycle."

"The precession is a conical movement that describes the planet´s axis drawing a complete circle due to the angular variation that occurs. The inclination in the rotation of the axis of the planet corresponds to a perpendicular to the plane of its traslation orbit. This movement generates the seasons of the year due to the variation in the angle of the sun rays. This inclination rotates and, it is that movement that is called precession. A complete cycle is the time it takes to develop an evolutionary plane. That is, one evolutionary cycle per astronomical cycle."

SECOND EVOLUTIONARY PLANE, THE CAVEMAN

"The main difference with the previous plane comes from the fifth dimension and the fact the population of human beings is much larger, the union of twin souls is obstructed. This also stimulates the instinctive need to find a mate, to protect and support it. Also, the protective instinct of their offspring, force the development of an intelligence that stimulates the imagination and thereby, speeds up its evolution."

"The needs generated by the living conditions in this plane, demand a more intense physical battle. They also stimulate the development of other charkas and the need to send evolving energy to superior planes through sexual charges of energy. The lack of a twin soul also invites violence, and at the same time, incites the mind to obtain what is needed."

"The average life span in this plane is also approximately 25 years, and it lasts another cycle of 25,000 years."

THIRD EVOLUTIONARY PLANE, FIRST LEVEL, THE MAN

"Man continues without the union of twin souls and is characterized by the perfection of neurobiological systems of mental control and synchronization of the human body. Man has learned, through experience, to use the elements provided by nature, adapting them to his needs. He manufactures cutlery and tools, plants, cares for animals for his use, and provides himself with a roof and nourishment. He discovers fire, organizes a society and manifests his religious inspirations with rituals and ceremonies. He begins to feel the need for spirituality through matter."

"Little by little, civilizations appear, as does technology and science. Man feels the need to learn the truth regarding his origin and his destiny. By intuition, he begins to comprehend the difference between matter and the spirit, but his lack of knowledge causes a vacuum. His physical brain, that is material, will try to fill that vacuum, caused by the lack of unity between matter and the spirit, through rites and ceremonies that eventually become customs. He not only tries to show his respect to the gods he fears through ignorance (rain, fire, wind, etc.), but also wants to satisfy his instinctive need for religion."

"He deifies everything he admires, fears or needs. But, his religious actions can be identified as idolatry from the beginning. We consider the three stages in the evolution of religions of the human being, as:

367

1.   Fear. It is the basis of the first religious manifestations of primitive man. He turns all he fears and admires into gods, in an attempt to please them.
2.   Superstition. Man is still lacking in knowledge. He is just beginning to develop science and technology. He presents his vital needs for love and affection on physical statues and figures to adore and please them, to mitigate his growing spiritual aspirations. He carries out new and elaborate rituals that he integrates into complex ceremonies that become traditions.

"All this gives man moral support, which he confuses as spiritual satisfaction, and accepts dogma without reasoning. On the one hand, because of ignorance, and on the other, because they satisfy his needs."

3.   Religious Hierarchy. This is the next to the last step of modern man in the religious evolution. No matter what religion he believes in, he feels the need to find his own spiritual identify with after life.

"He can feel his spiritual origin, but is still too materialized and only leans on what he knows. He, also, cannot understand the real and physical existence of his spirit, because he wants to find everything within his own material dimension. His spiritual needs can find fictitious support in dogma from any religion, but due to his own lack of criteria can fall into fanatism."

"Man should not be satisfied nor accept what others have thought, but must use his own judgment. He must use his will, intelligence, imagination and mind to find his own spiritual identity. Thereby attaining the necessary evolution to allow him to reach his own spiritual elevation to the next plane."

"In order for man to evolve, he must transcend to higher planes. This will be accomplished as he acquires full acceptance in his physical mind of a spiritual presence in his conscience."

"The average life span for man will increase as science and technology advance, and provide better health and a safer environment. This period lasts approximately 25 thousand years, also."

368

"Man on Earth is, at present, in this evolutionary plane. It should have been surpassed by this time, but this is not so. Unfortunately, only the minority have attained the required evolution."

"Ever since we met you have asked me several times just what exactly your mission is. Here´s the answer: your mission consists in trying to convince your brothers that, using their intelligence, they must look for their spiritual identity through their mind."

"How?" asked Eric. "Is this a religious mission?"

"Your life is a religious mission. I am only trying to explain that if your real self is spiritual and your physical body is only a temporary abode for your spirit, then your life is part of the path that takes you back to our Father. Religion is a link to unite and return to our spiritual origin."

"Everyone who can identify his own spirit, will reach the entrance to the next evolutionary plane. Each human being who attains his spirituality will be entering the New Era. The progress of mankind, physically and technologically, is subject to his own spiritual evolution."

"I have told you this before, you must renew your organization to survive. Only love will allow you to overcome problems that are a cancer destroying this humanity. To understand your spiritual origin is to begin to comprehend the reason for living and the Universe you inhabit."

"You must be willing to do so, and to obtain it you must have faith. But that faith must come from reasonable and intelligent thought, a product of mental analysis in which you have processed your knowledge supported by intuition. This, and the voice of your conscience, is something that comes from the most inner part of your being, which is the voice of your own spirit."

"Remember, blind faith is fanatism. It is man´s refusal to use his intelligence (which is a spiritual gift). It is a submission, due to weakness, ignorance and lack of character, to an unknown destiny. It is the acceptance of darkness."

"When a human dies, his soul is liberated from the physical body and remains in the fourth dimension, within an area near the planet where it continues subject to the attraction of gravity. This period can last from a few days up to 200 years, depending on its evolutionary level and the karmic conditions of the soul when it enters the fourth dimension. To be able to go from the fourth to the fifth dimension, it must have the necessary conditions to be able to clearly see its own situation. In the fifth dimension, with the help of superior brothers, it must prepare for the next life experience. If the spirit has already attained the proper evolution, it will enter the plane of SUPER-MAN."

"Whoever can accept his own immortal spiritual existence, will have to understand and accept that if spirits really exist, they have to be in a proper place in the Universe, in their own dimension. Whoever cannot accept this, it is because his concept of being is exclusively material and believes that everything ends at death. However, some day the time will come for them to understand as well."

"As a living being, the human continually suffers psychic alterations and emotions caused by the CONSCIENCE, that manifests itself consciously or unconsciously, when man uses his own free will."

"This causes discharges of energy in the charkas in his spiritual body. The discharges of energy form bands in the horizontal plane at the level of each chakra. These bands are called khans, which as they extend horizontally, (like the waves made by a pebble on a pool of water), intersect the aural cocoon and the vibrations of both (khan and cocoon), decompose into the emission of energy in subatomic particles. These particles keep the same vibratory characteristics of the energy integrating the khan and saturate the aural cocoon."

"Vibrations are transmitted to the mental spheres of the Being as they enter the physical body through the britis, already transformed to the third dimension (for example, healing energy). Remember, britis are points located on the soles of the feet and the palms of the hands similar to acupuncture points that exist on different places of the human skin. Except that britis serve only to attract vibrations of karma and darma, and as exits of positive energy equal to that of darma, but in third dimension."

Rahel stopped for a few moments to observe Eric´s reaction. Eric, obviously, was trying very hard to clearly understand all these concepts. Rahel asked, "Tell me, is this clear to you, up to now?"

"Yes, Rahel, I understand the spiritual brain controls the charkas. As it is in close contact with our own brain, it participates in the sensations that reach the senses and when these, emotionally affect the being, in any way, the charkas react emitting those vibrations. Is this correct?"

"Yes, it is precisely those sudden emissions in the plexus that are immediately identified in the affected physical organs, like the head, heart, liver, stomach and even in muscles, like a feeling of tiredness or pain, even when it deals with the emotions."

"The emissions of negative discharges are vibrations with a very high frequency, infinitesimal amplitudes and different polarity. These are produced when the voice of our conscience is ignored, and generally cause moral and/or physical damage to the being itself or others. These have a negative polarity and are called KARMAS."

"Vibrations of noble acts, generosity, and in general, love, as well as physical or moral pain, are positive called DARMAS. They are received in the mental spheres, where all karmas and darmas are registered. Due to their different polarity, they can be neutralized and only the charges that are left over are stored. For example, if a human being emits negative(-) vibrations in anger, let´s say that 10 units of karma, when these are disintegrated in the aural cocoon, these vibrations go to the mental spheres to be registered and stored."

"When that same human being emits love vibrations, let´s say 15 units of Darma, that is positive energy (+), these also are perceived by the mental spheres for their registration and storage. So,

Karma (-) 10 units
Darma (+) 15 units
Then: $-10 + 15 = +5$

So, there are 5 units of darma in his favor.

"Man will provoke negative discharges whenever he causes premeditated harm, from a small burglary that only gives him a high feeling, a lie to satisfy his ego, a humiliation to another human being, to bearing false witness, committing crimes for self-benefit, and even, murder. Negative feelings, such as envy and hate, even if not acted out, cause KARMA."

"On the other hand, through meditation, repentance for bad deeds, moral pain due to physical and emotional pain, and actions to repair harm, produce discharges of DARMA energy."

"As man evolves, he becomes more aware of his conscience."

"Would you please clear something up for me?" asked Eric. "You mentioned negative discharges that generate karma must be done in bad faith. Is this right? Now, for example, if someone hurts someone else unintentionally, will this become karma?"

"No, definitely not. This applies only when you act against your conscience´s recommendations. For example, you have a car accident and, either hurt or even kill someone, all the circumstances are evaluated. Whatever was your fault will cause karma. If, however, you are the victim, it would be illogical to think the accident will cause karma for you. Although, in the case you were driving under the influence of alcohol, then you must have been advised by your conscience, not to drive. Therefore, the result of your irresponsibility will add karma to your account."

"In days gone by, mankind regarded wars as good actions—for whatever reasons. Lack of evolution and ignorance led them to believe, it was a matter of patriotism and pride to kill. These were special circumstances of evolutionary and cultural underdevelopment, but nonetheless have spiritual value. You must realize you will be continually in risk of generating karma with every action you commit as in wars and any other violent situations."

"Let´s take another example, you suddenly find yourself in a situation that, to save your own life or someone else´s, acting spontaneously and in good faith, you hurt someone, say the attacker. The resulting karmas and/or darmas are difficult to evaluate at our level. The time will come for that judgment, you will be present, and then you will have all the elements to realize that, whatever karma you have caused, if any, will be justly applied. Divine justice is infallible, and of course, fair."

"Precisely because evolution and culture are important factors, wars and conflicts produce many and terrible karmic loads, although maybe these will serve as restitution for others to eliminate their own karmas."

"When we began this conversation, I spoke of the dimensions of our soul when joining the spirit, studies the results of the performance in life to return to a new life existence."

"But all that implies reincarnation," Eric interrupted. "Many religions mention it, but under different perspectives. They cannot believe in another life on the same planet in a different body. Some religions are of the opinion that it must be the same body, and others, just flatly reject this theory. If this message is for everyone, whoever does not accept this idea because of religious principles, will not be interested in the rest....."

Rahel raised his hand, indicating he understood the point Eric raised and continued, " Don´t worry, you are not going to be able to convince them of anything they don´t accept. Don´t forget nothing happens by chance. Everything has a cause and an effect. Anyone who is not ready will not be able to take advantage of the spiritual concepts, in fact, he will not even try to learn. It´s something like generating a spontaneous charge of darma, it obeys laws you cannot control and at most, you would like to understand. If it is daylight and someone is still in the dark, you will only be able to how him the way to go to see the light. To see the light, or not, is a matter of free will. Let´s continue."

THIRD EVOLUTIONARY PLANE, SECOND LEVEL, SUPER-MAN

"We are at this level now and it will be our duty to help you recuperate your level of cultural and technological development, in the case you have to suffer a serious setback caused by your own behavior, to be able to surpass the level of man. We will try to assist you, but this can only be done within the limits of your evolutionary freedom.

"At this level we continue to be human beings, that is, we have a physical body and we continue to live in evolving planets in the third dimension of space-time."

"The super-man possesses a clear concept of his personality, understands that matter tries to impose itself through the physical senses, but has already learned to listen to the voice of his conscience. His mental spheres, actively participating, help him understand his position in the Universe."

"The difference at this level lies in that there is spiritual conscience and there is harmony in their life. Intercommunication with our brothers in the next superior level is allowed. There is full consciousness of the spiritual presence of the soul in the fourth dimension."

"As there is harmony, there are more technological progress. At a certain moment, a twin soul will be found once again. Finally, when the time comes, both together will be able to rise to the next level."

"Mankind will live, at this level, a shorter length of time, approximately 1,000 years, which are enough for all twin souls to find each other. During this time, the twin souls will finish their third degree of evolution. Once this has been achieved, they will be synchronized in one last incarnation to be together in material life, as it happened at the first level."

"Mankind's life span is much longer. They will live an average of 160 to 180 years during the incarnations at the level of super-man."

"This stage is the end of life in the third dimension. Spirits will have their last experience in death. They will no longer return to bodies in the third dimension, except on special missions. They have earned the opportunity to proceed in their evolution towards higher levels, as participating spirits."

"Souls in the fifth dimension become part of a sexless spirit, possessing all the enriching experiences of the souls of both sexes. They have eliminated all their karmas and are ready to enter the next evolutionary plane."

FOURTH EVOLUTIONARY PLANE,
FIRST LEVEL, SUPRA-MAN

"At this level, beings are now spirits. Matter is only used to fulfill missions on evolutionary planets in space-time, but their physical bodies are very different from the beings on the planets in evolution."

"These special biocybernetic physical bodies, animated by the energy of the Universe, help younger brothers to evolve. The same way both they and we are helping you. They travel throughout the systems and galaxies of our Universe fulfilling missions to keep on evolving."

FOURTH EVOLUTIONARY PLANE,
SECOND LEVEL, DEMI-GOD

"In this stage, scientific and philosophical knowledge is vast. Missions include temporary life on evolutionary planets to help younger brothers. They are called this because the humans they help store the memory in their lives and deify them. Some of them have come to Earth and are remembered for their outstanding lessons and philosophies, like Mahomet, Quetzalcóatl, Buddha and Viracocha."

"They help in the development of humanity and try to make humans aware of their spiritual origin."

"As you have seen, knowledge and spiritual awareness have been taught for thousands of years on your planet. Although the minds of men in early civilizations do not understand and interpret revelations according to their capability and convenience, which is understandable. However, in a technologically advanced civilization such as yours today, you already can comprehend. Your will to do so, being blinded by materialism, is lacking."

"All religions arise due to the intuitive human need to find an explanation for their physical and spiritual origin and destiny. But, these religions have been transformed and materialized according to different cultures, for lack of spirituality. Instead of looking for a common denominator and rising spiritually, mankind has turned them into fanatic reasons for human discord."

Rahel paused to give Eric a break. Mirza took advantage and added, "This is very important, Eric. There is only one truth. However, each religion possesses, at least part of the truth, which is divine light. Even when they reach the spirit through different paths, each has their way of looking at that truth (even not being the real truth). Therein lies their differences."

"True religion must be felt with the spirit, without ostentation, hypocrisy, and miserly interests. It must be a "light" that shines upon the path for the evolution of the spirit on its way to God."

"When talking about religion, it must be about love, charity, wisdom and justice. The only gift man can offer to God is that of good behavior."

Mirza smiled at Eric to encourage him to continue listening and learning from Rahel, a gentle human touch!

"To keep on," Rahel said. "The demigods and Maitreya are almost the same. The only difference is that Maitreya, even though it carries out missions generally done by the spirits that help incipient humanities; it is, in reality, a very evolved spirit that, for some reason, is humble enough to participate in a task it has probably done thousands of years before. In the case of Earth, the Maitreya that came to help you was a MICAEL, the head of our local Universe."

FOURTH EVOLUTIONARY PLANE, THIRD LEVEL, MAITREYA

"They are very evolved spirits that can direct energies to help humanities in evolution. Given permission from higher powers, they can be born on evolving planets and physically be the same as the inhabitants, except they possess full spiritual consciousness. They take part in very special missions; their actions will be considered "miracles" by those human beings who still are not even capable to understand what is happening. In fact, the word, Maitreya, means "he who gives love".

"Almost 2,000 years have gone by since the last visit of a Maitreya. In life, his name was Jesus of Nazareth. His mission was to show you the way to end this level."

"You are privileged in spite of your backwardness, as I have told you. As you were visited by the highest spirit of our local universe: Micael of Nevadon, who is the Maitreya of this universe. NEVADON is the cosmic name of our universe."

FIFTH EVOLUTIONARY PLANE, COSMIC ENGINEERS

"As of this plane, the spirit keeps on evolving in the fifth dimension without new incarnations. From now on, it will operate only in the superior triad."

"With the knowledge and experience acquired during thousands of years, these spirits direct higher energies and control plasmatic germs to form new evolutionary planets."

"They prepare adequate systems for galaxies in the process of being formed, guide the transformation of energy into matter to keep the cosmos in balance, within the areas to create the super-universe. They have been working there for thousands of millions of years, although time for them, of course, has no meaning. At least not in the same way it does for us. As they are spirits, they are not subject to space-time."

SIXTH EVOLUTIONARY PLANE, BIOLOGICAL ENGINEERS

"The Father allows these wise and experienced spirits to direct the pulsating electric charges that give life (-9 to +6). Working with the Cosmic Engineers, they prepare planets and fill them with life as places for the evolution of humanities."

"These tasks take thousands of millions of years in the concept of space-time, but as the spirit is immortal, their time does not pass as ours does. They live spiritually in another dimension, and will continue to do so until the thirteen dimension."

SEVENTH EVOLUTIONARY PLANE,
MONITORS

"There are several different levels in this stage. The first is PLANETARY MONITORS. Their energy and dimensional body is enormous. They can give life to a planet and to all its inhabitants."

"At the next level, they will be SOLAR MONITORS. After having practiced how to direct, control life and transform stars for thousands of years, they have the chance to do this on a star within a planetary system which contains a planet with a humanity in spiritual evolution."

"In the next and final step, they will become GALACTIC MONITORS. They manage the energy of a galaxy, just as their name indicates. Of course, all the monitors have millions of helpers on lower levels. Million and millions of spirits cooperate with all their love and enthusiasm to keep the Universe going. As I told you the first time we met: we are all laborers of God."

"Spirits will get to the Island of Light or Central Universe, during their long journey towards evolution, after fulfilling missions and rising to higher planes and levels."

"In even higher dimensions than the ones I have talked about, spirits will be found in the spheres of the ISLAND OF LIGHT, integrating themselves with the Father Creator, who is ever more generous with his love. The love of the Father is that cosmic energy that covers the Master Universe with light and life."

"To illustrate this for you, try to imagine a gigantic planet, the size of a galaxy, surrounded by 21 spheres distributed in three concentric orbits. (Figure 77)

FIGURE 77

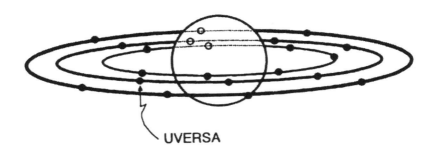

UVERSA

"In the first orbit, which is the closest, the spheres are known as the dwelling of the Sons of Havona. Havona is the cosmic name of the Island of Light."

"The spheres in the second orbit control each of the existing super-universes. The control of the seventh super-universe is found in one of them, known as the UVERSA, where we live."

"Ascending spirits, who possess a degree of perfection beyond our comprehension, are found in the third orbit."

"Now, imagine seven other parallel orbits, in addition to the ones we have mentioned, that are found at the equator level in the Island of Light. These seven orbits are spread out as if they were extensions of the parallels of that gigantic planet, full of similar spheres to the three interior ones. These spheres also contain highly evolved spirits coming from the seven super-universes."

"The orbit that has more spheres, probably the first super-universe created, contains 245 millions, and the orbit with the least, has 35 millions. The total sum of the spheres, at least when we were told, was 1,000 million in the orbit of the seven super-universes. (Figure 78)

"In all these dwellings of higher evolved cosmic spirits, there are conditions that spirits are our level of evolution cannot comprehend."

FIGURE 78

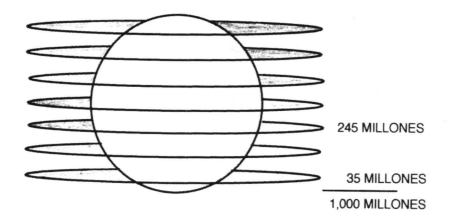

245 MILLONES

35 MILLONES

1,000 MILLONES

"Outside the orbits of the spheres of the evolved spirits, there are two perpendicular bands that serve as energy regulators that leaves the ISLAND OF LIGHT toward the MASTER UNIVERSE. The energy of those bands is beyond our comprehension. I can only tell you, as an example, they have a similar energy as that of the black holes. (Figure 79)

"The characteristics that prevail in those regions of the central Universe, have of course, the highest degree of:

Generosity	Wisdom
Truth	Spirituality
Beauty	Honesty
Love	Peace
Justice	Mercy

FIGURE 79

ISLAND OF LIGHT

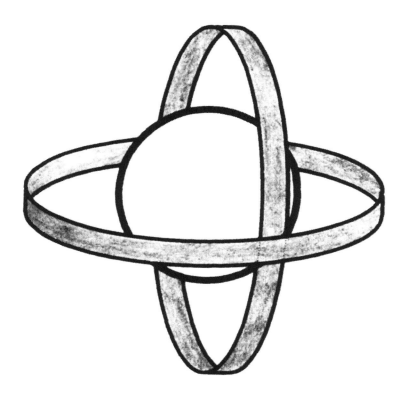

"We could describe the ISLAND OF LIGHT, as God's dwelling place. Our Father who, for the comprehension of those beings of minor evolution, has revealed himself in three persons, who are really as one. Each one represent different characteristics of same being:

The Father is the Creator of all things.
The Son is the Teacher, full of mercy.
The Holy Spirit is wisdom.

"The energy that floods the master Universe with love comes from that ISLAND OF LIGHT, and is the origin of all creation."

"The Father created the spirits with part of his own energy. Each spirit is a part of the Father. That is why he considers us as his children, and having come from him, must return to him."

"All this information was provided to us to have a very generalized idea at the level of our comprehension, as we are still not able to thoroughly understand the master Universe. We will not have the capacity to understand until we get to the fourth evolutionary plane."

"Just take this explanation as the most appropriate, at our level of comprehension, on the journey toward truth you will, someday, know."

Rahel paused, once more. He had finished with the subject intended for this encounter. He waited to see if Eric had any comments. As these were not forthcoming and it was getting late, he decided to end the conversation.

"Eric, it is now time for you to take your flight. Try not to think about what we have discussed today until some days have gone by. Then it will all be clear to you. Mirza will be in contact with you, and if next weekend, it is possible for you to visit Professor Krinnell again, it would be most convenient. We can talk about it later. Mirza and I have to go away. I´ll tell you all about this in our next encounter. Is this OK with you?"

After saying the usual affectionate goodbyes, Eric went to the terminal with just enough time to catch his flight home.

During the trip, he felt Rahel´s words as the beginning of a farewell. This alarmed him. His relationship with these friends from space had become most natural and commonplace. He felt their moral support. With this impending separation, he felt he must clear up several topics that had not been covered. So he tried to generally review these, but he was tired and decided to do this on another occasion. He fell fast asleep, just after take-off.

CHAPTER XIX

More than 2,000 years ago,
the Greeks began to learn about
the different areas of science,
and now these, have reached limits
that are difficult to comprehend.
The Theory of Hyperspace has been attained,
now the knowledge of other dimensions
will be the threshold to enter and the light
to guide this mankind in the New Era.

Pablo E. Hawnser

THE ISLAND IN SPACE

Eric, as was usual after his encounters, spent his days trying to organize his ideas and thoughts. He prepared questions regarding his doubts to ask Rahel or Professor Krinnell at their next meeting. This would be taking place in a week´s time, and since he had a feeling they would not be seeing each other many more times, this was even more important. He wanted so much to clarify all pending information as soon as possible.

He suddenly realized he had a message from Rahel in his mind. He didn´t know how or when it got there, but there was no doubt…he seemed to hear his voice saying, "Don´t worry too much. You will only cause yourself harm and may even confuse the issues unnecessarily. Let your ideas flow spontaneously and effortlessly."

"You do not have to convince anyone of anything. Your mission is to lightly touch the minds of your brothers and let their own conscience do the rest. Your mission consists in showing the bridge within us, to cross from mind to matter, from the physical aspects of this dimension of human and biological life to the highest of your spiritual being."

"It depends on the degree of SPIRITUAL EVOLUTION of each whether it is difficult or easy to attain. It has nothing to do with scientific knowledge, not even with cultures. Each person's perception is intimately linked to the way he manages his mental capacity, which is also linked to the spiritual development."

"Your mission is not to be a preacher. It is one of awareness. You are not going to offer anyone anything that is not already within their own mind. The only thing you will propose, is for them to listen to their conscience, to the Superior ID, and to comprehend that the reality of their existence is not material. All who listen to you and are able to understand this, will know by intuition, what they must do."

"The questions you yourself have made to us, and that probably will be made by others as well, are not important. I refer to the following:

Question: "Are there extra-terrestrial beings with you?"

"This is not new. Everybody knows or feels this is so. In any case, what they don't understand is how we got here and why there is no open contact."

Question: "Well, why don't you contact us openly?"

"We have already explained this to you, and we would like you to tell this to everyone."

Question: "Is is true there are different sized spaceships?"

"Just as many as there are types of cars. Their shape and size vary according to their use, just as you created many types of vehicles to suit your needs."

Question: "Do you come from different places?"

"Yes, many places, from very different and distant planets."

Question: "Are you green and dwarflike or giant monsters?"

"They only see the varieties regarding size, color and shape existing in their own planet. If these differences exist under the same ecological conditions, it is logical to suppose that there are a

384

greater variety in the Universe. Of course, not so extravagantly, just some minor variations to adapt to the environment."

Question: "Are we aggressive and a danger to humans?"

"We are humans like you, and we have come from very far away to help you. We did not come to take advantage of you nor to attack you. We are astronauts who have the privilege of being here. We have undergone severe physical and mental tests to be chosen to carry our these missions so far from our homes."

Question: "Who controls you?"

"You can imagine we have an administrative organization and a hierarchy adequate to our mission. We respect the laws as should be in a society made up of highly evolved beings which, by the way, is more advanced than yours."

How was it possible that these questions and answers were in the order he had lined them up in his mind? Well, using a bit of logic, he also had that answer.

The days went by quickly, and Eric waited for Mirza´s call with great anticipation. It finally came on Thursday at 8:00 a.m.

"Hi, Eric! Ready for our next visit?"

"Yes, Mirza, of course! I have to go to Puebla tomorrow. We could see each other there at the Hotel Meson del Angel at say, 3.00 p.m.?

"Great, you can leave your car there. Remember you are scheduled to go on a "quick" trip to see Professor Krinnell."

"I hadn´t forgotten. I am anxiously awaiting to see him. We´ll see you there then. It is great to hear from you again."

At 1:30 p.m. on Friday, Eric went to have a quick lunch near their meeting place. He was always conscious of their puntuality. A few minutes before 3:00 p.m., while he was enjoying his coffee, Mirza arrived. She was well dressed, and drew many admiring glances from the male population. Eric simled as he greeted her, and telepathically told her: "Have you seen how all these boys envy me?"

Mirza turned and realized there were a group of youngsters who couldn´t stop staring at her.

"Thank you, Eric. But they would be even more envious if they knew where you were going!"

"I´m sure! Where´s Rahel?"

"He's in the minivan waiting for us. We don't like leaving him alone."

"Let's go then." Eric went to pay and both left the restaurant. Rahel was near the minivan, and they all got in and left, driving towards to a semideserted industrial area.

They went along the wide Hermanos Serdán Avenue, and turned left, passing a welding plant to an empty city block at the back.

Rahel drove the car up the sidewalk and stopped. The three looked around to see if there were any witnesses, but no one seemed to be interested in them. Rahel then sent a ultrasound signal and 25 meters ahead of them, a cloud of steam appeared. Then, a space ship came into view underneath it.

Two sliding doors opened while it descended softly and silently. It stopped, floating about 1 meter above the ground. Another door opened, and a ramp rolled out. There were two dented rails on the part that touched the ground, where the sprockets under the car could be attached. Thus securing the car and bringing it inside the space craft. (Figure 80)

FIGURE 80

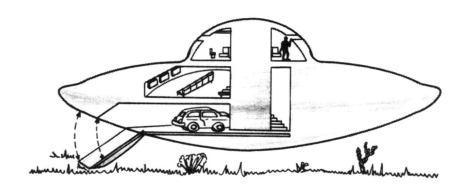

SPACECRAFT FOR LOCAL USE

Rahel drove the car to match the sprockets with the rails. As soon as this was accomplished, easily and safely, the car rolled in. In less than 10 seconds, it was secured on board, the rails retracted and the doors closed automatically.

They went up a small ladder to the next level and entered the first room facing that circular hallway. It was a spacious and comfortable room, triangular in shape. To the left of the entrance, there were three T.V. screens mounted on the wall. All three provided exterior views, the one in the middle towards the front and the clear sky, and the one on the left faced downwards towards the city.

As usual, when the vertical ascent got to about 150 meters high, it started accelerating as in a spiral. Although Eric had seen this before, he couldn't help feeling absolutely thrilled. The space ship didn't seem to even tilt, but the view from the outside confirmed the ascent and the leveling off.

There was a work table attached to another wall; on this there were monitors and a computer for two persons, and two armchairs, similar to the passenger seats. The vessel must be about 20 to 25 meters in diameter, judging from the size of the room.

Mirza and Rahel sat down and when Eric turned to ask a question, Rahel started, "This is a spacecraft for local use that will take us to a big vessel in orbit, that also doubles as a sub-station. You will see it and, what's more important, you will see something special. Right next to the place where we enter the station you will see another access for spacecraft entirely different to ours. Those belong to our superior brothers, the ones I have told you are already at the supra-men level, which is the fourth evolutionary plane."

"They do not have organic bodies like we do. They are superior beings with their own matter and functions. Even though they are in the third dimension, they do not have our physical faults. We could say they are bioelectronic beings, somewhat like robots, but possessing life and a soul. They are sexless spirits integrated into the fifth dimension, who carry out special missions like this. They control, give orders and authorize our contacts with you and supervise all their orders are carried out."

"Like which?" asked Eric.

"For example, the transportation, like teletransportation you have used on your astral travels to Professor Krinnell. A visit from you which could take a few hours, could mean upon your return that weeks, months and even years in your planetary time have gone by. This is caused by the relative difference that affects your time spans."

"We must not affect the normal passage of time of the planets. We cannot avoid this, they can. This is the way we have been transported as well. We are living in a similar time span as in our planet. When we travel these distances, and even if we are in the same galaxy, we could not return to our families and our humanity."

Eric couldn´t say a word, he was stunned. Mirza saw this, and added, " Don´t worry, Eric. Just look at everything as naturally as you have done up to now. Get over your surprise and take this as something perfectly natural. When you have traveled to another country, you accept and understand other races and cultures. You see their traditions, ideology and places with interest and curiosity, don´t you? Well, this is exactly the same."

Rahel was talking to the pilots and pointed to the screens. Eric had the impression of flying over the roof of an enormous factory covered with many differently sized and colored domes. Further ahead, there was a very big one, approximately 150 meters in diameter, that covered part of a high circular tower.

Rahel´s space craft lowered down to one side of the tower, 60 meters away and at a 45-degree angle. It was full of light. The "island" was situated in such a position to get the sun rays at the zenith. There were also two very similar smaller domes. The first measured about 50 meters and the other, 10 meters.

The space craft slid very slowly elliptically around the domes. The smaller dome opened, like a fan, a few minutes later. A brilliant sphere could be seen, of a color between silver and crystal, about 6 meters in diameter. It looked like an enormous pearl in its case.

It immediately started to rise softly. It appeared to be a soap bubble reflecting colors due to the decomposition of light on its surface, like that of a crystal ball. After a 20-meter separation from the dome, which had already closed, it appeared to levitate a few seconds and then left in a impressive burst of speed. It was not so much the distance, but rather, it just seemed to vanish.

After witnessing the exit and departure of the sphere, the spacecraft they were in moved to a platform with half-ring supports, where it rested. Soon after, a sliding door opened and revealed the entrance to a hangar where the vessel was pulled in. At that moment, the T.V. screen turned off and everyone got up to leave the ship.

They went through a hermetically sealed capsule, full of pressurized air. Once the air had settled, a door opened and they were able to leave. They headed toward this enormous hangar, full of spacecrafts of different sizes and shapes. A moving belt took them to the next building and, on their way, they passed a beautiful garden, full of tropical vegetation. The green leaves seemed to shine in the sunlight coming in from the domes. They went to a large comfortable room, where a hologram projector and a camera were installed at the end wall.

"Is this the projector you used to talk to Professor Krinnell and myself?" Eric asked.

"Yes," Rahel pointed to the place where the person being projected was to sit.

"They then went to the other side of the room, where there were spacious armchairs facing large windows overlooking magnificent views. It was like looking out to a range of mountains with lakes and forests. There were many, at different levels, giving an illusion of seeing everything in third dimension. Whatsmore, the air drifting in was cool and fresh!

They served themselves big cups of tea and sat down to chat. Rahel started, "Eric, in a short time I will have to return with my team to our place of origin. You are the end of our mission. I must tell you we have been successful in other missions we have carried out, and we will be very proud if this is also as successful. After this trip, we will see each other one more time to clarify any doubts. Now, you will go with Shem and Vanny. Mirza will meet you for your safe return home."

"Rest a while," Mirza indicated. "Close your eyes and relax. In a few minutes you will continue your trip."

Mirza turned to Rahel and spoke a few words in their own language via mental telepathy. Eric tried to understand, but fell asleep. He had no idea how long he slept, but when he opened his eyes, he saw Shem and his wide smile, filling him with friendship and trust.

"Hi, Eric, I'm happy to see you again. If you are ready, we'll leave. They are waiting for us. Look who's here!"

Eric turned and saw Vanny, who extended her hand in greeting. This made him react even more quickly!

"Vanny is a biologist, and she is working on a similar project to ours in another planet. She came to see the systems we have used and the type of illustrations Professor Krinnell developed to explain the subjects given to your planet. They are very useful because they provide instant understanding of the transformations."

They were in a small room, with direct access to the platform and spacecrafts. It could be the University's airport!

"Shem, is Kunn going to be with us, today?"

"No, Eric. He is not here now; that's why we were brought here directly from the station in orbit of our superior brothers for this system."

"Let me see if I understand. We came here directly from the sub-base on Earth?"

"No, from the sub-base you were sent to the base belonging to our superior brothers in orbit of another planet in your system. From there, you were sent, via teletransportation, to the base that is in orbit here, and from there you were brought here. Vanny and I arrived the same way. When we are through with this meeting, we will be returning together to meet up with Mirza."

After speaking to Eric, Shem transmitted his explanation to Vanny and she answered something, he translated to Eric.

"She told me to tell you that you are not the only ones. You seem to think that, because you are "men", you are the only ones in the Universe. But they will soon find out, as you have, that this is not so. Later, from our level, you will understand the next evolutionary levels more easily."

"It is like going to school, and you see classmates in higher grades. Even though you have no contact with them, you are still aware they exist."

"Have you had direct contact with them?"

"Very little, but it is a great experience. They are kind, generous and courteous...it's not easy to explain. You feel flooded with love when you are in their presence. Their aura is very strong, it invades you and you feel, though your own aura, a marvelous and unforgettable feeling of peace."

"But, tell me. How did you get in contact with them?"

"When your humanity fully enters into the New Era, you will change a lot. Morally you will find, once again, all those values you have put on one side because you do not listen to the voice of your conscience."

"Honor is to respect your given word and the truth. These two concepts, by themselves, require great change that involves so many other things. When people love each other, they do not cheat and tell the truth, out of respect for their own personal dignity, and that of others. Human relationships can change by this behavior, and everything is so much easier. Living in harmony helps understanding and, as such, evolution. Then, you will be ready to get in contact with a higher level."

"Believe me, the most difficult and complicated part in the beginning of these contacts, is ours. Especially when mankind, who should have already attained a certain degree of evolution, are so backward. Technology makes it easier for them to have an aggressive and materialistic humanity, whose goal is power to satisfy their egotism."

"Man, by instinct, is materialistic. He searches for power all his life, in every way. Often it touches men who, have spirits in a satisfactory degree of evolution, but power spoils them. They forget their conscience and do not use their highly developed human brain. It is more convenient to use their free will, make decisions and act without ever listening to the voice of their conscience, they have become deaf and indifferent to that inner voice. They consider themselves strong as they have overcome what they believe is prejudice to discourage the weak."

"Violence is a way to conquer your own natural spiritual inclination towards an unjust act, supported by falsehood, ambition or personal vainglory, and to let you happily go your own way for material gain. These human beings, who were possibly ready to attain the adequate evolutionary level to rise to a high plane, can fall into excesses and provoke a spiritual blockage which will prevent them from surpassing the era."

"To surpass the era is something similar to go from one grade to another. Not to pass means an enormous loss of time. It´s like flunking a grade, and having to do it over. Of course, your soul is immortal, but the other 75 thousand years that it implies to start over, are a terrible punishment for it."

"Higher entities who try to help, are in contact with the floating spirits that program new lives on Earth and to provide spiritual inspiration in the new beings as way of compensating for the delay caused by bad behavior and the karma it accumulates."

Vanny understood something and again spoke to Shem.

Vanny tells me that, in her era of humanity, the same problems occurred. Such was the pain and suffering it caused, that on the second try, they attained the necessary evolution, even before it was time.

While they were talking, they continued to Professor Krinnell´s office. He greeted them, effusively and affectionately as always. They took their places where the Professor had everything in readiness for them.

"Let´s see something, that may clarify and complement your knowledge of quantum mechanics. This information has also been given to Earth, Eric, though different contacts. We know there are several organizations of your brothers which try to make them known."

"It´s curious, but when knowledge such as this is received, societies seem to, little by little isolate it. That lack of interest denotes a lack of comprehension. When some people are faced with something they do not understand, they can feel motivated and eager to seek more preparation, but it can also work that full of confusion, they misunderstand and do not interpret correctly, falling into fanatism."

"Esoteric knowledge is very attractive to humans, although the majority of the time, they really do not understand, but it is exciting to participate in the magic. As they confuse astrology with astronomy, many are not prepared to learn more and do not know where science is separated from fiction. Then, they forget about the whole thing. They consider it to be a distraction to waste their time and energy which should be given to their own battle for power. Only a small minority understands and takes advantage of it for their own evolution, after conquering their religious fanatism and scientific ignorance."

The Professor paused for Shem to translate and then addressed Vanny, "It is very important for your selection of candidates to include people of different social conditions, age, sex and academic education. Remember you do not know the degree of their evolution, and many times the ones you think as the worst, will turn out to be the best of your students and will make your work worthwhile."

While Shem translated, the Professor prepared his cassette and inserted it in the hologram projector.

"Human beings are biological entities, as was explained in the quantum mechanic knowledge given to your planet, whose functions apparently without any benefit, are three:

1. The genetic pattern (it is electronic for reproduction).
2. The metabolic pattern (this is for self-protection).
3. The behavioral pattern (this is for self-impression).

THE GENETIC PATTERN FOR REPRODUCTION

The images of thousands of sperms appeared on the screen. Much like schools of fishes moving their tails as propellers. On the other half of the screen, a cell—which is the ovule, grew showing much inner activity going on. As it got larger, 23 deep-yellow-colored canelike tails could be seen. These represented the feminine chromosomes, indicating a positive charge (+). There was an extra one, in orange, that represented the sexual one. The sperm showed 23 male chromosomes in green, (indicating a negative charge) and a sexual one in red.

"As you know, Eric, reproduction begins when a negative-charged sperm is attracted by a positive-charged ovule. The sperm penetrates the ovule and discharges the 23 chromosomes, plus the

393

sexual one. They pair up with the 23 chromosomes of the ovule, plus the sexual one of each." (Figure 81)

"The ovule is then fertilized, the positive and negative charges are in balance, and no other sperms are attracted. You already know the process from now on, but let´s see how these cells are integrated to form a new life."

FIGURE 81

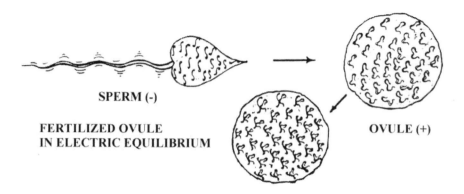

SPERM (-)

FERTILIZED OVULE
IN ELECTRIC EQUILIBRIUM

OVULE (+)

A chromosome separated itself and divided into the 2 small original canelike tails. (Figure 82)

FIGURE 82

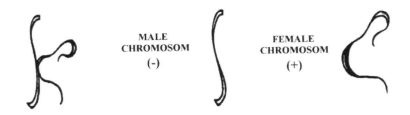

MALE
CHROMOSOM
(-)

FEMALE
CHROMOSOM
(+)

COMPLETE CHROMOSOME

When the small cane appeared alone on the screen, it disintegrated to show the elements of its makeup. The first was a DNA protective shield that shaped the cane; a double propeller held the packages of GENES. The shield´s cord had four shelves between each ring that represented pairs of biochemical structural unions of:

Adenine - Thiamine
Thiamine - Adenine
Cytosine - Guanine
Guanine - Cytosine

These intertwined in the gene packages.

The unions represented the structural spaces where the codes to assemble aminoacids and form proteins are manifested according to the genetic code.

As the DNA propellers shaping the small canes unwound and disappeared, one of the packages became the main actor on the screen. It was a GENE.

395

Its covering was a dense field of electric plasma that evaporated revealing an oblong cell wrapped by a cord. (Figure No. 83)

FIGURE 83

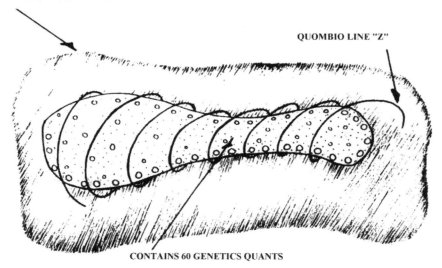

ELECTRIC PLASMA (PROTECTIVE MAGNETIC FIELD)

QUOMBIO LINE "Z"

CONTAINS 60 GENETICS QUANTS

When the magnetic field disappeared from the screen, the cord wrapping the cell, unwound as follows: (Figure 84)

FIGURE 84

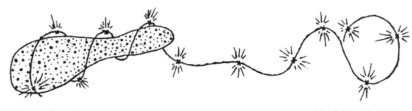

QUANTA CAPSULE

KAPPA CORD

Electric lines called kum and kemium are produced constantly in the sexual glands. These intertwine and form an electronic cord called KAPPA. When this kappa cord reaches a certain length, it forms a hoop and attracts four neutronium. These are integrated by positrons and electronegatrons produced in the gonads. (See Chapter XIV for more information) (Figure 85)

FIGURE 85

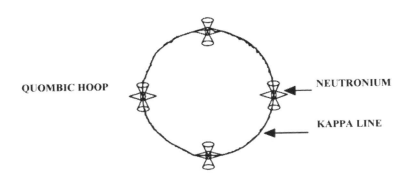

QUOMBIC HOOP

NEUTRONIUM

KAPPA LINE

Quombic hoops were integrated in a system of three intertwined hoops forming a quombic "Z", which is imprinted in the gonads with electronic charges. (Figure No. 86)

FIGURE 86

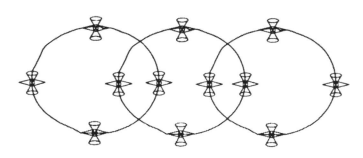

QUOMBIC "Z"

397

A genetic cell or capsule broke revealing its content of 60 genetic quanta. (Figure 87)

FIGURE 87

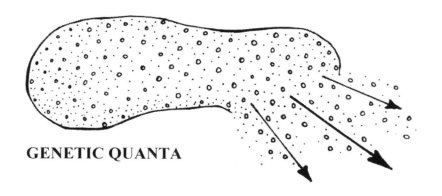

GENETIC QUANTA

The genetic quanta was integrated by six cytoembryos; two primary and four secondary. (Figure 88)

FIGURE 88

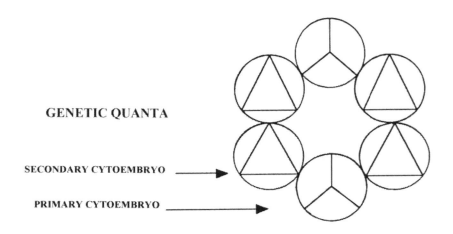

GENETIC QUANTA

SECONDARY CYTOEMBRYO

PRIMARY CYTOEMBRYO

The primary cytoembryo was integrated by a chain of 50 energetic quanta; when closing as a circle it started to turn slowly. The chain attracted another one like it, that approached turning in the opposite direction. Together they formed a cohesive field of energy that continued attracting more energetic quanta, until saturation, up to a maximum of 50 each. (Figure 89)

FIGURE 89

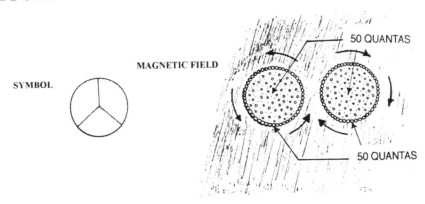

The secondary cytoembryo was also formed by a chain of 50 energetic quanta enclosed in a circle, and it also started to slowly turn. When two chains turning in the same direction met, they intertwined and also began attracting energetic quanta to saturation. (Figure 90)

FIGURE 90

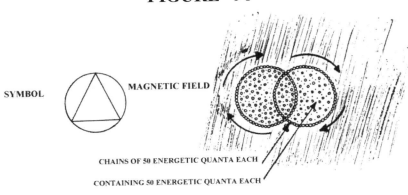

Each of these systems is called a distending static system. It attracts up to 50 energetic quanta—the saturation point—of each chain. When it is full of cytoembryos, these will stabilize in groups of six, 4 secondary and 2 primary, each integrated by a total of 1,200 energetic quanta. This new system is known as GENETIC QUANTA.

The internal activity of the energetic quanta could be seen in the animation. Each secondary distending cytoembryo dispersed the energetic quanta and freed the parton components. The primary cytoembryos, at the same time, gathered them together to form energetic quanta again in a sort of interior feedback.

The screen began to fill as more energetic quanta appeared. These, also, started to group together forming circles of 60 energetic quanta, known as a genetic capsule. This becomes a genetic system, when they unite and their magnetic fields are combined, to generate a plasma covering named a genetic capsule.

The genetic capsule attracted a quombic "Z", that split to form a cord. When it covered the capsule, the magnetic fields of each joined to form a GENE. (Figure 91)

FIGURE 91

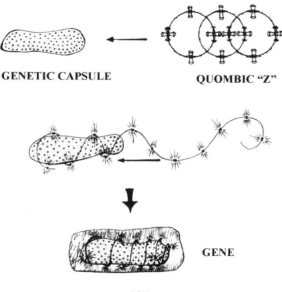

GENETIC CAPSULE   QUOMBIC "Z"

GENE

All the genetic commands given regarding the new being were engraved in the genetic quanta of the gene to be transmitted when the quombic "Z" was developed. The capsule of plasmatic energy was formed by the neutronium energies to protect the gene.

The genes continued to develop on the screen, and began grouping in the shape of small towers (ramas). These were protected by the DNA propellers forming small canelike tails, known as chromosomes. (Figure 92)

FIGURE 92

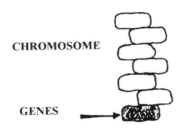

CHROMOSOME

GENES

When the canelike tails of each were linked together, inside the ovule, they formed pairs to become complete chromosomes. When they obtained the genetic information from both cells, these were known as VIDIC MERTANIC CHAINS. All the electric recordings contained in the genetic information form the genetic electronic pattern of the new human being. All this was done within 48 hours after the ovule has been fertilized.

THE METABOLIC PATTERN

Biologic entities such as man, need this automatic control to regulate all his vegetative functions. It is found in the brain, under the medulla oblongata, where it stimulates the cerebellum, the liver and the spleen. (Figure 93)

When the organism requires a certain hormone to be produced, it sends an electronic signal through the nervous system to the cerebellum from the organ that requires it. The cerebellum quantifies it and sends the production order to the spleen.

FIGURE 93

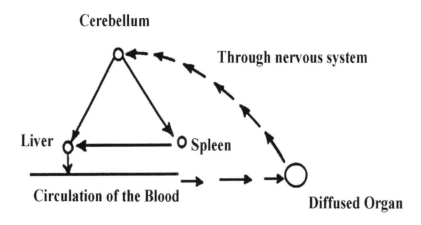

The spleen provides the liver with the raw material for the production of the required substance, the liver manufactures through the necessary biochemical reactions, and sends it through the blood to its destination.

Profesor Krinnell stopped the projector to explain the subject with more detail.

"To provide examples of these processes, let us suppose that a person, after eating, lies down to take a sun bath. On one hand, the digestive process automatically demands the production of the necessary substances for its function, such as the breakup of proteins, fats, etc. In addition to this process, transportation of the nutrients is needed throughout the organism through the blood and the endocrine system."

402

"On the other hand, the skin, through the nervous system advises the effects of the sun rays, receiving the whole range of contained energies, from ultraviolet to infrared rays. The temperature of the skin rises and automatically, the process of local protection begins, as sweat tries to protect the skin from burning."

"This information is transmitted through the nervous system, the metabolic pattern orders the cerebellum that, independent of the information that is already being received by the cerebral cortex for its conscious analysis, to send instructions to the spleen through the endocrine system. The spleen will provide the liver with the necessary elements to produce chemical substances to be sent through the blood to the skin exposed to the sun."

"You know this happens, it is NATURAL. But, what is "natural"? The fact it is automatic and occurs after receiving a stimulus or information through the nervous system in the form of electronic impulses."

"But, what is needed in order to react, issuing the proper orders, is the pre-recording that is not spontaneously generated. It is the result of previous study and experiences that have been provoked achieving cellular mutations. It is the proof of the foresight of the biological engineers, who are responsible for the design, adaptation and good functioning of the human body on evolutionary planets."

"The conclusion is to understand that the "natural" result of the process, even in the case of a chain of automatic reactions, is the end of something already calculated, designed and prepared by intelligent beings. It is not only the result of electronic, biochemical or electromagnetic reactions produced by chance at that moment. Everything has been previously thought out and designed to achieve the correct and useful function of this pattern."

PATTERN OF BEHAVIOR

"The control of this pattern is based on recordings by electric charges and is also found in the hypothalamic region of the brain." (Figure. 94)

FIGURE 94

LOCATION OF
HYPOTHALAMIC

This is integrated at three levels:

1. Upper or base level. The information coming from the physical senses is received here.
2. Middle or interpretation level. It works with the information it receives from the upper or base level.
3. Lower or distribution level. The information from the middle level is received here and its task consists in connecting and channeling it through the physical means at its disposal, so that the human can complete the analysis through the mental process that has taken place.

Life recordings are registered at the first level, which is a plaque of Ceroglobuline Beta, which is distributed as follows: (Figure. 95)

FIGURE 95

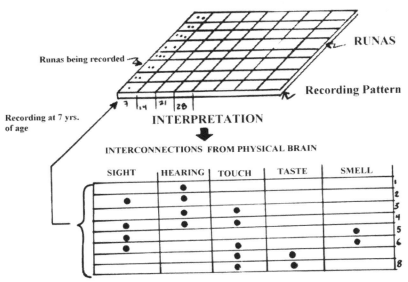

Runas being recorded

RUNAS

Recording Pattern

Recording at 7 yrs. of age

INTERPRETATION

INTERCONNECTIONS FROM PHYSICAL BRAIN

SIGHT	HEARING	TOUCH	TASTE	SMELL	
	●				1
●	●				2
	●	●			3
●	●	●			4
●				●	5
●		●		●	6
		●	●		7
		●	●		8

THE SYSTEM OF RECORDINGS OF ALL THE SENSES IS MODIFIED OR RECONFIRMED EVERY 7 YEARS.

"The recordings or RUNAS are vidic experiences that can have pleasant or traumatic effects on the psyche of the individual. Thus, they have to be re-recorded every seven years, to eliminate the unpleasant ones and improve the spontaneous reactions of the actualized register. The behavioral responses of the physical person are thus being perfected each time."

"For example: a child, whose first recording of rain was that of a frightening storm, will feel uneasiness every time he sees rain. When he is seven years of age, being more conscious of what rain, thunder and lightening are, he will re-record his new experience eliminating the fear of the first recording. Although, if there was something extraordinary that affected him deeply, and still exists even within the second recording, it will be associated to this and

405

will constitute a mental trauma that requires a process of self-control to be overcome or it will exert its influence until the next recording."

The Professor kept silent while Shem translated parts to Eric and Vanny. He then turned to Eric:

"There is a large amount of information in the genetic packages of chromosomes that would be the equivalent of several volumes of encyclopedias. The genes will send the necessary orders to the physical body through the developmental patterns but, also, will take care of the upkeep of the body and its repair."

"One of the missions of DNA is to carry the genetic instructions for growth in a code. This takes up less than five percent of the available DNA capacity, that is produced in the cells, because in addition, it has a thousand more functions as important as they are different."

"Through information received in the cerebellum from the central nervous system, and that coming from the charkas, when it is necessary to protect the person´s life, interconnections are carried out where the DNA has an important role. It also intervenes when there is mental stress caused by worry."

"Another of its functions is to participate in the recording of the influences of the environment, such as temperature, humidity, solar radiation and other influences as the electromagnetic and gravitational ones, which require the biochemical actions in the organism. These would be the reconstruction of DNA chains to prevent mistaken messages in the generation of proteins and enzymes for the reproduction of cells and to revise the DNA molecules in all the body."

Shem attended to Vanny, who had some doubts, while Eric pondered some questions on the subject. Then, he asked Shem:

"Is there any reason why, if everything is so perfectly thought out, we have so many physical faults, such as cancer and other sicknesses that could also be controlled by genes?"

"Everything has been, as you say, foreseen carefully. If you analyze this a little further, you will understand that IT IS INTENTIONAL. Nothing, absolutely nothing, happens by chance."

"The problems are designed to provoke errors or faults to serve a spiritual purpose. Suffering, physical pain, etc. can serve as restitution to be free of karmas generated in previous lives. They can also be motives for the development of research and study as an incentive for the human need to progress, to develop intellectually and scientifically to reach this level of evolution. These apparent imperfections are a means to motivate evolution."

"Then, is suffering necessary for human life?"

"No, but it is an alternative for evolution. Besides, it can be an element of restitution. As you know, the spirit is not going to perish as the body does. The spirit belongs to another dimension and time; its time is different."

"It must evolve through Divine Law by its own efforts. Each time a new body is assigned to it to continue its evolution, is an opportunity to advance, learn and eliminate its karmas, through sacrifice and pain similar to what he has caused others. Besides, sooner or later, with love, the spirit learns it is the best way to evolve."

"Remember that you are taking the first steps of evolution and have to learn, on your own, to know the physical body and understand your spiritual Being."

While Shem translated, the Professor prepared another cassette. Then Shem indicated:

"Now we are going to see a little about astrophysics."

The Professor proceeded by addressing Eric:

"You have had the opportunity to see processes that are beyond the scientific knowledge on Earth. We want you to acquire knowledge that is now being discovered on your planet. There will soon be a little more progress in the area of quantum. You have particle accelerators, although these are too small for the progress I am referring to."

The Professor was referring, without a doubt, to the cyclotrons that are working at the SLAC at Stanford University, the Fermilab in Chicago, the CERN in Switzerland and the one in Germany

"Although," he continued, "they are already preparing one with sufficient power. You have probably heard about it. It is the SSC of Texas in the U.S.A., whose results will surprise you!"(1)

"Also, the inaccessibility of the microuniverse is also an obstacle for biochemical research. Much has been done, but there are many answers still in this area not within easy reach of your science. Work must be carried out with faith and mental comprehension of the biochemical transformations in order to reach energetic phenomenon that go beyond the third dimension. As you see, again the spiritual part of the being makes contact with the physical one."

"It is also necessary, in the cosmos, to open the mind to accept the presence of the Creator in the manifestation of his laws and in the marvelous transformations. These are the presence of his children in those evolving planes, where they work to show the immense and infinite kindness and wisdom of our Creator Father."

"To speak of thousands or millions of light years is to talk about measurements of the Universe, that we don´t know and we only try to understand. Facing such an overwhelming reality, our Being can only overcome this immensity by being conscious of his spirit."

"The human being will only be able to conceive the immensity of space and eternity with the help of his spirit. The spirit alone has the capacity to understand everything."

"The speed of light is a parameter of dimensional differentiation. Itt is like talking about a parton, of relativity, of the deformation of space and time in the "zero" interval."

"This depends on the acceptance of being eternal and ever more capable, with the tenacity and desire to understand everything, or be as small and meaningless as the physical body it inhabits considers the only reality allowed to be understood."

----

(1) The SLAC (Stanford´s Liner Accelerator Collider) is 3 kilometers in length; the FERMILAB TEVTRON in Chicago, is a closed circuit of 6.5 kilometers; the CERN, the European Organization of Studies for Nuclear Research in Geneva, is an Electron-Positron Collider with an oval 27 kilometers in length; the SSC is a project for a Superconductor Super Collider of 87 kilometers to accelerate particles to the speed of light, but due to budgetary reasons, it was suspended by the government of the United States.

"In the end, everyone will know and understand the truth. But, when? The Father is in no hurry. Time is of no essence to Him. It is your decision to take advantage of this New Era to evolve, or do you prefer to start over?"

Yunner Krinnell turned on his projector. An aspect of the cosmos appeared on the screen. Little brilliant lights could be seen. The image slowly centered on a galaxy in a spiral. Professor Krinn stopped the projection and explained while pointing out the black area that surrounded the galaxy and filled all the intergalactic spaces.

"Here, there is mass and energy that act on the galaxy´s mass, not only are there neutrinos. There are also a large variety of energetic particles according to the type of galaxy where they came from. The system of particles and the primeval energy that started them, fill the space and constitute the manifestation and presence of the Creator."

"You combine the effect in the spectrum that you call Doppler, with the observation of the stars you call Cepheus that act as a cosmological constant to calculate interstellar distances. But I can assure you that soon you will acquire elements to contradict your own theories."

"The Big-Bang that is calculated to have happened between 15 and 20 thousand million light years ago will bring surprises. Your scientists will find offspring older than their mothers. So they can´t be their children, can they?"

"Well, we are talking about galaxies which are older tan 20 thousand million light years with different physical characteristics to those already known. The information obtained from such galaxies will constitute a paradox for the theories now in use. This will occur as you increase your knowledge of our local Universe and are able to detect galaxies that belong to other local universes."

"In any case, as I have told you before, the transformation phenomenon strictly obeys the behavior of energy and its interaction with matter according to Universal Law. From a subatomic particle to a galaxy, each are in the position, place and acceleration they are supposed to have."

"Only living beings can move with certain freedom, but only acting within the conditions necessary for their survival. Everything else is, moves and transforms in strict obedience to Universal Law."

"One of these is the Law of Cause and Effect. This explains that everything that happens is the effect or the result of a cause that originates it. It is the explanation for the effects over matter that are the result of causes and/or energies still unknown to you."

Yunner Krinn activated the monitor again. The image of the galaxy went away. Different types of galactic constellations paraded by. Some were ovals; others, rings with fire cloud centers, others were elliptical with perfectly defined bands of distinct textures that reminded them of the rings around the planet, Neptune.

Finally, everything went black. A cosmic cell called QUANTUM appeared in the center. This was a gene of energy at a cosmic level. (Figure 96)

FIGURE 96

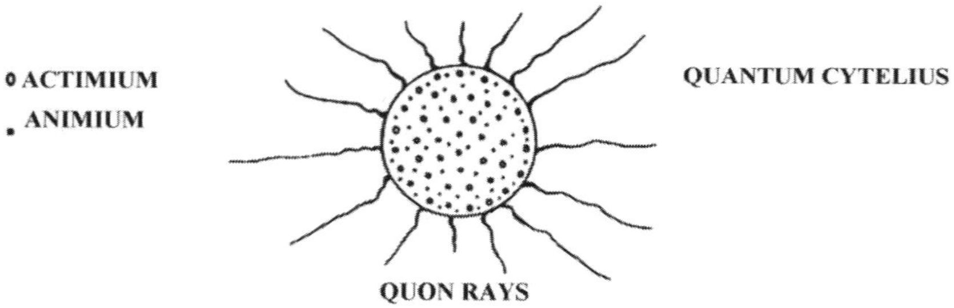

o ACTIMIUM

. ANIMIUM

QUANTUM CYTELIUS

QUON RAYS

"The quantum is a cosmic cell known as cytelius," continued Yunner Krinn. "It has the form of a sphere. The surrounding membrane allows an energetic emission called citobaric rays to exit through the pores, called perilios."

"Inside the cytelius, there are two elements—actimuim and animium—that react to each other. When the cytelius is saturated with cosmic energy, then the animium liquefies and reacts with the actimium. This generates a pulsation due to the attraction and rhythmic repulsion produced by their different polarities. The pulsating energy that results is the QUON RAY.

"The quombion or cycloquon is a sphere formed by three luminous arches perpendicular to each other. Each one lodged 12 energetic cosmic compressors with a quantum in the center." (Figure. 97)

FIGURE 97

QUOMBION OR CYCLOQUON

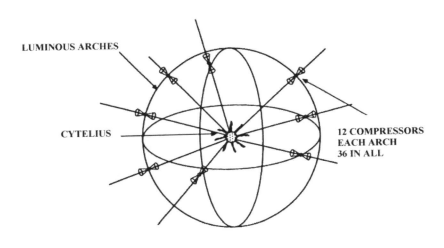

411

The compressors were formed by the integration of two intersected elements in the shape of a cone. These were a mesobaro and a fotosbaro. (Figure. 98)

FIGURE 98

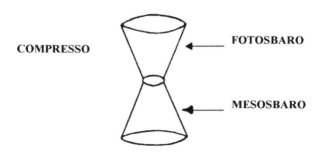

COMPRESSO

FOTOSBARO

MESOSBARO

The compressors attracted the cytobaric rays coming from the cytelius and expelled them as vibratory filaments named quon rays outside the quombion. (Figure 99)

FIGURE 99

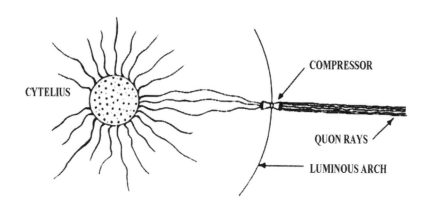

CYTELIUS

COMPRESSOR

QUON RAYS

LUMINOUS ARCH

These quon rays of electron energy 12 constitute the maximum strength of energy there is in the cosmos. (Figure 100)

FIGURE 100

QUOMBION OR CYCLOQUON

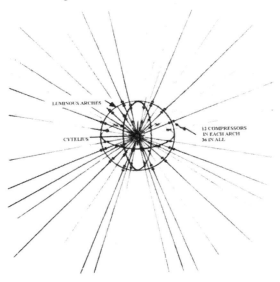

The quon ray, extending into space, looses speed and its filaments condense forming an energetic sphere called QUANTAR at one end.

As the rings of the quombion rotate, the sphere moves and generates its own rotation and forms a field of electrothermal energy around it. When the quantar is saturated, the quon ray subdivides forming four more spheres known as QUASARS. (Figure 101)

FIGURE 101

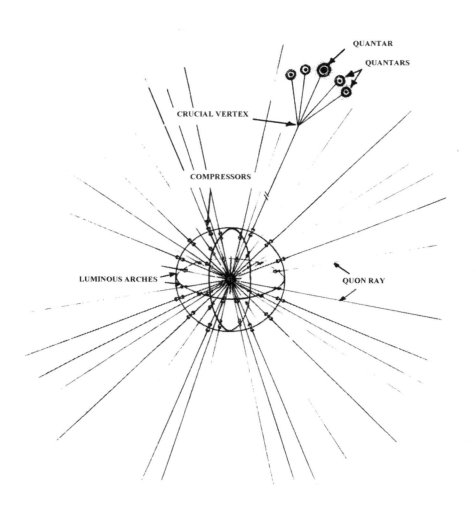

Each cytelius generates 36 groups of quantars with their respective quasars, that will give origin to 180 pulsar stars.

After the pulsar stars are integrated, when the quon rays bounce off the stars saturated with energy, they generate other bodies called germs of plasmatic matter. They are cocoons approximately 10,000 kilometers in diameter, (approximately the size of Earth) and one kilometer wide. (Figure 102)

FIGURE 102

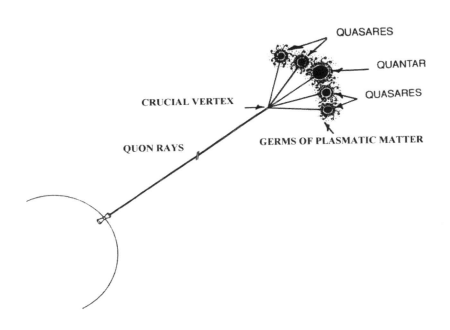

To sum up, each cytelius gives origin to 36 quon rays, and each forms a pulsar star, at one end, with an energy of cosmic proportions called a QUANTAR. When the quantar is saturated, the energy that can no longer enter, saturates the quon ray of the star coming behind. At a certain distance, the saturation forms a concentration called the crucial vertex. At this point, the ray divides into 5 rays. The main one forms the quantar, taking only one fifth of the energy that continues arriving to the star, but as it is already saturated with energy, it bounces back forming more germs of plasmatic energy.

The other four rays will also start to form, at one end, pulsar stars that reject each other, causing the feeding rays to deflect at the vertex 90 degrees from each other. (Figure 103)

FIGURE 103

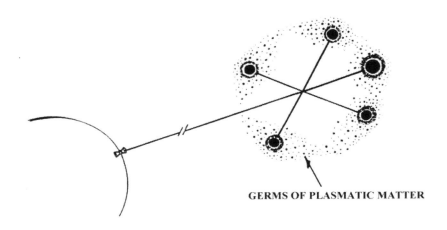

GERMS OF PLASMATIC MATTER

The pulsar stars that are formed at the end of the rays are known as quasars. When saturated, they will also start to emit plasmatic germs, but of a different structure that those of the quantar.

When the quantars and quasars are formed, the plasmatic germs become groups of spheres. As they integrate gravitationally, their interior is saturated by subatomic particles, from loose partons up to marsins, mertaners, etc. and paralfic chains that trap quanta. Energies are integrated by different polarities and with them, the thermal and luminous energies that form stars.

After translating, Shem added, "Due to the large variety of sizes in their formation, there will be stars of different intensities and sizes. You know them as Blue Giants, Medium Yellows (like your sun) and White Dwarfs."

416

"The quon rays, after starting the pulsar stars will break up and capture plasmatic germs of quasars and quantars. Thus forming some tubes of positive, negative and netural germs called Mauri´s tubes. These are associated to a star starting a system of planets."

"The transformation process is long and complex, but planetary systems like yours, are the result of these combinations, which have only one sun with 12 planets."

"Energetically evolving for millions of years, each cosmic cell will originate 36 systems of quanta with their respective quasars and an infinite number of germs of plasmatic matter. When the energy of the quon rays has been spent, the quombion disintegrates and the new systems absorb what is left to group around quasars and quantars. All these systems establish gravitational links and place themselves in the areas as satellites of the cytelius."

"The quon rays, converted into incandescent filaments of energy, loose their position. The break up as they deflect forming sections that link up to other stars and generate true constellations of stars with Mauri tubes, which will evolve for millions of years. These groups will form the galaxy. Two types of galaxies will come about depending on the participating energy. Some will have gamma rays as their main energy and will be sterile. Others will have alpha and beta rays. The combination of these energies will produce negative voltage lines −9 combined with +6 voltage, which is the combination of life in the Universe."

"The sterile galaxies originate energies that are projected into space and in other galaxies are transformed as part of the energetic elements, that are the origin of material life."

"Evolving stars with Mauri´s tubes could give origin to planetary systems, depending on their mass volume. This star, around your sun, can be seen here." (Figure 104)

FIGURE 104

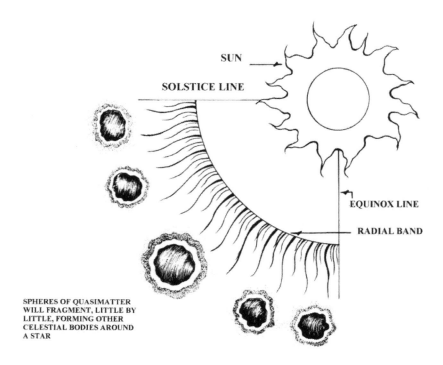

SUN

SOLSTICE LINE

EQUINOX LINE

RADIAL BAND

SPHERES OF QUASIMATTER WILL FRAGMENT, LITTLE BY LITTLE, FORMING OTHER CELESTIAL BODIES AROUND A STAR

A) Two spheres with an electric covering began two primary planets.

B) Two spheres with an electric covering (known as Van Allen Belts) originated 10 secondary planets.

C) Four spheres without an electric covering originated 96 satellites.

D) 24 spheres with an electric covering that started 3,240 planetoids.

The primary planets are similar to the main star, in as much as the elements that constitute it, except for the quantity of hydrogen found ignited in the star to be transformed into helium (fussion). The majority of the plasmatic germs of these planets come from quantar. The spheres that originated them do not break up and emit large quantities of physical energy of the third dimension. These combined with that of the Sun, define the energetic influence over the rest of the planets of the system, but also have a strong emission of energies of the fourth dimension that exert their influence on the spiritual field.

The other two spheres do break up and form the other 10 planets in the system. The gravitational forces make all these bodies find their positions, little by little, in compensated equilibrium and become a stable planetary system. In your solar system, one of the secondary planets that was already in orbit between Mars and Jupiter, due to internal energetic pressures and external gravitational ones slowly broke up in small rocks that went into orbit to find their positions of equilibrium. Jupiter and Saturn are primary planets. Here is your system. (Figure 105)

FIGURE 105

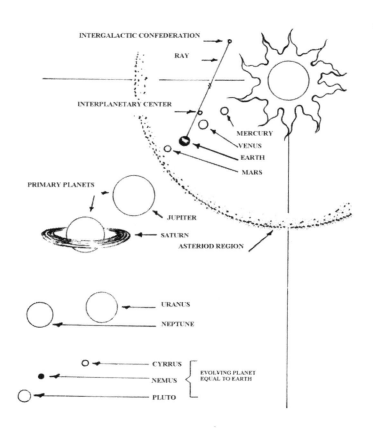

"As I told you in the beginning, the one sun systems have 12 planets. You still have to discover planets 10 and 11, whose names in this illustration are Cyrrus and Nemus. These names were given by the Intergalactic Federation when they were found while studying your system. One of them, Nemus, may have the adequate conditions to evolve. I am not authorized to give you any more details."

Eric raised his hand, asking permission to interrupt. Shem paused to listen to the question.

"Shem, the possibility of life on another planet of our solar system has been considered, but up to now, none has been found. Is it within another planet? Is there a human civilization on Nemus? Also, what is this federation you mentioned?"

"As I told you a moment ago, I am not authorized to give you direct information on your system. What I can tell you is that a planet can have vegetable and even animal life with unicellular organisms, and not contain a technological humanity in evolution. But, there are also planets with evolutionary humanities that live under difficult conditions due to the natural characteristics of the planet, such as temperature and hydrologic system, but have managed to adapt. Their technological development has strong limitations because of these hardships, but you will be surprised to know, that spiritually they have overcome in a short time, the era of the first level, and upon joining the federation, were transferred to a more suitable planet like ours, to live their next level, which with help, have quickly reached a technological development in less time than Earth.

"Nemus is very similar to Earth in its physical make-up. Due to its position in the Solar System, its characteristics limit its capacity to have an evolving technological humanity. However, the decision for it to be suitable for human habitation belongs to the superior brothers. They are the monitors who, through the cosmic engineers make all the necessary arrangements for the planet to be a proper home where humanity can fulfill an evolutionary level."

"As to your next question, there is an Interplanetary Galactic Federation that controls the relationships between evolving planets in our galaxy. It is the contact with the Intergalactic Federation which is the organization that supervises the relationships between the Galactic Federations of the universes. Your planet still does not officially belong to the federation as it has no representation. The federation determines the number and quality of contacts with beings. That´s why there can not yet be an open contact with you— only limited and controlled so as not to interfere with your development."

"It's up to our elder brothers of the fourth evolving plane to decide when a humanity has surpassed the necessary objective. When this occurs, they will permit us to begin open contact, to invite you to belong to the federation. Then, we will be able to help you to raise the level of your scientific and technological progress to ours and so continue together in evolution."

"You will understand from what I have just told you that it is not as important for you to worry about technological and scientific development. We could help you in that area. You need to overcome your weakness for material goods and take advantage of your resources with love, instead of using them to destroy each other. You must end the hatred and recover the values that allow you to evolve positively. You have to discover who you are and love each other."

"It is sad to say, but you still don't have a voice nor a vote in the federation because, although you as a humanity are on the threshold of the next level, you still don't fill the necessary requirements to be invited to belong to that organization. Mainly because your behavior is immature and not conducive to the spiritual evolution you should supposedly have. This is manifested by your selfishness, rebel attitude and dangerous for your own spiritual development. This is why our mission is so important."

Shem softened his reply with a smile, which Eric appreciated. Yunner Krinn continued with his usual gentleness, "Let's finish the subject of planetary systems. There are also systems with several associated stars. These can be four or eight containing 24 or 48 planets respectively, in addition to the satellites and planetoids."

Once he ended the explanation for Eric, Yunner Krinn turned his attention to Vanny and her questions. Shem and Eric left them to talk and went to the window where night was falling and offering a grand spectacle of the planets. There were two moons in different phases, stratus and cirrocumulus clouds lit up in tones of yellow and gold caused by the reflection of the sun, already hiding beyond the horizon. It was truly a symphony of color.

"Listen, Shem. Does physical life evolve in a similar way on all the planets?" Eric was thinking how alike he and Vanny and Shem were, although they came from different planets.

"Biophysically, life evolves everywhere in a similar way, although it depends on many natural ecological factors of the planet itself. Basically it is the same when animal cell evolution is obtained, when you have the same scale of RNA, enzymes, proteins, DNA, peptides, etc. It follows the evolutionary scale, but there is always an important RNA base in the cells of the ribosomes. In the chromosomes, it is the DNA which takes care of the genetic development."

"Rahel must have already explained to you that our superior brothers take care of organizing evolution, prepare the genetic recordings, etc. Millions of years ago, they were like us. Now they work as biological engineers. However, even in that degree of evolution, they also are on the road towards wisdom and perfection, following the Universal Law of the Creator Father."

"Within the physical evolution of man, you and your brothers are the result of the evolution of the species on your planet—from the primate to primitive man to the man of today. As you know, there is not intermediate "link". The change occurs when the spirit is implanted, separating animals from human beings."

The Professor and Vanny joined them. As Yunner Krinnell got close to Eric, he said, "We have a small surprise for you. We sincerely hope it will be to your liking. Let's go up."

CHAPTER XX

The idea of space—time
can seem a closed surface, without limits,
since it has deep implications in the role
God plays in matters of the Universe.

Stephen Hawking

OUR SMALL UNIVERSE

The four of them left Professor Krinnell´s laboratory and took the elevator went to an upper floor, where they exited at the lobby of an amphitheater. It looked out over Birken. Eric approached the windows to enjoy the sight and noticed there were different types of antennas on the roofs of neighboring buildings. Some parabolic to receive signals from satellites, others to receive communication signals by horizontal transmission of microwaves. The dome of an azimuth telescope could be seen on the adjoining building.

They entered the comfortable and elegant amphitheater, which was really a fantastic planetarium with space for more than one hundred spectators. Eric felt glad that it was very similar to the planetariums on Earth. He and Vanny sat in the seats assigned by Shem, who sat behind them so they could hear him better.

The Professor took his place at the control panel. He darkened the room and projected a marvelous sky on the screen, and began his explanation as Shem translated:

"We are watching a live take of the entire scope of the telescope. It is a panoramic view that allows us to select the area we

424

want to see in more detail. We can receive and project images from the telescope we have here, as well as from the telescopes in the space stations. We can even combine simultaneous takes of several and project them as if we had a wide angle lens, or select a zone and amplify it through special instruments."

The show was breathtaking. A multitude of stars twinkled everywhere. The intensity made the picture more exciting and alive. It was like watching the sky directly without interference. Some stars seemed to give off blue or violet lights, then they changed to yellow or green. Some were so small, that in spite of their brilliant twinkling were lost among the others.

The Professor projected a small circle that had a double red net. He went over the screen highlighting several of the brightest stars, stopping at a special one. Shem caught Eric´s attention, saying, "That one is Andromeda, as you already know. It is a spiral galaxy similar to ours, on the opposite side of our actual position within our galaxy. That´s why it appears to be so small."

The Professor then changed the image from the optical telescope to a computerized one. The small area was limited by a circle, about 5 centimeters in diameter. It grew to the size of the whole screen. Different stars could be seen in complete clarity. The slider moved and pointed out a twinkling star with yellow and white sparkles.

"That is your sun, Eric."

Eric was stunned, as he watched space and the star they said was the Sun. Shem continued translating, while the Professor moved the slider again towards the left. He then framed in another star, similar in size and brightness as the Sun, and said, "This other is the one you call Alpha Centaurus. Its partner is the star you know as Proxima, that is closest to your sun."

He moved the slider slightly to the right and pointed to a small bright dot twinkling in red and orange. "Look! There is the closest star to you. It has only small planetoids, where there are plants but no evolutionary life."

The sky´s image changed and a group of bright stars seemed to be under Andromeda. "Look, Eric. There is our home on a planet in that group of stars you know as the Pleiades."

"Do you really come from so far away, from the area of Andromeda?"

"No, Andromeda is another galaxy, although it is one of the closest to ours, it is still very far away. From here, it seems to be in the same direction, but the Pleiades are in the Milky Way and we are neighbors in the area."

"What is longest distance your spaceships can travel?"

"We can travel interplanetary distances in one system, but when it is a matter of interstellar distances, it would take us years. It is necessary to surpass the limits of the third dimension and the speed of light for these distances. This can only be done from another dimension. When you can understand other dimensions and the existence of the spirit, then it will be as natural for you as it is for us. I know you are doing your best to believe me, but it is hard for you to accept. Do not worry, Eric. The time will come for you and your brothers. You only have to put your will and your faith in our Universal Father."

Professor Krinnell then made some close ups of several stars and of Andromeda as a special gift. It was so impressive to see so many stars. The disk was leaning almost 45 degrees to the left and downwards. It was possible to see the main disk because it was also inclined toward the front at almost 20 degrees. This permitted a perfect view of the galaxy. The halo of stardust could be seen entirely on the plane of the central disk. The intensity of white light made it look like a luminous heavenly body with myriads of lights.

The spectacle of the system of all the galaxies could not be described. Eric was entranced by the marvel of being able to see the immensity of those creations of billions of stars in immeasurable spaces. He felt so small, so insignificant, that he could almost not conceive the infinitesimal of our surroundings. He had no words to express it and so preferred to keep a respectful silence before the greatness of Creation.

Professor Krinnell then showed them a galaxy in spiral, with one of the spirals going down and the other up, not on the same plane. They seemed to be the wings of a bird ready to land.

"The material universe is made up of galaxies formed by groups of stars in varied forms. If you look at the entire system, you will notice a certain synchronization in their rotation and in the position between each of the different systems. Each galaxy must keep a gravitational equilibrium."

"We must not loose sight that all the galaxies are gravitational units. But there are also constellations, which are larger systems formed by interrelated groups of galaxies. All together they form a super system that is the local Universe. Of course, the local universes also are interrelated forming the "wheels", which integrate the super-universe."

"Matter that can be seen is only 10 percent of what gravitationally acts in the systems. The local Universe is 100 times larger. Only one percent of the available matter in space can be measured by mass. Only a tenth of this one percent is visible. The other nine tenths are in the form of molecular hydrogen and in simple structures of carbon radicals, such as methylene, ethylene, acethylene and others as hydroxides and ammonium. They are in chains that can't be obtained in laboratories, of up to 13 carbon atoms and water. There are several thousand clouds of molecular dust in a galaxy, some up to 300 light years in diameter. All this is inside the galaxy.

"For distances in space, you use a measure called "astronomic unit". This is the distance from the Earth to the Sun (150 million kilometers). For interstellar distances you use the PARSEC (30 billion kilometers, equal to 3.26 light years). Using these units, we can estimate that if our galaxy measure approximately 100,000 light years in diameter, this equals 30,000 parsecs, or nine hundred thousand billion kilometers. It is shaped like an immense flat disk, with a thicker central part, as can be seen in the diagram.The largest concentration of matter is seen looking at the disk from above, from the Sun´s position towards the center of the galaxy." (Figure 106)

"However, the outer area has TWICE the matter that can be detected on the inside, as it is necessary to consider that what it included in the sphere surrounds the whole galaxy. The galaxies interact among themselves and correspond to energetic interactions that affect the speeds of intergalactic movement. You can watch these through the Doppler effect of movement towards the infrared in the spectrum. The distances and distribution of the galactic masses seem inconsistent to you, as you do not know of the invisible gravitational elements. You perceive that the value of the radiation is constant in any direction of the Universe."

FIGURE   106

GALAXY
THE MILKY WAY

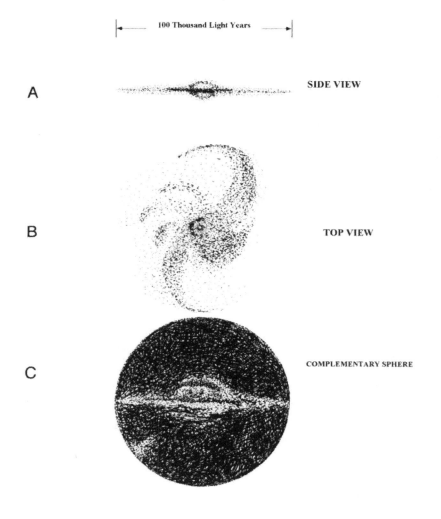

|←——— 100 Thousand Light Years ———→|

A · SIDE VIEW

B · TOP VIEW

C · COMPLEMENTARY SPHERE

Professor Krinnell paused and addressed Eric directly, "You can tell your brothers to try to comprehend the message that is a wonderful treasure. They only have to find it wrapped in the NEUTRINOS OF UNIVERSAL COSMIC ENERGY."

Eric watched Yunner Krinn, while thinking that those words must really be a revelation. He acknowledged his gratitude by nodding and replied, "Thanks, Yunner, I will take your words with me and hope that the scientists now studying all these cosmic phenomenon can understand the message."

Professor Krinn said no more on the subject and ended his explanation by saying, "All is in order in the Universe in accordance with Universal Laws, but a chaos due to the ignorance of many of the elements needed to be able to understand its function."

Eric felt so impressed and so small after what he had just seen, he kept quiet trying to absorb all that in his mind.

Professor Krinnell turned off the equipment and the four of them left the planetarium and went to Yunner's office to say goodbye. Eric couldn't avoid feeling saddened knowing this time it would be the final farewell for the Professor. He cast a last look around, and soon felt comforted by Yunner Krinn's gentle expression and his hand on his shoulder.

Shem translated his words. "Eric, it has been a pleasure meeting you. I wish you the best and I am sure that some day our spirits will meet again. Until then, may our Father bless you and be with you."

Eric shook his hand with love and gratitude, but couldn't find words to respond. He only nodded and put his hand over his heart to express his feelings. It was thoroughly understood. Shem and Vanny also thanked the Professor. Then all hurried to take the elevator and stop the emotional farewells.

In a few minutes they reached the airport waiting room at the university. The transfer vessel was already there. Eric missed Kunn. Shem explained that he was with Elim and Rahel's team waiting for their return.

While they boarded, Eric addressed Vanny via mental telepathy: "Are you going with them?"

"Yes, but I am going on my mission to another place in my constellation," she answered.

429

"She comes from the constellation known by you as Orion," Shem said. "It is very large and has a planet in evolution similar to Urania, the name your planet Earth is known in the Universe."

"Shem, are we being visited from many places?" Eric asked.

"We have seen missions arrive from at least 10 different places to visit you. On one hand, you are very privileged; but on the other, you are very backwards. Therefore, you do not have a very good interstellar reputation."

Eric thanked Shem for the explanations and couldn't avoid thinking about the "reputation" of the evolutionary humanity on Earth. He then turned to Vanny. He couldn't find in her anything that would betray her origins from another constellation of stars. She looked like one of millions of young women on Earth. *"Can I ask what your age is?"*

Vanny hesitated as she didn't completely understand the question. So Shem stepped in again, "Eric, you have to be more objective in telepathy. It would be better to asked her how old she is."

Vanny understood this and smiling answered telepathically, *"You have already asked me this. Do you remember? I have not reached the midpoint of my life yet. Our units are different, but an entire life is approximately twice the life span you now have on Earth."*

"Her planet has different movements and rotations," Shem continued. "Its orbit perimeter is a little more than twice that of Earth. The speed of movement is similar. It takes one year to complete approximately two of Earth's years. If their average life span equals 160 Earth years, they are equal to half in "their years". If she is at two thirds of that half of your 80 years, it would be two thirds of her 40 years. This is more or less 27 years, which would be about 54 Earth years."

Vanny agreed and added, *"I told you 55, do you remember?"*

"Her sun is bigger than yours," Shem kept on. "Due to this, the orbits of its planets are naturally very large. But the rest of the conditions are very similar. There is a giant red star very close to her system, of such a size that, if it were in your sun's place, the orbit of the Earth would be inside the star!"

Vanny paid close attention to Shem´s remarks. She understood and transmitted, "It is a very beautiful brilliant star in our sky that shines like a moon at night."

The access door to the vessel opened and the three of them entered the passengers´ area. There was space for 40 persons on this ship. The captain greeted them and explained something to Shem. After the friendly welcome on board, he invited them to tea and left to go to the cockpit.

While they settled down with the cups of tea, the ship initiated its departure. The screens showed the lighted panorama of Birken´s installations and, in the distance, some city lights could be seen. The ship started its helicoidal ascent at full speed. Eric closed his eyes trying to feel something---some vibration, inclination or acceleration…but, nothing! Only a sliding sensation that was more mental than physical. He felt a little sad and nostalgic as he understood this marvelous experience was coming to an end.

Wanting to get the most out of it, he turned to Vanny; *"Is the planet you are going to visit from your constellation?"*

"Yes, Eric, it is in a system of a star very similar to your Sun."

"And, does that humanity have a degree of civilization similar to the one on Earth?"

Vanny paused and looked at Shem, who rephrased the question. Vanny watched him attentively and then she addressed Eric, *"By civilization, referring to technological development, it is less; but they are more advanced in their spiritual evolution. In fact, I expect to obtain an opening for them in the New Era, so we can openly visit them as soon as they are accepted."*

Shem added, "We have not been able to do this with you. Evolutionwise, you have gone backwards because of your rebel attitude. However, Rahel and all of us believe that you have a chance to advance. This is why we continue struggling."

"We hope your entry could be like the one of Vanny´s planet. We will be very sad if pain and suffering becomes necessary to make you react spiritually. Although, to be honest, and I am sorry to say this, Eric. Your brothers seem to be blind and deaf to this. Their behavior is based on ambition and lies, on one side; and on religious

431

fanatism on the other. They are forcing panic, desperation and pain to make them evolve."

"There is no option. Already the time to comply with the minimum of necessary evolution is coming to an end. Believe me, we sincerely prefer to come to you openly, and welcome you to the interplanetary community as our brothers."

Eric was deep in thought. He leaned back in his seat. He knew he would soon say farewell and tried to think of something useful for him in the future.

"Shem, will I continue to be in contact with one of you? Who will be left in your place?"

"No, you will be alone with the experiences and knowledge you can recall. We will think about you a lot. If the results are good, we will know and be very happy."

"And…what must I do if I am not able to achieve anything, even if I have done my very best?"

"Nothing, you can´t do for your brothers what they won´t do for their spiritual evolution. It is a private and personal matter between humans and their conscience."

"We will return to our homes, after having done our best in the missions we came to fulfill. Don´t forget that we are like you in every way, except for the difference in our behavior manifests our spiritual evolution. Our scientific knowledge is superior to yours, but this is not really important as we have all eternity to keep on learning."

"The main difference is that you believe greater knowledge will make you change your spiritual attitudes and it exactly the contrary. Without spiritual evolution, your scientific progress will not occur. What is worse, if you don´t reach your goal, you will be swamped in a morass or even regress, which would be truly regrettable."

Again, Eric stopped to ponder his words. He then asked Shem, "I don´t know if I will have an opportunity to talk with Rahel again. Could you clarify two points I wanted to discuss with him? If I can speak to him, I am sure I will have other questions by then! Will you help me?"

"Of course, ask me what you wish to know, and if it is possible, I will do my best to answer."

432

"It is clear the evolution of the spirit is the same as culture and education is for man in the third dimension. Do you agree?"

"Yes, I agree."

"Well then, how do the experiences of past lives intervene in human life? Does the spirit's evolution influence conscious behavior of the person? I did undestand the intercommunication between the physical body and the spiritual being."

"Remember when we talked about mental spheres? We showed you that the human being is continually transmitting from his physical brain to the spiritual brain of his soul in fourth dimension. This is done through the interdimensional transmitting station."

"All the information your body receives through the sensorial organs of the third dimension. Every emotion that you experience, every generated thought—absolutely everything—as soon as it is generated is automatically registered consciously in the spiritual brain."

"Your soul, which is the physical part of your spirit in the fourth dimension, has a registry in its spiritual brain of life's happenings, experiences and acquired knowledge during his evolution.

But those memories are blocked out at a conscious level as a convenience to life shared with the human being it inhabits. However, they do influence the subconscious and supraconscious, making him prefer a certain type of behavior as something natural—as part of his character and his way of being. When certain information reaches the spiritual brain, it is necessary to inform the physical body. It is "transmitted" to the person's brain where it is perceived as intuition, a thought coming from the subconscious. When the "transmission" is emotional or sentimental, the chackras vibrate an energetic emission to flood the aura, and it affects the plexus of influence of that chackra in the physical body of the third dimension."

"This is how the person receives information mentally from his soul. The transmission arrives directly from his spiritual brain to his physical brain, and through it affects behavior according to the evolution he possesses."

"The result is reflected on people´s lives as it has a positive effect on their conduct and way of being. They are receptive persons, aware of their CONSCIENCE. They have a remarkable development of their spiritual gifts as is shown in their moral values."

"When a soul is going to continue its evolution in a new incarnation, the most convenient physical body is selected spiritually. A baby about to be born is chosen in a place where certain social and economic characteristics can be foreseen to develop and take advantage of opportunities, or have physical and/or moral sufferings due to family conditions or social surroundings, or even an organic disfunction. This physical and moral pain is what sometimes what the soul seeks to provide the DARMA it needs as restitution or opportunity to continue its evolution. The person, even not being aware of this, will accept the spiritual influence of restitution with positive resignation and love for others. Thus enduring his own grief with incredible human fortitude."

"Remember material lives are lessons and restitution for the soul. Equally, a spirit without evolution will not be able to help the human being it inhabits, even having a material life with all the advantages. He will show a total lack of moral values. He will accumulate karma and afterwards will have to atone. All these are lessons to evolve."

"The behavior of the physical person in the third dimension has the help of the subconscious, which supports the development of his level of evolution. In any case, the action of physical beings of the third dimension will always be his responsibility, using his spiritual gift of free will, but always guided by his conscience."

"Will this explanation clear the process of intercommunication between a human being and his spirit? It is important to understand this process because it is the path followed by your prayers."

"When a person wishes to get in touch with God, he prays. Prayer is a thought directed to his own spirit. This thought is a mental process where a dialogue is established within oneself. Everything goes to his own spiritual brain without editing. Communication is perfect. Even words are not needed. They could

434

be ideas, wishes and emotions. They will be received in their entirety by the spiritual brain of the being."

"Information received as "intuition" is the contact with the spirit through the physical brain of the third dimension. It can even come from the fifth and/or the seventh dimension. Besides, depending on the spirit´s evolutionary degree, continual guidance by the conscience is reinforced by its influence, through the aura, plexus and mental spheres. All this makes up the behavioral pattern of the person. In life he can be affected beneficially by his strength and fine spirit."

"Just as man is aware of the voice of his conscience, his behavior subconsciously manifests spiritual influence by positive feelings and virtues in accordance with his evolution."

Eric went over all this in his mind for a few moments. Shem added, "Keep in mind that man will always be guided by his conscience. His interests, feelings and degree of evolution will decide whether to follow the personal advice from his spirit and with his free will, will decide his actions."

"TRUTH is so difficult to define as it is easy to understand. Truth can not be changed, but can be interpreted, and this can be done in either good or bad faith."

"Truth is what it is. The way it is interpreted can be distorted. Besides, remember that everything comes from a series of transformation which can be perceived differently. What is received through your senses can be distorted depending on your physical organs. Then, it has still to be transformed into energy. When you analyze and think about it, it also can be different. Everything is vibration and quantically a fiction to begin with. From the time of its generation, conception, transmission and understanding, it can be altered even by your own brain with a mistaken result."

"My advice is: trust your conscience, the only true and direct information you get because of its spiritual origin. Don´t become a judge, because the basis for your judgments can be deformed. And, always, even in the case of doubt, act with LOVE.

"I hope this explanation will help you to better understand a phrase of the master of humility---Maitreya incarnated in Jesus of Nazareth who said: "I am the Light, the Truth and the Way."

435

"It was really very difficult for a man in that time to understand that LIGHT is the energy of energies, the origin of everything, the love of God. TRUTH is a fact, his life, teachings and material example, which cannot be altered or interpreted. The WAY is the spiritual path for evolution towards the Creator Father, God or whatever name He is given."

"Was my explanation clear to you?"

"Yes, thank you very much."

"And, what is your other doubt?"

"Well, you´ll see.....I understand that man must fulfill a certain evolution to be considered to be at the level of super-man. Is that when the New Era begins? How will we know when this happens?"

"The NEW ERA will come about during this time and consists in recognizing the power of the spirit and the faculties of matter without confusing them."

"We participate precisely in the guidance of mankind to acquire consciousness of his own spirit. This is necessary to be able to enter the new humanity."

"The new humanity will be that of SUPER-MAN, when man has reached the required level and his awareness will mark the beginning of a NEW ERA."

"And, do you believe that all humanity will be able to achieve it, more or less simultaneously?"

"Once it has started, it must be completed in approximately 25 years. This is serious, because if all humanity doesn´t enter through evolution, Nature itself will intervene directly to help. Remember a phrase of your Bible: "WHEAT AND WEED WILL BE CUT IN THE HARVEST. WHEN THEY ARE SEPARATED, THE WHEAT WILL BE PLANTED AGAIN.""

"Now, do you understand the wider significance of those wise words?"

"For example, the harvest can be a natural phenomenon taking many lives. Whoever has managed to evolve will be the wheat. A useful seed to be reproduced and multiplied. Whoever has not evolved will be the weed—useless. Of course, this is a metaphor. The spirit will continue living and will be taken where it can start another cycle to keep evolving. On the other hand, those considered "wheat" will only need a new body to continue on the path of evolution and spiritual elevation."

"Mankind can chose its evolution through its own behavior to allow their spirit to become "wheat". Spiritual harmony is the trait of SUPER-MAN. In this way he will be able to come in contact with others who dwell on other planets and consider them "brothers". He understands their common origin as children of God, although not all are at the same level of evolution."

"The fruits of the tree of life are experience, knowledge and evolution acquired by great efforts, tears and love."

"All this permits him to rise to his divine origin, the essence and end of his destiny, and in that knowledge, he will find peace. The only doorway to this new knowledge is recognizing the existence of his own spirit. In order to have spirituality, he must renounce selfishness, false pride and base instincts."

"Spiritual evolution is the result of a harmonious union of material and spiritual life. To elevate the spirit to develop its gifts, it is necessary to follow divine law and seek the most complete and profound knowledge of science and what exists beyond your planet."

"The man of the NEW ERA is one who identifies with his spirit. His degree of education does not matter, as he must develop and evolve spiritually. His age or gender are not important. He is a being of the new humanity that will inhabit, little by little, the planet from now on."

"A New Era man is conscious of his spirit. His mind, intelligence, knowledge and intuition make him understand the duality of his existence, both in a physical body and an immortal spirit."

"From infancy, he shows his potential and starts to develop his gifts together with the knowledge or memories filtered to his physical brain from his spiritual brain."

"Today's humanity on Earth lives in a time of change. It has to adapt to learn, understand and live correctly with the offspring of super men of the New Era, who are beginning to incarnate this new generation."

"Man has been spiritually lethargic. He has created imaginary hells and heavenly glories to explain life after death, even without having a clue as to his own material or spiritual existence, as he lives in darkness. He can not understand God without materializing him."

"Men have searched for the origin of life and the why of everything around them since the beginning of humanity. They have used all the strength of their minds and the light of their intelligence in this effort."

"First came philosophy, then science. But the human mind is very limited. The spirit is needed to comprehend the truth. Man´s science has managed to discover little of this truth."

"God is spirit. Whoever wants to find the fountain of life, the light of truth, the origin of creation will have to first find his own spirit, and thereby understand God."

"They must learn to communicate with their own spirit to rise above the weakness of matter through prayer and a willingness to learn, and also, love and serve their fellow beings. God is the creation of knowledge, truth and love. They have to be inspired in that love to get close to Him."

"God is our Creator Father, and we were created spiritually to his image and likeness. It is our spirit which has divine attributes."

"Man will first have to stop being a slave of the flesh. The Father can grant him wisdom to illuminate his spirit and enter a superior life. He will have to prove his comprehension that intelligence alone cannot understand the nature of creation. Only love can give his spirit the harmony to deserve new knowledge."

"Perversity, selfishness, false pride, vice and lies have darkened human life. These must be overcome by man of the New Era. This is the promise of the New Era. It will be a time of understanding, mental and spiritual light. Man will finally search for his origin in the spirit as he acknowledges his material insignificance."

"All the religions on your planet are paths that man has found to look for truth. In general, all of them are standards of behavior generated by people, with different degrees of intellectual, cultural and evolutionary development to identify and satisfy their spiritual instincts. They all developed under different conditions, supported by evolved spirits like Jesus, Mahomet, Buddha, Krishna and many others."

438

"Afterwards, each religious organization solved whatever they weren't able to understand by "Acts of Faith". They invented rituals and ceremonies to enrich their traditions and preserve and increase their followers. Religions and sects of all sizes have spiritual leaders. They are known as the clergy—be they guides, priests, pastors, gurus or whatever name given to them. Many of them speak of spiritual life offering beautiful heavens or threatening with horrible hells that are far from being spiritual."

"Meanwhile, wars rage between brothers causing pain and bloodshed. Have these guides come together with humility, love and concern to search for the truth….and erase differences? No, they allow hatred to generate more hatred and violence. They have a great responsibility on their shoulders. Many already have the necessary education to understand that the Universe is not like a planet with many countries having their own kings and laws. On the contrary, they must understand the Creator Father of the Universe is their God. And, the God of all other religions, since there is only one God."

"How can they remain indifferent, and not feel responsible for wars and hatred amongst brethren, by keeping separate religions, stating "their God" is the true one?"

"Religion means the union of man with his God, with his Creator. All men, regardless of color, race or where they live, are brothers and, as such are all children of the Creator Father."

"If the leaders of a religion tolerate, allow or incite hatred towards other religions, a time will come when they will have to answer to that responsibility. If they truly are spiritual guides, they should, through love, work towards one single religion for all. Ignorance, intolerance and fanatism should be attacked. Remember rites and dogmas support the separation. They are human beings looking for a material advantage of their power and their organizations. They preach for followers to obey them, in which the rejection of brothers of other religions is implicit."

"Heads of state should encourage a unity of nations and even abolish frontiers. The ideal would be only one country with only one language and under the same laws. True equality treats different persons in a different way, but with the same rights and obligations."

439

"Spiritual guides will have to unite in the New Era, to be able to guide humanity spiritually under the Divine Universal mandate of love. The Father asks only that man listen to the voice of his own conscience and live in love and peace. The conscience of humanity will awaken in its need to receive the light of truth, through each individual spirit."

"Remember Jesus was a humble man. He preached in the hills, in the desert, in rivers and valleys. He didn´t need temples nor special ceremonies. He made each person find his inner temple wherever he went, as each heart opened up as a flower blooms in the Sun."

"By uniting spirit and mind, man at last will be able to spiritually search for the truth of his origin and his destiny. He will understand that through science, the Father allows him to know his place in the universe. This is the NEW ERA."

"Let the spirit guide the mind. Don´t allow the mind to be enslaved by flesh and matter and be carried away by greed and base passions that only satisfy the physical senses, turning a deaf ear to the spiritual invitation to act with justice and love."

"Man now has to understand his spirit is immortal; and an integral part of the cosmic spirit that is God Himself, created with the mission to evolve through time and space in order to attain wisdom to permit him someday realize he is a child of God."

"A man must understand and accept that "God" is infinite wisdom, pure energy, the origin of all energies, of matter and all creation. The master Universe is the result of his love. Man must be able to see himself as a product of that infinite love to understand that his spirit is part of God. And, therefore, is His son."

"Man will accept, through knowledge or intuition, his physical body and the world where he lives are the result of physical evolution guided to perfection by God Himself. He is given the means to obtain the experiences and the knowledge needed for his spirit to evolve."

"When man becomes aware his physical and spiritual life are in temporary symbiosis, he can understand his responsibility to his spirit in the fulfillment of their evolving mission. It is then when man turns into SUPER-MAN. He can answer, "Who am I? Where do I come from? And, where am I going?"

Eric couldn´t think of any more questions. He suddenly felt the need to rest and closed his eyes and was soon sound asleep.

While he was unconscious, his friends transported him back to the base of our solar system. He didn´t know exactly how they did it. Maybe they even made him walk. But there was no conscious memory. He only felt he had been in deep sleep. He didn´t know how long, but was very rested as he little by little recovered consciousness.

Suddenly he heard Mirza´s voice speaking to Shem. He was not fully awake and to lazy to react. He had the impression that they were traveling slowly on a dirt road. So he opened his eyes and tried to see where they were.

"Hello, Eric. I thought we would have to wake you up when we got to your car," Mirza said as he sat up.

Eric only smiled. He suddenly realized they were on the space ship going from the station in orbit to Earth.

"Did you say goodbye to Vanny for me?"

"You will do it yourself next time."

"Really?....When?" He asked thrilled to know they would soon meet again.

Mirza turned thoughtful, paused and said, "Our mission is practically over. We are excited about going to our homes. Life visiting planets is interesting, but we are human beings and have the same emotions. Soon we will return to our loved ones and our life. But, we will remember this mission with special affection. Thanks to you, it will be a success. I believe a lot can be achieved if your brothers will it...I also believe they urgently need it."

"Rahel told me to ask you if you are going on a trip next month to contact you there. What are your plans?"

"Yes, I plan to go to Monterrey on the Thursday after the Independence Day holidays. I also have to go further north of Monclova."

"Well, I will call you to confirm the exact date of your trip. If it not possible then, we will meet again upon your return. Rahel will not leave without saying goodbye to you. I will let you know as soon as I know our departure date for certain. We still have some things to arrange and await our instructions."

The ship had settled silently and softly at the same place they had left. It was really an ideal and discreet location. Mirza, Shem and Eric traveled on the Mini that had descended on the ramp from the ship. Some seconds later, it was just another car on the avenue. Eric got down quickly when they reached the hotel. He didn´t want another long farewell. So he only said, "I will expect your call, Mirza. I will think about what to ask you, not Shem because he is like Rahel. He doesn´t let me think!!"

Everyone laughed at the joke and bid their farewells. They signaled they would wait to see him leave, so he entered the hotel and asked for his car. His friends followed him up to the circle to make a "U" turn and return to the highway. He looked at the clock on the dash board. It was just 8:30 p.m. It seemed unbelievable that, in so little time, he had gone so far and learned so much. He waved goodbye as he accelerated. The small car of his friends turned around and disappeared."

He tried not to think about anything and concentrated on driving. Before he knew it, he was at the toll booth of San Martin, but it was impossible to put all his memories aside.

After several days went by he managed to control his thoughts of this last trip. It was though he had been programmed. He could put these memories away or bring them to mind at will.

CHAPTER XXI

People who believe in physics
know that the difference between present,
past and future in space
is only persistent Fiction.

Albert Einstein

THE FINAL ENCOUNTER

As time passed, Mirza´s last words became even more painful for Eric. His affection for all of them had become so strong it was as if he had known them all his life. Although he didn´t know anything about their private lives, he felt he knew their spirit. He enjoyed their trusting and serene friendship. He was a little afraid of being left without their companionship, in addition to the responsibility of transmitting the knowledge and experiences he had acquired with them.

How to make men understand that the difficulty is not the acceptance of the "supernatural", but to comprehend the existence of something their minds can not yet visualize?

Mirza had not called him, so he assumed she was now on the trip she had mentioned. He sincerely hope she would get in touch with him wherever she was and they would meet during his next business trip.

He had just left Monterrey. Since he had left home on this trip he had spent most of his time thinking of them. He had gone through all their encounters---their real experiences, the induced

443

dreams and astral tele-transported travels. He knew it was about to end.

He became fully conscious of this reality as he drove down the lonely road. It ran parallel to a chain of mountains and the arid landscape added a sad note.

He scrutinized the sky looking for the possibility of rain. The high clouds made it a good day to travel on the highway. The car responded marvelously and he relaxed while driving calmly. He was on his way to Nueva Rosita to the north and as he passed through some little towns, he thought of stopping for breakfast. But he really wasn´t hungry. The snack on the plane would suffice until he got to Monclova, where he would have lunch.

The long straight road was lost in the horizon. Little hills and desert rocks made the road less monotonous. He passed two buses and a pick up truck. The desert road just kept on and on.

Suddenly something made him react. He felt his heart racing while detecting Rahel and Mirza´s voice in his mind. He slowed down while watching the horizon on all sides. All of a sudden, there it was…..Rahel´s spaceship!!!

It was a repeat of the first encounter. It was directly in front of him. A vertical light was turned on which, in broad daylight seemed a ray of sunlight. It crossed over the highway 50 meters above ground and disappeared behind mounds of giant rocks on his right.

At the crossroads, he located a road leading to a clearing and followed it. After a left curve, he saw the ship!

It was 25 meters in diameter and similar to the first one, except the dome was little different. The little windows were open through which he could see his friends. He got out of the car after parking it in front of the ship. He locked it and saw the access ramp descending.

It was a strange feeling to remember the first time, when he saw Mirza greeting him. But now, he was going to go up also. The space ship alone had impressed him so deeply due to its extra-terrestrial origin. Now, on the other hand, it felt so natural, so commonplace. But, above all, just to think that those persons were his friends and they were waiting for him!! Extraordinary!!!

Kunn appeared at the hatchway as Eric went up and greeted him with a firm handshake. The most enthusiastic of all of them, Kunn seemed to be an earthling, from the north of Mexico. In fact, he reminded Eric of his friend, Eleazar, whose son looked like Kunn, living in Monterrey. They went in to join Mirza, Rahel and Shem who were waiting for them in the center hall. Elim also came down from the control cabin. He now did the piloting with Kunn.

Rahel told him, after an affectionate greeting, "You have already had many experiences on board spaceships. But this time, you will be fully conscious during all the trip. The ride we will take today is our farewell gift to you."

Eric felt as excited as if it were to be his first voyage on a spaceship!!

"We will show you your own planet and something else!"

Kunn and Elim went to the control cabin. Mirza invited him to take a seat to watch the take-off. He felt paralyzed by his emotions. The ship started to rise with its characteristic zooming. Through the screens they could see his car, then the road and the landscape.

"I know you want to go up. Let's go so you see everything live!" Rahel suggested. The four of them went up to the cabin. Shem opened the exterior cover of the little windows.

They continued the vertical ascent softly. Eric could see the landscape as if he were in a panoramic elevator. They kept on rising. He could not feel the speed. The altitude could only be estimated by the view. He glanced at his watch. Eight minutes had passed. He calculated they must be at an altitude of 3,000 meters.

"At what altitude are we?" He asked Kunn.

"Four thousand meters....right at this moment! There is air traffic nearby, so we'll go up faster." Elim commented as he changed the helicoidal ascent. In two minutes, it stabilized at approximately 10,000 meters.

They saw a commercial airplane passing, surely on route towards Mexico City. They floated during some minutes and saw three more airplanes. They had kept the little windows transparent until then. The ship turned slowly like an observatory. Elim focused the television camera on the third airplane in front of them. They could clearly see the pilots as if they were ten meters away from the windshield. They seemed to be joking and you could almost read their lips.

"Can they see us?" asked Eric.

"Yes, but the sun is behind us and they don´t seem to have seen us." Rahel answered. Then he told Elim, "Show Eric his planet."

Elim closed the windows. The spaceship started to gain altitude with remarkable speed at an approximate 40-degree angle. It made a semi-circle towards the northeast. In two minutes, the line of the Gulf of Mexico appeared clearly.

"Get close, Eric, drive with us." Kunn invited.

"To drive" seemed a bit too much to ask. But he did want to sit at the control center table to maneuver the angle of the cameras, to see what Kunn and Elim did. He turned to Rahel, who nodded his approval.

Eric then took the third place at the control table. He looked through the cameras, controlled the direction of the lower one and applied the telescope. He distinguished a city on the Texas coastline. He recognized it was Galveston because of the bridge to the island. It was so clear he could swear he was flying over the city in a small plane. He changed to maximum close up and to his great surprise, even read the ads on the buildings. He seemed to be no more than 500 or 1,000 meters away. He could be on a hill top looking down. Elim enjoyed Eric´s fascination with the wondrous spectacle!

"How far away are we?" Eric asked.

"About 200 kilometers away and about 80 kilometers high." Elim calculated after checking the instrument panel.

Kunn maneuvered the ship into a vertical position and a section of the windows cleared to see through. It seemed as if they were admiring an enormous mural map. There was no light outside due to the altitude. Only the immense map of color in that part of the Earth he could still see, and a black sky full of stars.

Kunn closed the windows again and brought the ship back to its normal position to use the camera with the telescope. He darkened the windows and again opened the exterior covering. Then they could watch the Sun as an immense ball of fire through the polarized lenses. It was the size of a football, strikingly impressive and beautiful. It was stunning to be able to admire the greatness of the Creator in that star.

"That's enough for now. Remember that we are in space and the sun rays, even with filters, are very strong...Look at it through the monitors." Kunn advised.

"Now we will ascend to 3,000 kilometers to follow a geodesic path around the planet. The relative cruising speed will be 60,000 kilometers per hour," Elim explained.

"Ascend to 10,000 kilometers or a little more so that he can see the entire Gulf on the monitor," Rahel suggested. "And then high enough so he can see all the planet. While we ascend, go south over the American continent to the South Pole."

In five minutes, the entire Gulf of Mexico could be seen, from Tampico to Miami, New Orleans and Merida. The beginning of the Great Lakes and the whole Atlantic coast of the United States could be seen by just turning the camera to the north. Returning the camera to its vertical position, they saw they ship was over Panama, reaching South America.

For each 10,000 kilometers it covered going south, it went up 10,000 kilometers. This took five minutes. Therefore, 15 minutes after leaving Galveston, they were cruising over Buenos Aires at an altitude of 30,000 kilometers. Using the telescope at its maximum opening, all of South America, both the Pacific and Atlantic Oceans on the Earth's curve could be seen.

When the setting was changed, the view was dramatic. Earth was a beautiful balloon floating in a black abyss marvelously flooded by bright twinkling lights of different colors. The planet appeared somewhat covered by clouds in the panoramic view, but when the close ups were made, rivers, mountains and cities could be distinguished clearly.

"From an altitude of 30 kilometers, using a telescope with this capacity, you can read the headlines at a newsstand. At approximately 10 kilometers in height (33,000 feet, which is the cruising altitude of a jet airplane), you are able to see details which you would see 2.5 meters away!" Elim explained.

They were above the Strait that separates Tierra del Fuego from the Antartic Peninsula at an altitude of 40,000 kilometers. The planet was clear on the monitor. Towards the north, the southern tip

447

of the continent and towards the south, half of Antartica could be seen. Then, they headed on a straight line to a land just starting its day. The morning´s first lights of dawn offered a show hard to describe. When Eric turned a monitor towards the sky, he felt a similar sensation that reminded him of Professor Krinnell´s planetarium. Only this time, it wasn´t just an image, not a memory nor a dream. It was real and live!! To be able to see the immensity of space and the numerous galaxies with their millions of brilliant stars was more than he could take. His eyes filled with tears.

Dawn was just breaking in New Zealand. Darkness still covered western Australia and New Guinea. The spectacle was breathtaking. The islands as well as the coast of Australia stood out in the moonlight. They could clearly see the cities of Melbourne, Sydney, Brisbane and a chain of minor lights towards the northeast, along the Coral Sea.

Eric admired the immense desert in the central part of Australia shining golden in the dark. He was surprised to find a very large rocky mountain range in the geographic center of this island/continent.

After passing over the Philippines, dots of light were only detected by the telescope, except for the city of Manila that Elim pointed out. Far away, were the islands of Japan. Eric looked at his watch, it was 11.00 a.m. It seemed unreal, but one hour had already gone by since he boarded the spaceship!

Elim adjusted the telescope and pointed out the countries and cities as they appeared. Nagasaki, Hiroshima, Osaka, Nagoya and Tokyo. More lights could be seen towards the north, but Elim turned to the left, directly towards China, crossing the Sea of Japan. The coast of China was totally dark, until the lights of the city of Pyong-Yong came into sight. Further north lay Korea, Seoul and Pusan.

They crossed the Yellow Sea and passed over Tiensin and Beijing. Huang-Ho or Yellow River became a silver thread on route towards the sea. Towards the west the impressive heights of the Himalayan Mountains in Tibet, followed the plains of Mongolia. The Gobi Desert covered almost 15,000 kilometers from east to west, separating Russia from China.

There were few signs of civilization in all that stretch, but further up, around the Caspian Sea, dots of lights started signaling cities, especially in the oil fields of Baku. On the opposite coast of the Black Sea, in Turkey, the port of Sebastopol stood out as a very large city, as Istanbul did, further ahead, between the Mediterranean and Aegean Sea.

The ship changed course towards to southwest. They flew over the coast of Syria and the island of Cyprus until reaching Jerusalem. The city lights of Damascus, Haifa and Tel-Aviv were on in full swing as it was around 8:30 p.m. there.

The spaceship stopped over the Lake Tiberius, which joined the Jordan River to the Dead Sea by a silver thread. It floated softly while Elim pointed out Jerusalem and the area where the great Micael had lived and preached as the Son of God, Jesus of Nazareth.

"Is it true you took part when Jesus was on Earth?" Eric asked Rahel.

"We didn't, our elder brothers did. This is as true as you and I are here. Nothing happens by coincidence, Eric. Everything must be done according to a plan, in which many persons participate. And, that was no exception. On the contrary, Micael's coming was well thought out. It is a pity that, with your intelligence and knowledge, you close your eyes to reality."

"Man instinctively searches for his spiritual origin. That's why, in his ignorance, he looks upon things he doesn't understand as almost magical—as astrology, occult sciences, esoterism, parapsychology and mental control. He thinks these can guide him to the path of truth he consciously and unconsciously seeks."

The spaceship continued its voyage. As they cruised south of Cairo, Eric could see the Red Sea, the Suez Canal and the Nile River. They crossed the desert towards the Mediterranean Sea, exiting in front of the island of Crete. Everything was seen in its normal size on one of the monitors. The other one, adapted to the telescope, followed the important areas marked by Elim and seemed to be a section of a map. They recognized the lights of Smyrna in Turkey and Tessalonica in Greece. Infinite lights lined the cost of the Ionian Sea, the mainland, Crete and the rest of the Greek Isles.

449

On the north cost of Africa, Slim identified the cities of Tripoli, Tunis and Biserta. Towards the west, far away, Portugal could be seen, already in broad daylight. They then turned towards to northeast over Italy, completely sprinkled with lights—Reggio, Taranto, Naples, Rome, Livorno, Pisa and Florence. On the other side of the Apennines, Bologna, Padua, Venice and from Nice up to Turin and Milan, near the Alps.

On the left, towards the west all the Iberian Peninsula, between Gibraltar and Corruna and Barcelona could be seen. Then cities of Switzerland and Austria appeared; towards the north Berlin and several large cities and many smaller towns up to the Peninsula of Denmark. Oslo lit up the horizon.

They stopped for a moment over Paris and with the telescope, it seemed they were flying on a small plane ove the City of Light. Dusk had just settled in and lights were already being turned on to shine upon the Seine River in small stretches, as if it were cut in sections.

They cruised over the United Kingdom of Great Britain: London, Birmingham, Liverpool and further ahead Plymouth and Southampton. It was as if they were above each city when focused. As they passed over Dublin in Ireland, they could also see Glasgow in Scotland. A brilliant blue ocean of light shone towards Iceland, where it was full daylight. A band of volcanic lava crossed Reykjavik all the way to the sea.

The spaceship turned southwest to fly over Greenland and the Peninsula of Labrador, through Newfoundland, directly towards the Great Lakes. On route Montreal, Toronto and Buffalo were included. From there, south over St. Louis and Dallas. It was possible to see all the cities on the Pacific coast of the United States because of the altitude they still cruising. They started descending as they flew over the American continent, and had gone down to almost 1,000 kilometers when crossing the Rio Grande. Then proceeded to the helicoidal descent towards it departure point and softly penetrated the Earth's atmosphere. From a cruising speed that had reached 60,000 kilometers per hour, it slowed to a speed of descent before touching the ground that could be controlled with a precision of up to one millimeter per second.

It was noon when the rotors zoomed to a complete stop. Shem opened the hatchway and Eric peered out to see the car that had been left for two and a half hours awaiting his return.

"Thanks to you and Mr. Einstein, my watch has gone nuts!" Eric told Kunn as he looked at it. All of them laughed. Eric found it hard to believe he was really in the company of persons from another planet. They even had the same sense of humor.

"It is curious," Eric reflected. "If traveling west, we gain a day, how come we lost it upon our return? When did this happen?"

"Yes, it´s true," Mirza commented. "But only for a moment, when we crossed the "time line" until we went over the Antipodes, where day was just ending. We came back that same day. Remember that time is measured arbitrarily by you, and it is relative."

"Thank you, Mirza. I still cannot recover from this incredible and amazing trip. I feel as though I had gone to the movies during the morning in my childhood. After the picture ended and I left the theater in daylight, I would loose control. This was like a movie, but live!!"

"Yes, a fantastic reality!" Shem commented. "And, in truth, this planet is very beautiful."

Kunn offered Eric a cup of tea, which he gladly accepted. Then he realized Mirza didn´t have a cup, so he passed it to her, saying, "Take it, Mirza, this is an earthly courtesy."

They laughed again and while everyone had tea, Eric couldn´t refrain telling Rahel something he had wanted to mention to him for some time. "Rahel, thank you so very much for granting my wish. I am thrilled by this unusual trip, that I waited for, for so long. There is something I would like to ask you, may I?"

"Go ahead, Eric. If it is possible to answer, you know I will."

"I really don´t know exactly how to explain this to you. In a nutshell, I would like to be able to share this experience on a spaceship with some people--my loved ones who I know think like I do and will help me with the mission you have entrusted to me. Among them are my relatives and friends who will understand my situation and will share this mission with me. Do you think it is possible? In any case, it is the same if one person has lived this, or

451

20 or 50. Probably, no one would believe us. You know how most of the people on Earth are."

"I think you will be successful and more people than you imagine will use your experiences for their evolution," Mirza mused. "We have worked in many places and in different ways, depending mainly on the knowledge and degree of evolution of the person we contacted. This doesn´t have anything to do with the cultural or socio-economic position."

"We have been present in many places throughout a long time. We have been taken to be gods or devils. We have even been in danger. A few communities have not had the chance to see spaceships and we have been doing exhibitions for their awareness, but you know the reactions."

"There are many organizations in Europe that want to contact us openly, but you know that it is still not time, and that´s why we haven´t done it. Authorities, apparently offended by not being the ones who officially received the invitation to participate have, curiously, all reacted the same way."

The leaders of the more advanced countries know of our presence, but they deny it. The most outstanding scientists, who could use their influence do acknowledge us, but do not do so publicly, for fear of being discredited and ridiculed. As, according to their scientific knowledge, there is no possibility of this occurring, they continue waiting for our arrival in a mysterious way."

"There is really no mystery, only lack of knowledge. The main problem is the delay in evolution and the lack of spiritual learning. Excessive materialism block the manifestation of your spiritual gifts, and an aggressiveness born from your selfishness and greed. Remember that all this has to change in order to evolve towards your spirit."

"You need to share the good will and love taught you by our Micael. He, as we have explained to you, had special love for you, by coming in person incarnating Jesus of Nazareth to show you the way. If humanity doesn´t change its attitude, well.....then it will be necessary to force it by pain and suffering. The time allotted to reach the goal is practically over. Everything, in the Universe, has a time."

"I believe one of the main problems," Shem interrupted, "for the acceptance by human beings from other planets among you, is there have been beings from other places who have come to see you as though you were being exhibited at a fair. Apparently some of them did this to seek scientific goals, to compare them with evolving humanities on planets from distant constellations; but, they exceeded the limits designed by our superior brothers, who watch over the final development of this planet. If this did happen, you can be sure they were punished, and have been expelled."

"What is true is that people who did see them could have been scared by their odd appearance. If they were using some special equipment for breathing or pressure or infrared eyeglasses, all this contributed to create horror stories of kidnappings, abuses and other fantasies. Remember that even through we are all humans, there are physical differences in size, color and features as there are between yourselves. The same general design is adequate for the development of the human in a society that will develop science and technology, and has been so, even before our galaxy existed."

"As to your initial question, Eric," Rahel answered, "I agree, but for the moment, it will not be possible. We will do it on another occasion."

"We are to return to our homes, but I expect to return to congratulate you for the success of your mission, and then it will be the right time. If I don´t return, I will ask whoever does to fulfill my promise. Do you agree?"

"Great! Please accept in my thanks in the name of those who will be awaiting it."

"Changing the subject a bit, why is it you are not more open when you are on exhibitions of awareness? For example, before we left, do you remember the plane that was coming towards us? If we had flown by its side, everyone would see us. Then we could have made signs. All those passengers would talk about this and it would spread everywhere."

"Well," Shem said, "That would be considered a general open contact, which is still not permitted. You must think and reason. We want to encourage your evolution. That direct and open contact will occur when you, alone, reach this objective and behave at the level of the third era, when you become Super Men, which is totally different from the Superman on the comic strips of absurd fiction!"

"When you care for each other as brethren," Mirza intervened, "Without deception or abuse for material advantages--when you become sincere in your love for each other--when you accept the presence of your spirit and listen to the voice of your conscience, then your spiritual gifts were awaken. You will find happiness in living to help one another, and all together overcome the physical and mental shortcomings of the weak."

"Then everyone will have a proper level of dimensional conscience and mental condition to comprehend creation."

"Instinct stimulated man to begin his evolution," Rahel added. "He made deities of all he feared and admired, but his mind evolved, and now he must understand that the clearest manifestation of the Father, is man himself. But, his behavior must be in keeping with that of a son of the Creator Father, in all the moments of his life."

"Religions have been your spiritual guides inviting you to be good. So that, in the "other life", (because you already assume there is a spiritual life), you will go to "heaven", which is described as a earthly paradise. But, man is already an adult and fairy tales are for children. Although, believe me, that in the case of "heaven", reality is far more beautiful than any tale. You only have to made a small effort to see it within yourselves and give love as children of the Father. The satisfaction you will have will awaken your spiritual conscience. The spiritual satisfaction will make you feel peace. That spiritual peace is sublime—a sparkle of the happiness you must strive for."

Rahel stood up and said what Eric had feared was going to happen at any moment: "Eric, we must go now. I wish that until we meet again, you will be happy for the success of your efforts. Many thanks for helping us. May the memory of our talks caress your heart and be an encouragement to your spiritual evolution, that will take you closer to our Father and feel his love."

Then he gave Eric an affectionate hug with his usual happy smile.

"I will always remember you, Eric, and hope to see you again."

"May our Father shine upon you!" Shem said, as he also embraced him goodbye. "You have seen only a small fraction of the Universe, but you have comprehended the greatness of our Father, and that will be inspiring."

May you have great success and I hope to see you again!!" Now it was Kunn saying goodbye.

"I will talk to my loved ones about you and your planet. We will send you our love and our Father will made you feel it. May you have happiness with your loved ones and all your brothers!" said Elim. Eric had had less chance to talk to him as he had been in charge of coordination.

Mirza stood up and approached Eric. Her brilliant blue eyes shined with emotional tears of farewell. She embraced him and kissed him on the cheek. "Remember us as we will remember you, with much love. May our Celestial Father accompany you always. It was a pleasure meeting you and I also hope to see you again. Vanny has already gone on her mission. She asked me to say goodbye to you and to tell you that when you need it, just look up at the sky towards us and you will feel our love."

Eric felt a knot in his throat. He smiled and felt a tear falling down his cheek. A tear that showed his friendship, his gratitude and his human sadness at the parting of ways.

"Thanks to all of you for this unique experience, for your friendship and for all the teachings you shared with me. I promise that I will do my best in taking your message to this humanity before it´s too late. I will also carry memories of you in my heart. I will anxiously await the day when I will see you again. May our Father bless you forever!"

He glanced at all of them with one last look. Without another word, he turned and went down the ramp. He crossed over to the shade of the rocks on the other end of the clearing to see the windows. When he turned around, the hatchway was already closed. The silent spaceship made him remember his first encounter. Then the soft sound of the rotors announced the imminent departure. The little windows opened. He listened to Mirza´s voice in his mind: "Now you can tell everyone about your experience! Until next time!

455

Valim Alek!" He managed to see Rahel and Mirza raising their right arm in a farewell wave.

Eric raised his arm and transmitted: "Have a good trip! You take with you, in my name and that of all my brothers who will use your teachings, our gratitude and love for everyone. Valim Alek!"

The supporting columns raised softly; the ship did not move, even an inch. Then, it started to float upward. It increased its speed and turned on the light. In a few seconds, it was a shining dot in the blue sky, where rain clouds slowly covered the whole valley.

Eric continued waving goodbye. He knew they were watching him as if they were right beside him. The dot curved and disappeared.

He lowered his arm and leaned on the wall of rocks. He felt desolate, as if an immense weight was crushing him. But, at that moment, a thought came to his mind. He must really be happy. His friends were going to be with their families and friends after a long mission. And, besides, they had left us a message of love. How many people cared about us! And we.....are not even aware of it!!

Thoughts, wishes, good intentions and responsibilities that he had been given kept spinning in his mind. There were so many things, not one specially stood out. Until his mind said ENOUGH! He shook his head to get rid of all the churning ideas.

My gosh! The car was an oven after having been parked there for so long! He opened all the doors and turned on the motor to connect the air conditioning, while he waited for it to cool off.

He remembered the words of Richard Dawkins about an exclusively material world in a cold universe: "A Universe of electrons and genes blindly obeying, indifferent, physical forces and cold reactions to cause and effect, without finding a reason for order, justice, design or purpose, of good or evil. Just a total indifference."

How different that cold universe was from the one his friends showed him. The one of an evolutionary world is life, love, in harmonious transformation of energy. It is the physical manifestation of an immense and marvelous creation, filled with generous kindness. Our Father has given it to us to discover our Spirit, our true Being and to begin to understand our origin and our destiny within Creation.

When the car finally cooled off, he started moving very slowly, as if he didn't want to leave. He gave one last look around and headed to the road towards Monclova.

He turned on the radio to get his mind off things. He found some country music and smiled happily. The heaviness in his heart was fading away. At that moment he heard the words of a song:

"......what goes up, and what comes down,
what reaches the end,
where will the dead go,
Lord, where will they go?"

He began to sing along, while the car cruised nicely on the road. He began to relax and thought time would put all his emotions and ideas in order. In fact, his task was just beginning......

AWAKEN

The rooster crows announcing
A new dawn,
He greets us,
And exclaims with pleasure.

Open your eyes now!
Our stay is brief,
Don´t accept a life on your knees,
Strive for the fragrance of life!

Do not wait to be able to see
Until you become white frost,
As life, once it has left,
Will never more return.

Open your eyes now!
Sharpen your minds,
Within the mortal body,
Let reason make you conscious
Of your immortal Being.

Oh, the threat of hell
That baffles so many!
Oh, promise of heaven,
Only thing is certain.

You have been of this world,
And must close the gate,
As the flower that today bloomed,
Tomorrow will be dead.

But your soul does not perish,
Still will continue being alive,
And your unwanted body
Will soon be rigid.

That is why I sent my soul
To go and investigate, and to see
If there is a heaven filled of peace,
Or a hell to fear.

I received a tender message:
I already went to investigate and saw
That heaven and hell
Are within you.

Heaven is hope,
Light, peace, life.....
Spiritual evolution that goes forward,
Happiness never felt.

Hell is darkness,
Shadows, and oblivion,
It is living in a fog,
That has covered the soul.

When the soul is transparent...it flies!
In its heaven of light, shall be eternal.
The wicked, afflicted and in vigil,
Will remain in the depths of their own hell.

The invisible infinity
Is the limit of the spirit.
Only a sensitive soul can know
That Truth is the beginning and the end.

The rooster crows announcing,
A new dawn,
He greets us,
And exclaims with pleasure!

Open your eyes now!
Open your minds,
In such a way,
You are aware
Of your immortal Soul.

Pablo E. Hawnser

NOTE: The first quatrain belongs to a poem of Omar Khayyam, but it served as a beginning for the author to sum up in this small poem, the essence of the message contained in "Eric´s Story".

BIOGRAPHY OF THE AUTHOR

The author of this book, Pablo E. Hawnser, is a Mexican, with more than 40 years experience in different areas of Engineering and Administration.

He studied Petroleum and Civil Engineering at the UNAM (Mexico´s National Autonomous University). He was professor of Mathematics and Physics before going into private enterprise.

He worked in Calculus and Design as well as in the field, from a Residency in Construction to Administration and Management in different industrial companies.

Physics and Cosmology that explain Nature have always been his hobby. He is a member of the Planetary Society of Pasadena, California, U.S.A., and the New York Academy of Sciences.

This work tells of the extraordinary experiences he lived, when contacted by extra-terrestrial beings. In addition, it is also a means to spread the message left by them for all Humanity, which was the real reason for their visit.